The Peacock's Feather

Also by Sarah Woodhouse:
A Season of Mists
The Indian Widow
Daughter of the Sea

THE PEACOCK'S FEATHER

Sarah Woodhouse

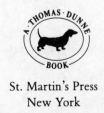

St. Martin's Press
New York

Library of Congress Cataloging-in-Publication Data

Woodhouse, Sarah.
        The peacock's feather / Sarah Woodhouse.
                p.   cm.
        "A Thomas Dunne book."
        ISBN 0-312-03908-5
        I. Title.
    PR6073.06164P43   1990
    823′.914—dc20   89-27057
                                                                     CIP

First published in Great Britain by Century Hutchinson Limited.

First U.S. Edition

10 9 8 7 6 5 4 3 2 1

For Jennifer

The Peacock's Feather

1

'Yes, sir, Westdene,' said a voice, 'most healthy place on the Suffolk coast. Many a gentleman is sent to Westdene for a cure.'

It was impossible to tell who had spoken, the yard was crowded with the usual hawkers and begging boys and listless youths. There was scarcely room for the old-fashioned, low-slung, clumsy, mud-encrusted coach just turned in under the arched entrance.

Several people stepped back hastily as far as they could, anxious for their toes. One of these was a short, lean, colourless man in black, with his hat on askew over an improbably old wig. He it was who plucked the scrawny young pie-seller by the ear and asked: 'Is this it? Is this the Westdene coach?'

'If you please, sir,' said the boy, twisting to lessen the pressure on his earlobe. 'It stand by the sea, Westdene do,' he added as his captor released him, 'old genl'men goo there for the cure. Hev a pie, sir, hev a pie. Good meat and strong gravy. My mother cook the best pies in Bungay.'

The Doctor, who could on occasion be endearingly sentimental, bought one but stowed it in his breast for future eating. Since he was currently engaged, so to speak, in prescribing himself a sort of cure, he struggled through the press to the ticket office and bought passage to Westdene immediately.

Thus into deepest Suffolk and all on a whim. Well, he was known to be capricious – his old patients could tell a score of tales of his irregularities of dress and manner and time-keeping – but he had never yet been called a fool. He gazed out at what little he could see of the country and wondered if now at last he had become one. But perhaps Westdene would provide the cure after all:

sea air, strangers, an enforced solitariness, a little time to ease these unacceptable hurts.

The road was lonely. On either side sorry fields of barley might be glimpsed beneath a grey pall of driving rain, barley which might never know the harvesters if the weather did not ease. The trees heaved, the ditches overflowed. The outside passengers huddled under tarpaulins, kept alive only by brandy and the hope of deliverance in twenty miles; twenty miles was the limit, the absolute limit, for one step further and they would fall into the sea. The insides languished too, but more warmly, and locked in a silence more hostile than suffering. There was a thin, pimpled, greasy, Pharisaical parson seated by the Doctor, and opposite a young, pale girl, grossly pregnant, and a well-dressed, impatient, heroic-looking man in his early thirties. This gentleman was rather tall and his long legs had to be accommodated diagonally.

After a while, another long while of deep ruts and miserably slow progress, the Doctor leaned forward.

'Madam, are you faint? Let me . . .' and he fiddled with the sash. A howling gale of the very worst August weather blasted through the open window.

'Damn it!' cried the tall man. 'You may mean well, sir, but you will have us laid out in our coffins. Put it up, man!'

The Doctor obliged. They settled back into the sour atmosphere in which they had already passed six weary miles. The parson pretended to sleep, the tall man got a paper from his pocket and read it thoroughly, frowning all the time, and the girl clasped her arms about her belly and closed her eyes. The Doctor retired under his wig, so ancient and so long unpowdered it had become something of a curiosity. He was aware of the tall man's scrutiny every time he lifted his eyes from his paper, a not unfriendly but wholly shameless scrutiny, and he suffered it sullenly, sinking back into his corner and wishing he had stayed on the London coach after all and was even now ordering something to eat in the chop-house he had frequented for years two streets from Guy's. This made him remember his pie, which he extracted with difficulty, the parson genuinely asleep now and leaning on his left arm. It was rather squashed and quite warm from being carried so long next to his heart, but though there seemed very little of anything that could be termed good meat there was a great deal of certainly very strong gravy.

They reached a village, as insignificant as any of four they had stopped at since leaving Bungay, and a large woman in a vast bonnet climbed in, clutching a basket from which emanated a strange, unenticing smell. She squeezed opposite the Doctor, puffing and complaining. The Doctor, making himself as small as possible and mopping gravy off his stubbly chin, reflected idly on the exquisite difficulty of finding the bone in such tremendous corpulence, even with his newest and most furiously sharpened scalpel. The fat woman did not care to be stared at, however, especially by slovenly little men in verminous wigs. He let his gaze slide aside to the girl, hearing her sharp intake of breath. She would deliver any day, he suspected her unearthly pallor and disturbed breathing told the usual story. The tall gentleman – her husband? – appeared to notice nothing, had not addressed more than two sentences to her since leaving the inn. He was altogether something of a mystery, for his skin was very tanned, his accent was strange – a Devon man perhaps? – and his clothes were exceedingly fine, almost flamboyant. Yes, he was really far too good for such a rustic coach, a coach that wallowed through the very pigsties and stopped at every crossroads to pick up or put down, to tie on hams, ducks, sausages, and bags of live geese.

The smell from the basket intensified until it became unbearable. The Doctor leaned forward.

'Do tell us what is inside,' he said. 'Would it not be more convenient to put it in the boot? More room, you know.'

As he spoke he touched the stick that held the catch

and to his intense horror it sprang out and the lid flew up. A ranker, even more penetrating reek . . . and a pair of sleek, fat, cunning polecats leapt forth, leapt with the unadulterated joy of the long-confined, and landed together on the lap of the suffering girl.

The devils in Hell and all those on earth too, the Doctor was later to say, could not have made more noise. The girl screamed and screamed – he suspected she had pent up a great many such screams over the last few miles, polecats or no – and the large woman cursed without drawing breath, and the tall gentleman gave a shout and bent double to dive into the filthy straw and bring up first one and then the other poor animal, suffering two bites and a knock on the head from the parson for his pains. The noise was so terrible the driver pulled up, and the curious faces of the outsides peered in at odd angles from above.

'I suggest we hurry on to the next stop,' advised the Doctor when he could make himself heard. 'This young woman is in labour.'

It was effective shock treatment but three pairs of hostile eyes regarded him with distaste – the girl's were closed. He chewed a stray rat's tail of his wig, unabashed and unrepentant. 'I am a surgeon and besides have spent many years in country practice. If it is a first child we need not worry overmuch. It *is* a first child, is it not?'

'I assume so,' said the tall gentleman since the girl did not speak. 'A surgeon, are you? A midwife might be more use.'

Not the husband then, thought the Doctor, no indeed. The fat woman assumed an air of superiority at this point and informed them her sister was a midwife, she could not abide these so-called surgeons, tooth-pullers and horse doctors all of them, no better at cutting off a limb than she was. The parson, peeved at having been woken, chimed in with his own unflattering view of medical men, officious sawbones all, and had just got into his stride when the coach apparently fell into a pit and they were all five catapulted together into the straw. The girl was

8

crying softly now, and the tall gentleman restored her to her seat quite lovingly and held her tightly clenched hands in his large ones. 'God save us!' he cried as they were all flung sideways again and one of the outsides screamed. The rank smell of ferret wafted about them.

'God save us indeed,' said Dr French, whose wig was practically over one eye. 'We are in for thunder and lightning; the sky is green.'

The sky was certainly livid, gangrenous and threatening. Far more threatening was the condition of the girl, who sagged heavily on the Doctor's arm all the way up to the cleanest, most private room the inn could provide at such short notice. It was little more than a tap-house, a paltry country drinking place – the coach did not even change horses there – and it was with real disappointment, bitter disappointment, that he watched that dreadful vehicle set forth again without him. He was no midwife, had already sent for the local practitioner in that art from the village – hamlet would be nearer the mark: farm, four cottages, two strange dwellings like primitive mud huts – but he had assured the girl's companion he would see the business to its natural conclusion in case of unforeseen complications. The gentleman seemed anxious at being abandoned in this remote place where they could not understand his language nor he theirs. He had offered a substantial fee to the Doctor and been sharply set down for it. Indeed, the Doctor told him he was determined to take as little part in the proceedings as his conscience allowed, he was not interested in childbirth and in his opinion normal deliveries were best left entirely to the women. The tall gentleman obviously thought him a fool and might have said so, having a direct, bellicose nature, but the look in the Doctor's slaty eye dissuaded him and he meekly let the matter drop – as meekly as he could, that is, not being naturally meek in any particular.

He was, on the contrary, naturally commanding, partly on account of his height: he was four inches too tall for any of the inn's public rooms; partly on account of his exotic appearance, exotic for rural Suffolk, to be sure. He was a deep mahogany tan from his hairline to some indefinite point well below his cravat. He had been abroad then, certainly in hotter sun than was currently trifling with Eastern England in this grim mid-August. His name, he said, towering over the Doctor in the parlour, was Jardine Henry Savage.

The Doctor did not ask why Mr Jardine Savage was travelling on a country stage with a girl fifteen years his junior who was about to give birth to her first child in less than ideal circumstances. He shook the man's hand and introduced himself as Alexander French, late of High Common in the county of Norfolk, a miserable, under-worked, overqualified country doctor, sometime army surgeon. No, he had no definite plans to return to the army, he had simply become intolerably bored with so much necessary idleness, no interesting cases, no new faces. He did not mention that he had been crossed in love, a mortifying confession for a man of forty-four who had supposed himself and Cupid on no kind of terms at all.

'I am on my way to look up old friends at Guy's,' he said in reply to Savage's inquiry, 'but I thought perhaps a week or two in the sea air . . . Westdene was recommended' – by the unknown voice? – 'I believe it was once prosperous, fishing, a harbour: all gone, or nearly gone; and it is not fashionable in the least, but . . . Yes, yes,' as the landlady put her head round the door, 'is the young woman any further along?'

'Mrs Bond sent down to ask if you could look in, sir, at your convenience. She would value your opinion.'

This was a polite translation of what the midwife had actually said and the Doctor, whose ear could detect urgent anxiety and even mild panic, rose at once.

'First confinements are generally tedious,' he said to Savage.

'She's young and healthy,' was the offering from the far side of the room where Mr Savage was gazing mourn-fully out of the dirty window.

10

'Oh, childbirth can be a protracted, sapping business.'

A quick look, a snapping together of dark brows: 'You have no premonitions?'

'Dear me, no. I only recall some instances I have known . . .'

Mr Savage hoped he would not recall them aloud and in detail. He rang furiously for shrub, for brandy, for anything to raise the general temperature and his flagging spirits. The Doctor excused himself and went upstairs to the midwife. The rain beat with renewed vigour at the small greasy panes and lightning lit the coast from Lowestoft to the Orwell estuary and shrub came and went, came and went, and the fire blazed up and died away, and night fell. The Doctor descended for toasted cheese about eleven but was no kind of company, running upstairs again still clutching a crust and muttering about defective human anatomy, the peculiar inability of some women to produce with ease, the very devil of a hard labour and nothing to show for it.

But in spite of the Doctor being no kind of midwife and the midwife slothful and lousy, by two in the morning there was something to show for it after all: a mewing, crumpled, downy-haired scrap of a girl-child, the very palest brown all over like a lightly roasted coffee bean. The young woman, whose name was Hannah, turned dark, drowned eyes on them in which Alex French detected momentarily not gratitude but a piercing hostility, and then she looked away. He patted her hand, left the midwife to clean up, and went down to tell Mr Savage he had a daughter, a normal healthy daughter as likely to live and thrive as any other baby in the kingdom.

Mr Savage was only a little worse for the shrub, the great quantities of shrub he had consumed all the long hours of his night watch, so that it was not drunken indignation but a cold formal sense of affront that chilled his tone. 'I assure you, sir, the child's none of mine. Why, I never saw the girl until she came on board in Kingston.'

'Kingston?'

'Jamaica. Kingston, Jamaica. The ship got in scarce

five days ago and she and I have been on the road ever since.'

'Which accounts for such pitiable exhaustion. But I do not understand how you come to be travelling together.'

Mr Jardine Savage, who many times in his career had been brought to give an embroidered account of the truth to awkward questions, looked directly into the Doctor's eye – such a cold, hard, compelling eye – and then shrugged and said wearily: 'God knows she is nothing to me, though you may believe what you like. She embarked alone, returning to relatives in Framlingham, and it was ten to one she wasn't married even if she wore a ring and called herself Mrs Brown. We had an overlong passage, light winds all the way, and the captain, poor devil, was all a-tremble she would deliver while we were still at sea. The other passengers were no friends to her, sour puritans every last one, as quick to spot an irregular state of affairs as terriers spot rats, and the only other woman was sick the whole voyage and kept to her cabin. Then when we reached England . . .' His expressive face told in an instant every hard fact of that dismal landfall. He had done his Christian best – and he had not had a strictly Christian upbringing, he informed the Doctor, had run wild as a boy on his uncle's plantation, had been sent as punishment for certain crimes, youthful crimes, to the steaming hell of Brazil – yes, he had done his best to help a young woman in distress, only days from the birth of her first child, and all he had had for it so far had been sly averted looks and unworthy asides, and now, now a medical jackanapes, a slovenly apothecary, thought the child was his!

The medical jackanapes looked mildly contrite.

'I beg your pardon, but you must admit the evidence was against you. The young woman has not spoken, you understand. She has screamed, the poor young thing, it was only to be expected, but she has said nothing of an ordinary or personal nature – except to tell Mrs Bond her name was Hannah.'

'I did not know. She was only Mrs Brown to me.'

12

'But you are not on the road for Framlingham, Mr Savage, though to be sure it is not many miles distant. This is the road for Westdene and the sea.'

'As if I did not know,' in the voice of a man who has suffered much in a dubious cause and suspects he must suffer more. 'I have been to Framlingham already. And what an abominable place it is, a real country retreat, it might be unchanged since Canute was king in these parts. The girl had not been home in ten years, knew nobody, had scarcely more than five guineas in the world – what was I to do? Leave her in London? And so near her time, and no idea how to obtain a ticket for the coach ... So I brought her up here in a wretched disobliging post-chaise with springs like nutcrackers, most improper no doubt and open to the vilest interpretation – but what was I to do? I'd as soon leave a kitten at the mercy of a crowd of spiteful boys.'

'I am sure you acted only for the best,' said the Doctor, who had not yet seen any signs of an amorous nature, 'and the long voyage would have knocked her up, privations, discomfort, no friend on board.'

'Quite so. A sidelong look, rather amused. 'In any event we flew into Framlingham scattering the hogs and hens, but where were the relations? Dead, or moved away, or unable to take her in. We had the door shut in our faces, can you credit it, and the two of us up to the chins in mud and no civilized meals since Kingston. There was nothing for it but to discover the grandmother who had gone to Norwich, but when we arrived there it seemed the old lady had only gone to Norwich to die – I cannot blame her: the rain! the mud! the disobliging natives! – which left an ignorant scrub of a cousin who looked like a rat and gave as much offence. He refused to take her in as well, said she was a harlot, could die in the street before he'd allow his womenfolk to clap eyes on her. I could have knocked him down.'

'I see, I do indeed. Oh how seldom is virtue satisfactorily rewarded! But how come you are on the road to

Westdene? Not more relations? They will be no more charitable than the others, I fear.'

Mr Savage sat down, stuck out his long legs, and crossed his ankles. There was wry humour in his smile. 'It is I who have property at Westdene. Lord, Doctor, what would you have me do? Whatever her cousin may say I could not leave the girl in the street. It was filthy weather, she was hysterical, and the baby . . .' He paused, as if any moment he might hear the cry of the newborn from above. 'So I took a post-chaise again but it broke a wheel just the other side of Bungay and could I hire another? No. I scoured the town. This place did not keep any, business had fallen off so much lately; that place had one, spoken for; that two, both out on the road. I would have to wait. Well, you can tell I was in no mood for waiting, not by then. The coach came, someone said Westdene, we climbed aboard. And now look – we should have stayed in Bungay at a decent inn.'

The Doctor was deeply conscious of Mr Savage's burning impatience to be gone from this rural retreat, so deeply rural it might be supposed the midwife was only a step away from witchcraft. Well, he had spent years in and out of country practice, the odd bone and dried toad and incomprehensible chant did not give him a moment's pause, but he could understand a man used to another climate, other manners, eager to be off.

'The girl will not be fit to travel for a while,' he said quietly, keenly aware it was the last thing Savage wished to hear. 'Not tomorrow, perhaps not the day after. She has had a sad time of it. But then, maybe it was to be expected. After all, the absence of a husband, the attitude of her family, the lack of sympathy, all must have a bearing on the case. We are emotional creatures, say what we will.'

A look of pure vexation, involuntary and consuming, passed across Mr Savage's face. Then he sighed, ran a hand through his thick dark hair, and gave a huge laugh.

'What a trial we are to you, Doctor. You are as desperate to quit this place as I am.'

14

The Doctor grinned. It was simply an excercise of the muscles, however, for his inner self, his inner professional self, was closely engaged with the girl upstairs and he had grave fears, a deepening instinct. But he grinned, and busied himself lighting a pipe, watching the smoke curl. He watched it for a long while, pondering life and its bewildering excursions – the particular stroke of fate that had brought both Savage and himself to the Westdene coach, and thence to this place, this low dark room smelling of damp wood and slopped wine, this chair with the horsehair escaping from its torn seat, this mood of gloomy premonition.

'I have been in the West Indies myself,' he said at last as the clock struck four, 'I was there in '93.'

'That slaughter! Merciful Heaven, I don't envy you then. But look how late it is – dawn, even was you able to rub a clear place on the glass and manage to look out. Will you take anything before you turn in? They are still carousing down the passage by the sound of it.'

'There has been a wedding in the next village. Some of the young men are walking to every ale-house within five miles and making a night of it.'

'And a day too if they do not soon turn in. But how do you know these things?'

'The girl told me earlier, the poor skinny little wretch they keep to scrub and polish.'

Mr Savage gazed about in surprise. 'I would never have guessed they knew the meaning of the words. But come, will you take another glass?'

'I may yet be needed. I will take some coffee if any can be found.'

'Needed? Upstairs? Surely not?'

'She is very weak, and shock and loss of blood . . .'

'I had supposed that once safely delivered . . .' And then, for he was neither slow nor insensitive: 'You mean she might die?'

'Well, there is no medical necessity for it,' said the Doctor, 'none at all. But I have known it happen before

15

for no apparent reason. And it is always a bad sign when the mother will not look at the child.'

'I see.'

He saw too much – or he was beginning to – said his tone, and he wished himself a thousand miles away. He stared very hard at the Doctor, as if trying to come to a true understanding of his nature, his reticence, his very real fears. He found that lined, secretive face absorbed in watching the smoke rings rising to the blackened ceiling. And after all, he too had seen men die because they had been told they would, and seen men live miraculously for as little reason. He sighed.

The clock ticked. After a while there was a creaking silence in the rest of the house, the young men snoring in the tap-room and everyone else abed. Then morning – at least, a dirty smudge behind the window panes – and the landlady in a frowsty old wrapper and a man's turban asking about breakfast, speaking of chops and liver and nice fat bacon. The two gentlemen turned red and weary eyes on her, speechless. But the smell of cocoa stirred them to reply: they would take a jug, a whole jug and very hot, and perhaps a little toast.

The Doctor did not wait for it but went upstairs. He found Mrs Bond asleep at the bedside. The girl was shrunken beneath the coarse sheet, shrunken and grey. He did not like it: weak pulse, fever, no true sleep. The child lay in the crook of her arm but she did not feel it there, had never, from its first cry, asked to look at it. It opened its eyes at the Doctor, however, and gave him one of those immense, intelligent, direct stares so startling in the newborn.

His mind ran on practical matters: wet-nurses, draughts, clysters, blood-letting. He put a hand on the girl's burning forehead. It was an unnecessary gesture; he did not need confirmation of her fever.

It struck him as he went out that it had been an unconscious valedictory act, a formal goodbye from one stranger to another. Instinct told him he would lose her.

*

16

He lost her. He lost her at noon, quite quietly, the pulse simply fading under his gentle fingers. For a moment, standing by the bed, he raged and raged at her with all the bitter fury of which he was capable, and that was a very great deal. But he did so silently, and nothing in his face betrayed the depth of his feeling. Only when he spoke to Mrs Bond, giving instructions about the child, did his voice sound ominously chill and there was a glitter in his eye that made her drop a curtsey, a respectful curtsey. Then he went down to report to Mr Savage that medical science had been defeated by willpower, a shameful admission.

'She wished to die,' was all he said at first, as Savage looked up at his entrance. 'I wondered if she might when she would not look at the child. No doubt she hoped they both might die together. For sure she hated me, poor dear, when I laid the baby in her arms and told her they would both do famously. Had she spoken to you about the father? Was it a love match, an elopement? Is he living?'

'She told me nothing, she scarcely spoke.' It seemed Mr Savage was darkly angry, drawing his brows together above his broad nose, studying his fingernails minutely as if he could not bear for a moment to look about him. He had been a poor champion, he was thinking, and how he wished he had knocked down that despicable Norwich cousin after all, his whole being had craved the satisfaction at the time though he was not intemperate or ruffianly in the general way. He flung away suddenly and yanked open the tiny, dirty casement, breathing in the fresh air. It was a fine afternoon, perhaps the finest afternoon since his arrival in England, only wisps of cloud left to streak the deep and deepening blue of the sky he had thought might be forever filled with rain.

'If I had left well alone . . .' he began, and then: 'But she had no-one, had five guineas and no idea how to find the Suffolk coaches. And the child . . . She was a child herself. What was she? Seventeen? Eighteen?'

'The child lives,' was the Doctor's dry comment from

across the room, 'and I only recommend you do not leave her here, the helpless creature, for there is nothing so suspicious and superstitious as a village. Her looks will mark her out if nothing else.'

'You mean she is deformed? Birthmarks?'

'No, nothing of the kind. She is as perfect as she could be. But she is a most exquisite brown.'

Jardine Savage slammed the casement shut. 'Oh, was that it? I did wonder at the vehemence those niggardly dogs showed, even her own brother making her stand out in the street. Some cruel letters, some filthy tittle-tattle, had obviously preceded her. But what use have I for a newborn child? Black, brown, canary yellow – what difference does it make to me?'

'I believe we should keep her until we find her a home. I do not care for babies in the least, but she is even more helpless than her mother, poor scrap, and as we've helped her into the world I fear we must help her on in it.'

'What noble sentiments!' was Mr Savage's sardonic remark, but he smiled, and it was evident his native optimism, so hard to put under, was rising again moment by moment. 'But you would do well to watch out. It don't do to take chivalry to any great length, look at the consequences. I suppose we could always parcel the child up and send it to Norwich. It is their responsibility, not ours, for God's sake. On the other hand . . . On the other hand I would not trust a python to the kind hearts in that house. What are we to do?'

The Doctor's own optimism, never buoyant, had sunk without trace. Lack of sleep had told on him, and the unremitting anxiety, and the huge effort of will he had expended trying to make that unfortunate girl recover some will of her own. He hated to lose patients, though he had lost hundreds perhaps in a long and bloody career. He especially hated this kind of loss, unnecessary, avoid-able, and therefore doubly cruel.

'Is there any coffee at all in this dreadful place?' he demanded. 'Is there a single bean, a single genuine bean, in all the country roundabout?'

18

'I had a sackful in my baggage, sealed and double sealed, sent on ahead to Westdene when we landed. If it is not stolen or impounded or in any way destroyed it will be waiting there.'

'But Westdene is Westdene and this is' – a sour glance round – 'wherever it is. And we shall be here some few days more, I fear, unless you wish to be put to the huge expense of carrying the body on with you. We must arrange the burial, Mr Savage,' and then, leaning to pull on the bell, 'and the christening. It would be as well, I think. Let us get all the formalities over.'

Much later he was aware that Savage had climbed up to see the child – and the corpse too, perhaps. At any rate he came down with a grim, contained expression and spoke very little, ate very little too, all the rest of the evening. All he did say, at bedtime and through the hideous fug of the Doctor's pipe smoke, was: 'And I do not even know if Brown was her real name. They were called Fairhead or Fairley or something in Framlingham.'

'I am not sure it matters,' replied the Doctor, 'I cannot see them galloping post haste to claim her as their own.'

2

The Doctor was fond of declaring he would not die of melancholy but it seemed to him that sometimes he came near it, he came very near it indeed. There were times he had found life insupportable, for his bland expression and eccentric wig hid a sensitivity rare in a man of his calling – a butcher's calling, he had often thought. His answer to a sore heart – such a thing as he had never hoped to have to do with again – was to pack his bag, close up his house, abandon his patients to a promising young doctor from a neighbouring town, and seek Consolation, whatever it might be, as far from the undulating green county of Norfolk as he could go.

He had firmly believed he was sunk too deep in bachelor habits ever to be struck by a desire to marry. Of necessity all his relationships with women had been of the temporary variety except one, long ago in his youth. His had been an inconstant, wandering life. He had spent many years in and out of India, and on that grim excursion to the West Indies, and to those sad parts of Europe trampled by the Allied armies. He had known deep affection and flagrant physical attraction and every shade and degree in between – but only in passing, as it were, on the wing. He had only ever proposed marriage to one woman and she had refused him, refused him with a laugh; he did not care much for the memory.

He had rather cynical views on marriage, but after a few settled years in High Common he had found his opinions modified by a young lady twenty years younger than himself, very vigorous in mind and body, galloping haphazard all over his carefully guarded emotions just as she galloped across her own wide acres. He had left her on the point of marrying a saturnine young attorney, his own friend, had absconded most shamefully before the wedding even came off and with nothing but a terse note of farewell in execrable handwriting. He had hoped he might be able to behave with more decorum, more sense, but found he could not. So he gave his Lascar cook to a neighbour, put all his medical instruments into a bag, and had slunk away before it should be noticed. Old and influential friends were calling him back to London, to the once well-trodden courts and passages about Guy's Hospital. It would be pleasant to renew acquaintances, discuss the latest techniques, the latest fashion in techniques. And then? Perhaps the army again? In any case he must go somewhere where he might be sufficiently occupied to put all thoughts of Ann out of his head. It was not as if she even knew, even part-guessed his feelings. His feelings? His feelings now were a steady blur, a sense of loss, that unreal sense of loss when the object lost was never yet possessed.

Breakfasting alone the third day of his stay in Suffolk, Mr Savage's voice booming from above in outraged condemnation of some other dirty habit he had discovered in the newly acquired wet-nurse, he wondered if fate were about to tip him fortune or disaster. The toast was tough, the coffee owed a great deal to ground acorns or beech nuts, and the bacon was greasier than any bacon he had ever encountered. The weather too had taken another turn for the worse, the sunshine of forty-eight hours ago a fond memory. The rooftops gleamed with rain, the heavy rain that had fallen for hours from a weirdly lit and furious sky.

Mr Savage entered, looking as his name.

'I have never met such a slattern. What is to be done? She swears like a sailor's whore, thank Heaven I can only understand the half of it.'

'She told me an hour ago she intends to leave, she has no intention of nursing a mule.'

'A what? A mulatto, I suppose. And what are you going to do about it?'

'My dear sir, I think it ought to be your decision.'

There was a pause during which Mr Savage poured

21

his coffee into the fire and scowled into the emptied cup. 'The sooner I get to Westdene and my own beans the better,' he said, and then: 'I've never had call for dealing with wet-nurses, with blasted lumps of ignorant girls who sell their milk as if it were liquid gold. And I wager were it gold indeed you could get it with half the hysteria.'

The Doctor glanced at the dark, furious face, at the blazing blue eyes- ordinarily blue, at least, but now so deeply angry as to be indigo – and a gleam of humour lit his gloomy soul. 'Mr Savage, pray calm yourself. After all, there is always the Parish.'

'The Parish? I know nothing about the workings of the Parish. I have not set foot in this country for nearly thirty years and at the moment, I don't mind telling you, I am strongly inclined to leave it and not return for another thirty. But in any case, would not the Parish quibble at being handed an improvident scrap whose mother came from abroad?'

'Oh, there are always quibbles. It is the nature of Poor Law committees to quibble, they would not function without dispute, would feel deprived. However, you have a natural repugnance, I can see that; you mean to do your best by the child.'

'Well, it was you advised me against leaving it here. And I have no intention of handing it over to that filthy girl, milk or no milk.'

'Oh, she would simply pocket your money and smother the baby. I have known it done before.'

Mr Savage glared into the fire. 'What a damnable world it is.'

'Damnable indeed. You can depend on nothing in deep country like this but that they will resist change and kill anything unusual.'

Silence. Above a distant screeching in the kitchen and the rumble of a barrel being rolled across the tap-room floor they could hear the gentle, monotonous thrumming of the rain.

'We had better quit these wild parts tomorrow, Doctor, and travel on to my house at Westdene,' said Savage

22

suddenly, poking the toe of his boot at the fire which was dying by the minute – for why should the gentlemen want a fire in August, the landlady had cried when they had ordered it on their arrival, fires in August were wicked indulgence. 'We will take the baby with us.'

His mother had come from Woodbridge, he explained, a fine old family now extinct, though there was still a female cousin in the vicinity – a distant cousin, so distant he could not for the life of him work out the genealogy. It was all in the book at Helen's Mount, of course, but until recently Mr Savage had not bothered with such things. Helen's Mount was the plantation where he had grown up. It had belonged to his uncle – great-uncle in truth – a withered, depressed old man and no friend to Jardine though he had taken him in as a child.

For a while Mr Savage spoke lovingly of the house – built in 1760 by his grandfather, another Jardine Savage. It was close to the north coast, some distance from the plantations, standing alone amid its rich pastures. He himself had been born there, for his father had been killed by pirates when his mother was but a few weeks away from her delivery and she had naturally sought shelter with her husband's family. But she too had died within eighteen months, and such was the way of things, one sorrow often hard on the heels of another, the grandfather, his last surviving son and that son's infant daughter Rose, had all been lost before the baby Jardine was five years old. That left his great-uncle to inherit Helen's Mount and three great-aunts, elderly spinsters, to cope with his domestic comforts.

'I suppose I should be glad he never married,' reflected Mr Savage while his toe still stirred the tired fire, 'I would have been turned out for sure then. As it was I had to live with Aunt Ginny in a house in Montego Bay, the old man never got on with her and sent her into a kind of exile there. We never had any money and she went barefoot along with me, but she was never less than a lady and she made sure I never went hungry. She told them all I was the rightful heir to Helen's Mount so I was invited out to all the big houses.'

'And were you?'

'I believe I should have been, but there was some dispute over Grandfather's will and in the end it was considered best if my uncle ruled the plantations at least until I came of age. That was the theory. I don't believe anyone thought he would turn me out of the house. There was some small protest when he did but it was small enough, and he told them all in Kingston I had been sent away to school. When I was about eleven he took me back – and poor Aunt Ginny, who was really quite as mad as he was, though a sight more charitable – and from then on I lived about the place like a . . . like a stray dog, I suppose, that you feed occasionally and kick occasionally and never bother to chase off. Only he did chase me off later, time and again. I believe now that he might have had me done away with if he had had the courage, but too many people would have been suspicious.'

'It is an old story,' remarked the Doctor, 'and makes a mockery as always of the old contention that blood is thicker than water. Disputing families are the cause of much of the world's misery, I have long thought so, yes, long thought so. I gave up hoping for relations many years since when I pondered what sort and condition of people they might be and how they would rejoice to see me off, how I could be nothing but a cruel embarrassment, how they must hope I had never been born.'

Mr Savage looked sympathetic. 'Aunt Ginny used to say kin were the very devil, she would give her teeth and hair to be a solitary man. But then, she had more cause to be bitter than most, for it was her own brother turned her out to live like a pauper among the fishermen and the half-tamed Indians. She paid him out, of course: she never wore a pair of shoes again till the end of her life, used to come downstairs to a ball at Helen's Mount in a gorgeous gown and bare feet. The gentry thought she was simply touched in the head, a poor eccentric, but I

24

always felt she did it on purpose to make the old man blush.'

'Pray God none of my relatives were as strange as that,' said the Doctor. 'I believe my grandfather on one side was a clergyman – nothing there to rejoice in – and on the other . . . On the other prosperity, immense respectability, the largest farm in the district and six fine tombs in the church. But my mother ran off with an unsuitable jack-in-the-night and fetched up on the rocks of disillusion. She never went home, perhaps she never tried. She died when I was three and I was brought up by a schoolmistress she had befriended. But there, time canters on' – consulting his watch. 'It will not do to sit and swap old stories all day.'

But with his hand on the latch of the door he turned, amused interest in his face. 'But what became of Helen's Mount? You're uncle is dead, I believe you told me.'

'The estate has gone to Aunt Cissie's son – she was the only one of my great-aunts to escape and marry. Not that her marriage was much better than a prison but . . . Ah, well, all I know is hearsay. Her son is a man about fifty, a lawyer, and though there was talk of my great-uncle's will being invalid and much more in the same vein, he took care to tie my hands with his damned red tape so that I could claim nothing except by a long and costly suit. He gave me my mother's money, of course, for he found he couldn't touch it – that must have made him choke on his spleen – and my aunts – the dear Aunts – had all left me their portions, and then he had to pay me off, make sure I was not going to make a fuss . . . I can't say I was ashamed to take the money though to all intents and purposes it was a bribe and I was thinking of quitting the island anyway: I thought of all the years he had treated me worse than his house slaves – and he was no kind master to them. I took what he offered and turned to privateering with a friend I had in Falmouth who was mad for ships and a quick fortune. I suppose it was a breath from being a pirate but I can't say my conscience troubled me about that either. The dear old

25

Fortune served us well enough for a year or two and then we fitted out the *Helen*. They are in Barbados at present. I sold out, all except a half share in the *Fortune*.'

The Doctor considered all this, smiling inwardly. Mr Savage would have made an honourable and cheerful pirate, he thought, depositing his captured crews on the beach and entertaining them to grog and baked clams. However, since the world did not admit honourable pirates, the term being a contradiction, he supposed he must bid this happy vision adieu: the truth was probably sinister and depressing. For all that Ann owned a privateer, the *Sable Island* of Guernsey, a strange and providential bequest of her first husband, he had mixed feelings about letters of marque and the licence afforded private ships to prey on the so-called enemies of the king. In theory privateers were all very well, the *Sable Island* herself a prime example of a fine, well-run, disciplined ship bent on chasing the French off the seas; but what a gulf might exist between theory and practice, what an abysmal gulf in some most sordid cases.

'How did you come by this property at Westdene?' he asked, thinking that the sooner they left this stinking place the better, it was a far far cry from Jamaican plantations and privateers.

'I was in need of a change,' was the quiet reply, which could have meant anything, anything at all; the Doctor found Mr Savage's eye could be quite as slaty as his own. 'This is my mother's country and it seemed as likely a place as any for a spell of respectable living. To tell the truth it would never have crossed my mind but I met a lawyer in Montego Bay who was abroad on his client's business, another inheritance gone damnably astray, and he came from Westdene, said it was famous for crabs and cures for lung disorders. I might have been in drink when I asked him to look out for a property, but he took it seriously enough, wrote with the particulars of this place and at a moment I was sick to death of . . . of everything.'

'So you have come here on a whim.'

'I suppose I have, as much of a whim as yours, I fancy.'

'I fear your past life has not fitted you for the part of a country squire in deepest Suffolk.'

'Not as far as I can tell.' A grin, a flash of blue eyes.

'But then you have a great deal of money and you are a ship-owner, a plantation-owner by right. It is a start, some kind of start.'

'I slept in the stables more often than not and was sent out with the field gang. I have cut the cane and picked coffee and found my evening meal in the slave huts. It was no sort of apprenticeship for living with the gentry, though my Aunt Ginny made me promise to comb my hair of a night and morning . . .'

The Doctor saw that the real Mr Savage, Mr Savage delivered from the discomfort of an antique stage and the drama of childbirth and shattered good intentions and sudden death, was a naturally commanding, self-reliant, puckish gentleman whom he could come to like. Then an outrageous hubbub above was suddenly pierced by a baby's rising cry.

'Damn them,' said Mr Savage, 'can't a man have an hour's peace?'

'It is ever the way with family men. There is no more quiet once children are in the house.'

A fierce look, and then the expected laughter, deep and unaffected. 'Is that what I am come to? A family man? To think I have avoided it for all these years and now find myself a father by proxy, by adoption.'

The disturbances increased and a moment later the slatternly girl was in the doorway, the landlady behind with the bundle that was the baby. There was confusion, and shouting, and the sort of language the Doctor had hoped to hear only on the lower deck of a man-of-war. Jardine Savage, unable to draw himself up to his full height, remained seated but reached sideways for the poker; silence fell at once.

'Get out,' he said in a low, cold, terrible voice: 'Out, the pack of you. And leave the child.'

The child was thrust into the Doctor's arms, the door

27

closed, a subdued shuffling and a few mild screams faded down the passage. Mr Savage showed his teeth.

'The whores on the Kingston waterfront behave with more restraint. Do we leave at once? Speaking for myself I have had more than enough of this place.'

'You must find another nurse,' remarked the Doctor, whose gaze was fixed on the round affronted face of the baby, barely visible among the layers of wrappings. He always found babies disturbing: they could not be ordered about, nor could they understand rational argument. He was not, however, taken in by their apparent fragility, having seen them safely born on battlefields and surviving the kind of deprivations that would cast down grown men. He consequently looked at the child in his arms with some respect, and the child looked back, her mouth puckering for a hearty yell.

'There, there, we shall find your luncheon directly,' he said, rocking the bundle. 'Mr Savage, you must swallow your pride and run out and offer that miserable young baggage a guinea to stay until tomorrow. I know a Dr Bridges of Beccles who could be relied on to find a clean honest woman to take her place. You might send to him, sir, and mention my name.'

'You are leaving?' cried Savage, detecting the false note of the traitor in the Doctor's voice.

'I am expected at Guy's and have lodgings to find.'

'But you said yourself you were contemplating two weeks in Westdene, sea air and solitary walks!' Mr Savage stood up, paced to the window, paced back again. He appeared to be composing his face in the hope of looking humble and shyly hopeful, but anatomy and temperament were against him. His was a bold, strong, tenacious face. 'I would be infinitely obliged, Doctor, you would consider a week as my guest before you make haste to London. The house is large and rambling, baby ...'

'needs a wet-nurse, hardly a surgeon.'

'I am pushed for decent company and you are a

man who knows about these country places, how to behave, how to get things done . . .'

'You would be disillusioned. I have the reputation of an eccentric, and worse, I am not known to care for protocol, for precedent, for the fixed order . . . I am quite the wrong person to introduce you to country society.'

'I would pay your fee. If you prefer to come as a professional man and not as a friend, I would pay whatever is your due.'

The Doctor would not hear of a fee, stamped out at the very thought of such a thing, and Savage had to duck after him, calling out apologies. The Doctor ran to ground in the tap-room and when his pursuer burst in stopped him dead by handing over the bundle that was the baby, saying: 'Here, she is yours. By the way, what is she called?'

Mr Savage puckered his brow. He had not looked on the baby as any kind of person until this moment, not a real person, with character and feelings and a given name. Brown? He stared into the child's dark eyes, quite dark, though as yet more of a steely grey than an unequivocal black. No, not Brown. Had Brown been the mother's name at all? Or Fairstead, Fairhead, Fairley? He shuffled her awkwardly to his other arm for he was left-handed, and frowned more deeply.

'Perhaps she should be Hannah after her mother but I don't care for the name. My nurse was a Creole called Henriette, the dearest woman, joy of my heart. What if we call her Henriette?'

It occurred to him that the featherweight in the crook of his elbow was a mental millstone; he did not want her but he could no more abandon her than he could have left her mother sobbing in the Norwich rain. And the simple act of giving her a name, and one close to his heart, had somehow bound her to him as if it was some ceremony of adoption. But: 'Do come to Westdene – a week, a bare week, Doctor. It will see me settled and give me a chance to repay in hospitality what you will not take in . . .' A difficult moment as the Doctor stepped back. 'I beg pardon for mentioning it. But you will come? You will come in the capacity of a friend, I hope. And I will send to Beccles for the nurse. And you must not call me 'sir', we are become too well acquainted. You must call me Jary.'

At this point Henriette began to cry in earnest.

'Quickly, quickly,' advised the Doctor, 'run after that girl, offer her anything you like. The child needs nourishment.' And with a sly look at Jary Savage's alarm, 'And we need peace and quiet.'

3

The house was a quarter of a mile from a village called
Stretfield on the Westdene road. The post-chaise bearing
the Doctor, Jary Savage and the baby with her new nurse
turned in at a lugubrious trot.

'I bought it for next to nothing,' said Jary, struck by
the magnificence of the avenue of old oaks but unable to
see what was at the far end of it. 'I have lost as much in
an afternoon at cards.'

They crossed what seemed to be a pretty stone bridge
over a small river, the River Wiss that flowed out into
the sea at Westdene.

'There it is,' cried the Doctor, who had abandoned his
wig and thrust out his bristly head. 'What did you say it
was called?'

'Ramillies.'

It looked very fine in the watery sunlight of a fretful
August afternoon, of faded red brick – though it had a
noble entrance in the same stone used in the bridge –
and with a front that owed much to the fashions of the
early 1700s. As the chaise pulled up on the weedy gravel
Jary leapt out, staring about, his hat in his hand and his
companions forgotten. He vanished under the porch and
they heard him thunder on the door.

'Well, it all looks promising,' remarked the Doctor,
helping down Mrs Bloy and Henriette. 'I had feared the
worst, for if ever a man bought a pig in a poke it was
Mr Savage. A trifle of paint, and some energetic work
with a hoe ...'

The place was certainly charming, damp but charming,
though the Westdene attorney Mr Calloway's sketchy
description of it as large and rambling was something of
an understatement, for it was in fact two houses, the
newer attached at right angles to the original. This was

31

a sixteenth-century building, mullion-windowed, which had once had its own gracious entrance, and drive, and avenue of elms, all leading in a different direction. The housekeeper, Mrs Clark, an Ipswich woman engaged by Mr Calloway, told them the 'back house' had once been known as the Priory, but that was all she knew, beg his lordship's pardon, for she had had her information from Millett, the manservant, and he could barely be brought to speak to her, she was a foreigner.

'But you are a Suffolk woman!' cried Jary, roaming about the entrance hall of the newer house as he spoke and looking into the dark corners and concealed cupboards. 'How are you a foreigner?'

'Oh sir' – and she gave a flushed, shy look at the Doctor, whose immense shabbiness and remarkable muteness almost unnerved her – 'was you to come from Woodbridge you would be a foreigner to these people.'

'Oh . . . Yes, I see. But then, I suppose it is to be expected. It is human nature for a man to love his own few feet of ground the best.'

But it seemed the people hereabouts were abnormally insular, abnormally proud, and abnormally inclined to distrust others. Westdene had always been cut off by marsh, heath and wood, but it had been an enormously prosperous town and had simply turned its back on the wilderness. It had looked seaward, not landward, for the majority of its provisions. If the harbour had not silted up it might have continued to flourish, to grow like Ipswich, to become queen of the coast: but the harbour silted, the ships no longer came, and the town decayed.

'Should I make a negus, sir? It is so chill for the time of year. The beds are all aired but the windows downstairs should be opened, the rooms have been shut up so long. I've sent Hattie to light fires but it will be evening before you feel the benefit.'

'Yes, yes, a negus by all means,' said Jary, who threw his hat on to the knob of the stair post and climbed away into the upper regions. A little later: 'I'll wager there are dead birds and rats, even owls, stuffed up there,' as he examined a bedroom chimney. 'It is all in a sorry state.'

'I have been to the kitchen and found a strange dark woman who calls herself Mrs Fipson. She is making pies in your honour. I believe she is your cook. She told me the house has been empty five years. That accounts for a great deal. I saw Millett too, he has been here since he was a child and is all the groom, stable boy, coachman and gardener you have.'

A gloomy tour of the bedrooms followed, the ancient bedrooms in the oldest part of the house. 'Well,' said Jary, after a long time of looking and poking about in rather shocked silence, 'which would you prefer? The front and the Chinese wallpaper or this back with plain white walls and a view of the knot garden?'

'Is that what it is?' asked the Doctor, peering through the casement. 'I believe I would prefer it here, it has a charming simplicity and there is not a level floor in the place, but I fear this side of the house has not seen a hot brick or a warming pan for many more years than five. Let us repair to the front directly.'

There they found a charming morning room with a splendid fire, so charming that the years of neglect had been as nothing. Mrs Clark brought in the negus. The baby, she told them, was already up in the nursery with Mrs Bloy, that so very capable lady from Beccles – Heavens, how foreign Beccles must be, so many miles to the north, a very frontier post indeed!- and the girl Hattie had been sent into the attics for the cradle long ago laid by. Mrs Fipson, whose family lived only the other side of the park, and had done for countless generations, said that every Rayner for a hundred and fifty years at least had been put to sleep in that cradle, that it would be an honour for any child to lie under its oak hood.

'I did not buy the house from anyone called Rayner,' said Jary, opening more cupboards concealed in the panelling and finding a collection of empty rum bottles, a snuff box, and a piece of very old cheese.

'I believe the Rayners lived here before Mr Treadgold,

sir. There was an old Mr Rayner who died in debt and the estate was sold up.'

Jary closed the cupboards. 'Perhaps it is an unlucky house,' and then more cheerfully, 'but it was very grand once and deserves to be so again. What do you think, Alex?'

'I think it is too big for a bachelor and will soak up your money until you too die in debt. But with a wife and family and servants and determination you might live in tolerable comfort.'

Jary grinned. 'Well, I have the beginnings of a family up in the nursery, sleeping in the ancestral cradle. Come. Come, we must inspect the gardens.'

They went out, and found a wilderness. Jary strode on, muttering about shears and billhooks and spades. The stables, separated from the house by a short gravel walk, yielded nothing of note but the hostile red face of Millett, a fat old pony with yellow teeth – he showed them all when approached – and a plain, honest, unexceptional horse rather high on the leg.

'Another of Calloway's finds,' said Jary, inspecting it thoroughly. 'I wrote to ask for a good sound riding horse, nothing flash or fancy.'

'Then the admirable Calloway has delivered what you asked for. He is plain enough.'

'But is not that leg a little thicker than the other?'

'Well, to be sure, he has four. Does it matter?'

Jary rose from his stooping position. 'I can see you have no knowledge of horseflesh, whatever your virtues as a medical man.'

'No, no, none at all. Horses are an impenetrable mystery. Still, he has a kind eye,' the Doctor ventured, 'and that makes up for a great deal.'

'In the general way, but it cannot make up for a lame leg. Well, I will try him later. I suppose if he is a local horse Millett will know all about him. By the way, what about the doves? There seem a great many.'

There were certainly more than enough. They picked their way through cloud upon cloud of them to reach the

34

iron gate into a walled garden. The whole stableyard was full of doves, doves which apparently all tried to cram into the small triangular dovecote high on the coach-house wall and which stained everything with their droppings and filled the air with their incessant calling.

'You would think they might have ate some,' remarked the new owner, flapping his arms. 'We could have a squab pie or two perhaps.'

The Doctor feared there were so many birds they might tire of the pies before the numbers were substantially reduced. It was obvious that after Mr Treadgold, the last inhabitant of Ramillies, had gone into retirement at Bath, the doves had been left to breed apace; and Millet, who lived over the stables, was obviously not partial to pigeon.

'Partial to rum,' said Jary, wrenching open the gate and stepping through into a peaceful green jungle which must once have been a splendid old-fashioned parterre. 'The entire stables smell of rum. I wonder the horses are sober.'

Together he and the Doctor crossed the thick wet grass, looking up at the old part of the house, once obviously the front.

'I suppose it saw Queen Bess,' said Jary, poking his toe at a rampant box hedge, 'was she so foolish as to try her luck in these parts. Look, a sundial. Here, you are the man for Latin, I never had an hour's schooling in my life. What does it say?'

'Make haste, the shadows fall.'

'I wish I had not asked. Is that a statue over there in the bushes? It is a woman with a bow, and she has some arrows, by God. I like the flowing hair. Do you not prefer a woman with her hair loose? But there is more Latin. Come, let's make for the river in case this is as melancholy as the last.'

They passed round to the new front and struck down across wide lawns to where the unpretentious little river sparkled between its overgrown banks. To their right was a small wood, a copse of hazel and birch and willow, then a mass of elder and a steady deterioration into scrub, a boggy expanse, elders, and a pool. It was a sausage-shaped pool with water a most unnatural green. It had been made long ago by means of a simple sluice on the main river and perhaps it had been intended as ornamental, which would account for the out-of-hand copse and another half-hidden statue and the bridge, a peculiar rustic bridge of poles and old oak.

'There are fearsome algae here,' said the Doctor, stooping to watch the scuttle of waterboatmen and the sudden plop of a fish rising.

'Fish!' cried Jary. 'Look! What are they?'

'Tench perhaps. Who knows? You will have to bring a rod. They are all yours now whatever they are, poor dears.'

They stood side by side on the peak of the bridge – it rose sharply in the middle – looking back at Ramillies, a rather lovely house seen across this green, neglected distance.

'Still,' said Jary, whose thoughts had been turning on more practical considerations of his new home, 'I can understand why Treadgold flew to Bath after a year or two. An old man's joints would seize up in a place like this. But it will do for me. I will try it for a while and see if I cannot restore its old glory.' He turned a rapt, dreaming face to the rustling tops of the willows and dropped the handful of pebbles he had been carrying into the pool below.

'You have brained a fish! Look, he is rising.' But there was only a flash of scales in the sun and then nothing but a long ripple on the emerald water.

'We are a long way from Jamaica, dear Lord,' was Jary's odd remark as the ripple died away.

They walked back in silence. On the rough lawn in front of the house they came across Mrs Bloy with the baby in her arms. She had taken to heart, she explained, the Doctor's vehement exhortations to give the child air, as much air as possible. She curtseyed deeply to Jary, quite in awe of him, and held the tiny morsel out for inspection.

Jary peered between the ruffles of the baby's bonnet.

'I daresay she will grow up quite comely,' he said carefully, touching the silky black hairs that escaped here and there. 'She is just a little dark in her complexion.'

'She is a dear,' said Mrs Bloy, who had grown amazingly attached to Henriette in the three days she had cared for her. 'She is the best baby I have ever nursed, sir.'

Jary looked gratified, as if the compliment somehow extended to himself. He looked again into the tiny nut-brown face with its huge dark eyes and a stirring of something more than sentimentality made him bring his brows together in a sort of frown of astonishment.

The Doctor saw the instant of his falling in love and turned away to smile and grope in his deep pocket for his pipe and tobacco.

'Let's hope the beds *are* aired,' said Jary, after Mrs Bloy had made off across the lawn with her charge, 'for if they are not by now I wager they never will be: we are going to come a sad second to Henriette. All those clothes she was wearing came out of a box in the attics. Mrs Clark has been busy on her behalf fetching out the long-lost Rayner heirlooms.'

The beds had been aired but perhaps longevity and damp were indivisible. Doubtless the mattresses were old, very old, and bedpans and hot bricks were powerless to come at their lumpy and mouldering interiors. The Doctor slept badly, waking once to find he had forgotten to blow out his candle, and later to a howling draught, and later still to what sounded like a committee of owls in the chimney. Often he thought he discerned the bright sparkle of rodent eyes and several times heard the patter of rodent feet. In the morning, however, he woke to find two grey cats on the counterpane who did not even condescend to open an eye between them when he stirred and spoke – and there was a dead mouse in his clothes cupboard, skilfully beheaded.

Downstairs Jary had been up some time, had feasted

on kidneys and bacon and perfect toast, all kinds of preserve, kedgeree, chops and a sausage, and his own marvellous coffee hand-nursed from Jamaica. He smiled at the Doctor, pushing the coffee pot over the white cloth.

'Dear Mrs Fipson has surpassed every expectation,' he said. 'Try some of this raspberry on your toast. I hope you don't mind eating in the morning room but I have taken a liking to it and besides, it's a good stone's throw nearer the kitchen. Mind you, I am not sure I care for all these dead Rayners watching every mouthful.'

The Doctor looked about. 'Are they Rayners? Are they not Treadgolds?'

'Mrs Clark has it from the cook that every last one is a Rayner. Old Treadgold never touched a thing, bought the place with every stick of furniture the Rayners hadn't sold elsewhere and every member of the family still hanging on the wall. Do you think he had no relations of his own and adopted them, so to speak? Some of them are very grand. And look at the lady the far side of the fireplace. I would like to meet such a female as that, I would indeed.'

The lady in question had been painted in her best grey silk, a small dog under her arm. She was not strictly a beauty but an ardent, impatient character seemed stamped in the decisive bone. A pair of green-brown eyes offered a challenge. The mouth smiled and yet withheld a smile, not coyly but as if the lady knew a great deal more than she was prepared to say. The Doctor reflected sadly that he had met several young women of that stamp and they had been the very devil.

'She has a broad, pugnacious nose,' he said eventually, feeling a comment was called for but not being a man to flatter.

'But interesting. Don't you find it an interesting face?'

'Who is she? Have you consulted Mrs Fipson?'

'Now you are pulling my leg. I have not consulted anybody. Perhaps she is the late lady of Ramillies.' And then, glancing again at the deep bodice, the cuffs, 'Maybe not, maybe the lady before that. She has a great deal of hair.'

'A despicable, unhealthy fashion, powdering the hair. How much better if she had left it as God intended.'

'That's rich coming from a cove in a wig like that,' declared Jary with a stab of his fork.

'Oh . . . I had left it off,' said the Doctor miserably, who had spent some long time in front of his mirror admiring the effect of leaving it off but whose courage had failed him at the last moment. 'I had resolved never to wear it again, though it is against the grain – against the custom of my profession indeed. But I thought you would be offended by my rude bristles.'

'Rude bristles! Bristles be damned! You look ten years younger without the dreadful thing. Why not throw it away? It has seen better days without a doubt, it is due for honourable retirement.'

'I have another, more respectable.'

'For best? Oh well, do what you will. For my part I would rather have the bristles.'

There was sunshine outside. Far away down the lawn was a small bent figure with a scythe, cutting and pausing, cutting and pausing, now and again rubbing its back.

'Who is that?'

'That?' Jary looked up from deep contemplation of several old maps. 'Oh, that is Millett. I told him I wanted the grass cut. He said it would take till Candlemas to cut it all, so I told him in that case he had better make an early start. I shall try the horse this morning. I have a mind to ride round the estate. I found some old maps in a desk upstairs last night and they have every copse and ditch and every field name on them. Did you know there is a place called Paradise only just outside my gates? All the meadows between here and there are called the Meeting Grounds.

The Doctor paused with a piece of kidney on his fork while his brain wrestled with a complicated joke which involved these unlikely places, but he gave it up, and a moment later asked: 'Will you be out all morning?'

'I suppose I will. You could join me on the pony. We could amble about together.'

'I would rather remain unacquainted with the pony. No, no. I shall find myself a rod among the many tossed down in the boot room and shall catch a fish for my supper.'

Jary approved. He felt that perhaps the Doctor ought not to be seen roaming the countryside on the grass-cutting pony; they would have to find a more suitable mount – they would have to apply to the inestimable Mr Calloway. Jary rang for Mrs Clark, sent a message by her to the scything Millett to have the brown horse ready in half an hour, another to Mrs Fipson congratulating her on the breakfast, and then did not omit, the Doctor noticed, to climb to the nursery to see Henriette before leaving. Then outside to the depressing gravel sweep – more weeds than was botanically possible, said Jary – and into the saddle of the polite brown horse.

He had no sooner gone than a lady in a carriage called, a Mrs Jewkes. The Doctor scuttled for the back regions, calling out that he was from home, he and Mr Savage were from home. It was not his place to entertain Jary's callers, it was true, but it was an undignified retreat. Mrs Clark chased him into the kitchen and found him talking bait with the cook, who was all for mutton fat and sultanas.

'I hope you will not waste sultanas on those old fish!' she cried. 'I have seen them, they are all as plump as can be. It is Mrs Jewkes who has called, she is the tenant of Foley, the house by Lower Paradise. I really do think . . .'

But the Doctor was unmoved by social obligations. They were not his, in any case, they were Mr Savage's. And what would Mrs Clark recommend then in place of the sultanas?

'Oh! Oh, they will rise for a crust!' was her affronted cry.

And they would have done too. They had not been pursued for many years except by infrequent, trespassing fishermen and Millett's old half-blind spaniel. The

40

Doctor, who sat on a riverbank primarily for the profound peace and opportunity for meditation, was distracted by their readiness to rise. In the end he hung his rod in an elder growing right down by the water and smoked quietly in the shade by the rustic bridge.

The sun rose higher. It was time he returned but he made no move. The wind trembled the leaves of the sallows and brought him a whiff of sour elder wood where he had skinned a branch with the rod. He closed his eyes.

A faint splashing attracted his attention. He opened one eye, sighed, and groped his way awkwardly towards the sound. The rod was bending with the force of the fish's withdrawal. He pulled it out almost savagely, damning it for interrupting his dreams, guilty dreams of Ann, and yet as he did so he wondered he had left it so obscured in reed and grass, so hidden by the hanging branches. He did not remember doing that. Then, across the water, a sharp voice, a female voice, cried: 'You have landed my fish, sir! Have you not enough of your own?'

He looked up, his dulled senses returning to normal. He saw a shape on the opposite bank, waist-deep in willowherb. And he also saw, some yards away, his own rod dangling from the elder bush.

'I beg your pardon. I had forgot I took my rod out of the water. You may have him with my blessing.'

She had gone, was crossing the bridge. He could hear the swish swish of a skirt through the grasses. She ducked under the elder branches and fetched up a little distance away, more wary now, as well she might be seeing he was wigless, coatless, his shirt sleeves rolled up and her fish, her fine fat fish, wriggling about in his hands.

'You should not be fishing here,' were her first words, a very faint nervousness apparent in her clear, authoritative voice. 'You are trespassing. All the land on this side of the river belongs to Ramillies and no one may fish this pool without permission.'

He hesitated. His mischievous spirit was kindled. She had spoken to him as if he had been a schoolboy, and that small, insignificantly small part of him still desirous of being admired by women, any comely woman, rose to the bait as readily as the poor dear fish.

'Is Ramillies not empty?' he asked mildly.

'It was. The new owner arrives any day, so they tell me. And he is a great nabob and will hang us all by the heels for poaching.'

'Not a lady, surely? He would not persecute a lady?'

She gave a glance down at her damp hems, her galoshes, her dirty hands, and the rueful smile that broke slowly across her face was the most delightful thing the Doctor had seen in quite an age.'I doubt I would pass for a lady if I were paraded in the parlour by an irate water bailiff.'

'You mean, there is a bailiff patrolling the bank?'

'Not yet, but there may well be. Rich men are so jealous of their privileges, have you not noticed? But here, give me the poor fish. It is cruel to let him suffocate.' And she dispatched it neatly, and quite as if the Doctor could not possibly be trusted to do it.

She was as tall as he was, for he was not a tall man, and she had fair slippery hair piled up anyhow under a very old straw hat. For a moment she reminded him of someone he had recently met but for the life of him he could not think who it was. She was nothing like Ann at least, there was none of Ann's slight darkness, her beautiful eyes. And this girl was older, hardly qualified as a girl in an age when twenty-five was past the prime of life. There were faint telling lines about her mouth and eyes; he could see them as she stepped into the sunlight, the unkind sunlight, though it blazoned on her hair and turned it to pure gold.

'I have not had the pleasure . . .' he began.

'Oh, I would far rather remain anonymous,' said this surprising female, starting back for the bridge, her fish held expertly with two fingers. 'If we do not know each other's names we may not be tempted to peach upon each other.'

'Of course,' he called as she put her foot upon the first

plank, 'I might be the new owner of Ramillies,' and waited for the riposte that would surely come.

'You have a hole in your frock,' she said, 'and your shoes are a disgrace, and would any man who was a nabob bait his hook with cheese?'

'Appearances can be deceptive.'

'I am sorry to hear you falling back upon commonplace maxims.'

'But you see I have always been careless of my clothes. You should not judge me by them, you should not indeed.'

'You seem very careless of your wig as well,' was the retort, 'I should carry it home and air it well or you will surely get a cold in the head,' and she vanished into the alder scrub without a backward look.

The Doctor cast about, bewildered, and found his wig among the rushes and the bogweed, waterlogged. He tried to wring it out but without much success, and was forced to wrap it in his coat to take home as if it were some damp misbehaved animal.

'I have met a neighbour of yours,' he told Jary, whom he found in the stableyard with the sweating brown horse.

'Not the one from whom you ran away so rudely just after I went out? Millett says it was a Mrs Jewkes from Foley. Apparently everybody saw you running away down the back lawn.'

'No this was not Mrs Jewkes, I fear, but certainly a lady.'

'On the riverbank?'

'With a rod, a very good rod, no willow switch with string. And I would say she was most assuredly raised as a lady though her present circumstances are difficult to guess. She wore a very old petticoat but it would once have been fine enough to curtsey to the king. I suspect she is a frequent visitor to your pool.'

'Well, I'm not a man to grudge a fish or two, but why are you half undressed and what is that bundle? It is dripping.'

'It is my wig. It is past resuscitation, I believe. I shall give it to Millett to burn.'

They walked to the house. Jary, it seemed, had had adventures of his own, having found the brown horse too much of a gentleman to be true, and having become bored with him. He had therefore jumped him over a couple of fallen elms and then set him alight across the grass, but an old fellow had risen up from under a tree and there had been no chance of avoiding him.

'His leg was trodden on so I brought him back riding double. He is in the kitchen. He has a theatrical line in howling, you would think he had been disembowelled at the very least.'

By the porch they paused, looking across at the swathes of cut grass where Millett had been making reluctant inroads on the jungle.

'You know, I have always wanted a sort of water garden,' said Jary. 'There were fountains at Helen's Mount. Of course, it stood by the sea, one was never out of sight of water . . . But if we dredged the pool, made it bigger, dug a ditch there . . . No, there . . . Yes, and then another pool.'

A low lupine wail came from within.

'Lord, the old man,' cried Jary. 'We must go in.'

The Doctor followed, damp and wigless. 'I hope you do not mean to provide me with a patient every day,' he said.

4

Fanny Jewkes returned to Foley and gave her friend Lizzie Rayner her unrestrained opinion of shabby little men in threadbare coats who crept out under the very noses of their visitors – and clutching fishing rods and a basket! She had a pleasantly passionate nature and she felt she had been deliberately snubbed.

'And there was I,' she finished with a sigh, 'hoping for a handsome baronet, a man of fashion and property.'

They were in the garden and it was twilight. Lizzie had been out all afternoon painting one of the children from the cottages at the Diddlers whose mother sometimes helped in the Foley kitchen, and her lap was still stuck with dismembered daisies and dandelion petals. The evening was damp and sharp, the smell of autumn already in the earthy waft of air from Frenchmans Hill and the dark reaches of Beke's Wood on its summit. There was the *queek-queek* of an early hunting owl making his way down the ditch that separated Foley's orderly garden from the stubble fields and the flat, faintly misted acres of grazing along the river that had been used in ages past for village meetings, witch trials, football, cricket, coursing hares, pony races, dipping sheep. These haunted levels, full of snipe and – down in their watery extremities – bitterns and reed warblers, divided Foley from its grand neighbour Ramillies. They were still known as the Meeting Grounds, though successive squires at the big house had discouraged their use over the centuries until now only the most eager and discreet lovers met there in the lush growth of June and July.

Lizzie, seated on the garden bench, Frenchmans at her back and the valley unfolding in front of her in shades of grey and mother-of-pearl, gazed across the intervening distance – half a mile, perhaps less – to the invisible

Ramillies. She did not care who might be the new owner of that lovely old house, she did not care in the least. Her jaw stiffened with the great effort of not caring, and her eyes burned tigerishly under their slender pale brows.

She glanced sideways at Fanny, who had been mother and sister, friend and companion for more than ten years now. Dear generous cunning Fanny, who lived on gossip and was reputed to take to her bed in its absence. In a small rural community what was there but gossip to sustain interest? For much of the year they were cut off from the diversions and urgent considerations and even the daily news of the greater world. The grandest event of the year was the Assize Ball, a trip to Ipswich or Norwich the talk of six months. At any rate it was commonly believed not a mouse could stir between Diddlers and Westdene but Mrs Jewkes would know of it before anyone else.

'There is not an unattached female for twenty miles,' Fanny was saying, 'not praying he is single and tolerably good-looking – and then to find him in a ragged coat, a mean skimpy little man, horribly shifty!'

'How sad for you all!' said Lizzie with an unsympathetic laugh. 'You will have furbished up your best gowns and used up your elder-flower cream for nothing – though of course he may still be single and he *is* a man of property.'

'I would not consider him were he to kneel at my feet. I shall not call again.'

'Well, either way, single or wed, he is your landlord and master of half the village besides, so we shall all live by his smiles and sneezes, as humble folk do everywhere who are at the mercy of the rich.'

'Lizzie! Have you been reading more of those strange pamphlets? Sir James will have you taken up for sedition! Why, your own father was a rich man, and put his money to good use, was loved by every man, woman and child in the valley and beyond; put *most* of it to good use, I should say, save what was diverted into those foolish investments and the harbour scheme that was bound to

46

come to nothing. Those mud-flats will ruin more honest men than will ever be counted.'

Lizzie brushed at the flower petals on her skirt. 'What of the Whiteleys? Can you say their influence is benevolent? Would you want to be a tenant of theirs? Mrs Whiteley cares nothing for duty, responsibility, even common charity. How could she, and sit in her grand parlour with an easy conscience while people live and die in hovels at the Diddlers?'

Fanny, seeing the quagmire of social conscience ahead, veered abruptly. 'Of course, Mrs Whiteley is bound to call at Ramillies.'

'Only if the gentleman has impeccable references and a very great fortune.'

'How could she find out? Calloway would not tell her were she to grovel at his feet. His only virtue is that he despises her thoroughly and does not care to hide it. Nobody knows the man's name, or where he has come from, or how much he is worth.'

The light was dying away. Lizzie said in a low strained voice: 'Perhaps he will make great changes.'

'Perhaps he will. You must try not to mind it. Anyway, it is better the place is lived in than that it crumble to dust as a sad reminder of the past. Your father would have hated that. But I will not call again, no, no, I will not.'

'Then how will you ever know if he is single and rich? How you would hate to receive every scrap of information from Mrs Stone, who is certain to call even if he is repulsive, for she has too many daughters to be nice.'

The owl had crossed Little Piece and was hunting down the hedges towards Paradise, the big farm beyond the ford where the steep lane to Stretfield crossed the river. Lizzie could not hear his wings but she was aware of him, of the soft blur of his passing and of his getting farther and farther away.

'*You* could call,' said Fanny all of a sudden.

'At the door? Boldly? "Miss Rayner has called to see

47

what mountebank has taken her father's house. How dare you move the portraits, they are all relations! And put back those bedcovers, sir, my great grandmother stitched every one by candlelight!" Fanny! How could I call? But perhaps I could be so shameless as to peer through the hedges when I am out walking.'

'Lizzie, I did not . . . You are teasing . . . But yes, I suppose you could. You walk in the park still and you could take your brushes and paints so 'twould not look as if . . . He would not even notice you.'

'Unless he were standing on the roof with a spyglass, but if he were he would hardly be the romantic hero you desire. I have never heard of one, at any rate, who behaved so curiously.'

There were moths in the tall grasses by the hedge and above them the sky had deepened to cobalt. Soon the moon would lift over Paradise. There was a little dark shape flitting by the ash at the end of the lawn, and another and another . . . Fanny gave a squeak and jumped up.

'Bats! Lizzie, bats! I must go in. Quick! Quick!'

The following day saw Lizzie finishing her commission at Diddlers and Fanny wavering in her decision never to cross the threshold at Ramillies again. At noon Mrs Stone, who liked to think herself the most important lady in Stretfield after Mrs Whiteley – considered herself the equal of Mrs Whiteley but could not truthfully claim Mrs Whiteley's astonishing income – called at Foley on her way home from her own expedition to call on the new gentleman now in possession of Lizzie s inheritance. Since it added nearly three miles to her journey to circumnavigate the Ramillies park in order to pass secluded Foley it was obvious she had news of some interest. She was a great fat cheerful woman, an old, old friend of Fanny's: they had known each other intimately twenty years. Fanny had never had children though both her brief marriages had been happy ones; Mrs Stone had five daughters and two sons, none of whom were safely settled.

'I did not see him,' she said as Fanny ushered her into the little square morning room. 'He was out, Millett said, out about the grounds. I did not even climb down from the carriage. Millett met us in the drive and spoke to us. He admired the whiskey, said he thought it must be very fashionable. Belinda says it makes her sick, it sways such a great deal,' and here a reproachful look at her eldest daughter who had put on her best bonnet to call at Ramillies, and all to no effect. 'I went on to the house and left my card, and the housekeeper came out, was thoroughly pleasant, gave us to understand the gentleman was foreign.'

'Foreign from where? Of what nation?' cried Fanny, who saw herself doomed to disappointment on all counts.

'Well, all she said was that Mr Savage – Mr Savage! – was busy riding about the property for he had lately arrived from abroad and was not acquainted with the English countryside. There, what do you think of that?'

'Perhaps he is not foreign at all,' said Fanny hopefully, 'but is newly returned from . . . from India, say.'

'But never seen the English countryside?'

There was a movement outside the window. 'What a great disappointment he is proving,' remarked a tart voice, 'perhaps it is ever so with heroes. Perhaps they never measure up to our expectations of them. It is a sad thought, but maybe they are best left between the pages of books where we never know how they deteriorate after the last line and become quite sinful and human after all.'

'Lizzie!' and Fanny rushed to close the window, finding Lizzie with an armful of roses, no less, and looking her best for a change, a circumstance that made her if anything crosser than ever seeing that Lizzie so rarely looked her best and was seldom to be found surrounded by flowers.

At dinner she admonished her more severely. 'People

will take it amiss, they will say how eccentric you have become. And uncivil.'

'It was only a chance remark. And surely "people" are used to me by now – Mrs Stone has known me since my cradle. Surely you can see the amusing side? How you are all hanging out your tongues for a glimpse of this poor creature at Ramillies. No doubt he is a perfectly ordinary man, dressed in a perfectly ordinary coat and with perfectly ordinary spectacles.'

'Spectacles! Heaven forbid! But he is a foreigner.'

'So is anyone who comes from beyond the turnpike. And Beccles or Woodbridge or Framlingham might be the far side of Cape Horn.'

This was evidently true, for Fanny subsided. Of course she could see the amusing side of half the country agog to see what sort of man had taken Ramillies, but in such a remote place it was the equivalent of the Assize Ball – it would keep them from running mad with boredom for some months.

'But Lizzie dear, he is excessively tall and dark-skinned and he gallops everywhere – he galloped over Tom King in the park. Tom called this afternoon to chop the faggots and told me all about it, told Lussom anyway, who told Kitty. He was taken up as if he were a feather and carried up to the house where he was treated by a doctor, a qualified man by all he could understand, but in shirt sleeves and smelling of a duck pond.'

'Tom King has no business in the park and deserves to be galloped over. But why should a doctor smell of a duckpond?' and here Fanny might have noticed Lizzie looking rather sly.

'How should I know? I have no experience of doctors, only old Plesset, and you could not prise him out of his wig and frock or his breeches and stockings if Bonaparte himself were to land at Westdene.'

Lizzie considered. Fanny had still not noticed that roguish little smile. 'Dear Fan, I believe you must call on Mr Savage again; put on your new pelisse, swallow every prejudice. Why, the master of Ramillies might be a mean little toad of a man but the doctor – the Doctor might be Paris and worth a tidy fortune.'

Fanny rang for Lussom, and when the manservant appeared – a gangling, squinting, ugly man who had been with her years and years – she said: 'I will want the carriage tomorrow. How is the mare's foot?'

'Oh,' 'twill get her as far as Ramillies, never fret yourself, mum,' was the innocent reply, and Lizzie, who cared nothing for dignity, went off into a peal of laughter.

Lizzie had been to Paradise with cheese – the Foley kitchen was renowned for its cheeses – and was returning with a basket of eggs. It was a dull heavy louring day, the sky a dense dark grey over the cornfields, a threatening stain of watery yellow beyond the Meeting Grounds. For a moment, standing under the dripping elms after crossing the ford by the rickety footbridge, she mentally arranged her palette so that she might begin a tremendous summer storm scene in just these violently heightened colours: the sky so dark, the uncut barley so unnaturally blond, the trees vivid green.

Just before Foley a bend in the lane brought her to a clear view of the burnished levels, over which not a lark was singing in all the ominous quiet. With sudden decision she set off at a brisk walk, leaving her eggs in the hedge by Foley's wicket gate as she passed, and continuing, not up Frenchmans but along the road that skirted the park at Ramillies. After a while she passed by the old plantation at Cuckooland and a hundred yards more brought her to the end of the old elm avenue that had once been the entrance. Now all that remained were the two rows of great trees, many of which had fallen to age or storms, the drive between returned to the original grassy ride of Elizabeth's day. The gates had long ago been removed and the gap filled with stout poles. It was the cattle's stamping place; they were there now switching off the flies and hanging their heads in the unbearable humidity.

Lizzie leaned on the fence. Ramillies; poor old trees;

poor avenue, almost ruined; at the end of it was the walled garden that had been her mother's special place. Before the wall had been built, enclosing it, carriages might have trotted right up to the gravelly terrace, to the old low doorway of the Elizabethan front. Before the river had been diverted to make the pool, before wide sweeps of grass and rustic bridges had been fashion, Ramillies had looked this way, to Frenchmans, the Meeting Grounds, and Low Paradise.

Low Paradise was a village no more, the church a heap of stone in a copse, Foley and three cottages all the rest. Plague or riot or flood perhaps had caused the people to move across the river to Paradise which was really just the outpost of Stretfield.

Once, years ago, Lizzie Rayner had felt that she would do anything to secure Ramillies again, that two hundred and twenty years of amiable ownership should not go for nothing. She had thought seriously about the possibilities: marrying wealth in order that she might buy it back; becoming wealthy in her own right as a painter, ditto; becoming wealthy through the legacy of one of her Woodbridge cousins who on his deathbed repented having cast her out. Knowing it to be foolishness, still she had hoped. Perhaps such hopes had kept her alive, had kept her chin firm and her brown-green eyes blazing, had calmed her outrage and despair. How well she had taken it, they had said at the beginning, how well, how astonishingly well . . . But how could they know what it was like to be left at seventeen with one's whole world disorder, debt and degradation? How would they feel to be sent a curt note on the morning of their father's funeral to say that the man they had been going to marry was constrained to call off the wedding, he had been led to unreal expectations, that in the absence of the agreed dowry the contract was void?

Lizzie climbed over the poles. She would never have Ramillies now. A few large spots of rain fell on her as she passed between the elms. After a while she saw the garden wall and the roofs and chimneys of the house. If she sat here on a fallen trunk, and listened, she would hear the murmur of the doves in the stableyard and the stop-start exhortations of the wood pigeons above her. There was a bee in a patch of bugle at her feet and the patter of rain on leaves.

It had been a great loss – father, home, lover, all in four days – but nothing like so great, she had sometimes felt, as the loss of her own self-respect and every last vestige of her innocence.

Jary, on a tour of inspection on the roof of his new purchase, paused in his gloomy perusal of the decayed lead and missing tiles and glanced down over the oldest portion of the property. He did not have a spyglass but then he had keen eyes.

'Millett, there is a woman sitting in the park. I swear it is a woman. On the fallen tree.'

Millett removed his cap the better to improve his view. 'Oh, that'd be Miss Rayner, sir. She were brought up here. She come and goo as she please.'

'Does she? Oh, does she!' cried Jary. It occurred to him as he dodged the chimney and made for the ladder that she might be a direct descendant of the lady who so enchanted his breakfasts and luncheons and dinners, might have been rocked in the cradle now so charmingly occupied by Henriette. But when he reached the small door in the knot-garden wall and forced his way through she had gone.

'You did not hear me,' accused the Doctor, finding him casting about in the long grass with an air of defeat. 'You were too intent upon your quarry. What was it, by the way?'

'A woman; a woman with fair hair.'

'Oh. Have you never found it does not do to be too obvious when pursuing women? They only laugh, aware of their power. Would it not be prudent to maintain your distance for a while?'

'Ha, ha. Your old jokes become tiresome, Alex. I was not pursuing her, at least, not in the way you mean. But

53

Millett said her family lived here years ago. She is a Rayner, a relation of my lady in grey silk. And I have just found some drains. Drains – can you credit it? I did not think this place knew what plumbing was.'

'I had been told you were on the roof.'

'That was just now. This morning I hunted round the front of the house and found drains – they must lead to the river, but where? Where? I am beginning to wonder if they are responsible for the algae on the pool. When I saw this woman Rayner I thought . . . I thought she might know where they led.'

The Doctor sat down on Lizzie's tree trunk and his laughter grew a little uncontrolled. When he had croaked to a stop he found Jary staring at him, infuriated.

'You find it amusing, no doubt. But she used to live here. Do you not see? She may know all about the land, the damming of the river, the sluices; she may be able to advise me on my water garden.'

'And she may slay you,' said the Doctor, 'for desecration. Has it occurred to you that you are living in her house?'

5

It was a close-coupled little, sharp little, witty little horse, the sort to out-think the majority of riders in a twinkling; he had the Doctor's measure the moment the Doctor's foot was in the stirrup.

'I thought he would be just the thing,' said Jary, a sad strain of doubt in his voice, 'he seemed so suitable when they trotted him out.' He scanned the Doctor's deficiencies with anxiety. How stiffly he sat and how very short his reins were, witness to an insecure seat. It might not do to have too insecure a seat on this particular pony, he had the cunning of generations between his incurving ears.

'Lengthen your reins,' was all the advice he felt able to offer, 'he resents being held up so. Perhaps you would do better on this old fellow, he is undeniably a gentleman.'

But after a while they got along in better order, for the Doctor's fault was not fear but a natural inability to balance, much as some people are tone deaf. The pony, finding him inept but impossible to unnerve, gave him a ride Jary afterwards described as 'sprightly', a gross understatement: his heart had stopped several times. But: 'One would never fear for one's liver on this brute,' was the Doctor's only comment at the time, jogging from rut to rut and occasionally disappearing sideways up a bank or turning tight circles in the hedgerow.

'Not your liver, but what about your neck? I wish I had never clapped eyes on him, but he came when they called and walked out like the proverbial lamb.'

'I do not mind him,' cried the Doctor, grabbing a handful of mane as a pheasant clattered out of the undergrowth and the pony stopped dead. 'He has no malice in him, I am sure of it.'

It seemed to Jary he might have used this phrase of Mr Calloway, who had not, as yet, put in an appearance at Ramillies, but as time went on he was becoming less inclined to give Mr Calloway the benefit of the doubt. He had had a trying morning, not improved by receiving a note to the effect that Mr Calloway was unable to call – again – owing to an old lady twenty miles away needing him to attend to her will. The entire absence of apology in this terse letter irked Jary considerably as he read it and still irked him an hour later after half a dozen muffins and a whole pot of coffee. Henriette too had been in an irascible mood, screams of temper could be heard even in the morning room, a prodigious feat for lungs so small. It was therefore in a rather ominous voice that Jary had ordered the horses brought round for his visit to his distant cousin.

She may have been distant by blood but she was by no means distant in miles, for she was the dread Mrs Whiteley about whom the Doctor – he had not said anything to Jary – had so far heard little good. She had not yet called at Ramillies so Jary had sent a note over to her house, Stretfield Place, begging leave to call and naming an hour and day; he received no reply. This too rankled along with everything else as he and the Doctor rode down the back drive and into the lane that led to Foley.

'I have not been this way before,' he said, 'I thought instead of riding through the village we could bid Mrs Jewkes good day and come at this Stretfield Place the back way.'

'Have you met this Mrs Jewkes?'

'She has not called again, if that is what you mean.'

The chestnut pony pranced and plunged but the Doctor sat tight – at least, he could not be shaken off. It was just as well for he was dressed very finely. Jary had insisted he abandon his ancient bottle-green coat and put on a decent black – not the mildewed black of the stagecoach – had lent him a spotless stock, had seen that his breeches were brushed and his boots cleaned.

56

'We don't want to make a rum impression, you know what old ladies are. The elderly are always puritanical though they were rogues and libertines in youth. It don't do to turn up on a doorstep looking like a pair of low coves who never shave.' This was a pointed reference to the Doctor's chin, which received attention once a week and sometimes once a fortnight.

Jary was eager to see what he supposed might be his only living relative this side of the Atlantic Ocean and he paid particular attention to turning himself out well. The result, as the Doctor was amused to see, struck a joyful compromise between the truly elegant and the totally vulgar. Jary dressed up was a sight to behold, for he was not to be confined to the dull blues or blacks or buff of the current fashion. He belonged in spirit to the previous century when a man could get himself up like a peacock and be proud of it. His coat was magenta and extravagant in style. It had been made by the best tailor in Kingston and in its way was a masterpiece, but its way was not the way of Stretfield and deep Suffolk.

'I was once sat upon her lap as a baby,' he was saying now, patting the neck of the brown horse. 'My Aunt Fray — her name was Francesca but we always called her Fray — brought me over when there was a case brought about my mother's money. Perhaps my uncle had told her to get rid of me on the Woodbridge relations. In any event there were none, just an old uncle half-senile and this cousin Maria.'

'I daresay she would not remember you,' said the Doctor, conscious of the inexpressible gulf between Jary as a baby and Jary in the magenta coat.

'Well, she ought to give us sherry at least,' mused the new squire of Ramillies, gazing now at the broken-down palings around the park which he would have to replace, and now at the Doctor falling on his pony's neck. 'She ought to do that out of common civility. I wonder though that she made no reply to any of my letters. But then, you never can tell with old ladies.'

'No, you never can. Your aunts were eccentric, of course.'

'I suppose they were, but perhaps it was simply that they had had hard lives – they did indeed, though Helen's Mount looks like a palace. They had never been beautiful or charming, they were all near six feet tall, a dreadful disadvantage in a woman, and my uncle treated them worse than his dogs. They were always good to me, saved me titbits from the grown-up dinners when I was too little to attend, and salved my hurts when my uncle had taken a strap to me, and once they kept me secretly in the summer house for a month when I came home from sea after being turned out. They were all the mother I ever knew, the dear aunts and good old Henriette. Most of my money came from them, they left all they had to me, and each time one of them died Uncle spent a week ranting at the lawyers to undo the will and told the whole island I was a blackguard and a pirate and tried every trick he knew – and he knew a few, the old devil – but all for nothing. The old dears may have been mad but they wrapped up their affairs in double-rove knots not even a Kingston lawyer could unpick.'

They had reached Foley, which was a long low house looking down across the Meeting Grounds, its back to the lane.

'Let's go that way,' cried Jary, turning his horse to the left and up Frenchmans Hill.

'But that is the wrong direction. Stretfield is this way and across the river.'

'Millett said that halfway up Frenchmans we might turn right and come down through Beke's Wood to a place called the Diddlers and then across the river to Stretfield Place. Come on. This is all Ramillies land and I have never ridden to the farthest boundary.'

If he had hoped for a view from Frenchmans, a fine sweeping view across the whole of his estate to the village, to distant Westdene and even to the sea, he was disappointed; there was no view at all, the trees came crowding thick and fast, they were in dense wood in a moment.

The road to the Diddlers was nothing more than a stony track leading down between steep banks, the dried-up path of a stream in effect, and the trees met over it so that everything was dank and still and gloomy. The horses were subdued as if they too wished themselves in a kinder place out in the sun. And then suddenly they heard the raucous barking of geese and the lowing of some desolate calf, and the smell of woodsmoke wafted to them on the quiet air.

'I suppose I have seen worse,' said Jary as they emerged from the trees on to level ground and pulled up, gazing about him at the rough common, the waste, the sour dying grass. There were half a dozen mouldering cottages, scarcely much more than crumbling mud walls and decaying thatch, none of which would have been declared fit for the Ramillies pigs. There were two tethered goats, the forlorn calf, the suspicious geese gathered about a swampy hollow, and smoke rising from only one chimney, rising straight up into the air and then flattening and drifting down to tickle their nostrils.

'This is rural decay,' said the Doctor, who had also seen worse, far far worse. 'An indifferent landlord, no doubt.'

'The slaves at Helen's Mount were housed in mansions compared with these,' cried Jary. 'And you forget, the indifferent landlord is myself – this is Ramillies land.'

'This poor neglected place can hardly be laid at your door, you have scarcely settled in. But I thought Millett told us the Diddlers – perhaps it is not the Diddlers after all – was on Mrs Whiteley's land. How strange her boundary should run alongside yours.'

'If this is Whiteley land I shall speak to her about it.'

It did not shock them, such sights were too common, but they were moved by the deep, burning indignation of humane men. Jary especially felt a keen anger that such misery should exist on a property of his, and he kicked his horse forward as if he hoped one of the inhabitants might be found to give him an explanation. But he was conscious of secret scrutiny and an unnatural silence, as if the very birds in the rotting thatch were suspicious of strangers.

'Is there nobody here?' he asked, as his frown deepened. The ground was very wet and several times the brown horse stumbled.

'Of course they are here, but they are keeping out of sight.'

'What are they anyway, crouched away down here between bog and woods, no decent grazing anywhere, no proper road? How do they live? How do they feed themselves?'

There was no answer. The Doctor, having clapped his heels into his pony, had found himself on the damp earth in the wink of an eye.

'Damn it! You are not safe to be let near horses!' and Jary caught the rascal and brought him back, trying not to grin.

'I have been told so,' said the Doctor, with a sharp memory of Ann, who sat a horse as straight and rode as stylishly as any woman he had ever known.

Jary's irritation had drained away. He hoisted the Doctor into the saddle and they turned their backs on the Diddlers, though aware for some time that their slow progress along the increasingly muddy track was being followed by more than one pair of hidden eyes. At last there was the ford, no footbridge and a remarkable trodden quagmire. It was nothing more than a summer crossing place. What did they do in winter, Jary demanded, keep a boat for a ferry? There was no bottom, only mud, the thick glutinous mud, and a great deal of weed, and a strong current. Even now the water came over the horses' knees.

'I suppose this is the road to Westdene,' said Jary, as they scrambled up through an alder thicket, as dank and boggy as alder thickets can be, and finding himself on a made road.

'It is the way we came in the chaise,' said the Doctor. 'See, there are the roofs of Stretfield ahead. Your cousin's house is this side of the village. Is that not it behind those oaks?'

It was a square, grand house, not more than twenty years old, set back behind railings and with a noble sweep for carriages.

'She has done very well,' was Jary's dry comment. 'She was a spinster for years, so Aunt Fray said, was brought up so starched and corseted no man could come at her. Then she married a local fellow, someone she had known all her life.'

'To be sure he was prosperous.'

But at the door they were told Mrs Whiteley was not receiving visitors and with a curtness that suggested this was never a welcoming house, that Mrs Whiteley did not care for visitors in general. Jary, undaunted, put his large fist on the door. 'Tell her it is her cousin from Jamaica,' he said, 'she would be most upset was you to turn *me* away.'

'He cannot believe you are respectable,' the Doctor whispered as they stepped into the hall. 'It is the way you wear your hat.'

'Well, I have taken it off . . . But dear God, you look a knave without your wig! And your necktie is adrift. What kind of impression must you be going to make?'

'It was you said you preferred the bristles,' was the indignant reply, 'and I was hoping light and air would encourage them to grow.'

Jary stared. 'Is that a fact, a scientific fact?'

'No, it is wishful thinking.'

The boy in dingy livery returned: Mrs Whiteley would see them in the library. They noted twenty yards of false spines and a fine revolving globe before their eyes could make her out, a dim little figure in a chair by the hearth.

'Cousin Maria!' hailed Jary, hurrying to pluck her up and kiss her, a fate she avoided by visibly shrinking back and saying shrilly: 'You are nothing like Susannah Howton, sir. I trust you have credentials? '

The Doctor saw with amusement that Jary was put off his stroke, and being a naturally bluff and genial person

61

could not get back to it at once. 'But of course I am your cousin. I favour the Savages in looks, pray God not in temperament. I was in petticoats last time I saw you, or you saw me for I was too young to remember. I have written twice' – rather harshly for it had been a tremendous effort – 'and had you forgot I was to call today? Your boy did not even seem to know my name.'

'Indeed,' said Maria Whiteley coldly, though it was not clear whether she meant indeed she had received his letters or indeed she had not told her servants to expect him, 'I must confess I would never have known you. Was your father so excessive tall?'

The Doctor could see Jary struggling with his good manners which, like the polecats in the coach, were growing tired of confinement. Eventually he managed to say in an almost normal voice that all the Savages were of an uncommon height and all swarthy, even the women, which perhaps accounted for his great-aunts remaining unmarried when they all had good portions. They had not believed in sunshades, he added, their complexions had been only a little lighter than his own.

'How disgraceful!' said Mrs Whiteley.

She was not more than five feet high herself and her skin was transparently pale; against it her little black eyes looked brilliantly malevolent. Under her cap her hair was carefully curled and yet the effect was neither pleasant nor interesting. Her hair was as the rest of her: dry, rigid, artificial. Jary was just wondering if she wore a wig when a discreet murmur behind him brought to mind the Doctor, whose awful head was all too real.

But the Doctor bowed with extraordinary grace, all the more extraordinary since he was in muddy riding boots and looked like an escaped felon. He could be gently witty when he cared, and urbane, and though he was not good-looking he had a fine, cultured voice and had many times wooed less amiable women than Mrs Whiteley to take notice of his advice and, ultimately, pay his bills.

'What a fine house you have,' he said after a while, a

while during which the lady softened remarkably and even rose to point out some particular of the view to him through the tall window.

'My husband was lucky in his investments and also inherited a large sum from a relative in the East India Company. He has been dead four years. I live here quietly with my husband's nephew who was left without parents as a small child and whom we took in as our own. I have never had a child. He has been a son to me, the best of sons.'

She rang for refreshment. She smiled on the Doctor. Jary thought even her smile artificial but he supposed she could do no better, and it seemed hard she did not smile on him, her own relation, who had crossed several thousand miles of furious ocean and might expect a more cordial welcome. He brooded over the strange fact that, apart from his three aunts, he had not liked any of his relations, and how it was fate dealt some families such a preponderance of rogues and misers. Then the door opened and Mrs Whiteley's nephew, her 'best of sons', came in. He came in with a pasty, disobliging girl carrying a tray, and on the tray was only tepid tea and little biscuits the size of a man's thumbnail. Jary was not to have his sherry, not in this house.

The nephew was a long-armed, long-legged, long-necked young man with a tight little mouth and stiff manners. It was quite probable he was almost as old as Jary but a quirk of nature had given him a face, and that thin, pale hair, which remain the same for a decade or more. He stood on such ceremony – either from distaste or a feeling of natural superiority – that even the Doctor had trouble finding any subject for a conversation, the Doctor who could be relied on, Jary was finding, to get the best out of any man. Jary kept up a desultory and painful exchange of information with his cousin: what acreage was Helen's Mount, how many slaves, distance from Kingston, kind of horses, cattle, house servants; how much less tedious than life in a rural backwater, all mud and disobliging tenants, hardly a breath of civilized social intercourse, hardly a family worth knowing except of course Sir James Braile's, did he know of Sir James Braile?

'I never cared for Ramillies,' Mrs Whiteley remarked at some lull, 'I never did.' It was doubtful she had ever cared much for anything that was not or could not possibly be her own. 'The late Mr Rayner let it go, never spent a penny on it, though he had no family to support – only one daughter and she was educated at home, scarcely educated indeed – and thought of nothing but the estate. I am afraid he sank his money into wild schemes perpetrated by scoundrels, hoping to make a vast fortune if the harbour at Westdene were dredged . . . Well, it was not dredged nor ever will be and the ships go to Lowestoft and Ipswich and everywhere but Westdene. And Henry Rayner died in debt and the place was sold up.'

'What became of the daughter?'

'Elizabeth?' and here a covert glance at her nephew, who looked away. 'She lives at Foley – you have surely seen Foley, it is one of your properties – with a Mrs Jewkes. She is past her prime now, poor child, not that she was ever thought good-looking, and her father's death left her with nothing, nothing at all, so she must be resigned to living on with Mrs Jewkes for a great while yet. I doubt very much if you will meet her unless you call at Foley and find her willing to receive you – she is no friend to society, shuns us all, does not visit, does not dance.'

Edward Whiteley, breaking in as if he did not wish to hear any more about Miss Rayner, suggested a walk about the gardens.

'The gardens at Ramillies must be overgrown,' said his aunt, looking fondly at her own immaculate hedges. 'I have not been there since Rayner died. Mr Treadgold was a recluse and soon left for Bath. It was a grand old place thirty years ago, I could not bear to see it come to ruin.'

Jary detected a false note. She is jealous, he thought,

she once coveted Ramillies for herself. But before he could pursue this she had stopped, pointing out the pond, and had changed the subject.

'I do hope your affairs are not in the hands of Mr Calloway,' she said, knowing as well as any man, woman and child in the whole district that they were, 'a most obdurate, forward sort of man without the least idea how to behave in society.'

'I am sorry to hear it,' said Jary, 'I am beginning to have grave doubts about him altogether.'

'What a shocking pair!' was his verdict as he and the Doctor rode home. 'I shall never call again. Did you notice how she could not bring herself to be civil when we were announced? Well, I was expecting more of a greeting than that; what a mean, miserable old cat! I hadn't the heart to mention the Diddlers . . .'

'It would not have been politic at your very first meeting, certainly.'

' . . . because I knew at once she would not have been moved, would perhaps even deny the place existed. And as for that boy, that degenerate boy . . . I have never so longed to bloody a man's nose.'

'Sure, your digestion is upset. It was those biscuits.'

'It is nothing of the kind. He disliked us on sight, would have had us turned from the house had it been his house and had he had the nerve. As it was he kept those suspicious pop eyes on me all the while and toadied disgracefully to that dreadful old woman, giving her his arm every two minutes and running about for her stick. Stick! She no more needs a stick than I do!' and he dug his heels into the brown horse so that they cantered purposefully through Stretfield, giving the inhabitants their first glimpse of Ramillies' new master, an improbably tall, dark, scowling man in an all-fire hurry. It was only when they had left the village behind and Jary had slowed to make sure the Doctor was still with him that he spoke more normally.

'What was all that about Prince? I kept looking about

for a dog but there was never the hair of a dog. Did you catch the drift?'

'I believe,' said the Doctor, who was riding with two handfuls of mane and no reins, 'that the nephew is called Edward Prince Whiteley and that your cousin has always chosen to call him Prince instead of the less exalted Edward. This may be a kind of maternal vanity or a preference of the boy himself – I can hardly believe it is sarcasm though to be sure she cannot be blind to all his faults, and though princes are held in low esteem these sad rebellious times you would go a long way before you found a man less fitted to become one.'

There was a damp autumnal scent, an instinct of coming storm. Jary drew rein at the church, which, like Low Paradise, had been abandoned by social change and now stood alone on a grassy rise between the village and the front gates of Ramillies.

'She disparaged it hugely but my dear cousin envied me Ramillies. Perhaps she had designs on old Rayner in her youth and he was too cunning and too wise. Did you notice how she could not speak of his daughter with any charity?'

'My dear, old feuds and family fallings-out are the stuff of life in villages. But I would be interested to know why the nephew refused to speak of her at all.'

'My God!' cried Jary, remembering. 'That damned high cravat and all that talking through his nose!'

'That may be a catarrhal condition . . .' began the Doctor, but he spoke to air: Jary had already tossed his reins over the gate post and was halfway up the path to the porch.

It was a large church but it was not very clean and it smelled very strong: old books, old wood, damp, damp, more damp. Jary climbed into the pulpit, climbed out again, explored behind a torn curtain that hid the dim mirror where the parson peered to set straight his wig each Sunday, opened a box of candles, opened an old chest of vestments – and looked more and more cast down.

'It is in a sad state,' he said at last, walking back to where the Doctor was reading a memorial tablet on the wall. 'Do you think it would be taken amiss was I to pay for a spring clean?'

'Sorely amiss. You must wait and be patient. If you stay here long enough and go about quietly and appear respectable there will come the day they will ask you for a donation – and then you may order your spring clean and new bell ropes and whatever you wish. But look, what do you think of that?'

'Of what? "Amelia Elizabeth Rayner, wife of Henry Dane Rayner of Ramillies . . ." She died young and of the smallpox. What of it? Or do you think she is my lady in grey?'

'No, I believe she is the present Miss Rayner's mother, or was, poor child, was a great while ago. You know, the terrible Miss Rayner who does not care to take tea with the other ladies, and does not dance, and lives retired with the unspeakable Mrs Jewkes – did you not receive the distinct impression Mrs Jewkes was unspeakable?'

They went out into the churchyard, warm in the sunlight and full of strange little butterflies. Jary flapped his hands at them to see them rise in a cloud from the rusty sorrel and bent grasses. All around were Rayners.

'This is their corner,' said Jary, reading the eighth or ninth. 'The tall stone by the holly bush is Henry Dane himself. Still' – looking about with a sigh – 'it is a pleasant place to lie.'

They could hear nothing but the bleat of sheep and the rustle of dry grass. Then Jary's eye was caught by the swift movement of a human figure down the path by the gate, and he saw a woman start towards them and then hesitate and turn back. She paused by the elms however to hold a conversation with the Doctor's pony who was interested in the contents of her basket.

'She has gone,' said Jary, who had hurried after her. 'How could she have vanished?' It did not occur to him she might have taken a path into his own park on the other side of the wall.

'You may find she has put a spell on him,' he said a moment later to the Doctor, who mounted quite easily, the pony apparently subdued, 'though I must say it might be for the better. They are all strange people in this part of the world. Did you see her hat? It must have been the fashion forty years ago.'

'Oh, I am no expert on hats and forty years ago I believe I was more interested in pebbles and mud pies and what was to eat. But there was something familiar about her, I must confess.' He had certainly seen that disreputable old straw before.

'I don't believe in witchcraft,' said Jary, turning the brown horse in through the gates of Ramillies and gazing with sudden affection at his oak avenue, 'though there is a witch at the Diddlers, Mrs Whiteley told me so,' and seeing the Doctor's raised eyebrow: 'No, no, I said nothing untoward about the Diddlers, never even asked her whose land it was. She only said there was an old woman in the woods by Frenchmans, a Mother Henham, who stirs a pot and keeps black hens and sells love potions on the sly. No, she did not mention Diddlers by name. I tell you, I would not be surprised if she pretends it does not exist.'

They slowed to a walk. The afternoon was golden and still, only that vague whisper of bad weather yet to come. It lifted their spirits and they turned up their faces to the sun and breathed in the humid air and felt that overwhelming affection for everything that comes with a sense of well-being. Even when the pony shied the Doctor off going over the bridge they passed it off lightly, and Jary heaved him up again with a laugh. A little way from the house they met Mrs Bloy walking the baby, and the baby was awake but content, waving her fists in the air and making small animal noises, and Jary had to dismount to admire her, absurdly doting, every harsh line his erratic life had put upon his face smoothed away in a moment. Mrs Bloy approved such tenderness and smiled conspiratorially with the Doctor over Jary's bent head.

In the stableyard Millett was stamping among the

doves with buckets of feed but even he, struck by the
wreathing smiles the gentlemen bestowed on him, was
twenty times more gracious than usual when leading the
horses to their supper. In the house Mrs Clark had left
cheese and cold meats and rabbit pie on the sideboard
in case the gentlemen should feel peckish before dinner,
and they did, for the Stretfield Place biscuits had been no
kind of midday meal. They sat and ate in hoggish and
rapturous silence for a long while. When Mrs Clark came
in with a venerable bottle of port which had to be opened
– would Mr Savage care to draw the cork himself? – Jary
said briskly through a mouthful of pie: 'Have you heard
of Miss Elizabeth Rayner, Clarkie?'

'Oh,' said Mrs Clark, blushing, for she was not
expecting anyone to take liberties with her name. 'Oh
yes, sir. Millett often speaks of her. He seems very fond
of her. I believe she lives at Foley and often walks across
the park.'

'Millett worked for her father?'

'Yes, indeed, the old squire who broke his neck
jumping the park railings. Millett helped carry him home
on a hurdle. It is the only thing . . . He is still moved
when he speaks of it, sir.'

They could not easily imagine Millett moved by
anything more tender than indignation. Mrs Clark curtseyed and began to withdraw.

'I suppose no one offered to marry the poor girl after
she was beggared,' murmured Jary, turning the port
bottle over in his huge hands. 'That might account for
her secluded life.'

Mrs Clark paused at the door. 'Millett says Mr
Whiteley was to have married her, but he called off the
wedding the day after her father died.'

The door closed. Jary looked up.

'So that was the meaning of those silences and sly
looks. But I wonder how she came to be engaged to that
insolent dog in the first place.' He was disposed to feel
sorry for Miss Rayner but he could not bring himself to
admire a woman who had once been in love with Prince

Whiteley. She had every attribute of a romantic heroine – he assumed she was good-looking and had the most endearing smile – and it seemed to him no true heroine would look twice at a man like Whiteley.

'Perhaps you should call at Foley and ask her yourself.'

'How could I do so? But I may call. After all, Mrs Jewkes rides about in a carriage. A carriage! Miss Rayner might have done worse than find a friend in a rich widow.' And then, thoughtfully: 'And she might only be thirty, and pretty.'

'I was not aware you were in need of a rich widow to mend your considerable fortune.'

Jary went to the sideboard to see if there was any pie left. He grinned, unbuttoning his waistcoat. 'Widows are so much more fun than single girls, there is no silly shyness and always being watched and treading on etiquette at every turn.'

The Doctor looked cunning. 'I'll wager you a guinea she is neither thirty nor pretty, and I'll wager you another Miss Rayner is a nervy, bookish, sardonic sort of person with a pugnacious nose.'

6

Mrs Stone had reported that she had heard a baby crying at Ramillies.

'I shall call,' Fanny told Lizzie Rayner. 'Why, he has never been near Foley. He entertains Lavinia Stone on sherry wine and plum cake but he does not condescend to knock at my door.'

'You should have gone the other day. You ordered the carriage.'

'But the mare was still not quite right, and Kitty had such a sore throat I had to call in Plesset in case it was something dreadful, and then Miss Pawle from Hopes called . . . and Mr Hook about the smoking chimney . . . But I will go today. I will see if this Mr Savage is as charming as Lavinia says he is, she was never a good judge of a man's character.'

'Is that a reflection on Mr Stone? He is a dear, harmless man.'

'Oh, a dull homely creature with very moderate appetites. I believe it was not judgement led her to marry him but luck, simple good luck. They have been very happy and I am glad of it.'

Lizzie would not go to Ramillies, so the mare and her three-year-old son — far too young, of course, and still headstrong and uncouth — were put to the carriage, and Fanny was driven the short distance alone in a fluttering anticipation. There was no answer to Lussom's ringing at the front door, but half the windows were open and the scream of women's voices could be heard in the distance. Mrs Jewkes, being a practical woman, stepped down and walked round the house to where she could see the entire domestic staff gambolling about with sheets and towels and tablecloths as if every linen cupboard in the place had been ransacked. Mrs Clark, flushed and

71

disordered, was writing in a small book as each new article was shaken out for her inspection.

Fanny slipped away and made for the stableyard, for a furious masculine dispute was stirring the myriad doves to a frenzy. She came upon Jary superintending a general clearout which had apparently produced several surprises such as ladies' hats and a trunk of rusted stirrups, a gross of walking canes, a dozen bee skeps, and a mysterious canvas holdall full of peacock feathers. It was these last tattered objects that were causing the dispute, for Millett had declared them unlucky, they should never be brought into a Christian house, and he was not having them thrown on the rubbish heap in *his* stables. Jary, who was not superstitious but would never mock another man's foibles to his face, had lost his temper mostly because he was in a bad mood, such a bad mood even the Doctor had had to take refuge behind the coffee pot at breakfast. The brown horse was suddenly lame, the man Hawke, sent for to give an estimate for the water garden, had quoted an absurd price, and a peremptory command to Mr Calloway had produced nothing.

'I oont hev them in my yard,' cried Millett, more red in the face than anybody had ever seen him, 'not if you put me in the pill'ry.'

'They have been in your yard twenty years or more by the look of them. Well, if they can't go on the rubbish pile they must be burnt on the kitchen fire.'

But, 'Oh no,' said Fanny, treading through the doves, 'you really must not bring them indoors. It is not permissible. Who knows what bad fortune you might not bring down on the house?'

She walked straight up, holding out her hand, aware that she was at last talking to the new master of Ramillies. Jary saw a short, plump, middle-aged figure in an exaggerated hat and bright red pelisse.

'Mrs Jewkes, I am so very pleased to meet you at last,' when she had introduced herself, 'but what am I to do with all these feathers?'

'Make a little fire for them in the orchard.'

'It seems an odd thing to make a funeral pyre for a heap of old feathers but it must be done, I suppose.'

'I do believe they must be from poor Henry's peacock, a solitary pining bird which never had a mate. It may have died of a broken heart.'

They gazed at the feathers with some emotion until the Doctor, who had been sitting by a pile of ancient harness, rose and came forward. 'I have dissected a great many hearts but never yet found one that was broken. On the other hand, I would not care to pronounce on peacocks.'

Mrs Jewkes gave him a level look but her mouth twitched up. Jary said, 'You must ignore the Doctor, ma'am. He is inclined to feeble jokes and childish humour.'

And: 'You have lost your guinea,' said the Doctor to the sky, his face turned up with a smile.

Jary frowned. 'Do not mind him,' he told Fanny, who was certainly past thirty and though pleasant had never been exactly pretty. 'Come across to the house. You have caught us at a disadvantage. Only there is so much rubbish thrust into every corner, moth-eaten, broken, old-fashioned rubbish.'

Fanny, running to keep up, was bold enough to say as they reached the house and went inside: 'A word of warning, Mr Savage. Do not presume to mock the squire, the old squire Rayner, nor local custom, however absurd.'

Jary paused. 'The Doctor has already cautioned me. The old squire was much thought of, I understand?'

'He was greatly loved. He was a foolish man in many respects and he was a poor hand at figures and never could recognize a rogue but he cared for his land and the people on it. He is now a legend in Stretfield, and even in Westdene. All his faults have been forgotten long ago or are only spoken of with affection. I fear you will find Ramillies haunted by his shade.'

Jary, who was beginning to appreciate her quick smile, her quick sharp way of speaking, her sense of humour, gave an irresistible smile. 'I do not believe in ghosts.'

'No more do I. And yet I would not walk in Beke's

Wood at night, lantern or no, for fear of meeting the hanged boy, though he was hanged a long while ago and was the sweetest, most obliging creature while living. But I think you will find the old squire more difficult to avoid.'

They crossed the hall. From upstairs came the thin wail of a baby woken and distressed. Fanny cocked an ear.

'That is Henriette,' said Jary cheerfully, calling for Mrs Clark. 'She generally wakes about now and leads us all a dance for an hour or two. Do you care for babies?'

Fanny might have said no, for she had never yearned for children and as nature had given her none she had never had occasion to try her maternal instincts, but a glance at Jary's adoring face, lifted towards the distant nursery made her a little cautious. 'I am sure I would think yours the prettiest thing,' and then, with a gleam of her eye: 'Whether she were or no.'

'It would be polite to say so,' said Jary with a grin, seeing that this Mrs Jewkes was a woman he might get along with, 'but she is not mine, you know. Not mine by . . . blood.'

Mrs Clark appeared. A Mr Fisher had called, she had put him in the library, she hoped she had done right. She hoped particularly- though she did not say so to Jary – because Mrs Fipson, whose local knowledge could never be faulted, had told her that Mrs Jewkes would not care to meet the gentleman, that there was some kind of connection, or lack of one, which meant it was prudent to keep them apart. But she need not have worried, for Jary had decided on a pleasant half-hour with Fanny alone and did not wish to be at home to anyone else. He bore her away to the parlour with the instruction that Mrs Clark was to keep his other guest well supplied with whatever he preferred until such time as he could see him.

'Oh, and Clarkie, tell him I may be twenty minutes. He may not care to wait,' was his parting remark.

The Doctor, wandering in from the scouring of the stables smelling of musty hay and damp all overlaid with a general pervasive horsiness, met Mrs Clark on her way to the library with a bottle of madeira and a solitary glass on a tray. He took it from her. commanded a second gllss, and went in. He had expected to find Jary alone or perhaps Jary and the vivacious Mrs Jewkes, but instead he found a small spare man who radiated an intense eagerness like a very young puppy, and who bounded from the hearth at once, his hand outstretched.

'Mr Savage! How glad I am to meet you at last!'

The Doctor begged pardon and introduced himself. Mr Fisher's amiability fell away in an instant to leave a pathetic melancholy, a hypochondriacal melancholy. The Doctor was on his guard at once. When, after some inoffensive remarks about the weather, Westdene, sea bathing, Mr Fisher asked the Doctor's opinion, his medical opinion, of his elderly father, the Doctor was ready with a bland, smiling refusal to have any opinion at all.

The door opened. 'Ah,' said Jary, apparently in high spirits, 'there you both are! Mr Fisher, good of you to call, sir. You must join us at once. I believe . . . What in Heaven's that . . .'

A shriek of anguish, fury, horror, extreme indignation, rose in a terrible continuing note from below. Mrs Clark emerged from the kitchen and with her acrid smoke and another inhuman howl.

'Someone is being waked,' said the Doctor.

'More like roasted alive,' said Jary.

But it turned out simply to be the cook's reaction on finding that the new stable boy, an undernourished, unhandy boy consumed by a desire to please, had thrown all the peacock feathers on the fire after all instead of burning them in the orchard. He had now brought bad luck on the lot of them and, which was worse, was quite unrepentant, being unable to understand that he had done wrong. The distraught Mrs Fipson had chased him outside with a poker and had returned to a kitchen full of smoke, Heaven knows what evil in attendance.

'You may as well believe in goblins,' was Jary's

unsympathetic comment. 'Do tell Mrs Fipson I am sure it is all a great deal of nonsense.'

He was about to lead his guests into the parlour when he caught sight of Mr Fisher's face as he gazed ardently at Fanny Jewkes, and became aware that the lady did not reciprocate such a feeling, but rather shrank from it, if anyone of her character could be said to shrink at all. With a knowing look at the Doctor and a command to keep Mrs Jewkes amused for a 'few minutes, Alex, only a few minutes', he drew Mr Fisher away to look at the garden, talking fountains, lakes, canals, anything that suggested itself. Perhaps Mr Fisher understood the mechanics of fountains? No? But Mr Fisher would surely give his opinion of the plans, would pace the ground and imagine the finished effect? Mr Fisher hesitated. Jary swept him to the door.

The Doctor sighed. 'It will be like Timon's Villa,' he said mournfully.

'Oh, surely not,' said Fanny. 'He is a man of common sense, besides which he is not a raw boy come into a fortune. He has been used to money and may be trusted to spend it wisely.'

'Indeed you are right, but I tremble for the view, I cannot imagine what it will be like with fountains playing and little bridges dotted here and there. What is suitable in Jamaica by a coral strand is not always happily transferred to . . . to places such as this.'

They went into the library where they had two great windows opening on the lawns, and stood a moment to watch the two receding figures, the one striding forward throwing out its arms, the other hanging back.

'Mr Fisher is from Westdene, I understand,' said the Doctor.

'Oh yes, his house sits practically in the sea. He brought his father here for a cure fifteen years ago and never left, poor man. I feel for him most deeply. The father's whims and fancies rule all. But I must not speak out of turn. I may be a horrible old gossip but I hope I am never malicious.'

He was turning to reassure her he could not imagine her being malicious when his eye was distracted by another figure crossing the lawn towards the gesticulating Jary and the reluctant Mr Fisher. This time it was a tall man in drab brown, youngish so far as could be made out at such a distance.

'Jary will be gratified' – he gave Fanny a wry smile – 'his audience increases moment by moment.'

'Oh that! That is Mr Calloway the lawyer, such a mean, pinching, puritanical . . .' She was about to say 'hound' when it occurred to her she was prejudicing her claim to be entirely good-hearted. 'His father dealt with this estate,' she continued after a difficult pause, 'and was the man who told my Lizzie she was beggared; now the father is dead it is young Charles who knocks on my door to remind Lizzie how beggared she remains.'

'He acts for her? There was something saved?'

'Saved! Dear Doctor, everything was to the four winds, not a penny left. All her mother's money gone too. She received a small annuity from her Woodbridge relations, thirty guineas a year, hardly a fortune' – in a harsh, unforgiving undertone – 'but they stopped it immediately she . . . Well, they did not approve of her coming to live with me.'

They looked again at the trio outside. There was a more subdued air about the proceedings as if Jary found his audience somewhat unappreciative. They were walking back towards the house.

'I will fly,' said Fanny, 'I will leave you men together to . . . to . . .' and she wrinkled her round little face, remembering: "To consult the Genius of the Place in all." '

' "That tells the waters or to rise, or fall." Yes, yes. Only I fear Mr Calloway is obviously not interested in waters, look how he stands and scowls.'

Mrs Jewkes took his arm, his dusty, hay-seedy arm. 'How can you see a scowl at such a distance? But yes, I do see what you mean. Oh, never let him cast you both down,' she implored as they crept together like thieves to the garden door in order to reach her carriage undetected,

'Young Mr Calloway has a cold pessimistic outlook on life. I only say it,' she hastened to add, 'as a sort of general observation. He is very thorough and painstaking, I am sure. He is most thorough, yes, and most painstaking, a man of undoubted integrity, I would never hesitate to recommend him as a legal prop and adviser . . . but such a melancholy disposition, so very very quick to dampen the highest spirits.'

From the house behind came the sound of Jary in argument, his voice raised.

'You see,' said Fanny Jewkes, letting the Doctor hand her into the carriage and smiling down into his solemn face, 'it has begun already.'

The Doctor was to leave for Guy's at the end of the week. Meanwhile he was withdrawn, mulish, prickly, and no kind of company. He left Jary renegotiating with Hawke the enormous estimate for making a cut, a large pond, and a sort of interconnecting string of watery wonders, and he rode to Westdene and surveyed its narrow streets, its fine old houses, its silted harbour, its pleasant stony beach. They grew quite used to him at the Admiral, putting him to dry in the chimney corner and plying him with veal pie and pork cheese, for he seemed so innocent and kindly and always forgot his wig.

The truth was he had received a letter from the most excellent avid learned young man he had left in charge at High Common, telling him of the progress of his more difficult patients. Familiar names, familiar symptoms, the signs of familiar hypochondria, brought back other memories the Doctor would rather forget. He spent a great deal of time – when he was not at the Admiral – pacing the lawns where the workmen were already busy with pegs and spades. He often fell into experimental channels and random bore holes and once or twice, thinking of Ann or trying not to think of her and wondering if he should return to India, he moved the sacred pegs and came in for sharp reproof.

'I shall miss you,' said Jary one evening over their usual

supper of bread and cheese – though he would certainly not miss this irascible devil the Doctor had become – 'We have had a pleasant few weeks. What is this lecture you are to give?'

'The surgery of wounds sustained in battle. In St Thomas's theatre. It is a singular honour.'

'You have never lectured then?'

'Not in exalted company. I have harangued the hopeless callow dogs sent me as assistants and if they heard one word in ten I was grateful, but it is a different world, the battlefield is a different world ... I expect were several great surgeons removed from their hospitals and sent out among the cruelly wounded they too would turn out hopeless dogs.'

'Have you ever published any papers? I always believed it was how a medical man built up his reputation.'

'Oh, what would life be worth without pamphlets!' cried the Doctor, spearing his cheese and waving it ecstatically. 'I have a great many. There are some would interest even a layman, even you, dear Jary, to whom all doctors are quacks or warlocks. But my own contribution is slight – a brief note on the incidence of scabies in the army.'

'Scabies!' Jary laid down his knife. 'Well, I suppose I never did meet a soldier who did not itch.'

'There have been interesting theories as to the cause. But the crowding together and general low treatment compounds the rate of infection.'

'I suppose Guy's... I suppose the United Hospitals are too lordly to give the itch a passing thought. But I can see it is an honour to lecture them on wounds.'

'Stone-gropers,' murmured the Doctor through a mouthful. 'They have their patients presented cold, so to speak, lying waiting on their pleasure. Trauma is not a word often heard among them. It is all rich idle men paying for a lithotomy.'

Trauma was not a word often heard at Ramillies, nor was lithotomy. Jary made a careful study of his last piece of cheese before he spoke, unwilling to ruin his meal by straying too far among medical minutiae. He did not want a minute by minute description of a lithotomy to pour forth and spoil his happy feast. He did not care much for strangulated this or putrid that, or boils, or baldness, all of which had at one time or another intruded into conversation at mealtimes. He said: 'I am sure you will be an enormous success. It will be a salutary experience for the old rogues to meet a practical man, I daresay. By the way, old Hawke says you moved his pegs again this morning and spoiled all his calculations.'

'He follows me about in case I misbehave. I am not a man to give unsolicited advice, but is he sound? He has a strange, foxy face, and a foxy manner to go with it.'

'I thought you were the one said "Do not judge by appearances".'

'Well, there must be times when the outer appearance mirrors the inner man, and I very much fear this is one of them.'

There was a knock. Mrs Clark entered, frowning. Was anything wrong, asked Jary, was Henriette ill? No, it was not Henriette, it was Mr Calloway, she replied, Mr Calloway on business.

'What a damn inconsiderate time to call,' cried Jary, jumping up as the door shut. 'To begin with he never comes and now he comes at a ridiculous hour – it has chimed ten o'clock, what is he doing out so late? Did I tell you he poured scorn on my water garden? He was only glad, he said, I had sufficient funds to indulge in such frivolous ventures. Now he is badgering me to act upon some overdue monies I have told him may wait until Michaelmas. He is not the most amenable of men.'

'But remember what an excellent housekeeper he found you, and cook, and riding horse. He carried out all your instructions to the letter.'

'You have not seen his bills. I tell you, Alex, it is only a matter of time before Mr Calloway and I fall out.'

The day before he left for London the Doctor was invited for a dish of tea at Foley. He put on his black coat for the occasion and was just putting his foot in the stirrup when Jary appeared in the yard and gave a broad delighted grin. 'My, how fine you are! Do give Mrs Jewkes my kindest regards; and Miss Rayner if you see her. How Millett has polished that little devil, he shines like gold.'

The little devil seemed aware of it himself and turned round several times to let them see the full effect. When the Doctor had finally gathered up his reins Jary was sitting on the mounting block, laughing.

'You are not safe to be let out together but there, I suppose you will come home again one way or another. I am off to the Diddlers later. I wish to consult Mother Henham if I can find her.'

'For what? A cure for warts, an aphrodisiac, a curse on Mr Calloway?'

'No, I only want to know why they all pay rent to the Whiteleys – if they do – for I am sure the land is mine. I have spent hours with the maps and I can't make out a case for the Whiteleys having any land just there, not even half an acre.'

The Doctor wished him well, but he meditated deeply on the Diddlers all the way to Foley, gazing now and then between the pony's polished ears at the fertile Meeting Grounds and remembering the waste below Beke's Wood. Were any rents paid? And if so, how much or how little might one man owe another for the use of such wilderness? The land was wet, the trees encroached all round. How had cottages come to be built there? Squatters? No sane countryman would pitch his house in a swamp. And it was a settlement as hidden and solitary as the charcoal burners' on the far side of the wood, and as shunned. Only Mother Henham was welcome in the village and only she was visited at the Diddlers – there was a bush, Mrs Fipson said, where one tied a red kerchief for a consultation, if she was home she came out at once when the children brought word that a stranger was about and if she was away she would turn up at the back door within a day or two.

81

'Mother Henham?' asked Fanny, ushering him into her warm sitting room. 'Oh, she visits frequently. She is so much more reliable than old Plesset, though you must never tell him I said so. And she treats the animals too, thinks nothing of visiting the pigsty or stitching up a dog's ear. Of course the parson has a little medical knowledge – he really wanted, poor man, to help those unfortunates who could not afford Plesset's fees – but there is not a soul will call him while Ma Henham is about. I feel rather sorry for him sometimes, I am sure his intentions are invariably the best, but then he is such an upright, preaching man I cannot feel sorry for him for very long. Do sit down, do. Look at all these roses. Lizzie will stuff them all in any jug she can find and then says I have ruined the effect when I try to . . . to arrange them a little.'

The roses were charming, said the Doctor, but where was Lizzie? As he spoke the door opened slightly, as if someone wished to know who was in the room before entering. Fanny gave a small laugh.

'Lizzie dear, it is only the Doctor. Dr French, not Dr Plesset. He has been admiring the roses.'

The door opened further. The Doctor looked up and saw his bold racy lady of the riverbank.

'I believe we have met,' he said.

'And where was that?' asked Fanny with a mounting suspicion she had been kept in the dark.

Lizzie smiled. It was a cosmetic smile for her eyes were darkly serious. 'Oh, we met upon the rustic bridge at Ramillies. We admired the pool together.'

So the fishing trips were secret even from Mrs Jewkes. The Doctor gave a slight bow. 'We saw a great many carp,' was his dry comment.

Half an hour in her company brought him to the conclusions he had come to long ago while facing her amid the rushes: here was no kindly, naive, downtrodden girl languishing in obscurity, periodically wounded to the heart by Mr Calloway's insensitive reminders of her penury. To begin with, though she avoided local society, she seemed to know a great many people in London, nearly all artistic, and if she was not personally acquainted she carried on a correspondence. Oh yes, she painted, she had always painted, she told him, spurning Fanny's muffins but dealing swiftly with a dish of cooling tea; she had painted since first she had been old enough to hold a brush and had once been soundly thrashed for decorating all the endpapers in her father's library with comical portraits – if the Doctor cared to look he would find a few still there as evidence of the heinous deed. She had taken to painting portraits as a living, was it not a splendid way to make money, ten guineas a head and shoulders? But now she had been invited to submit some work for hanging at the Royal Academy, *perhaps* for hanging at the Royal Academy, she had wondered whether fifteen guineas might not be more the price.

'It was the picture of the Admiral that brought her to their notice,' Fanny struck in, aware that Lizzie at her most arch and sardonic was not Lizzie at her best – when was Lizzie ever at her best?

'He had come to visit Sir James Braile, they are old friends, and when he spoke casually of having a likeness done Sir James was good enough to recommend Lizzie. It had to be done in a tearing hurry, of course, he was only in Westdene ten days, hardly any time at all, but he was so impressed. . .'

'He has the gout,' said Lizzie flatly. 'When the pain leaves him for an hour or two he is ready to admire anything.'

'Liz, you do not do yourself justice.'

Lizzie looked stubborn, her underlip pushed up. The Doctor suspected she always looked so when she was embarrassed, that she never blushed but grew fierce, exceedingly fierce: she had a fierce and contrary face.

'And where is Mr Savage today?' Fanny asked when they had exhausted all the trivia they could think of, Lizzie contributing nothing but staring intently at the

Doctor's face as if she were assessing it in some way, as a professional challenge perhaps.

'He is at the Diddlers consulting Mother Henham.'

'Oh, is that why you asked after Mother Henham? Good Heavens, surely he cannot have business of that nature already?'

'Of what nature?'

'Oh, cures and suchlike, pills, wicked syrups. But perhaps his horse is ill, we had heard . . .'

'I believe he wished to know about rents, about why the cottages are built on Ramillies land but owe rent to Mrs Whiteley, who, as you must know, is a very distant cousin of Mr Savage . . . yes, very distant indeed. Dear lady, if any wicked syrups were called for I am perfectly capable of making them myself.'

Fanny laughed. 'Of course you are, indeed you are. But I had always understood the Diddlers was Whiteley land.'

They both looked at Lizzie as if hoping she might resolve the problem with a word, but she only shook her head, a gesture that might have meant anything, that she did not know or did not care.

There was a commotion outside. A strong cheerful voice could be heard in the passage. Kitty opened the door for Jary with a wild glance upward, crying out that he should mind his head, And Fanny jumped up, nearly knocking over all the cups, and the Doctor saw Lizzie's face go pale.

'I was on my way home and thought I would step in to bid you good day, Mrs Jewkes, and to ask if the Doctor would care to ride along with me. Miss Rayner, delighted.'

She had regained her composure, nodded to him gravely like an elderly matron, said how do you do in a low firm voice. If Jary found her unimpressive he did not show it, he was polite and amiable and attentive. Only when the Diddlers was mentioned did he grow a little passionate.

'I am going to consult Calloway. I do not care how

84

those hovels came to be on Ramillies land but they will not be there much longer.'

'They have always been there,' was Lizzie's quiet remark.

'Well, it is time we gave the people sound roofs and dry floors and a little bit of land.'

'How philanthropic!' exclaimed Fanny admiringly, though there was the very slightest tone of doubt.

'You will find the past is not so easy to dismiss in the country,' said Lizzie, 'and I tell you, they have always been there, always, and why they are there is lost in history.'

For a moment the Doctor thought Jary was about to reply with some strong words, but after a second he turned from Lizzie and made some innocuous comment on the roses.

In ten minutes they took their leave, Kitty running with the Doctor's hat. There were rags of cloud above the Meeting Grounds and the smell of rain. The swallows were skimming low across all the flat meadows between Foley and the river and now and again the wood pigeons broke out in mournful cooing and then abruptly fell silent.

'Bad weather coming,' said Lizzie, at the gate to say goodbye.

'Miss Rayner.' Jary had stepped forward, was determined to be friendly: 'Miss Rayner, I would be honoured if you could step over to Ramillies, give me your opinion of the new water garden. The Doctor says you will think it desecration. They have only just started digging and the plans are not finished – there is some argument about pumps and sluices – but I have a sketch of how it should look in its glory. I am sure you must like it.'

'I am sure I must,' she said, meaning, by the look of her flashing eye, that she would never give her approval to any scheme that involved the alteration of her former home. When the Doctor bid her farewell she looked at him for several seconds without seeing him, her eyes all angry tawny, but she recovered to say, 'I hope the baby

85

thrives. Fanny told me Mr Savage is very fond of her, that she is called Henriette.'

'My dear, she is a perfectly ordinary baby but he has taken her to his heart. Her story is a strange one, even romantic. But I fear she sleeps in your own cradle, you must not mind.'

'Why should I mind? What can I possibly want with a cradle? In any case, I am glad there are to be children at Ramillies. It has been too quiet and full of old ghosts too long.'

They were brave words. He felt he could see her heart physically contract with the effort of speaking them.

'I am away to London in the morning,' he said, doffing his hat in admiration and taking the pony's rein.

'But you will come back?'

'Never doubt it. I will be back in the spring if I am not called abroad. I have promised to be here for the opening of the water garden, for the first spurting of the fountains, for the . . . ahem, baptism.'

She laughed. It was a purely delightful laugh, no bitter ring to it. For a moment there was no jealousy in her, no cynicism, none of that angry challenge which habitually blazed in those bold eyes.

And: 'What an odd woman,' said Jary as they jogged homeward, the swallows skating the lane almost under the horses' noses and an ominous darkness coming on, 'I felt she did not like me. Not a womanly female either. It must be hard on a girl to be plain and sour together.'

They turned in at the back gate and ambled up the overgrown drive between thickets of hazel and elder, oak scrub and nettles. A distant rumble of thunder made the pony flap his ears.

'I thought her very like the lady upon your morning room wall, the lady of whom you are so inordinately fond,' said the Doctor.

The first large drops of rain began to fall.

'She is nothing like!' cried Jary, astonished. 'How could you think so?'

7

'I see you still carry van Swieten,' said Grant, idling among the Doctor's pamphlets. 'And what is this? *Variolae Vaccinae*. Cow-pox. You take an interest in the latest methods, of course. But what about surgery? Nothing here on surgery.'

'The best part of my library is still in Norfolk.'

'I am surprised you wished to leave after so many years. You are too old for change, Alex, too old to go tramping after your wretched soldiers. Not that I would not recommend you as a surgeon in the field, the best, the very best. But there comes a time when we must give way to younger men.'

'I had not noticed you had done so.'

A dry laugh. 'Yes, I will take another glass. You always inclined to admire Larrey, did you not?'

'I approved his method, his humanity, his *ambulances volantes*.'

James Grant looked at him over his spectacles. He had known Alex French long enough to detect the warning tone. And after all, he meant no criticism, he was no surgeon himself though he had a lively interest in pathology. He was deeply attached to this unpredictable man who had shown such brilliance on the battlefield and today had demonstrated uncanny skill and nerve in front of a distinguished audience at Guy's when invited, on the spur of the moment, to take over an amputation. Tonight, October streaming beyond the misted windows, he had come to Alex's lodging, a noisome little room in the Crown a quarter of a mile from the hospital, to share a bottle and discuss the day's events.

'A benign tumour,' he was saying now, feeling that a change of direction might lighten his friend's mood, 'but a wretched presentation: too deep, oh far too deep. No chance, poor fellow.' An amount of gruesome detail followed and the results of the post mortem. Alex nodded, asked a few pointed questions, and gazed deeply at his wine against the candle. He was not himself. His mental state was akin to the night: cold, dreary, pitch black.

The mention of Larrey, a man he had so admired, could not move him, nor could the benign tumour, however unusual, nor the praise heaped on his head by Dr Hunter when he had finished with the amputation that morning and now repeated verbatim by Grant who had thought it well deserved. After Grant left, very very late, so late it was almost day, he roused himself only to remove from his writing case a letter, a letter obviously read over several times and grown crumpled in the process though it had only been delivered that morning in his absence. It lay on his lap as he turned to pour another glass of claret and when he came to peruse it again the frown deepened between his brows.

'How could you do such a thing?' was Lady Barsham's initial demand, a preliminary flexing of her scriptorial muscle. 'To leave us at such short notice – no notice, forsooth! – and give us all into the hands of that smiling, raw, officious, clever, expensive young man. Have you no conscience, no pang of guilt? You have departed hurriedly before, yes, have exchanged us for several thousand poor soldiers on a whim, but never with quite such lack of consideration. How are we, who thought ourselves your friends, to construe a brief note and a moonlight flit?' And then, more mildly, 'Dear Alex, of course I know why you wished to leave the neighbourhood, your sound reasons – though I do not usually advocate a man run away from what he does not like. But could you not have found the courage to say goodbye?'

The Doctor laid down the letter. There was another sheet, not quite so full of recriminations as the first, but packed with news of Ann, with Ann's bewilderment on hearing he had gone. Had she guessed his reasons? He doubted it. He had been very careful, very circumspect.

He folded the letter very small and sat looking at his name upon the front of it. He had a sudden vision of Louise Barsham sitting writing in her lovely drawing room. He had delivered her babies, treated her husband's excesses, eaten at her table for years, and he had a deep affectionate regard for her, her charity, her profound common sense, her unflagging good humour. Her letter cast a shadow over him, for he had been severely rebuked by someone whose opinion he valued. He had spent a long and tiring day in the company of great men, behaving himself, operating under their super-critical eyes, giving his second lecture on the surgical treatment of severe wounds. He had walked the wards with Grant, and though he had no place there, no official standing, no connection at all with the patients, he lingered now and again so that some junior student had to be sent to find him, to chivvy him on. He had not been in a large hospital for a great age, and he had never cared for them, it was true, for he had a great dread of the infections that periodically swept such institutions and which had often carried off those patients he had believed saved by skilful use of the knife. He did not care for the system of nursing, for the inevitable squalor, for the diet, for the general atmosphere. But he had let himself be overwhelmed by the atmosphere this time, had taken a keen, determined interest in everything. He had felt the need to be occupied, to be thoroughly occupied.

And then to return to his charred chops – two hours overdue and what was a poor woman to do, no notice being sent? – Grant in attendance, and find Louise's letter by his plate.

'I will answer it tomorrow,' he thought, slipping it in his pocket to keep company with the seven-toed cat's paw – not a genuine article, he felt, but possibly a taxidermist's joke, he had found it in a curio shop – the handkerchief upon which he had wiped his bloody hands, and a small piece of cheese given him by a deranged old man in one of the wards who had assured him he must eat it at once to avoid it being stolen. 'I will answer it tomorrow,' he repeated, crossing to open the shutters and find tomorrow there, clear and wind-riven, beyond the tumbled rooftops. He rubbed a hand over his bristly chin.

In another hour Mrs Glissop would bring in his breakfast. In another hour she did so, knocking loudly and marching in before the reverberations had died away, for she had grown used to his oddities in the weeks he had lodged at the Crown and one of those was to sink into a torpid state by the fire, lost in some learned book or medical pamphlet. He kept none of the usual hours, being as likely to be up scribbling notes at midnight or at four or six as to be abed at noon. He left books all over the floor and coal on the table – which seemed more perversity than eccentricity – and often and often she had to run after him with forgotten objects: sandwiches, handkerchiefs, his watch. But on the whole she found herself tolerably fond of him and thought that if he could be got to shave regularly and to wear a better coat and leave off polishing his surgical instruments and demonstrating their use in graphic dumb show when her wondering eye fell on them, she might grow very fond indeed.

'I have a nice piece of kidney pie, Doctor,' she said this morning, depositing her tray and noting that he appeared to have been out of bed all night, 'and there is honey for a change. The toast will be up before you have finished your meat.'

He was deep in an unscientific, prolix paper on intestinal worms and only grunted.

Mrs Glissop sighed and departed. She had made the pie herself and had given him the lion's share but she might have known he would be indifferent, he did not appear to notice what he ate. A moment later a hammering on the street door preceded the tread of heavy footsteps up the stairs and a further hammering on the Doctor's door, which half opened under the onslaught. The shrill voice of Mrs Glissop could be heard remonstrating, the Doctor was still abed, the Doctor wished to be left undisturbed. The Doctor, sunk in the mysteries of ascarids, looked up to find Jary filling the doorway.

'It is all right, Mrs Glissop. Mr Savage is a friend.'

'I am sure I did not know, sir, the gentleman brushed past me on the stair. But why, you have not touched your breakfast yet, and the toast on its way!'

'Then send up some more pie for my friend, and hurry the toast, Mrs Glissop. And a jug of coffee. I will indulge myself this morning.'

She went out. Jary hesitated, glancing about. 'How glad I am to find you. I have had the devil's own job down all these alleys and low courts. You are in good spirits, I hope?'

He asked with the merest trace of anxiety, for his instinct, not entirely overwhelmed by his pleasure at discovering the Crown at last, warned him all was not well. There was an air of distraction, of gloomy withdrawal about the Doctor, and it was clear he had not been to bed and was in desperate need of barber and valet. He reduced his own good spirits by a superhuman effort and said calmly: 'I hope I have not intruded. It is simply that I have a problem and you are the only person in this blighted country to whom I might turn for . . . for help.' And then, as the Doctor said nothing, 'You have a snug hideout here, though how you stand this stinking city . . . What are those?' looking suspiciously at some specimen jars ranged on the mantelshelf. 'Good God! Umm . . .' as his eyes focused on the foetus floating gently in its alcohol.

'Is Suffolk proving troublesome?' asked the Doctor, picking up knife and fork and waving Jary to a chair. 'Ah, Mrs Glissop, you are the best of women! Is that not the rest of the pie, the entire pie? And toast for a regiment. Pray put the coffee here, and tell the girl Tizzie I will have hot water and clean towels in an hour.'

'Not Suffolk,' said Jary when Mrs Glissop had withdrawn, gratified, 'though the wind blows something cruel and a strange malady has wiped out half the fish in the pool . . . No, not Suffolk. But . . .'

He took a mouthful of pie, chewed it, swallowed it, took a deep breath. It was a very deep breath but if it was intended to steady him it failed, for his face was suddenly suffused with the ruby glow of distress.

'Hell and damnation!' he cried. 'I am to fight a duel.'

'Is that all? I have been called out myself in the dim past.'

'You have? *You*? But you cannot understand – it is the most ridiculous ... oh, far worse than ridiculous situation.' His eye had fallen on the paper on worms, took in a sentence or two, and his red flush receded to be replaced by a pinched grey distaste. 'I am to fight Prince Whiteley over Lizzie Rayner. No, do not laugh! I know you are about to laugh. I can scarcely tell how it all came about but there is no humour in any of it, I assure you.'

The pie was excellent, and the bacon and chops which had accompanied it, the toast was hot and crisp, the coffee was as fresh as any coffee that could be had in all London, but the whole meal might have been dust for the two men who ate it, solemnly, face to face across the small table. The Doctor made no reply to Jary's suggestion he might stand as his second, but chewed with a serious and unhurried doggedness. At last, when all was finished, and Jary had grown rather fearful of the outcome, he rose and stretched and scratched his head.

'You had better tell me how it came about, even if you are not sure yourself. It strikes me you have chosen ill to call out Whiteley. Was there no one else offered you a quarrel?'

'You like to mock, I know. Do you think I would not have avoided it if it were humanly possible? And how did you guess I had called him out? He was all wound up, in a fury, he would have slain me on the spot if he could.'

'Oh, I doubt his courage would have carried him to challenge you when it came to the point.'

The worst of it was, Jary confessed, while watching the Doctor begin his tedious barbering, that the quarrel had been at Sir James Braile's, at a dinner given, he had supposed, in his own honour as a newcomer. Sir James was a fat, florid, loud sort of man, all nose and a gross ulcered leg and self-importance, but as honest and upright as any other man who was of an old decaying family and was a local magistrate. His wife had always been a good friend to Lizzie Rayner, so Lizzie had been present too, a dull, extinguished Lizzie among so many glittering gentry decked out in their best to meet the exotic Mr Savage. The Whiteleys had been there, of course, and the odd Mr Fisher and his father, whom Jary had thought an invalid but who had been quite hearty enough to eat steadily through seven courses. There had been a Mrs Stone and several pretty Misses Stone and a Master Stone of the most unbelievable dullness like an automaton. All had gone well until the girls – Mrs Stone's delightful girls – had been prevailed on to play a little, and Jary, who did not care for this kind of entertainment, took advantage of the audience's polite attentiveness to slip out into the hall. From there he had wandered to a library, whose double doors stood open, and by the table he had found Prince Whiteley, writing in a pocket book.

'Computing debts, no doubt,' said Jary harshly. 'He looked white when he saw me as if I had caught him at some game or other. He made no reply to my remarks on the party, on the hospitality of the Brailes. He was shifty, put his little book away with one of those rabbit looks, that little jerk of his head. He does it when he is nervous, I think. Anyway, just at that moment who should pass the door but Lizzie Rayner – strange how dull she was, almost as dull as the Stone boy, but I suppose she felt awkward being at the same table as Whiteley. I doubt they have spoke since he called off the wedding. I did wonder at first that the Brailes would have invited them there at the same time but then I thought well, it happened years ago, years, and they must meet about the village to give each other good day, and people cannot nurture hurt feelings for ever. But do you know what he said after she had passed – she was in full view because of the doors being open, and she glanced in, and a real fiery look when she saw who it was, not like the mute downcast Lizzie of the dinner table – he said . . .' Jary drew breath, remembering, and his eyes glowed. 'He said: "Thank God I did not marry that vixen. She was too high a price even for Ramillies." You can imagine I remonstrated, quite gentle then though, you know the kind of thing: "Come, sir, you ought not to insult the lady, she does you no injury," and he cocks his mean little head at me and says: "What's it to you, Savage? You cannot have designs on her, she has no looks and no money."

' "I do not like to hear a lady abused," says I, all stiff and foolish no doubt but getting hot. I could have bent his nose for him, believe me.

' "Ho, lady is it? What makes you think she may be called a lady?" he asks, getting hot himself. "Just because she grew up at Ramillies and has a family tree. Did she tell you how she ran away with a soldier when she was twenty-one or so? Lady! She is nothing better than a slut." '

The Doctor stopped shaving, his razor poised over the last square inch of soap on his smooth chin. He said nothing, asked no question, made no noise of encouragement.

'I lost my temper,' said Jary slowly, 'I told him he had insulted a friend. Well, Heaven knows if I may claim Lizzie Rayner as a friend but Mrs Jewkes is an excellent neighbour, an excellent tenant, the dearest woman . . . I told him I would have satisfaction unless he withdrew his remark. He said he would not. I own he hesitated before he replied as if a push might make him think better of it, but I said: "Well?" and he said he would not, I had better find myself a second, and walked off, the dog, just walked off without another look.'

It had been more than awkward, Jary said, for it was not his custom to pick quarrels while out to dinner and it was evident to the entire company that he and Whiteley had been going at each other like fighting cocks, though

94

no one knew the slightest of what had passed. And now it was all out, and it was to be pistols up in Beke's Wood, there was some well-known clearing always used for this sort of thing – did the Doctor think duels were so often fought in Stretfield that a clearing must be kept specially? – and Mr Fisher was acting as his second, quite capable in spite of appearances but too fussy for Jary's taste, though he meant well. Would Alex consider coming up to Suffolk to see him through this business? He had hoped to shrug it off, to look on it as the price he must pay for his own unreliable temper, but two days ago he had sat in the library at Ramillies and felt damn lonely and dispiritingly unsure of the outcome. And of course he was not thought much of for falling out with neighbours – cousins, even – and Sir James was offended, and Lizzie . . . Well, Lizzie!

'She wrote me a note,' said Jary, and the Doctor emerged from his towel with a grunt that might have been humorous. 'She wrote this damned little note, straight black writing, venomous stuff, she had nearly scored through the paper, to say she would be grateful if I could call the whole thing off, she did not care to be defended. She did not care for it! Is that a way to treat a man who has hazarded his life on her behalf?'

'To be sure,' said the Doctor, brushing energetically at his short hair and suppressing a wicked desire to laugh aloud, 'she did not ask you to hazard yourself. In any case, will not Whiteley call off and apologize? He surely does not want to meet you in Beke's Wood, the whole district agog for the outcome?'

'He has shown no sign of it. If anything he is more belligerent now than he was three days ago. The matter is to be fought out next week – Whiteley has business in Ipswich which cannot wait and will be away until then – a dark, resentful look and a flash of barely contained frustration – 'he is off to practise with his pistols, no doubt.'

The Doctor put on his coat. It was his black coat and in it he looked a new man. Jary fell silent, suddenly shy.

They were, after all, almost strangers, three weeks in each other's company could not contribute much to an undying friendship – three weeks and several sharp moments, minor misunderstandings, criticisms, differences of opinion. At Ramillies, sitting alone with the feeling that he had taken up an intolerable burden by challenging Whiteley in such a manner, it had seemed a comforting thought that Alex would soon be with him – it had not occurred to him until he had stood on the threshold of this very room that Alex might refuse to come. He had felt a strange fondness for the man, a happy anticipation of having him at Stretfield again. Now, looking at him as he slipped on his shoes, gave the finishing touch to his immaculate linen, and took up his cane, he was not so sure. The Doctor did not invite friendship and in his present mood . . . Who knew what he was capable of in his present mood?

'I have an appointment,' he was saying, searching for his gloves. 'I have a very important appointment with the Inspector General of Army Hospitals.'

Mrs Glissop was at the door again. It was raining hard, she informed them, and would they care for a hackney to be called? The Doctor would spoil his best coat even with his umbrella over, the wind was something terrible, and his stockings – his stockings would not survive a yard. The Doctor agreed to a hackney-coach; he was certainly fearful for his stockings. He had a great admiration for Dr Franck and would not like to appear slovenly before him.

'You are going back to the army then,' said Jary, reaching for his own hat and cape, thinking of the long, hard, lonely road back to Suffolk.

'Oh, it is not decided. An old friend assured me last night I was too old to follow the army, to suffer the deprivations of battle hospitals, of operating on a hundred poor souls in a space of hours. Perhaps he is right. Perhaps I might find a position superintending the welfare of the men, the day-to-day welfare which is so neglected. But I am not known for a conforming man, I have no

96

patience with committees and boards and chains of command. They will smile falsely and show me the door.'

They walked downstairs together. Mrs Glissop was by the street door with the umbrella. Outside in the blowy wet a drab vehicle waited, the horse understandably hanging its head.

'Is the weather as bad in Suffolk?' The Doctor did not ordinarily mind the weather but he could see that, hackney or no, his stockings would suffer this morning.

'Possibly worse. The ford at Paradise is impassable.'

'I cannot be at Ramillies before Tuesday. Is that too late?' A great sense of relief swept over Jary. He had not felt so lonely for a very long time, perhaps not since the first days of his exile in Brazil. He had thought that cold ache, that sense of rejection, had been peculiar to eighteen, to those distinct circumstances, to a special loss and to continually unfair treatment... But he had known it again in Suffolk. He remembered what the Doctor had said at the inn where Henriette had been born: They hate change and will kill anything unusual.

'Come, share my cab,' cried the Doctor now, seizing his arm. 'After it has set me down you must go on to the Fighting Cocks. I will meet you there in' – getting out his watch and shaking it gently as he always did – 'in an hour. It will scarcely take them an hour to tell me they have nothing for me.'

For five minutes they threaded their way through teeming traffic. Then, gazing at Jary's face in the dim light – there would never be proper day through this determined downpour – the Doctor said: 'It is not like you to be a pessimist. Why do you fear the outcome so?'

'Because I believe it is their way of driving me out. I have made disapproving noises about the Diddlers, consulted a lawyer, spoken harshly to Mrs Whiteley – I did, though I never meant to when I called, I was the model of politeness for a good ten minutes – ruined the park at Ramillies, and have the audacity to bring up a black baby in their midst. They mean to see me off, Alex. They would all rather Ramillies fell down than that a stranger had it.'

8

It was not possible for Mrs Jewkes to fly into a passion, she lived her entire life in a state of cheerful excitement, but she was angry, a deep blazing anger – she blazed in all emotions, she could do nothing else – and her face was paler than usual when she called at Ramillies that squally Tuesday. She called to give Jary a piece of her mind: grown men to fight like boys, antiquated nonsense, the victor possibly taken up for murder, the lady in dispute entirely against it. What was the world coming to? What were they coming to, who professed themselves gentlemen, and civilized? And she swept in even on being told by Mrs Clark that Mr Savage was not at home, her eyes kindling at the falsehood, for the post-chaise had been careering away up the avenue as she arrived; she would give him not at home.

Her entrance into the library was meteoric, she knew it was his hideout and she would not be denied. But her darting eye beheld only the Doctor, still in topcoat and boots, apparently looking up something in a book.

'Good day, Doctor French, and how do you do? You must forgive the intrusion. I have presumed on a short acquaintance to behave very ill, very unbecoming. Did you know Mr Savage is to fight Prince Whiteley and all over Lizzie, which is absurd! Absurd! Oh no, pray do not leave off, continue, continue. I shall be gone directly. I have no wish to disturb you from your studies.'

But he had closed the book and tossed it down. He was looking frowsty, a peculiar colour, as if he had not slept, but he made a bow, said calmly: 'If you hoped to move him, madam, you will not do so.'

'No,' and she flung up her head so that he saw her bright little eyes and wide rueful smile, 'No, you are right. One might as well go wave a handkerchief at men engaged upon a battlefield. But could a woman move him by guile? Yes, we ought to try guile. Though who? Lizzie will not speak to him – will not speak *of* him, my dear – and has no looks, she don't attract him, so could only have an effect by sobbing on his chest, and Lizzie don't sob, so that's an end of it.'

The Doctor gave her his arm and led her to the morning room where a lively fire paid tribute to the howling westerly outside.

'What are we to do?' asked Fanny, with a sideways look at his harsh, drawn face. She admired him immensely, and instinct told her he was formidable when roused for a cause, though for what causes he might be roused was as yet a mystery.

'We must let matters take their course. Mr Savage has a notion he may wing his opponent with such precision there will be but a teaspoon of blood and an honourable withdrawal.'

'I have never been present at a duel,' said Fanny, untying her bonnet ribbons, 'but it strikes me they are sad affairs in general and the outcome unpredictable. A teaspoon of blood indeed! La, what fools they are to be sure.'

'To be sure. But the day after tomorrow will see it over.'

'Are you his second?' – with sudden blushing suspicion, as she watched him fold his coat over the back of a chair and realized belatedly it had been he and he alone in the chaise.

'Dear me no, I am the attending physician. The Whiteleys have agreed to it. His second is Mr Fisher, who has proved most efficient.'

Fanny coloured a little at the mention of Mr Fisher, whose awkward gallantries she had rebuffed for a year or two now, and striking off to safer ground said: 'Poor Lizzie! She has scorched off to Westdene for some paltry shopping; woe betide any shopman who crosses her. I believe if she met Mr Savage in the road she would strike him.'

'He would be at a loss to understand such indignation.'

'Well, I can understand it, I can sympathize . . . She hates to be talked of, cruel nonsense, old envy, all the past brought up again. There was so much of that the last time . . .' and she stopped, aware she was about to say too much.

For a moment they sat staring into the fire, both contemplating the nature of their sympathy for Lizzie, who never asked for any and was a temperamental recipient of even common civilities. As if she read the Doctor's mind Fanny looked up to say gently: 'She was not always so sharp, you know. Always passionate, yes, even as a child. But never . . . Well, you must have judged for yourself. Now and again when she smiles I can see the girl I knew at Ramillies all those years ago. She lost far more than that old house when her father died.'

'She lost Mr Whiteley, I understand, that same Mr Whiteley who now abuses her.'

'A good thing too, what a marriage that would have been! I told her father at the time it was wrong, a dreadful mistake, but the old fool had been unwell that winter and was thinking on death and settlements and how his Lizzie would fare without him. He was excessively depressed. The truth is he knew he had made bad investments and had lived the last ten years entirely on credit. I believe he also knew Mrs Whiteley – not Mr Whiteley, poor persecuted soul, such an amiable, helpless man – would buy up Ramillies when he died, and his setting up of Lizzie with young Prince was a way for her to keep what was rightfully her own. But I always thought it was a terrible thing for him to do – a man who loved her dearly – to encourage her with that scoundrel.'

'And what did Lizzie say?'

Fanny laughed. 'Lizzie had very little chance to say anything, it was all so sudden. And she was very young, seventeen, and Ramillies her whole world. My dear Doctor, I assure you there have been times since her father died she would have married a monster had he money enough to buy it back for her and knowing full

100

well what she was doing, but at the time I think she never considered . . . never, how can I put it? Never thought about regard, affection, the day to day afflictions of living with a man she did not like. She had known Whiteley since they were children but he had grown up when he returned from Oxford in the spring and he rode over to Ramillies every day and courted her most conscientiously – I expect his aunt had threatened him with disinheritance if he did not. And Lizzie had no one else whispering in her ear and holding her hands and begging her to marry him. Charles Calloway called her a termagant at the Assize ball and wished Whiteley well of her. But then old Henry was carried home with a broken neck and that was the end of her whole world.'

Her relations in Woodbridge had taken her in, Fanny said, and Ramillies had been sold to Treadgold. Mrs Whiteley would not match his price. She had been expecting Ramillies for nothing, or for the trifling consideration of making Lizzie unhappy in a loveless marriage, and the very natural disappointment had made her meaner than usual. Anyway, with Ramillies gone Lizzie was packed off to Woodbridge where she had been hopelessly unhappy. The aunt had been a vain, silly creature, the uncle a bullish man, autocratic; he had never won her confidence and certainly not her affection. She had been rather confined, rather *watched* as Fanny put it, and she was forbidden her brushes and easel: at least, it came to that in the end. She took painting beyond the limits of a ladylike occupation, she talked of exhibiting, she corresponded with Lockinge. It was not the thing for Woodbridge, not the thing at all. Eventually there was a row.

'And you offered her a home?' asked the Doctor.

'She was confused and homesick and ripe for rebellion. There would be mischief enough in a twinkling were somebody not to step in and prevent it. Foley was a lonely barn of a place, there was room and more for two spinsters and an easel. I offered, she accepted, it was as simple as that.'

101

It had not been quite so simple, said her bleak expression, but they no longer dwelt on all that. Indeed, Lizzie had done her best to blot out every last memory of Woodbridge, still grew pale if it were mentioned. But if Fanny Jewkes suspected a deep and continuing wound she had never remarked on it, nor ever would.

'I must leave you,' she cried now, springing up. 'Pray don't ring, I can find my own way to the door. Why, I played in this house as a girl. No, no tea, nor ratafia, nor sherry wine. I have intruded too long, I have sunk to being a mindless old woman, rambling on without consequence.'

The Doctor bowed gravely over her hand. How enchanted she was with such old-fashioned manners! She almost regretted he had left off his wig. He said, 'I had heard about an escapade with a soldier. Was that a lie?'

'Lizzie and a soldier? Is all that trouble to be brought out again? Yes, there was a soldier, and a very handsome one too, and I do believe as honourable as he was handsome – though we shall never know now, shall we? But I never break a confidence, Dr French; though I am guilty of a great many miserable sins I will never do that, I hope. If you wish to know more about the soldier you must ask Lizzie herself.'

He smiled, knowing full well the impossibility of such a thing, and she smiled back, knowing it too. And she thought that if only he had been more alluring physically she might have set her cap at him, for she was sure she would always enjoy his company, his informal, cultured, stimulating company, were he to throw off his reserve and become just a little romantic. Alas, it was unlikely he was ever romantic, the tough old bird he was.

Jary, meanwhile, ordinarily level-headed, had discovered in himself a great capacity for the romantic. It was true he had offered to fight over the insult to Lizzie only because training, indignation, and his swift temper had brought him to it, for he had not until that moment even regarded her as a true woman, rather as a strange and

102

slightly repellent being, asexual. But it seemed to him, though he did not think too deeply about it – Lizzie Rayner was nothing to him after all – that under the unbecoming smock she wore for painting must beat the heart of a woman, not very different perhaps from the hearts of other, more desirable, more accommodating women he had known. The act of fighting a duel over her lent her a femininity she had not possessed before in his eyes. He came more and more to see his defence of her as a romantic gesture and he applauded himself for it, not in a vain, overbearing way but with simple cheerful satisfaction. He had behaved well. It was seldom he recognized when he did so, seldom the wrongs and rights of a case were so clearly exposed that he could make a choice and be sure he had not blundered. And now the Doctor had said he would come, the result of the fight was not the terrible weight on his conscience it had been; and though the whole district was against him he would not take the hint, he would not run away.

He rode into Westdene in this sunny, defiant mood, but he could not fail to notice some interested looks from those who had caught wind of the encounter. The cause of the quarrel was imperfectly understood, only that it involved the notorious Miss Rayner: many thought it was Savage who had insulted her and Whiteley who had called him out. Jary was aware, therefore, of some keen scrutiny as he rode slowly towards the Admiral on the corner of the market place. It was as well he could not hear what was being said: that he was a man of the world, had owned plantations, a thousand slaves, coconut trees, elephants, a whole nabobbery of suchlike wonders; that he was as mysterious as he could be without being inhuman and poor young Mr Whiteley had better watch out.

Jary stabled his horse at the Admiral and was about to step through to the public room to see if Mrs King could find him any of her famous veal pie before he strolled round the corner to see Calloway about the Diddlers, when a venomous eye caught his own. It belonged to Lizzie Rayner, sitting in a private room with her feet up on a little pile of packages.

'Miss Rayner, how do you do?'

'Furiously, thank you. The whole town is talking about me and my two ferocious lovers.'

Jary pulled the door to behind him; there was a gathering of little boys down the passage all eager to do anything for sixpence, even eavesdrop.

'He insulted you. I only did what seemed fitting at the time.'

'Oh, Mr Whiteley is always insulting me, I think nothing of it. It is probably a guilty conscience. Has it occurred to you that if you kill him you will be hung for murder?'

'I shall take great care not to kill him.'

'You sound very confident.'

'Well, it may be Mr Whiteley who is taken up by the constables, I shall do my best to come through unscathed. Has it occurred to *you* that this may be your last sight of me alive and cheerful?'

She did not smile; if anything, she looked angrier. 'How can you jest? How can you take it so lightly? Sir James will clap you both in irons at the least hint of a wounding, the slightest scratch, the very slightest fuss. Though *he* pretends not to know, the countryside for miles around is fully aware you and Whiteley quarrelled in his house, which puts him in an unenviable position, the poor donkey. He likes to keep up appearances, to set a moral tone. If one of you kills the other he will be . . .'

'Is that where your sympathies lie?' Jary broke in. 'You pity the magistrate for having unruly guests! Well, it is between myself and Mr Whiteley. And I might say that if Sir James Braile had been present when Whiteley spoke of you as he did I would have considered him a dog not to have defended you himself, though it would not have come to pistols in that case. Your servant, madam.'

He had his hand on the latch when she spoke. 'I am sorry if you think me ungracious,' and 'Ungracious!' Jary shouted, turning round, so that she took a sudden deep breath before going on. 'They have been waiting for years to catch me in some scandal again.'

How could there be scandal, he wondered, and what did she mean by *again*?

'I am sorry for it,' he said, 'but I do not care, forgive me, for foul-mouthed scrubs, and he is one, nor do I care for a parcel of gossips trying to frighten me out of the county. Good day to you, Miss Rayner.'

A message, curious in the circumstances, was galloped up from Ipswich to inform them that Prince Whiteley was indisposed, had taken to his bed and was receiving medical attention.

'For the pox, no doubt,' said Jary, who was eating his breakfast. Mr Fisher, who had refused a chair, blushed deeply. 'I believe it is . . . I believe he has caught a bad cold.'

'Well, it will be interesting to see how long it keeps him in Ipswich, this bad cold.'

'Cold feet, more likely,' he said later to the Doctor, whom he found teetering on the edge of the new pond, a saucer of mud surrounded by pegs and twine. 'Do you mind kicking your heels about Ramillies for another few days?'

'Not since I received this . . .' was the answer, and the Doctor passed over a sheet of paper, closely written but in a faultless official hand, of which Jary could make out the words 'very much regret' and 'posts vacant' and 'future employment'.

'Is it from the Inspector General?'

'From the same, or his department, his minions. Well, it is not his fault, he is an able man and as far as I can tell, as fair as any other man in such high position. I cannot say I was not heard, that I did not air my views. Alas, my views were too well known already: chickens will not invite a fox into the farmyard, even chickens are not so foolish.'

Jary handed back the paper and the Doctor stuffed it in his pocket. After a while, moving round gingerly to the other side of the pond and looking down the new cut, he said: 'I am unemployed, on the beach as sailors say.'

'You could return to High Common.'

'I could.' They looked at each other. The Doctor walked on a little and the wind, the rising wind, blew off his hat and bowled it down into the swamp.

'You must put it to dry and then brush it,' said Jary, hooking it out with his toe. 'It's a good thing it was already stricken in years, it will never be the same again. I take it . . . I suppose there was a lady in the case?'

'What makes you think so?' snappily. 'What have I to offer a lady?'

'They all smile on you and call you "dear Doctor", and you are not so bad when you have shaved though you will be better when your hair is grown a trifle longer.' It had reached the stage where it gave the Doctor a startled appearance, standing up all over his head.

'But I wanted to ask her to marry me. Think of it: marriage. What would a young woman of twenty-six, quite wealthy in her own right, quite lovely . . . what would she want with an old bachelor with no money and none of the attributes of a hero?'

Jary tripped over one of Hawke's markers. 'Damn! Look, you do not need to be a hero, only to Miss . . . Miss?'

'She will be Mrs Claverden by Christmas.'

'Oh, you had a rival?'

'How could I have a "rival"? I never sued for her affections. We were friends, as close friends perhaps as a man and woman can be without . . . She never guessed. In any case she was in love with William Claverden. I . . . brought them together.'

Jary tramped on, occasionally looking back to see if he could make sense of the pegs and holes and mounds of spoil. 'You would do well to stick to lopping off legs and arms, to be sure you are no good at mending your own affairs. Why bring them together? By God, *I* could not have done it!'

106

'But she loves him.'

They were almost at the river. 'Yes, well,' and Jary stopped, gave an affectionate, crooked smile, 'it would not have done then, keeping them apart. Look, there are the herons. There are sometimes ten together on the far side. When I marry I hope my wife will be amiable, affectionate; I could not do with unrequited passion, nor yet no passion at all, but . . .'

'Broadmindedness,' declared the Doctor, coming to himself at last but forgetting his hat was muddy and clapping it back on suddenly without a qualm. 'I mean your wife must be exceptionally good natured, as good natured as a woman can be . . . Or else what will become of Henriette?'

A succession of clear sunny days, blasted only by the tremendous wind, put Jary in an unassailably good mood. The wind made riding about an anxious business but he contrived to pay his compliments to Fanny Jewkes and to the Stones, dined with Mr Fisher in Westdene and left a short, harsh note for Charles Calloway, discussed with the builder the necessary alterations to the stables, and organized the draining of the pool, an operation of much confusion, loud oaths, wetness and surprise. His good spirits never abated, not even when Fisher rode over again, straw and leaves in his hair and his cloak half torn off, to tell him the appointed hour was six-thirty the morning of the following Tuesday and the appointed place that curious haunted level within Beke's Wood where the gipsies invariably camped and someone had once, so legend said, hanged himself for love.

As the wind rose so did his state of high excitement. He loved the wind, he told the Doctor, it reminded him of Jamaica. Whether it did or not, whether the memories were happy or not, the Doctor could not tell. But the wind increased and increased as if it were determined to blow as like Jamaica as possible, and the wind beat them, the duel was put off. The wind beat them and rejoiced, howling across the country scattering the debris of everyday life as it went, throwing down so many elm branches in the clearing in Beke's Wood that only the very agile and extremely foolhardy would attempt to cross it with a loaded pistol, and it reached an intensity whereby a man might be blown over if he did not crawl along hand over hand like an inverted sloth.

The Doctor went out, however, called to a curious coma, a coma so curious he had no hesitation in facing a hurricane to view it. Jary, who was puzzled as to how one coma might differ from another in even the minutest respect, watched him go with the anxious exasperation of a parent whose child is bent on some feat beyond its little strength, sure to end in tears.

Some moments later: 'The Doctor has left his cheese and cake,' said Mrs Clark, coming in on the heels of Mrs Bloy who had brought the baby down for her daily inspection. 'Should I send Millett after him?'

'No, no. He will not die for want of a snack between here and the village. Dr Plesset will feed him. They are off to see old Colling or Cullen, I forget which.'

'Old Mr Culling, sir. Mrs Fipson says he had a fit two days ago and now sits upright, stiff as a board and with his eyes open.'

'Mrs Fipson is remarkably well informed always, seeing she never leaves the kitchen. It sounds a practical impossibility to me, being struck rigid sitting up and staring. Are you sure he is not dead? I have known a few poor souls pronounced dead by doctors who subsequently sat up and ate shark steaks with relish, so I would not be astonished if they were to make the same mistake t'other way round,' said Jary, holding Henriette on his knee and looking fondly into her dark eyes. She was a pretty baby and her black hair was very fine and straight, Indian blood perhaps, or Spanish. She could have been his own daughter after all, they were equally swarthy, and as delighted with each other as always.

'Oh, I do hope the Doctor is safe.' Mrs Clark rose from mending the fire. 'I do believe the wind is rising yet.'

'It will serve him right if he ends up like old Culling. Clarkie, run and fetch Millett, will you, and the stable account book.'

He felt cheerful and confident. He did not mind the duel, the weather, local opinion. He handed the baby back to her nurse and pulled out the plans for the new stables, smiling down on them. He was giving new life to Ramillies. He looked up and out of the window. The view seemed very familiar, as if he had known it all his life. It was not Helen's Mount of course, they would not stand comparison, but then Ramillies might become what Helen's Mount had never been, for all his brutalized sense of attachment, his sense that it was rightfully his and was where he belonged; it had occurred to him more than once that Ramillies might become a home.

The oaks up the avenue were plunging wildly, the last leaves streaming from the branches.

'Oh sir,' and Mrs Clark was panting in the doorway. 'Millett cannot come, sir. The ash tree has fallen on the paddock fence and the horses are all abroad.'

On the way back from his coma the Doctor called in at Foley, a Foley surrounded by broken trees and tumbled fences and yards of uprooted hedge. Fanny was lying down, she had a headache, the wind affected her so.

'So many tiles off the roof,' said Lizzie, appearing unexpectedly and showing him, equally unexpectedly, into her studio, 'and every one of them smashed in the fall. There will be builders and bills for months. It is enough to give anyone a headache.'

'Yet you sound cheerful.' It was true. For once she was softer, more approachable.

'I have been working all morning and have finished Mr Fisher.'

'May I see?'

He stepped forward and round the canvas. 'It is the very man.'

'You sound as if you expected much less. Have you met him?'

109

He felt it was a just rebuke. 'I beg your pardon. But I had been expecting . . . competence; this is talent.' He gazed at the hook nose, the libidinous little eyes, the tufted eyebrows. He had only seen him once in the flesh, in Westdene, being pushed by a manservant in his invalid chair. Stephen Fisher had been with him, had performed hesitant introduction. His tremulous 'My father, Mr Fisher' and the father's direct, disdainful stare had told the Doctor a very great deal.

'I am no critic,' he said slowly, wondering what innocuous phrasing might or might not offend her, 'but if I were looking for an artist to do my own portrait I would engage you without hesitation.'

She leaned forward a little, studying his face, though he had turned from the light and was in concealing shadow. There was a sour smell of fresh paint.

'I would like to paint you. Would you sit? You will find it tedious, I expect. But two sittings, three . . . And you may come to be exhibited in the Royal Academy.'

The Doctor declined to be exhibited, Mr Fisher would grace a wall much better – or Mrs Jewkes in a tantalizing lace cap. But he agreed to be painted for a trifling sum, a sum to be agreed upon at some vague and distant date – she did not care for money, she said, she cared only for an interesting subject. It was a lie, for she was very conscious of her debt to Fanny if nothing else, and the Doctor knew it was a lie but did not mind it.

'Ah, still here, Doctor, I am so glad,' Fanny exclaimed, walking in five minutes later. Mr Fisher had called, his carriage stood even now under the writhing elms, the horses scarcely able to keep their feet. He was feeling low, poor man, his father could not endure stormy weather, and he had come out of his way to bring Mr Calloway to Ramillies on urgent business, having met him with a lame horse on the Stretfield road. She had put both of them into the parlour with hot shrub and the latest newspapers but she did not feel up to the task of entertaining them alone.

Lizzie went to change. Fanny shut the door of the

studio with a sigh. 'This was the old drawing room but it faces north-east, Heaven knows why, for it is courting disaster in a house as chill as this one. It is entirely Lizzie's now, as you saw, and she has been shut away in it for days finishing the picture of old Mr Fisher. She had to go to Westdene to do the sketches, he refused to come here even in his own carriage, and she would have painted it in Westdene too but the wind saved her from such a fate. You will be civil to young Calloway, will you not? He looked very straight when I said you were here. Has he quarrelled with Mr Savage?'

He looked ready to quarrel with anyone when she opened the door to find him sharing the hearth mat with Mr Fisher, who was flushed with shrub, the glorious shrub. He was a great deal taller than Mr Fisher, though not as tall as Jary, and his darkness had a sombre quality. He always dressed conservatively, was scrupulously clean, and gave the impression of being a steady dependable reserved young man who would execute all his clients' business conscientiously, which no doubt was the impression he wished to give. He had been on his way to Ramillies when his horse had shied into a ditch and on scrambling out had wrenched off a shoe.

'Then he must have stood on it,' he said. 'He is very sore. He pricked his foot, I swear. I have left him at Paradise and Mr Fisher bravely turned out of his way to bring me here as I also needed to consult Mrs Jewkes.'

He spoke as Lizzie entered the room, a Lizzie in grey with a blue sash, still glowing from the relief of finishing the portrait, relief and achievement. Her eyes flashed at Mr Calloway, to whom she did not normally speak, the Doctor surmised, unless it was absolutely necessary; her eyes flashed with challenge but her smile was lovely.

'How do you do, Miss Rayner?' he said, as formal as could be, but somehow taken aback as if he had difficulty in recognizing her. Perhaps he had never seen her make such an entrance before.

'Come, Mr Calloway, come,' said Fanny, holding the

door, 'let us dispose of the business and then we may sit down to toast and madeira.'

'Toast and madeira!' cried Mr Fisher as the door closed behind them. 'I never expected such a bounty when I set out an hour ago on a simple errand. But I cannot stay long' – with a distracted glance at the mantel clock – 'my father will be expecting me home.'

It seemed pitiable that a man of forty should still be afraid of a parent's wrath. Lizzie, with rare charity, smiled on him and said: 'You must come and see the finished portrait. Come to the studio.'

She led him away and was back in a few minutes, alone, and with a definite air of intense satisfaction. 'He is amazed. He has pulled up a chair and is sitting staring at his father's face. Oh, poor man! He is so very fond of that horrible old villain who does nothing but make his life a misery. Why do kind, good people sacrifice themselves for such worthless causes? Or is it some weakness of their own? Is it all Mr Fisher's fault he is tyrannized?'

They could hear raised voices at the end of the passage. Fanny and Charles Calloway had had some difference over rents and repairs. Mr Savage's name was bandied about.

Lizzie sank into a chair by the fire. 'Do you know, Mr Stone asked me yesterday if I thought Prince Whiteley cared for me after all since he was to fight a duel for my sake. He had only the most garbled version of the story,' and she bit her lip, staring into the flames. 'Of course, they are all remembering some foolish business over years ago. Very soon I shall be spoken of as the notorious Miss Rayner and children will be hurried by on the other side of the street for fear notoriety is contagious.'

He said nothing. He wondered if she would go on, would confide in him. She had her face turned to the fire still, he could see the sharply carved bones, the drooping corner of her wide expressive mouth. He waited, shrunk into his chair like an old man, one who knew the meaning of integrity, who could be trusted to keep confidences.

'You look very fierce,' said Lizzie, turning. 'Have I said

something to offend you? I know I speak disparagingly of Mr Savage's gallantry but you do not know . . . It will not make him popular in the neighbourhood, this duel.'

'I had formed the impression it would not matter to you if he stayed or went, lived or died . . .'

'Thank goodness that is all over,' said Fanny, halting on the threshold at the whiff of disagreement. 'Mr Calloway says he must get on to Ramillies if he is to be home before dark. Where is Mr Fisher?'

Mr Fisher was emerging from the studio, and he came straight up to Lizzie and held out his hands, his thin pale face beaming with pleasure and gratitude. 'My dear Miss Rayner, I cannot thank you enough. It is splendid, splendid. It is far far better than I hoped. I never knew . . .' He had never, like the Doctor, guessed the depths of her talent. He hesitated, coughed, let her hands go with an embarrassed smile. 'You deserve to be famous, you deserve to be feted, to be another Angelica.'

It was an unfortunate remark though he could not know it, his was a simple, innocent soul. Miss Angelica Kauffmann had enjoyed a certain reputation: there had been malicious talk, scandal, heartache. Mr Fisher knew nothing of it however, he only understood the lady had been a famous artist many years ago. He thought he had paid a compliment.

'You are very kind,' said Lizzie.

Now if I had compared her with Kauffmann, thought the Doctor, she would have flown at me and demanded in what particular she was like, the artistic or the moral. And she would undoubtedly, undoubtedly have taken it as an affront.

Charles Calloway was at his elbow. 'Mrs Jewkes is to lend me a horse. Perhaps we could ride on to Ramillies together. There is something I would like to ask you before I meet Savage.'

The Doctor twisted his cuff, pulling idly at the buttons. His face was sober and alert. 'Not as a doctor, I hope,' he asked in a low, low voice.

'No! No, of course not! As a friend of Savage. I am

113

on a difficult errand,' and he turned slightly so that the others would hear nothing, his face bent close to the Doctor's own. 'It is about his will. I do not know if he has made one, but I believe it my duty to suggest he does so at once. I have only just heard this duel is to be fought as soon as the wind blows itself out. There is a great deal of property involved, a vast fortune. Perhaps you do not know how rich a man he is. He summoned me some days ago but I could not come, being in Ipswich, and I wondered if you knew why, I mean why he left such a peremptory note and without indicating his business.'

'I know nothing, dear sir.'

'I am sorry for it. I had thought perhaps you were his confidant.'

'But should I also be yours?'

The rebuke made Calloway blush scarlet. 'I did not . . . I do not suggest anything improper. I only wished to know why I had been commanded to Ramillies.'

'Commanded to Ramillies?' cried Fanny, coming over, 'who has been commanded to Ramillies? Is Mr Savage playing the prince? La, you must not mind it at all, Mr Calloway. A man who has commanded a thousand slaves and ten score pirates can think nothing of a poor country attorney, nothing.'

'Are there no amendments you would care to make, no codicils to be added?'

'Well, to be sure the whole thing needs drawing up afresh,' said Jary, looking into Calloway's cheerless face and finding himself glad the man had refused to stay and eat. 'There is Henriette to consider now . . . Perhaps you should take it in the library and read it through, see how it is all tied up at present.'

Calloway's saturnine face had softened at the mention of Henriette. He believed her to be Jary's own, as did the entire district, and although he strongly disapproved he could not help admire a man who seemed to wish to do right by his bastards, a rare soul indeed. He retired to the library more inclined to like Jary than hitherto, but

114

ten minutes with Jary's will was enough to send him back to the morning room, frowning horribly.

But in the morning room he found the Doctor and Mr Savage playing about with some wicked-looking pistols, squinting down the barrels and holding them out at arm's length. He had never seen Mr Savage so happy, a grin of pure delight, pure lustful belligerent delight, on his dark face. Calloway stopped, his hand still on the door knob, the will clutched to his chest.

'Ah,' said Jary, swinging about to face him, 'Good. Now you are here . . . There is something I meant to say. I have found another map, an older map. The Diddlers is marked plain as can be. It was pasture then so far as I can make out and there is a beck running out of the woods to the Wiss. Perhaps the river has risen over the years as the harbour silts up at Westdene; what with that and the grazing neglected for years, it is understandable the whole should turn into a bog. But the important thing is there was a building, a shed, a cottage, and it was all Ramillies land, there is no doubt of it.'

'You are determined to act?' Calloway sounded harsh, even aggressive.

'The place is a mess of unhealthy wilderness, the people no better than outlaws. If it is mine I am determined it shall be swept away. And more: there are ten cottages on the estate that have not been inspected or altered for fifty years, and the wells — half of them are suspect. The Doctor thinks they are the cause of these strange unremittent fevers. And then there is the common land by Low Paradise — Hartey's Green do they call it? — in a disgraceful state, overgrown and marshy. That ought to be restored to the cottagers to keep a cow or two.'

'A cow or two? I see. But I believe it has long been enclosed.'

'Then it must be un-enclosed.'

'You may find yourself entangled by Acts of Parliament.'

Jary laid down the pistol and drew himself up. All the good humour had gone from his face. This was the face of a man who was at home on the deck of a privateer and under fire.

'I see you came to ask some question about my will,' he said, in a low, cold, forbidding voice, so very low, cold and forbidding Mr Calloway took a step back. 'Pray, ask anything you like; the Doctor is a good friend and has agreed to be my executor, I have no secrets from him. Well?'

There was a silence. Perhaps Mr Calloway was struggling with a violent longing to bloody Mr Savage's nose; but Jary had too much natural authority and had led too adventurous a life among all manner of men, so often in danger of his life, that there was no question he could stare down any opposition.

'Come,' he said, and set Charles Calloway a chair by the fire.

9

The wind dropped. The interested parties removed the debris from the clearing in Beke's Wood and in the cold dispersing mist of early morning a subdued gathering under the trees had the pheasants clacking away into the undergrowth. The seconds conferred, there were some low urgent mumblings, neither principal wished to withdraw and there was no question of apologies. The mist dripped from the trees and now and again a twig snapped, and now and again a face – Prince Whiteley's face – peered out of the closed carriage drawn up under the oaks. The pistols were examined. Whiteley's second, who wore a strange worldly look of premature satisfaction, turned a little pale when Jary stripped to his shirt and picked up his dear Duvier with a gentle respect and cocked it with the unthinking ease of a man with plenty of practice.

'Dear Alex, you look ashen,' said this most self-contained Jary, the most self-contained the Doctor had ever seen him, as cool and deliberate and calculating as a man could be, as he had once supposed Jary could never be.

'I have my bag at the ready,' was his own laconic comment. Jary smiled, but it was the smile of a man whose mind is occupied elsewhere.

A man of action then, thought the Doctor, watching him stride away; he had seen such deadly control before in military commanders, poor, weedy, insignificant men some of them at home, beset with wives and babes and domestic responsibility, but on the battlefield what change! A clear eye, clear thought, instinctive grasp of all the rules and possibilities in this most vicious game.

He heard a question and answer from across the clearing, saw Whiteley in position, a much more slender man than Jary, and fair, and pale; he saw the seconds, only a little apart but standing as though a brick wall were between them; he heard a level voice say: 'Fire when you are ready' and in the next instant there were two reports, barely distinguishable as two, and everyone was hurrying forward, able to speak normally at last now it was all over.

'He fired a second too late and his aim was not true,' said Jary in a low voice, 'I believe I saw the ball go by. How seconds seem like minutes when one's life is in the balance.'

The seconds had met and parted, and Mr Fisher, his face all relief, trotted towards them.

'He has a flesh wound,' he told Jary, 'it is a trifle. The Doctor will bandage him up.'

'I prayed for it,' said Jary, and Mr Fisher did not doubt he had. One slip, one trembling movement, and it would not only have been honour satisfied, tragedy would have had her share as well.

The knot of stooping persons about Whiteley broke up and reformed. The Doctor's voice could be heard giving firm instructions.

'I believe we may go home,' said Stephen Fisher. He noticed suddenly that Jary looked grey, worn out, ten years older. He hurried away for his coat, for a blanket. He wrapped him up tenderly and Jary let him do it, and let him escort him back to the dogcart like a child. He did not even glance back for the Doctor, he felt so weary, so depressed.

'It is all such nonsense,' he said as the horse moved forward, but when Mr Fisher might have remonstrated he saw Mr Savage's head had sunk forward and that his eyes were closed.

Jary sat all morning by the library fire, an abominable mean hissing fire that would not draw, not now the wind had gone round to the north and had almost died away. As the hours passed he sank deeper and deeper into depression, a most unnatural state for him, coming more

118

and more to blame himself for a childish excess of zeal in defending Lizzie, in starting – no, surely he had not started it? – the whole silly row.

Mrs Clark brought bacon and chops, new bread. He ate it more for Mrs Fipson's sake than his own, and he tasted nothing. He had a very clear mental picture of that space in Beke's Wood, all grey mist and muted browns, and of Whiteley standing there, his arm raised . . . He did not care if he killed me or not, was the accompanying thought, he did not give a damn for being taken up for murder.

The clocks struck. They struck hour after hour. Jary stirred only to brandish the poker at the fire, at the failing wood and dull coals. He felt the chops sit leadenly in his stomach. He felt other things, equally burdensome: gloom, despondency, doubt, frustration, false hopes, bitterness.

It was five o'clock and a thin rain was flying at the windows when the Doctor walked in, smelling of the night: cold, wet leaves, horses.

'I can do no good here,' cried Jary, looking up, 'I believe I shall go back to Jamaica.'

'It is a natural reaction. It will pass. Let us hope today has seen an end of bad feeling between you and the Whiteleys.'

'I am afraid not. '

'The Diddlers? Oh, it will not come to a law suit. Even if Calloway is not certain of your case, to be sure Mrs Whiteley can be far less certain of hers.'

'Calloway is a mean pinching fellow. He nearly choked himself to death with indignation over the will. Why should I not leave everything to Henriette? I have no one else. And what is wrong with a bequest to Miss Johnson, I would like to know? It is none of his business who she is nor why I wish to leave her money; it is not for him to have moral objections.'

The Doctor closed the shutters. 'He is a conscientious man. He clearly sees it as his duty to warn you against leaving large sums to ladies of easy virtue. No, no, I say

119

nothing against her, but he has received the impression that that is what she is.'

'Well, she is not, not as he means it. But by God, I would rather virtue came easy than squeezed out drop by grudging drop as he would do, the puritan dog! Here, Alex, ring for Clarkie, will you? There is time for half a bottle of sherry before we eat.'

Lizzie at breakfast was a dull slow serious creature, looking her age. Fanny, who was used to it, took no notice but rang for more coffee and when it came urged her to have a cup, to have two.

'One of the Fipson boys came by early,' she remarked, beginning on her toast, 'and would you believe it, word is about that Prince Whiteley is at death's door and Mr Savage crying hallelujah!'

Lizzie splashed her coffee. Sense and intelligence returned to her face. 'Dying? No, surely not?' She had spent an extra restless night for no news had come to Foley the day before even though the carriages had passed their door in both directions.

'Well, no doubt the story has been embroidered here there and all round the cottages, but yes, they say Whiteley gasps for his life and Jary Savage has drunk half his cellar in celebration.'

'You cannot believe it! It would not be in the man's character.'

'And what do you know of his character?'

'That would be a meanness he would have nothing to do with. Can you see him celebrating murder?'

Fanny felt she had teased enough. 'How you defend him, and yet for two weeks you have only mentioned his name to curse it. How should I know if the rumour is true, though rest assured those Fipson rogues were hiding in the trees and saw it all. If they are right there'll be a pretty price to pay. Mrs Whiteley has enormous influence. She will have the Lord Lieutenant out, mark my words.'

Lizzie swallowed her coffee and excused herself to dress, to re-dress in effect, to change into a plain dark riding habit with a severe hat. Fanny, when she met her in the hall, pursed her lips and sighed. The girl still looked her age.

'You will be careful,' was all she said, depositing the required kiss on Lizzie's cold cheek. 'The pony does not care for the cold.'

Nor did he, but Lizzie was in no mood to brook contradiction. When she said go he went, mindful of her poised whip and the iron determination that reached him even through the bulk of the ancient sidesaddle. They went down the lane at a hearty canter, avoiding the Foley geese, the Fipson boys hiding in the hedge, and Tom King who was bringing the cattle off the park at Ramillies to graze Cuckooland and the Long Pightle on the edge of the Meeting Grounds. They turned in at the back gate, scattering the stones and shaving the ivy off the gate post, and they left several large hoofprints in the half-weeded gravel.

But the gentlemen were out, Mrs Clark informed Lizzie, twisting her hands in her skirt with sudden nervousness, for she found Miss Rayner incomprehensible and snappish. Both gentlemen were out, for Mr Savage had taken himself off very early with a map and the Doctor had been called out by Dr Plesset to a dropsical case: the Doctor had said it was a very ordinary dropsy, totally undistinguished, and had set off with a snarl.

There was no point in waiting. Lizzie sat there for a moment looking about. It was many years since she had come to the front door of Ramillies, only twice perhaps since she had been exiled to Woodbridge, but the changes she noticed were Jary's changes: the new paint, the builders on the roof, the scars on the lawns where the water garden would be. She bit her lip and her hand tightened on the reins so that the old pony chucked up his head in protest. And then from the doorway came the unmistakable protest of a furious Henriette, wrapped up in nine layers to brave the autumn chill, and Mrs Bloy's honey voice hushing her over and over, telling her it was all for

121

her good and Mr Savage would be back soon and wanting to know why she had not had her walk.

'How pretty she is!' exclaimed Lizzie, who had dismounted to see.

'And forward,' said Mrs Bloy, who had seven of her own, none of them able to hold a candle to little Miss Savage. The general progress of babies, the lack of it, the merits of babies Mrs Bloy had nursed in the past, were discussed as between long-standing friends. Lizzie, who had never had anything to do with babies, apart from sketching the poor wasted creatures at the Diddlers, found herself with Henriette in the crook of her arm. Mrs Clark, who had got over her fright and was all smiles, asked if she would not step in for some refreshment, would not step in and wait, Mr Savage had only gone to Paradise to look at a horse and a bull, she expected him home within the hour. But Lizzie shook her head. It would not do, sitting alone in the house she had loved, brooding on the past; and besides, the casual use of the word 'home' had struck some chord deep deep inside, a chord of anger and jealousy and, if she were honest, rank self-pity. She would call another time, she said, she would call on Henriette, and the two women laughed, and curtseyed, and watched her mount and ride away with cheerful, fond expressions.

She rode down the front drive – she might as well make a pleasant outing of it and describe a full circle, going home through the village – until over to her right she saw, or thought she saw, a green coat in the alder scrub down by the pool, the head and shoulders of a tethered horse. She turned her pony on to the grass. Yes, there was someone there, perhaps the Doctor. This was all familiar territory, the gently sloping ground, the cropped turf covered now by the gold and brown mass of dead leaves. The pony snorted. There was an answering whinny from the birch copse and a man stepped out.

'I called at the house,' said Lizzie, conscious suddenly of his height and breadth and the obvious consternation in his face.

'Oh, I have been over to Paradise, and then I thought I would look at the place where the new sluice is to be, the sluice for the water garden,' said Jary, seeing her puzzled look, 'and then there is this bridge ... Would you care for it in another place, d'you think? Over my canal, for instance?' He spoke quite civilly though he did not sound as if he truly valued her opinion and he looked as if he hoped she might shortly go away. It was clear he was not going to mention the duel.

'I hope,' she began, strangely devoid of the courage to challenge him directly now he was standing at the pony's head pulling absently at the pony's forelock, 'I hope Mr Whiteley survived your encounter.'

Jary frowned. 'Survived? I should hope he did. He could have done more damage falling off your pony. Alex went home with him yesterday though my cousin would not let him in, would rather have swallowed nails than let him in, but he said the wound was nothing, a scratch.'

Lizzie felt her muscles give way. The leg hooked about the pommel shook. 'It would have been courteous to let me know. I felt most closely involved.'

Jary felt it a rather unjust rebuke, for she had given him to understand her greatest wish was never to see or speak to him again, but he had several times thought of sending a message to Foley, only deciding not to because he had been so sure word would already have been brought, especially since at Foley they could most certainly have heard the actual shot. He had put Foley out of his mind and taken Millett to Paradise to look at Carter's bull and a horse Mr Stone wished to sell, and then had returned to plunge about the alder thickets and the swampy pool alone. He felt an odd resentment now towards this woman who had caused him so much heart-searching and unease, and had – though it was no fault of hers, it was true – shaken his standing in the neigh-bourhood. He did not find much to like in her, she was haughty and unfeminine, and all his cheerful, romantic fancies had died away with his good mood in that clearing in Beke's Wood. To think that he, whose women

123

had always been soft and round and generous, should fight a duel for the sake of such an old puss.

'I thought the news was all about the district,' he said.

'So it is, but the news has Mr Whiteley dying and you crowing on the dung heap. Has not the Doctor warned you about gossip? And Foley is quite isolated, we receive the news last and curdled with all the frenzied retelling. We would never dare stir from the house if half the tales we hear were one part true.

Jary stopped fondling the pony's ears. 'He would not have cared had he killed me.'

Lizzie leaned forward a little. 'His aunt is on the best of terms with the Lord Lieutenant,' she said with a wry smile.

'A silly spoiled vicious boy,' cried Jary in a venomous voice. 'I am surprised you ever . . .' and there he stopped, shutting his mouth firmly on the rest, looking away over the river to where a heron was flapping away above the reeds.

A moment later when he glanced up he found her pale and serious but still with that wry smile, which seemed to have become fixed and was entirely independent of her eyes. He said: 'Forgive me. I spoke out of turn,' and stepped back, thinking she would ride off. Instead she brushed her whip up and down the pony's shaggy mane and looked across as he had done to the old willows and brown reeds.

'The herons always fished that stretch,' she said. It was, in its strange way, the most gracious acceptance of his apology Lizzie Rayner was ever likely to make. He acknowledged it, his smile was warm.

'Alex believes you must be disgusted by my changes, by the lawns all dug about. '

To his surprise she laughed. 'Ramillies is yours, Mr Savage, it is nearly twelve years since I left here, and Heaven knows change was needed. My father loved this place but he did not spend his money wisely.'

'There are his cottages in the village. Most of them are

excellent. I understand before he had them built the people lived in thatched huts at Low Paradise '

'Oh well, the cottages. . . And he drained Cuckooland where your cattle are now, and he had a new cut dug by the mill to improve the flow, but taken together . . .' and her whip brushed up and down, up and down. 'We went on from year to year as we had always done. So long as the walls still stood and the roof did not leak the world was as it should be. It was a short-sighted view. I have often thought about it since.

'The Diddlers,' said Jary suddenly. He had been thinking a great deal about that place.

'The Diddlers? It has always belonged to the Whiteleys. All the land from the far side of Beke's Wood across the river beyond where Stretfield Place now stands was the Marston estate – there used to be a great old house, thatch and timber, but it burned down years ago – and when old Frederick Marston died Mr Whiteley bought three or four hundred acres and built the Place just outside the village. Do you not see? He bought the Diddlers from the Marstons. '

'According to my maps the place was on Ramillies land. If Marston or anybody else conveyed it to the Whiteleys he was a fool or a rogue for it was not his to convey.'

'Now I think of it there was some trouble over boundaries, my father was for ever riding to Westdene to see old Galloway about it. But that may not have been the Diddlers. It was all so long ago.'

A hallooing along the riverbank drew their attention. It was Millett riding the garden pony and leading a tall black horse. They did not seem to be getting along very well, the black horse pulling back and Millett hallooing at it to encourage it forward.

'That's not Jack Tubb's horse that Mr Stone had borrowed for Caroline to ride?' asked Lizzie, craning to see.

'Why? Is there anything wrong with him?' asked Jary suspiciously.

'Not that I know of, though his manners are not what they were. My father bred his dam.'

Jary sighed, watching Millett's difficult progress towards Ramillies. 'What a tight little world it is,' he said, 'I cannot move but I break with some tradition, or offend someone's cousin's brother, or stir up old memories best left forgotten. And I was just coming to enjoy the house.'

She looked down and saw a strange mixture of emotions in his face: anger, doubt, a definite wretchedness. She wished she had not mentioned the black horse's breeding; she wished she had not mentioned her father. She felt uneasy in the presence of this man, so amiable in general, even boyish and simple, and yet a man whom she saw now was perhaps difficult to know, a more remote and inaccessible figure than anyone would think meeting him for the first time.

Her eye fell on the pool, and after the pool the marker posts for the new sluice. 'Did you say you wanted my opinion on moving the bridge?'

His quick look, very piercing, showed her he was wondering what she was at, speaking so mildly, her face quite remarkably softened. He took a moment to decide how to treat this approach, which might after all only be the approach of a tiger whose good temper must be counted unreliable. Then he said, 'Yes. If you dismount and come up to the lawn I will show you the lay-out, the whole plan.'

Fifteen minutes later they had skirted the alders, made their way up to the lawns and back again, and were standing once more near the river. Though Jary was the only one who spoke, and a great deal of what he said was merely technical and therefore unquestionably neutral, Lizzie's face was occasionally lit by a sudden unexpected delight, as if she too, once or twice, had seen his fountains playing and all the ornamental waterfowl disporting themselves round about. Whether it was because he was naturally enthusiastic, or because he spoke as if all their past ill feeling was indeed past or had never been, would have been difficult to say, but he talked and she listened and when they reached the grazing pony at last she had a string of intelligent questions and no fault to find.

There was a fine view of Ramillies from down here, Jary was saying, but then he supposed she knew that already, had known it all her life, and then, what was that reddish animal flitting down the avenue? It was an odd shape and held its head in an odd position. For a while they stood staring. And then the foxy thing revealed itself as the Doctor's pony, with the Doctor on board, all hung about with packets and parcels and dead ducks.

'Ducks!' Jary exclaimed, waving an arm to attract the Doctor's attention and watching with growing merriment as the pony and its load turned off the drive and came across the grass.

'Miss Rayner, how do you do? Did I hear you say ducks, Jary? I believe there are three. Three ducks, two whole hams, some late biffins or pippins, I forget which, and two jars of the strongest cider ever brewed this side of the Orwell. They are all gifts from Mrs Stone, who obviously believes we run a house wherein domestic order is unknown. I am not sure if Mrs Clark will be astonished and delighted or infuriated by the slight on her house-keeping. Millett should have brought them along on your new horse but they told me he refused, saying the horse was trouble enough.'

'And did you see Mrs Stone?'

'I did. She was comforting the dropsy, a very old lady who had once been in her employ – and comforting with cognac I might add, though they both moved exceeding quick to conceal it the minute I walked in. I was forced to give a sermon on the inadvisability of strong drink in the circumstances and they both agreed like angels and never blushed. Mrs Stone gave me a list, asked me to stop at her house for the servants to put me up a basket, but when I reached there I found all the rest that should have come back with Millett, so I have brought it all. There there' – this to the pony who had begun to throw his head about – 'he does not like the ducks.'

Jary and Lizzie Rayner gazed together at this palpable evidence of Mrs Stone's regard – though it was quite obviously regard for Jary as a possible son-in-law rather than for Jary as a pleasant neighbour – and both began to smile.

'Dear Woman!' cried Jary, a vision of supper rising in his mind. 'Dear Woman, how I love you!'

'I take it Miss Johnson is an ardent, vivacious lady, possibly with a pugnacious sort of nose?' asked the Doctor.

'With a what?' Jary looked up from his toast, astonished.

'I simply wondered if she bore any resemblance to your lady in grey who has vanished so mysteriously from above the fireplace and might be found, so I am told, hanging in your bedroom.'

'Oh that,' and Jary seized the coffee pot. 'I sent all the other Rayners back to Foley, or rather, I sent them off there since I suppose they had never been there before. I thought Miss Rayner might like them, or one or two, I cannot say I would care for forty at once, some of them plain honest Johns and others quite scoundrels and all in damn unbecoming country wigs. The women were better than the men, more lively by far, but even so I would put them out of sight if I were her, if I were Miss Rayner.'

'And does she know you have kept one, and hung it lovingly upon your bedroom wall? To be sure it argues that either a man is of a feeble turn of mind to fall in love with a portrait or else the portrait reminds him of a lady that he knows.' There was the very faintest significance in this last word that did not escape Jary, who drank off his coffee and gave a false, horrible grin.

'Miss Johnson is tall and dark, and her eyes are grey. Does that satisfy you? She is an uncommon handsome woman, an intelligent, liberal-minded, gifted woman. She has money of her own and many influential friends.' He did not add: she was my mistress. If the Doctor knew this he was not a man to comment on it, unlike Charles Calloway, who had assumed the worst – he had considered it the worst – and had raised several ill-found objections to a man leaving any part of his fortune in the direction of a whore. He was to consider, Jary had told him, the very nature of whoredom, and if a discreet and thoughtful woman who shared her favours with a limited number of equally discreet and thoughtful gentlemen was quite the same as the girls upon the waterfront servicing half the Jamaica fleet. Mr Calloway unfortunately had replied that he saw no difference but that the one washed more often than the others. Since then, and since Mr Calloway's precipitous exit with Jary's strong, condemning voice ringing in his ears, no more had been said about Miss Johnson until now, until this particular morning when the absence of the lady in grey from the morning room wall had struck the Doctor so forcibly.

'So it is not Miss Johnson then,' mused the Doctor, finding some lumpy porridge in the tureen – Mrs Fipson was indisposed – and thinking he would do well to leave it there. 'The picture reminds you of another lady perhaps.'

'No, it does not. When did I last meet a woman in powder and patches? God forbid, I was a boy when those were the fashion. She is nothing like any woman I have ever had to do with, and a good thing too, she looks a disputatious, independent type, not for marriage and domesticity. And she is nothing like . . .' He paused, and a bleak look of bleak memory passed over his face. 'She is nothing like my first love.'

'Nothing?'

'Nothing. And I should know, dear Alex, for I was banished to Brazil on account of her. Here, read this, we have been invited to Sir James Braile's for a glass of hot punch and a mince pie come Christmas. I thought he would never have me over his threshold again. Do you think anyone will speak to me if we do go? I am still given black looks in Westdene and the duel was a month ago.'

'I believe Whiteley receives blacker ones, if it is any consolation. When the village thought him close to death he was up and away at some pony races; of course he was found out. You must certainly go to Sir James's and be as affable as you know how – he is the man to have on your side over this Diddlers business. He is the biggest landowner for miles and the Justice of the Peace and, which is more important, no partisan of Mrs Whiteley. If the law says the Diddlers is yours he will uphold the law in the face of ten Mrs Whiteleys, and it would take a bold man to do that, I assure you. By all accounts – yours included – he is dull but honest, a rare and I believe underappreciated combination; he will do his duty to the bitter end. Tell me, you are something of a nautical man, do you know what a bitter end is? I have the strangest feeling it is to do with ships. I believe I have heard it mentioned while floating about with all my poor soldiers in hellish transports.'

Jary might have given a very lucid explanation of the bitter end but Mrs Clark came in with the baby, who was being hurried outside to have her walk before the rain began, Jary rocked her on his knee and she smiled at him wider and wider. They looked deep into each other's eyes and approved of what they saw and smiled and smiled.

'Is she not charming?' Jary asked the Doctor. 'But there is definitely Indian blood. I wonder if it is cannibal?'

'I don't find babies charming. She has all her faculties, thank God, and she is plump and healthy. There will be time enough to worry about charm when she grows up. And' – dropping his voice – 'I would not mention cannibals, you will have the house in an uproar.'

With the departure of Henriette silence – except for the ticking of two clocks and the hiss of the fire – and the Doctor looking gloomy, reading his post. After a while he looked up and stared about at the faded wallpaper and the fine furniture and the litter of their breakfast. His expression was one Jary had seen before.

'You are thinking of that woman,' he accused, but gently, for he was very fond of the Doctor. 'How miserable she makes you.'

'No, no, it was not entirely that. I was wondering what I am to do now the army is closed to me, now I am thrown back upon civilian life.'

'Could you not set up a practice where you chose? Plesset will be retiring soon, or dropping dead. Do not mistake me, he seems a capable old man, but both times I have met him he seemed horribly short of breath and a dull colour. Is his heart sound? Or you could go back to Norfolk. This . . . girl will be married soon, as soon as this William Claverden is home from sea, you said, and you will find you do not lust after her so much when she is wed and bedded. There is nothing like seeing a woman you think you love deeply, frantically, growing plump and complacent bearing another man's child and smiling at his jokes and prefacing every sentence with "My William says. . ." '

'I know you are right. Yet in this case I fear it will not serve. You forget I have seen her married once before, and though he was a scoundrel she was certainly mad for him. And she is not the kind to grow complacent or laugh objectionably or take a reverent view of her husband any more than Miss Rayner would of hers, if she had one.'

'It is too late now for Miss Rayner by the look of it; she could flay a man with her eyes, let alone her voice.'

'But have you not noticed the resemblance to your portrait?'

Jary rose, hearing the clamour, the distant, rising clamour, that might just possibly be the arrival of his new dogs.

'Whose resemblance to my portrait?' he asked, not waiting for the answer. 'Are you coming? Alex, are you coming? Do you know anything about dogs?'

'Not in the least, except they have four legs and smell abominable when wet. I shall finish my toast and stroll out to see them later when they are safely behind bars.'

10

The Doctor sat for an hour and a half, growing in rigidity
until he thought he might never be able to move again.
Lizzie worked in bursts of furious activity and long,
intense pauses, during which she studied him with that
impersonal eye he knew so well; it was the eye of the
professional, the eye of one who judges a great deal by
the external elements. Just so would he look at Lizzie
were she to consult him in a medical capacity; she would
cease to be a particular woman and become all women,
indeed, no woman at all but an object of scientific
abstraction.

'You have been very good,' she said after the clock on
the mantel had struck the half-hour yet again, 'I have
kept you far longer than is usual, far too long. But . . .'
She ceased abruptly. But your face is so awkward, she
might have said.

As if to cover the embarrassing pause she continued:
'Mr Fisher called yesterday, mumchance because Fanny
was abroad in Westdene trying on bonnets – they must
have passed on the road. I do believe the poor man is
really in love.'

'I believe he is. Mrs Jewkes does not encourage him, I
understand.'

'I believe she might, though not with any great passion,
he is not exactly a passionate creature, is he? But she
says that to take on Mr Fisher would be to take on Mr
Fisher senior and that she could not bear.'

She spoke lightly, the words simply noises, polite
noises. She hardly knew what she said. She had struggled
too hard this last hour and a half, she was exhausted.
After a while she wiped her brushes and the intense,
white-hot fierceness died out of her face, and she became
simply Lizzie in a painting smock, a dull thin Lizzie with

faint lines of weariness and exasperation between her brows.

'I will tell Kitty to give you something to eat by the fire in the parlour,' she said at last, while he creaked to his feet, 'I am going out directly. I have promised to call at Paradise with a parcel of old magazines.'

He lingered in the doorway. 'May I not look at the sketch?'

'You may not. I never allow viewing until the work is finished. And I am going to lock the door.'

She bid him good day a moment later, candid and abrupt as ever, and he found himself by the fire with a tray of cold meats and new bread and apple pie.

'More ale, sir?' asked Kitty, returning a little later to find him engaged in taking out the insides of the mantel clock which did not keep time according to his own excellent Courvoisier.

'More ale indeed,' he told her, 'and some tweezers, dear girl. But my bag is in the hall. Fetch me my bag. We will operate and set all to rights,' and slyly, as an afterthought, 'Has Miss Rayner locked the studio?'

'Oh yes, sir,' with a curtsey, 'and she would kill us all, sir, was we to open it for you with the spare key.'

The Doctor could well believe it.

Jary had met Fanny Jewkes in the lane and they had held a pleasant rambling conversation through the carriage window.

'She said Lizzie was a daughter to her,' Jary told the Doctor that evening when they had shed formality and sat in stockinged feet smoking by the library fire. He spoke as if he doubted the truth of this statement, much as he admired Fanny and perceived the genuine affection between her and the tempestuous Miss Rayner.

'She is more dear to Mrs Jewkes than ever she was to her own relations, that is certain.'

'So it seems.' He had listened to a harsh, furious diatribe against Lizzie's family, who had apparently cut off some miserable little allowance, a pittance a year, when she had run off with a Captain Jervis, and had cut it off overnight – 'by return of post', Fanny had cried – not even waiting to see if the girl came safe home again, or married, or died. How cruel and cunning and stony-hearted relations were, and how rare it was to find true family feeling.

'How goes the portrait?' Jary asked after a long and gloomy reflection on his own close relatives.

'I am not allowed to see it.'

Jary laughed. 'I wager she never finishes it. Mrs Jewkes said a gentleman from London had written, some learned cove connected with the Royal Academy, and that Lizzie has been asked to paint a duchess. A duchess! There is no saying what she may do after a duchess. She will certainly have nothing to do with country doctors.'

'She is not so base, so treacherous, as to go to London and leave me without nose and eyebrows. But why the reproving tone? Why the hard look? I thought you and she were civil to each other the time you met by the river. Why, I saw you smile together.'

'Oh, we have discussed snipe and the replanting of the copse by Cuckooland and fountains and ponds. I would not care to say we are on good terms. And every time I see Hawke dig another yard of trench for the canal I think I feel her eye on me – was it the basilisk turned men to stone? She feels for the Diddlers, I grant her that, and she is not blind to her father's neglect, but. . . . Well, I would not trust a woman with that kind of passionate nature. You never know where you are.'

The Doctor pulled his ear thoughtfully. 'Can Miss Johnson not claim a passionate nature? I thought from your description. . .'

'Oh she is passionate for things I can understand: position, jewels, money, cutting a figure. Perfectly ordinary greed, you might say. No man could hold it against her, she is quite open about it. I believe that is why I have always liked her so much, she hates any hypocrisy so.'

They sank and sank into a state very nearly comatose,

for they had both been out and about all day, each exercising authority in his own inimical way, and the struggle against opposing forces had tired them out. The Doctor, having set the mantel clock to rights, had left Foley for a very private visit to Dr Plesset in his small house in the middle of the village. It had not only been a private visit – he had received a brief, touching note sent over with Plesset's boy to Ramillies after breakfast – but a professional one. He had gone through the motions of an examination only out of respect and the almost unconscious knowledge that a difficult situation is best got through with a certain ritual. It had been quite evident to him for some time that Plesset would very shortly have to leave his patients in the care of some other man, but that even immediate retirement would probably prove too late for his failing heart. Jary, on the other hand, had had the latest of several differences of opinion with Hawke, who had proved to be a man who would not stir an inch without being paid for two.

Now, in the flicker of their furious fire, the two of them turned over the events of the day, while far far away the thready wail of a wakened baby came and went, came and went.

'I wonder who this Captain Jervis was,' said Jary at last, his eyes closed, his dark head red in the firelight.

'I do not know. I do not even know what kind of captain he was, a sea captain, a captain of marines, an army man.'

Jary did not bother to open his eyes but a slow smile spread and spread. 'Whatever he was he would have needed to be a man of stout parts to carry off Lizzie Rayner. I do not envy him the attempt.'

It occurred to Lizzie, squinting, her brush poised, that she would never finish it. His face gave up no secrets, was contained and grave, a lean experienced face a little raw at present from an over-enthusiastic shave. It could have been the face of a judge, a man of business, a politician, were any of those noted for intelligence. Apart

135

from very obvious intelligence, present but indefinable, it was a mask, a very mask.

Lizzie sighed and bit the end of her brush. 'Perhaps you should rest,' she said.

There, there was life in the eyes, in the mouth: he had detected the note of desperation in her voice and had looked sharply, a spark of humour in the look.

'I would not mind buttered toast,' he replied, stretching.

'You may have as much buttered toast as you like, and jellied veal, and Fanny's uncle's sister's unsurpassable ham. And you must choose something from the cellar.'

'Will Mrs Jewkes permit it?'

'Fanny will be only too pleased. The late Mr Jewkes laid down so many bottles and barrels of this and that it would take an army to drink them up. There have been times when we have gone short of a crust but have sat over bottle after bottle of good brandy; I do not mean sat over to drink, I mean we have sat at our mean table knowing it lay under our very feet.'

The Doctor had edged round a little to catch a glimpse of his picture but she steered him away, talking of anything now, a false, harsh, gay talk, and she locked the door behind them. Going down into the dark cellar, Lizzie holding up the candle, he reflected that he might never come to see his portrait, even half-finished. Her perfume, a faint fragrance of violets overlaid by rich oily paint and the tang of spirits, wafted back to him, and then there were other smells: dust, damp, age, mice, mildew.

'Here they all are. You may choose what you like. Would anything in particular suit jellied veal?'

He had a cobwebby bottle in his hand but there was no immmediate way of knowing what it was. 'May I draw the cork? It could be anything.' It was the best burgundy he had tasted in many years. Lizzie sent Lussom down for another two bottles and pressed the Doctor to accept them.

'Your cellar must be worth a great deal,' he remarked,

finding that late afternoon was certainly the wrong hour to drink a great wine, and buttered toast and ham inadequate accompaniments.

Her look was sharp. 'Do you think so? But to whom could Fanny sell all those hundreds of old bottles?'

'Any merchant worth his salt would covet the half of them, but you might try Jary Savage – he is more knowledgeable about these matters than I am. Of course, the barrels may be spoiled by pitch and sea water, they may have come to grief being rolled up the beach in the usual great hurry and hidden here and there in strange places. On the other hand, the duty may have been paid, they may have travelled like princes, hand to hand.'

He thought her fingers paused in their swift dismembering of her toast but he could not be sure it was a significant pause. He could never be sure of her feelings except when she was actually painting, when she was all rapt attention.

Fanny entered on this scene of quiet domesticity half an hour later, taking in at a glance the greasy toasting fork, the strange and unaccustomed sight of Lizzie kneeling in the hearth with crumbs down her bodice and smuts on her cheek, and the glasses of ruby wine . . . And her first thought was: if this keeps up we might see some unbending, some warmth, some more natural behaviour; though what this natural behaviour might be and what part the Doctor might play was beyond imagining.

'What a pair!' and she moved to her own chair from which she could see for a certainty that they had finished at least one bottle. 'Doctor, you have dribbled something all down your lapels. Lizzie, what were you thinking of? No napkins and wine with buttered toast!'

'The Doctor admires your cellar. He would have us believe the brandy is worth a pirate's fortune.' Was this a reference to Jary?

A sharp look from the Doctor, and another from Fanny, for different reasons, touching her pretty curls and smiling her most artificial sweet smile. 'La, a fortune under our feet and we did not know it! I have never given Mr Jewkes the credit he deserved.'

At the door, seeing the Doctor off: 'I have never seen her so dishevelled. She is quite drunk. And I thought you such a gentleman, so trustworthy.'

'She is not drunk at all, she has been laughing. I told her about my mongoose and my Lascar cook. She has not drunk above two glasses.'

Fanny sighed. 'Only two, well, well. But tell me, how is she progressing? How does the portrait? Well, I know she will not let you see it, that is her eccentricity, but surely you can tell?' And then a lower tone, intimate, confiding. 'Does she look pleased? I believe she is hurrying to finish it before she goes to London. She has been asked to London, is it not exciting? I wonder she has not mentioned it, she was like a girl again when the letter came. But tell me, does she say nothing about your picture?'

'She bites her brush a great deal.'

Fanny looked taken aback, the light died out of her face. 'Oh dear,' she said.

'Oh, I will never get it right,' said Lizzie, gazing at it with a hawkish, furious, malevolent eye, 'he is too difficult a subject.'

'The Doctor? But he is perfectly innocuous, rather ill-looking but that don't detract a jot, I find, he can be so charming when he cares. But surely . . .'

Fanny looked at the face on the canvas, the only-half-finished, undelineated, amorphous face that was hardly the Doctor and yet hardly anyone else; there was enough of him to recognize but only as one might recognize an acquaintance on the other side of the street.

'It looks' – a pause, a warm thoughtful pause – 'it looks as if a great portrait were struggling to come to life.' After all, Fanny cared for Lizzie Rayner very much.

'Well, it never will. His face is wooden when he sits here, a perfect blank. . . there is no life in it, no . . . Alex French.' Her voice died away. Fanny was aware of acute disappointment: Lizzie looked as if she might pick up a brush any moment and strike the face through.

'Perhaps you should do Mr Savage instead. He would make a bold portrait, I daresay, being so dark but with such blue eyes and good-looking too . . .'

'You have designs upon Mr Savage,' said Lizzie, turning her back on the Doctor.

'Designs? At my age?'

'Mr Pemberton married a widow of sixty-five when he was twenty-eight and you said you hoped he would be very happy.'

'I was not sincere, surely I was not? I spoke with a curl of the lip.'

Lizzie swung round, laughing. '*You?* You would not know how to curl your lip! You believed he was genuinely fond of her and wished them well.'

'Fond of her as his mother, perhaps.'

'Well, maybe, but you could scarcely be Jary Savage's mother unless you had been a child prodigy.'

A momentary pause. Fanny looked again at the face on the canvas. 'You have made him very grave.'

'How can you tell? His mouth is nothing and his eyes are blank.'

'Well, it seems to me he is very grave.'

'And is he not? Anyway, medical men must look serious in their portraits, it is the custom. It would be considered inappropriate levity were a physician to smile.'

Fanny retreated. 'I have always found Dr French ready to smile.'

'You bring out the best in him, I bring out the worst. I cannot give him a smile, dear Fan, even if I wanted to because he never smiles for me, never moves a muscle, the wretch!'

This was worse than Fanny had suspected. She could not really understand the difficulty about the picture but supposed Lizzie was simply not in the mood, it would be nothing new. On the other hand, it may all have something to do with Ramillies and the old reopened wounds.

Still, Lizzie would never tell her and she knew the utter folly of asking outright. She said mildly: 'I only hope you have not charged him too much. I fear he will be disappointed.'

'I may not charge him anything. I may give it up. After all, there is London to consider. If I leave in the new year . . .'

'Then it would be kind to warn him in that case, the poor man, giving up his time and all for nothing . . .' And then, as an afterthought, 'It is not like you to be defeated, Liz. You are becoming a sad case.'

The day was cold, clear and cold. It was a winter clarity, a winter revelation, every field and hedge and tree etched and coloured like a child's painting, and over it all the intense blue of the sky, as blue as August but filled with a December flight of rooks and half a dozen scavenging gulls. The Doctor shrugged his collar up round his ears and gazed at Frenchmans and the sweep of land that ran down to the oak-fringed paddock and the squat gather of buildings that was Foley. It reminded him of another place, of Thorn smoking at the foot of its own hill and Ann calling a greeting across the home pasture. He frowned, discovering yet again what an effort was sometimes required to repel sentimentality. He frowned and spoke sharply to his sidling pony, who laid back an ear at the tone and shook his mane over his wicked eyes.

Mrs Jewkes was from home, she had taken advantage of the good weather to visit the more distant of her friends who might not count on another call until March winds dried up the roads. This was in answer to his clipped inquiry at the door, wrenched open at the last moment by Kitty, a red, perspiring Kitty who had run from an unseasonal turning-out of the pantry at the Doctor's knock. The young mistress was out walking, might be anywhere, had not been seen since luncheon. Kitty avoided the Doctor's all-seeing eye at this point, for it would not do to show too much relief, absolute

140

relief, at seeing the back of Lizzie, Lizzie in a queer, brittle mood, a regular passion.

The Doctor remounted and rode thoughtfully back the way he had come. It had occurred to him to creep along the path and try to get a glance at his portrait but such a caper seemed base and undignified. So he rode away, jogging back to Ramillies, the wind in his teeth.

He was conscious of a remote disappointment, but very remote, very far down. He was not attracted to Lizzie Rayner physically and yet he enjoyed her company, it was never dull, and he had learned through patient observation that when she was her most abrasive she was feeling her most vulnerable. He approved of her independent spirit, her hardiness. It was a quality Ann too had possessed, humour spiced with a sort of tough resilience, a bold realism. But he did not want to think about Ann, it only made him grieve to find how susceptible an elderly man might be – forty-five was certainly elderly in these circumstances. Celibate, celibate, I have been too long celibate, he thought suddenly, and the pony, catching his mood, played none of his usual tricks but grew slow and serious-faced, his eyes quite dull between the strands of his forelock.

But at Ramillies they were unexpectedly confronted by the spectacle of Jary standing on the great pile of frost-hardened earth thrown up by Hawke's men and gesticulating vigorously to someone below him in the canal. It was at its full depth now, the canal, having been dug out daily while the weather held, and the someone was invisible. The Doctor dismounted and let the pony wander off.

'Alex, Alex, come and explain to Miss Rayner how it is to be done. I cannot put it into. . .'

'Perspective,' said a dry voice from the pit, 'I believe perspective is a word often used by landscapers. '

The Doctor peered in. Lizzie stood on the oozing clay bed where next summer the carp were destined to swim, holding up her skirts. He reached down a hand to haul

141

her out just as Jary said: 'The water will make all the difference, and a bit of green.'

They all gazed round, trying to see the battlefield with uncritical eyes. Every day the Doctor was subjected to this impossible exercise, every day was told optimistically that when the plants had grown and the bridge was moved. . .

'Oh,' he said, spotting his pony's ears proceeding along the ditch that led to the canal, two ears and that golden-red forelock, 'Oh.'

'I guess gossip is saying I am digging up the lawn to bury the bodies of all the servants I beat to death,' said Jary, whose attempts to hire another servant had not met with much success in spite of Fanny's trying to help by asking in every likely family from Low Paradise to Westdene.

'Gossip is a natural element in the country, like rain and strong winds,' said Lizzie, 'and prejudice dies hard.'

'But I have Mrs Clark, and Mrs Fipson, and Millett. They are happy enough, they all recommend the place.'

'But Mrs Clark is a foreigner, and Becky Fipson was one of two Fipson girls who came to bad ends, so they do not count; and Millett has been at Ramillies so long he is not even considered.'

'I see,' said Jary, 'I did not know,' and he began to drift off among the heaps of spoil until, a movement catching his eye, he turned and saw what the Doctor had already seen. 'God's teeth, is that your pony? He has got in the canal. He will break the banks trying to get out. Catch him, Alex, catch him!'

The Doctor ran, flailing his arms. Lizzie covered her eyes with her hands and burst into unbecoming howls of laughter.

'It will not be funny if Hawke finds great holes in his banks tomorrow. He is the most temperamental, awkward, tight-fisted . . . I beg pardon, I was carried away. Dear God, what is that awful hooting?'

'The Doctor,' said Lizzie, wiping tears from her cheeks

and choking on a fresh wave of laughter. 'The pony has sat down.'

Jary's face broke into immoderate merriment of its own. The Doctor running was a sight to behold. There was a loud shout and a furious snorting, and for a moment two arms and the pony's head rose above the banks and then sank again, accompanied by a great deal of oddly mellifluous Latin.

Jary was looking at Lizzie Rayner with a sudden intense wary look, the simple joy fading from his face. For her part she was turning now to look again at the excavations, the lawns all dug up, muddy and forlorn. She did not look as if she minded, but then the amusement was still glowing on her face; another minute and she might look as if she minded passionately. She reminded him of someone, how she reminded him of someone, and he could not for the life of him think . . .

'There is rain coming, or snow. The wind is rising and going round to the north,' he said, 'I must tell Millett to get the gig ready. You will not refuse a ride home in the gig?'

But she refused at once, gathering up her skirts. 'Nonsense! I will walk back across the park.'

'But it will soon be dark, and the bullocks are back in the park.'

The Doctor, trailing the wayward pony, came up in time to hear her brisk: 'I am not afraid of the poor cattle, Mr Savage, and I could find my way across the park blindfold.'

They watched her walk away.

'Lord, how I hate women like that!' cried Jary.

143

11

Mrs Whiteley resisted Jary's civil requests for a meeting, she would never have him in the house again; he was not any relation of hers, he was not mentioned in her house. To make the point plainer still she brought in a plump, greasy, reptilian lawyer from Ipswich to write greasy, threatening replies to Charles Calloway's polite letters. It was already nearly Christmas and the Diddlers were still condemned to their damp and isolated settlement, what was more, they would not move from it though Jary promised them cottages over by Hopes, a farm in the next parish. The Doctor, who had ridden with him and had listened to his cheerful announcement, his subsequent arguments, his eventual harangue, explained gently on the road home that for them to be removed to the next parish was the equivalent of being transported, that since none of them had ever set foot in that neighbourhood it might, indeed, be Botany Bay, it was as little known, as little understood, as much dreaded. But, said Jary, there were no cottages free in Stretfield and though he had plans for building some those were unformulated plans for the future, they could not keep the Diddlers warm this winter. If it was proved the land and settlement were his he would take steps to move them out at once, he would play the high-handed tyrant, would brook no opposition; how would they care for that? They would resent it, replied the Doctor, and grow sullen and awkward, but they would go, for they were, after all, well used to high-handed, bloody-minded tyrannical overlords and Jary's right in the matter being proved they would acknowledge that right by shifting where he commanded.

Now, not to be seduced by the preparations for Christmas, by the smell of Mrs Fipson's mince pies, the absolute necessity of cutting the holly, Jary rode to

Westdene for his first appointment with Charles Calloway since their row over the will. He rode briskly as he always did, and since the sight of the cold heaving sea did not encourage dawdling, he trotted purposefully into the market place and up to the Admiral. He had a shopping list from the Doctor which included articles like waistcoat buttons and nightcaps, and this he gave covertly to Pamela, one of the charming rosy daughters of the inn, who assured him everything would be seen to, everything would be ready on his return.

Not if that rascal gives me a bare ten minutes and another sermon on the wages of sin, thought Jary, for if he does I shall refuse his luncheon; after a little, reaching the street door of Calloway's office, he added: if he offers me any, and banged three times with the knob of his whip, his face quite gloomy.

He had a great deal longer than ten minutes though luncheon failed to appear, none was offered, and his own plan of falling back on the Admiral and his projected 'Come, Charles, let us step along for a bite to eat' died before it reached his lips; he felt snubbed and affronted by such reserve, such mean inhospitable reserve. But he did go thoroughly into the Diddlers and read and reread the copious correspondence, all saying nothing in amazingly windy syntax, which had flown to and fro between Calloway and the Ipswich attorney for two weeks. For all his dislike of the business, for all his very genuine doubt Jary had a case at all, Calloway had been remarkably diligent. No, he could not be faulted in that department, but there would be no making friends with him, no intimacy.

Even his dark eyes seemed censorious; though his mouth smiled stiffly and his tone was not exactly hostile, his eyes disapproved. Jary, never a man to sit easily under unwarranted slights, became more and more formidable, his face darker and harsher and angrier with every letter he turned over in his hand, his voice growing colder and more authoritative, the accent more pronounced.

'Well,' he said at last, when it seemed there was nothing

more to discuss, 'now you know my mind about the new cottages and the problems of rehousing. You may press Mrs Whiteley for documents relating to the Diddlers but this Ipswich man seems determined to be belligerent about it, we must let him cool off a little and think what our next step must be. I never thanked you for the will, it was a noble job, everything as I wished.' This was the moment to say: what about the Admiral's veal pie? but Jary was damned if he would say it, for there sat that puritanical booby in his black suit and choking tight neckcloth only waiting for Jary to quit his office before he rang for that same veal pie to be hurried in.

Jary stood up and took his leave. Charles Calloway bowed very slightly: enough to show me his opinion of whoreson Jamaican planters, thought Jary, cramming on his hat and giving good day to the trembling clerk. He took the stairs two at a time ad strode with subdued fury towards the inn, only faintly aware that a cold thin mizzling rain, an almost sleet, was falling. He felt the cold though, he was not yet acclimatized, and he plunged thankfully into the hot fug of the Admiral, a delightful hot fug of tobacco, ale, hot pies, lemon shrub and the like. But in the passage he nearly collided with a figure he knew, a figure which retreated immediately several paces and stood staring belligerently.

'Mr Whiteley, I beg your pardon,' said Jary, removing his hat, 'I was preoccupied. How is . . .'

But Whiteley turned on his heel and made off, a childish sort of insult Jary shrugged off with a smile but which only added to his bad temper, so that while he pretended it meant nothing, it was the behaviour of a poor cowardly scrub, in reality it rankled beyond belief, coming as it did after Calloway's miserable reception.

'Oh, sir, we have had your own pie hot this half-hour and more,' said Pam, throwing open the door to the private room where he had often eaten before, 'and there are your packages. Mr Dye has put in a note because of the measurements missing but says he has made a guess and hopes Dr French will be satisfied, and the little package is the stockings. Will I put some string about them so you can carry them easier?'

The pie did not seem as tasty as usual and the drizzle had turned to real sleet so that Jary picked up his awkward load and went out to find his horse. In the yard he found a smart blue carriage just arrived, boys running to throw rugs over the two matched greys, and a small animated face thrust out of the open window.

Jary, who had always liked a plump dark pretty woman, inclined his head and smiled. She was nothing like Miss Johnson, though her eyes were certainly grey; she was much younger to begin with, and her bold stare was an innocent one, her experience of gentlemen being small.

'Frances, what are you about? Come in, come in, 'said a testy voice from the recesses, and the little beauty said: 'Yes, Mama,' and withdrew, but not before she had smiled in acknowledgement.

Jary's bad mood relented and left him. The memory of Thurza Johnson rose to cheer him and even the unexpected and dreadfully strong wave of homesickness that followed on almost immediately could not extinguish such a cheerfulness. He had never been in love with her but how fond he had been, and what happy hours they had spent, and how comforting she had been, always prepared to listen to his troubles but always scorning them to their right proportions. He had not minded that she entertained other gentlemen, she had made no secret of it, and while he was in Kingston she was exclusively his – presumably she made that clear to the other gentlemen. She was much sought after and always smiling, her bad moods simply wild tantrums – she often laughed while she raved and collapsed laughing when she was spent. It had been an ideal arrangement, perhaps, Jary thought, one all men would like: no possessiveness, no jealousy, no responsibility, no real commitment.

Ah well, he had had no one else to leave money to, only his partner in the privateers, and Thurza would spend it so much more stylishly, on clothes and jewels and good food. Now she had only a small legacy, small that is in relation to what she would have received before; before Henriette.

'How merry you are,' the Doctor said as his friend appeared humming, the parcels in his arms. 'I trust Mr Calloway gave you a hearty luncheon and you are on good terms again.'

'Good terms? We shall never be on good terms, he thinks I am a vile immoral . . . Oh, never mind. I will not let him get me down. I have a note from Dye about your shirts, and here are the nightcaps – why half a dozen? – and I suppose this packet is buttons. Here, open them all. I am going up to the nursery.'

He stood looking down at the sleeping baby, snug in her Ramillies cradle, and he thought that Thurza would be delighted with her if she could see her, that though she did not care for babies any more than the Doctor and though she had lost a fortune to this one, she was too good-hearted, too magnanimous to mind for very long about the money.

On the way downstairs common sense returned: no doubt he was idealizing both of them.

'If only all women were like Mrs Stone,' was his surprising remark to the Doctor as he re-entered the library, 'who gives a man three ducks and a quantity of strong cider and makes no demands on his emotions.'

The Doctor was obliged to hide his face in his new silk stockings. 'You may laugh,' cried Jary, laughing himself, 'but look what this Ann Claverden has done to you, look how you still grieve for her.'

And the damnable thing was that he did, he still did.

He did not give the impression of grief, however, when he and Jary were ushered through the door at Westdene Park for Sir James Braile's Christmas gathering. He was remarkably spruce, his old waistcoat partially hidden by a new black coat, and his hair, which had grown almost respectable, as much gold as grey in the light of a hundred candles. Jary was quite amazed at him, never having seen

148

him at his absolute best, far more used to a greasy brocade dressing gown and rich gingery stubble.

Sir James's greeting was a little formal, he felt Jary was that dangerous animal the unpredictable guest. Prince Whiteley was not present so they could hardly pick another quarrel, but there were people here who knew Jary only by repute and had not liked what they had heard. He was also a conspicuous man, for if his size could be temporarily disguised by sitting him down In some safe corner, his taste in clothes was unfailingly flamboyant. Twenty years ago he would not have been looked at twice, but emerald-green coats were not in favour this season, nor were such quantities of lace.

Lady Braile, a dumpy, brown, ordinary woman, a lesser Mrs Stone, apparently found the Doctor irresistible. Jary, watching her pilot him away to meet her dearest friends, wondered why it was so many women felt an attraction; though acutely conscious of his worth he could not see it. He moved cautiously in the Doctor's wake, speaking to those few people he knew, bowing to those he did not with an elegance that had them all talking about him within ten minutes. Eventually he reached a party of young people gathered about the two eldest Braile offspring, Eugenia and Frances, and not being a man to hesitate he engaged Miss Frances for the first dance after supper, smiling into her startled eyes when she recognized him as the man at the inn.

On the other side of the room Lady Braile had captured Lizzie Rayner and was towing her to the Doctor with: 'Dear Dr French, Lizzie tells me she is painting your portrait. I am sure you have a great deal to say to each other.'

She bestowed a hopeful smile and left them. There was a long silence, during which the Doctor thought of all the things good manners insisted he say. Instead he stared round at the chattering, sweltering crowd and loosened his perfect stock a little.

'Yes, it was indeed very crudely done,' said Lizzie.

'She meant no harm,' was the reply. In fact, said his

149

expression, she meant to do us both a favour, thinking I ought to be too old to be interested in pretty young women and you too brazen and intellectual to charm a younger man.

Lizzie did look remarkably fierce, but perhaps it was to cover a deep hurt. Her eyes flashed. Then she lowered them, and he saw one corner of her mouth pull suddenly into the wry smile he knew.

'I will take you in to supper,' he said, 'unless you are already engaged?'

'Goodness! Do you think it likely? Mr Fisher is the only man who would offer because he is so innocent he is never put off, and he is busy persuading Fanny, he has drunk enough punch already to give himself marvellous courage.'

They went to supper. The Doctor asked her about London, about her pictures. She replied mechanically, as if the joy of her life, the peak of its achievements, was nothing to her. He realized belatedly that hardly a soul in the room had spoken to her and that some had deliberately stepped out of her way. He touched her elbow and said gently: 'When you have finished your jelly we shall dance.'

'Do you dance?' A raised eyebrow, another flash of those eyes.

'I do, though I must warn you I have danced on only one occasion in the last fifteen years.'

For a man so out of practice he gave a creditable performance. And although she had drunk no punch and up until now had felt cold and miserable, his attention and obvious goodwill warmed her thoroughly. When he made her laugh and miss her step it was as if she came alive, so that when Jary, pushing to the front to find the Doctor, saw her bright face under that wildly curling fair hair he was pierced by her resemblance to the lady in grey, his dear lady in grey who saw him last in the evening and first every morning and about whom once or twice he had had warm hopeful dreams . . .

150

'Miss Rayner, are you engaged for the next?' he said as the Doctor handed her from the floor.

She was not engaged for any. She allowed him to return her with a sidelong, challenging look.

'I should have danced the first with little Frances Braile but she spilled wine all down her dress and has gone to change.'

'Frances? She will save you another.'

'You sound very sure.'

'Of course I am sure. You are the catch of the county.'

He laughed. He had made up his mind earlier in the evening, mellowed by several glasses of possibly the strongest punch ever brewed between Bungay and Ipswich, to get on better terms with this strange woman, and now she was making it easy for him. They were both accomplished dancers and as they danced she spoke openly and warmly of Fanny's many kindnesses, of the Doctor's courtesy and consideration — 'I do not believe anyone with real troubles would ever talk to him and remain uncomforted' — and of plump, hot, little Frances who was only eighteen and always ungovernable.

Meanwhile Mr Fisher, in a state of trembling and sweaty anxiety, had cornered the Doctor and was consulting him about the difficulties likely to be encountered by a husband, conjugal difficulties the Doctor must understand, encountered by an ardent spouse. The Doctor, understanding only too well, looked grave. They were very near the orchestra. The scrape of fiddles and the dull moaning of the poor assaulted cello hurt his ears. He said sharply that a supper party was no place to consult a physician and his accompanying look would have put off Agamemnon at the gates of Troy, but Mr Fisher was, as Lizzie had said, too innocent to be put off by anything. Besides, he was well fortified with punch, he could never approach old Plesset on such an intimate matter, and he had a deep admiration for the Doctor. He had long been troubled by a fear of impotence, the reality of which he could not test, having never in his life lain with a woman. He had just this evening asked Mrs

151

Jewkes to be his wife but he could not offer her less than her due, he could not offer her whatever it was he might be offering her, supposing his anxieties had substance.

The Doctor, who refused to discuss such matters while crouching in a dark corner, advised him to mention it some more suitable time, and escaped, skirting the dancers with his head down.

'Dr French, why are you creeping about?' and there was Fanny in blue, charming and fragrant. 'Don't you think Lizzie and Mr Savage look very fine? They have danced twice in a row.'

They did look very fine, in spite of Lizzie's dull green, in spite, presumably, of their not liking each other. There might even have been a faint regret in Jary's face when he handed Lizzie to Mr Fisher and found Frances at his elbow.

'Mr Fisher has proposed,' said Fanny in a low voice, watching him whirled in one direction while Lizzie whirled in the other.

'Am I to congratulate you?'

'No, no. I . . . Most certainly not.' Her face took on a strained, cautious look. 'Let us away to the punch, dear Doctor. It is not every day a woman turns down an offer of marriage to an ideal man – I mean, a man ideal in every way: kind, warm-hearted, prosperous.'

'It seems incredible you should refuse him,' with a long smiling look.

'I am afraid I find him very dull company, and besides, there is his ghastly father, who is not dull at all but selfish and lascivious.'

He was, and demonstrated it quite openly in the hall half an hour later when, amid the flutter and bustle of people leaving, he attempted to kiss Lizzie Rayner under the mistletoe. She avoided the dread outcome by clutching the Doctor's sleeve as he was passing and crying: 'Doctor, I have been looking for you. Tell me' – but her stock of lies, inventive, self-preserving lies, was very low, she was many things but rarely cunning – 'tell me . . .'

He saw her situation, removed Mr Fisher's importunate hand, said quietly, 'You are drunk, sir,' and watched the poor old man slink away.

'How good of you to rescue me,' said Lizzie cheerfully, but he could see in her eyes deep gratitude, heartfelt gratitude. 'He is always like that when he leaves his invalid chair.'

'It shows he should not be in one,' said the Doctor tartly, 'for a true invalid is not instantly revived by goatish thoughts.'

At this he stooped the inconsiderable distance to kiss the corner of her mouth. She was conscious of a hard cheek against her, no softness at all, none, no enjoyable sensation. She might as well have been kissed by a turnip. This thought came to her a few seconds after he straightened and she laughed. For a moment she thought she saw an answering gleam in his eyes, as in one who appreciates the absurdity of two ill-matched and irascible people stooping to the foolish conventions of Christmas.

'Oh there you are,' said Jary, coming on them suddenly out of the curious press of homegoers hanging in the doorway. 'Have you captured Miss Rayner?' He would far rather have captured a stoat, said the doubting glint of his eye, or an eagle perhaps. 'May I join in?' and before she could protest he had embraced her with all the large cosiness of a bear and had planted a cheerful, solid sort of kiss full on her mouth.

'Oh,' said Eugenia Braile from behind the Doctor, 'no one has kissed *me* under the mistletoe.'

Several gentlemen stepped forward to rectify the matter but she evaded them all prettily and sought the Doctor's protection and, in another second, the Doctor's kiss. Since Eugenia had been out two seasons and had turned down several offers from perfectly eligible young men, various interpretations could have been put on her odd preference: she might have been trying to stir jealous feelings in the breasts of her many followers, or might simply have decided the Doctor was a safer proposition than Jary Savage, who still stood there looking very large and self-assured; on the other hand, she might just have wished to kiss the Doctor.

'La, look at that,' said Fanny, pausing in her farewells to Lady Braile, 'I would never have thought it.'

Lady Braile peered about short-sightedly but had luckily missed the sensational moment. 'Look at what, Mrs Jewkes?'

'Dr French making love to Eugenia.'

'Nonsense!' Lady Braile looked astonished 'Only last week he came over with Plesset – he is not well, that poor man, he could hardly climb the steps, so short of breath – and examined her tongue and scolded her about that cream she and Frances put on their faces, he said it was most damaging, would make them old before their time instead of twice as pretty. How can you make love to a girl when you are on intimate terms with her tongue and her tonsils?' Apart from which, she could have said, he is a mean figure of a man and not rich, not anywhere near rich.

Jary was making the same observation as he and the Doctor rode home in the spirited dark, the moon vanishing so often behind great flying ragged clouds that it might as well not have been there.

'Why the prettiest girl in the room wished to kiss you, a learned, ill-looking cove with nothing to recommend him, I have no idea.'

'Perhaps she has fond memories of my examining her eyeballs,' was the dry answer, as the Doctor urged his pony on under the threshing trees, for a great westerly blow had come upon them again and small twigs were raining down.

'I hope you did not oscillate her chest.'

'Auscultate, auscultate. I should hope not indeed. In the circumstances it would have been most improper.'

By the time they had turned in at Ramillies the Doctor had dismounted to avoid being blown from the saddle and Jary had been forced to put his hat under his arm. In the stableyard the lanterns had blown out and no one was about. 'Rot his soul, where is he?' cried Jary, incensed. 'Millet!'

There was the far-away clang of a door, the house door. The garden pony whinied repeatedly from behind his necessary bars. The wind blew them the shuffling crunch of Millett's hurrying feet.

In the house there was a letter, come by a late post and brought from Stretfield by one of the Fipson children hoping to be royally fed in the Ramillies kitchen. Jary found it in the library on the little tray along with a note from Charles Calloway to wish him a merry Christmas, the season's greetings.

'The young prig,' was Jary's reaction, tossing the paper on the fire. He read the other letter carefully, smoothing out the yellowed, travel-stained page, tilting it to the candle.

'Good God! Alex, listen to this. My uncle has dropped dead and has left no will. At least, he has left a will but it is not valid, it has no witnesses or something – I cannot make it out, the ink has blurred.'

'I am sorry for it. But then I recall you did not like him, nor he you, and that he resented your presence in Jamaica, your claim on Helen's Mount.'

'He did, but he slipped up, it seems. This is from Collinge, who was his lawyer, not a bad man for a lawyer either. He says that unless there was another will, properly signed and witnessed, et cetera et cetera . . . Here we are. He must advise me – the artful dog, you can see him bowing and scraping as he writes – he must advise me that I am next of kin and will inherit.'

It was one in the morning. The Doctor wound his watch. 'Inherit what?'

'Why, Helen's Mount. Fate is going to give me Helen's Mount.'

On Christmas day, which was crisp and fine, they walked to church across the park and listened to the parson, Odbold, preach a strange sermon, not at all seasonal, comminatory to say the least: they walked home again to the crackle of Hell flames about their feet. Jary took refuge from thoughts of eternal damnation by playing with Henriette for the rest of the morning, coming to the conclusion that he did not regret his moderate fornication and that his life would have been the poorer without it. He had great respect for Odbold, who was not a popular man but took his duties seriously, yet he felt a Sodom and Gomorrah sermon on Christmas Day was not easily forgiven. He did not care for evangelical parsons, he decided. He told Henriette as much and was rewarded with a succession of ridiculous dribbling smiles that warmed his heart, so that it was a cheerful, boisterous Jary who put up the mistletoe and under it kissed the entire female staff of his household.

After dinner he and the Doctor played draughts, which was all their failing intellects could rise to after such a quantity of good claret and a plum pudding of unparalleled lusciousness. In the middle of their third game Jary remembered something and leaned to take one of the Doctor's pieces with an apologetic smile. 'By the way, a letter was delivered yesterday for you. Did you not see it? Clarkie found it in the hall this morning and thought you must have overlooked it. I put it on the small table in the morning room.'

'I have it here.'

'Is it . . . Is it a woman's hand?'

'I cannot see it is your business one way or the other,' snapped the Doctor with such a look Jary took another two of his counters without compunction.

Later, by the fire, in the companionable silence of surfeit, Jary saw the Doctor withdraw the letter from his pocket and open it again. Why did it disturb him so? His face was gaunt. It must be from this woman in Norfolk, the one who had broken his heart. Jary found nothing ridiculous in the thought of a broken heart, his own had been injured once, though it crossed his mind that life was apt to be a sad business if broken hearts were still in order at forty-five, an age when most men consider themselves past such hazards. He sank down his chin and closed his eyes and thought back to Nell and all that old bitter business, his uncle beside himself, the woman dry-eyed and mutinous, and then... Brazil. Nell ... Nell ... Was she dead now? If not, she must certainly have grown old, nearly fifty, all that fair bright beauty gone.

'I shall go back,' he said drowsily, 'I shall have to go back to settle Helen's Mount,' and then, his hand tightening on the arm of his chair, 'if it is mine.'

'When?'

'In the spring.' He would have settled the Diddlers by then, settled Mrs Whiteley, refurbished Ramillies, bought the new stock bull, tamed Millett to be a paragon of efficiency, seen the water fill his canal ...

The Doctor looked down at Ann's close-crammed pages. They were all questions, dashing, imperious, frantic questions: why was he in Suffolk? Why did he only write to Louise Barsham? Why had he been determined to miss her wedding? Between were stray lines of simple information; new purchases of stock for the farm, her cousin Tom's heady pursuit of Lord Barsham's daughter Charlotte, William's sudden promotion to another ship. Then, on the last page, all the recriminations he had dreaded, those he could never have answered to her face which was partly why he had absconded without a word to her, only a note, a brief, stilted, inadequate note. Was he not her friend? He had attended her first wedding to a man he had not liked, why should he refuse to come when the bridegroom was his own friend William? He had run away in the night like a thief. Would he please write to her, would he explain? And she signed herself 'Ann', nothing loving or faithful or even mildly affectionate, just 'Ann'.

The Doctor read the letter through twice and then laid it on the fire. He watched it blacken and curl and crumble to ashes with a drawn, detached look, and then poured himself another glass of madeira.

'Lizzie Rayner is an odd creature,' said Jary thickly from the chair opposite, returning from a far country

157

and a dream of warm and loving women. Why should he think of Lizzie Rayner?

There was nothing left of the letter, a puff and the ashes would disintegrate. The Doctor watched it hang, frail as frail, over the red void. Had she sat at her little writing desk to compose all those passionate sentences, struggling to produce the right effect, the balance between the old frank openness once between them and this new reserve, suitable for addressing a man who was almost a stranger? He could picture her dark head bent, the quill brushing her mouth as she paused, deep in thought. He could see the quiet room with its ticking clock and the ginger cat, and hear the distant squall of Miss Pennyquick bringing order to the kitchen. If he had spoken, the night they had dined alone together, or at the ball, in the library, if he had ignored his deep regard for William, the obligations of friendship, sacrificing both by speaking of his love, what would she have done? Would she have laughed? He could imagine that too: the quick laugh, fond and warm, the disbelief, the daring anxiety. But you are my friend, she might have said in a tone that would have told him at once how certainly she felt their friendship excluded carnality, you are my friend and you are old enough to be my father. . .

He remembered suddenly, out of a kind of stupor, that it was Christmas day. She should be married by now. But she had said nothing about it in her letter, had not written as Mrs Claverden. How strange, how very strange. Surely she was married. Louise Barsham had told him it was to take place the second week of December.

Jary woke, looked about, yawned, and bent forward to poke the fire. The letter fell to nothingness and was lost in the uprush of sparks.

12

The day Jary rode into Stretfield to see the parson about the Diddlers was a day never to be forgotten by the entire neighbourhood, so that for years afterwards small children were threatened with Mr Savage if they misbehaved.

'He is an innocent,' said Lizzie, 'or he is the biggest fool the age has yet produced. Do you mean to tell me he rode up to the parson's door and demanded he bring care and comforts to the outcasts in Beke's Wood?' She was standing in front of the Doctor's portrait sucking the end of her brush and looking distracted. Her subject was arranged comfortably in his chair and looked amused.

'He swears he only asked half a dozen pertinent questions, such as who should visit the sick and poor and bring comfort to the dying? Odbold naturally answered his curate, for that is why he pays him. But I fear it was not an answer to turn away wrath – not Jary's wrath anyway, Jary's wrath is of the sublime order, floods and plagues of locusts are nothing to it.'

'I almost feel sorry for the parson.'

Lizzie stood back, scowled, bit her lip, scowled more fiercely. Some discrepancy between the face glinting at her from the chair and the reconstruction of that face on her canvas struck her forcibly. Her brows came together. Another silence – they had weathered so many in these same circumstances – and the wet branches heaving a foot or two beyond the panes were strangely loud, along with the hiss of the damp file.

'You care for him deeply,' was Lizzie's abrupt comment after an inordinate while, 'Mr Savage, I mean. He appeals to something in you, you cannot help responding.' The Doctor looked up. 'How you frown! And you have moved your chin!' she cried.

He appeals to you too, the Doctor was thinking, though you bristle now when he is mentioned. Of course women were attracted to Jary for a variety of reasons, and in some no doubt he roused the maternal instincts. But Lizzie was not in any way maternal. She was a hawk when roused, as swift, as purposeful, as deadly. Was it a sexual attraction then? Was it that after all? If it was it was very slight and she was fighting it and apparently winning.

At last, casting down her brush, a very hawk indeed, she said: 'Perhaps we should have a dish of tea. I shall finish for today.'

A bare twenty minutes. Was she really finding his portrait so difficult? He had already sat for her much longer than she had originally deemed necessary. He did not believe his face was so very different from the Admiral, from Mrs Stone's daughters, from old Mr Fisher; it possessed the same number of features: eyes, ears, lips, nose, chin. What was it about his face that caused her so much inner turmoil?

Lizzie was at the door already, and he recognized a characteristic defensive pose, an angry tilt of her head. It occurred to him all at once that she was probably bored, and lonely, and fretting at being confined − for it *was* confinement, this endless village existence, a large prison but a prison nonetheless, its limits strictly delineated and stoutly walled. How she must long to escape to London. How she must long for the new year and the much-talked-of departure.

'How is my likeness?' he asked, walking to see. She flew to catch his arm, an urgent, desperate gesture, unladylike, unbecoming even in a friend. He could feel her fingers biting through his sleeve.

'No, no, you shan't see it! It is only half-finished, nothing like. It would give you pain to look on it now. You must . . . You must come for your tea.'

The Doctor watched her hand loose its grip and hide itself in the folds of her skirt. She was still so close he had a pleasurable sensation of warm skin and the faint

160

familiar scent of violets. 'Well, I shall see it another day, no doubt. But I must forgo the dish of tea. I have to visit a Mr Hinsey to look at Jary's bull.'

'You are not turned animal doctor?'

'Jary thinks it is anaemic, Hinsey says it is a naturally pale ®beast – or perhaps one should say it has always been an unnaturally pale beast. Jary has actually looked in its mouth and disbelieves it.'

'It does not seem the occupation for a man who has had Astley Cooper wring his hand and every student in London cheer his lectures. How bored you must be here.'

'I leave as soon as the weather improves. I have promised I will stay to the end of next week. I am to give a report to the lawyers on the sanitary deficiencies of the Diddlers.'

'You see, you could not resist his appeal. It will snow and you will be here till March.'

'I did not resist because I hope I am his friend.'

She bit her lip. He felt she might like to hit him. He went into the hall and found his hat, turned only to make a decorous bow. He suspected suddenly that she had spent the twenty minutes making a caricature of him, that she had drawn a grotesque likeness, exaggerated and cruel, with a bubble issuing from the cynical mouth in which were the words: 'I am grown old, lascivious and despairing and can doctor every ill except my own.'

'Damn!' he said, and let himself out.

The snow came. The Doctor broke the ice in his washing bowl every morning and gazed mournfully out at a waste of white in which even the tallest oaks were little more than white clumps, and the distant Frenchmans nothing but a white heap, anonymous, silent. But it was nothing out of the ordinary, it was expected. Only Millett grumbled because he could not turn out the horses, the snow came over their knees, and they grew bored and then furious at being confined.

After four days Jary was beginning to match them in mood, after five he could stand it no longer and wrapped

161

himself up in several layers of clothes, in knitted cap and scarf and two pairs of breeches, and went out to dig his way along the back drive where the snow was less deep owing to the trees being closer together. Whether the intention was to dig to Foley, his nearest neighbour, or simply to get some exercise, it was impossible to say. What was certain was that no one at Foley would dig towards Ramillies so there could be no cheerful reunion somewhere along the margin of the Meeting Grounds. The Doctor, going out to find him and tell him it was time to eat, came across a benign and smiling Jary who had spent all his frustration on the drifts and now leaned, resigned and pleasantly exhausted, on his shovel.

'There are some oaks will have to come down,' were his first words, and he pointed here, and here, and far over towards the unrecognizable Long Pightle. He led the Doctor on, floundering, to the broken-down gates, and spoke of their restoration, brushing the snow from their rusted ironwork. He was totally absorbed, every word expressing, though he might not know it, a deep and deepening affection for this remote and inconvenient old house. The Doctor, who sank thigh-deep occasionally, being so much shorter than Jary, hopped and jumped after him smiling inwardly at this and wondering if he had come to love Ramillies in an instant, as he had Henriette, or whether it had been a gradual bewitching.

A week later there was a partial thaw. Jary rode to Foley to see if all was well and found the ladies playing backgammon and eating toast and potted beef. He rode on to the village through Lower Paradise and called on the Stones who gave him game pie and claret, and the parson, who perhaps felt inclined to give him nothing but magnanimously shared his own luncheon of ham and potatoes. Thus fortified Jary turned for home past the church and through the front gate, having described a gastronomically rewarding circle. He rode in pink-cheeked and plainly happy, self-satisfied, replete. He put up his horse himself as Millett was nowhere to be found and stamped into the house the back way, banging his boots on the scraper. Inside was an unusual quiet, an atmosphere of expectancy.

'I am afraid Henriette is not well,' said the Doctor, who had come down on hearing him try every room in turn, ringing all the bells. 'She has a fever and a cough.'

'Yesterday it was nothing but a cold in the head.'

The Doctor thought it prudent to turn Jary's thoughts in a happier direction, there may yet be no need to worry about the baby. 'How were they at Foley?' he asked.

'Playing backgammon for guineas – they are using raisins for guineas. Lizzie currently owes Fanny Jewkes two thousand five hundred, there is a great pile of IOUs; she loses all the time, she is too impatient. They were very merry. The Hinseys only offered me a stirrup cup, he has not forgiven me yet for rejecting the bull: he swears it is as honest and capable a bull as you could ever find. Then I went on to the Stones, who are always cheerful, and to old Odbold. Now there is a most extraordinary man. I wonder he ever came to be a country parson. He says he took lessons from an apothecary so that he could act as doctor to the poorer people as well as priest – and there was I thinking he made little success at either, an unworthy sort of feeling when sitting at a man's table eating his meat. He collects moths, did you know? I believe his moths mean more to him than his parishioners.'

'But he unbent a little, you are on better terms?'

'Well, we exchanged some civil words if that is what you mean. He is not a bad man, only a little neglectful and foolish. There are ten rooms in that place and he inhabits two, his woman servant only the kitchen. I would not say it was squalor, it is too sparsely furnished for that and tolerably clean, but the fire was too small to do any good but suck in cold draughts and there was nothing of beauty, no pictures, no books. It struck me unnatural in a learned man. Still, I suppose the moths are all the decoration he needs, though they are shut away in drawers. He does not approve of me, he thinks I am a libertine. I know it. He is a rabid misogynist, barely

163

spoke to his servant, poor old crone, and whispered to me that there were strumpets living within a mile of my gates. Who do you think they are, Alex? Susan Fipson at Lower Paradise has had two husbands – do you think he meant her? Or Fanny Jewkes?'

'Fanny Jewkes for sure, and probably vexatious Lizzie who ran off with a soldier in a scarlet coat.'

Two days passed. The snow fell again. The Doctor gravely confirmed that Henriette had the whooping cough. How could she have the whooping cough? cried Jary, she never left the park. And how in January, such bitter weather? The Doctor must be wrong.

A week of listening to the painful agony of Henriette's coughing proved the Doctor right, and there was no medical remedy nor any other kind. Jary retreated somehow inside himself, so that it was only the shell of a man which walked from room to room, and his voice sounded unnatural and hollow when he spoke. He only lost his temper once, when he dashed the fried mice out of Mrs Bloy's hand and ejected her from the nursery crying witch and heathen, but he had to let her back in, he could not comfort the child himself and her pinched blue face, so thin and tiny, brought him to desperation.

'What do you know about coughs?' he shouted at the Doctor over supper one evening. 'You have only ever had to do with soldiers.'

'You forget all the babies of High Common. I have wrestled with the whooping cough before, oh many times, you may take my word on it.'

So too had Mrs Stone who, when the news wafted from Ramillies to Foley and from Foley to Paradise and Stretfield, came over to give them the benefit of her experience. Experience told her, as she picked up the child, that she had seen this extreme state before. She handed Henriette back to the Doctor, and her eyes met his and saw the rage in them: pure, vicious, helpless rage, though when he spoke it was mildly and very low: 'There is nothing I can do.'

164

Mrs Stone's kindly face turned away. 'I have lost two of my own,' she said, 'you do not need to tell me.'

The funeral was four days later. Jary had been to Stretfield to see Odbold among his moths and had laid claim to a corner of the churchyard as yet untenanted. It was on a slight slope and from the top of the wall just beyond a man on tiptoe might see into the park at Ramillies. It struck him that this was as it should be, that this was the spot for Henriette to lie. How deeply he grieved for her, no longer lying in her cradle up at the house, no one – except perhaps Alex – ever knew, for he took his grief off and dealt with it in his own way, marking the trees to be felled, measuring out the new pond, visiting the stockyards. He had wrapped the child up himself, and kissed her, and given her to Mrs Bloy to carry downstairs, and he had shut the door of the nursery and not set foot inside again. The Doctor had; he had sat on the low nursing chair and rocked the carved cradle with his foot and looked long and hard, though virtually unseeing, at the ponderous grey rocking horse Jary had carried down from the attics for future enjoyment. It had crossed his mind that Jary blamed him, that once again he had only proved that medical knowledge was not so much at fault as non-existent, that a child of five months with a common disease could defeat all his training and experience.

The morning Henriette was buried there was a north wind with flakes of snow in it. It seemed cruel to put anything into that hard, cold ground. Jary and the Doctor stood by the grave while Mr Odbold did his best with the brave old words, and the wintering gulls rode high up in the torn white sky. Afterwards Jary said he would walk back alone and did so, and the Doctor was left to shake hands with the parson and watch old Nudd and young Jerry Fipson begin to fill in the grave. When they were done there was just the little mound of frozen earth, scarcely bigger, it seemed to him, than a mole heap. It was lonely too, some distance from the other graves. The

Doctor gazed at it a long time and as he gazed it came to him that by burying Henriette, Jary had somehow laid claim to Ramillies, that he had, in a manner of speaking, taken seizin. Now he was not simply the foreigner who had fought Prince Whiteley, he had had his own grief, a common grief they could all understand; and his dead were buried in the churchyard. There would be future Savages to lie alongside Henriette, Jary himself perhaps, a clutch of children, grandchildren, other, luckier Henriettes.

Mrs Hinsey was at the gate. 'I will walk along with you,' said the Doctor, lifting his hat. 'It is a raw morning to be abroad, dear lady.'

She nodded back towards the churchyard. ''Tis a sad business, Doctor. Mr Savage takes it hard, no doubt.'

'Very hard.'

'And you too,' she said after a moment of studying his face, as they set off side by side through the slush. 'But there, we must accept what can't be changed. The poor mite's gone. And there will be other children at the big house.'

The Doctor took this unsatisfactory comfort in silence and trudged on through the wintry landscape. He let Mrs Hinsey run on about the farm, the stock, her own children, and he heard one word in twenty and grunted at it so that she believed he was listening. But at her own gate, turning to bid her farewell, a thought struck him.

'Mrs Hinsey, I have heard a Captain Jervis spoken of recently,' and this with a look of such innocence even those who knew him best might not have guessed his cunning. 'Do you know him? Does he live hereabouts?'

'Lord no!' and she gave an uneasy laugh, glancing about as if she feared they would be overheard. 'Lord, the Captain does not live in these parts, Doctor. You have misunderstood. He was from the West Country, I believe, and a very fine, charming gentleman he seemed, came to stay with the Mitchells in Westdene – he was a cousin, I think. Oh, Doctor, if you had been here . . . the

166

trouble that was caused. He and Miss Rayner fell in love, sir, and ran away together.'

'Good gracious – but of course they were not married? Miss Rayner returned.'

'She did not want to, I believe, but Mrs Jewkes fetched her home. He had abandoned her.' Very low now, and nervous. 'In some seaside place a long, long way from here.'

The Doctor promised he would never speak of it, he was distressed to have brought an old old secret to light. He bowed and bid her good day and plodded on towards the Meeting Grounds. He could see Foley momentarily as he struck out along the snow-covered path that led direct from Lower Paradise to Ramillies, it stood in the shelter of Frenchmans, a long, low, friendly house. He wondered about the two women within, who had played backgammon for pretend guineas, and he tried to imagine Fanny Jewkes in some squalid room in a seaport tavern pleading with Lizzie to come home to Suffolk, and he could not see it, he could not see it at all.

By the time he was wearily climbing the park railings his feet and legs were soaked and numb.

'Oh,' cried Mrs Clark as he came in, 'I will fetch hot water, the foot bath . . . But your hands! They are blue!'

'I left my gloves in the church,' he explained. He did not know how he had come to do it. At the mention of the church he saw her eyes fill with tears and she turned away quickly, making for the door.

'Where is Mr Savage?' he asked.

Mr Savage had come home an hour ago and had found a package left by Miss Rayner who had called a little earlier. No, Mrs Clark could not say what was in the package, it was very small, and thin, and wrapped up in paper and string. Mr Savage had opened it but he had not said anything, he had simply thrust it under his arm and climbed up to the nursery and they had not seen him since.

He came down at nine, carrying a candle, one of the nursery candles. He looked worn and haggard and spent.

167

He said nothing to the Doctor but smiled, a brief, affectionate smile, and dropped something into the Doctor's lap. The Doctor picked it up and turned it over and looked at it in the light of the flames, while Jary carefully went round lighting all the candles.

It was a small sketch, six inches square. On a note attached to it Lizzie Rayner had written: 'You did not know, I used to visit her, but this is all I ever drew. I thought you might like to have it. E.R.'

It was a portrait of Henriette.

Henriette hung in the morning room for it was the room Jary liked best, and indeed it was now truly his, for he had had the walls painted yellow and all the dull grey panelling done over in white. The curtains were new green brocade and sumptuously framed Jary's favourite view of the avenue. In all this bright cheerfulness the little portrait hung quite alone on the wall which had once been home to a dozen Rayners. Lizzie, true to her talent, had captured the essential Henriette, and the little dark head with its dark, smiling eyes was the baby as they would always remember her, not that cold wasted bundle Jary had kissed goodbye.

The thaw continued unabated, a week of mild weather leaving them stuck fast in quagmire. Unabashed, Jary organized the felling of two of the largest trees for both would be a danger in the furious March winds to come, and he spent three whole days watching the teams of great horses at their task, lending his considerable strength when it was needed, and learning how to handle the bullocks who were to drag some of the timber to Sir James Braile's sawmill at Westdene. He was fully occupied and therefore happy. If Henriette's death had cast a shadow over his life it was not noticeable; he was as good-humoured, as encouraging, as optimistic as ever. The men liked him, he gave them good morning, spoke to them direct, did not interfere in work they understood, and had hot food sent out from the house – for if it was mild it was only so by January standards, there was a fresh wind and raw cold.

On the third day Lizzie Rayner appeared just after the great old tree, split in several places from past storms and a hit by lightning, was being lopped up on the ground. She stood a while a little way off, watching the men swarming among the branches, listening to their talk and the dull thud of the axes and the stamping and jingling of the waiting teams. Jary did not see her at first and was alerted by Millett – who had ridden early to Westdene for the post and had returned sour and cold with none – saying: 'A sad sight, Miss. This here was an old tree before the house was built.'

'It needed to be felled. It was in a poor way,' was the crisp, quiet reply. Jary turned, seeing her beyond the patient grey head of the lead horse, and he stepped across, his boots cracking the twigs and small branches scattered all around.

'I came to thank you for your kind note,' were her first, disarming words, 'I am glad you liked the picture.'

She was in blue, with a fur hat and muff. She looked different, and he realized he missed her hair, her pale thick wayward hair, tucked up under the hat.

He did his best to be friendly, aware that she might shy away at the least excuse or fly into a passion. He asked her about her journey to London, the delay, the pictures she might exhibit, the Doctor's portrait. Eventually he ran out of subjects and being Lizzie she did not help him find any but said after a long long pause: 'I suppose you have not seen the portrait of my grandmother? It used to hang in the morning room.'

'A lady in grey, with a small dog?'

'Yes, yes. She's still there? I am so glad. Only Fanny swears she never saw it, and I have all these cheerless old dandies in full wigs and shocking shoes with bows, and no end of ladies in disarming décolleté, but no Julia. It is a good picture, very fine work. I would have liked to have it more than any of the others.'

Jary sighed. Had the Doctor told her? Was this all

done to embarrass him? But she was grave, a grave inquiring face under the soft fur, not the least sign of that mocking humour he had often seen in her eyes.

'I am afraid I have kidnapped her,' he said at last, 'She is . . . She hangs in my bedroom.'

Lizzie laughed suddenly, and it seemed to him there was definitely mockery there now. 'She would have appreciated that, Mr Savage. I can still remember her, she was a very dashing old lady, had been a very dashing young one once. She left my grandfather twice, dreadful behaviour, and might have stayed away altogether but she had to return for Ramillies' sake, my grandfather having no feeling for the land or the tenants and everything going to ruin. Of course, that is legend. The truth is she was probably abandoned by her lovers and that's why she came back.'

There was a difficult moment where Jary gave his attention to the tree fellers and Lizzie stared hard at his broad shoulders, waiting for him to name the day he would have the notorious Julia sent over to Foley. At least, he thought that was probably what she was expecting, was probably why she had come over, it was all nonsense about the note. Why, if one went about thanking people for their thanks and so on and so on the world would come to a stand. He turned back to face her as cheerful and polite as before, but he said: 'I am sorry, I would very much like to keep the picture myself.'

He saw disappointment plain in her face, and something else, more elusive: rage? Now, he thought, she will make something more of her attachment to the old woman, spin out some tale of how she used to sit on her knee and be told stories of Ramillies in the great old days, will do everything she can, in short, to make me feel guilty at depriving her of one picture among three score. He waited, but she did not speak. He waited a little longer and told her: 'I will look after her very well. If there comes a day I have to leave, for good, I mean, I will not take her with me. I shall give her to you, of course.'

170

She was biting her lip. Was she really at a loss, or was it anger that seemed to be making her dumb?

'Mind yourselves,' yelled someone, and twigs flew in their direction. Jary was so bold as to seize Lizzie's arm and lead her away, far away under the trees that still stood.

'I am having a headstone carved,' he said quietly. 'It will only be very small, of course, just her name and the date. Strictly speaking I should not call her Henriette Savage but what does it matter? The Doctor tells me the whole neighbourhood thinks she was mine, and so she was, though not in the way they mean. I would have brought her up as mine, Ramillies would have been her home, and she would have been a sister to my other children. So there it is. What would you do in my place?'

If she had been angry over the picture she was not angry now. He saw the sudden shining of her eyes as she turned away. She said: 'You are right, what does it matter? You were all the father she had ever known.'

He felt a great chasm of grief but he grasped his ledge firmly, he would not cry to this straight-backed, unpredictable woman who a moment ago might have scratched out his eyes.

'The Doctor tells me he has asked you to paint my portrait. Is that true?'

'Yes' – a pause, as if she were gathering her wits – 'Yes, it is true. And I suppose there is no reason why I should not start it right away, there will just be time before I go to London. I shall expect you . . .' another pause, but now she began to walk away, only adding over her shoulder: '. . . the day after tomorrow at ten o'clock in the morning. I hope it is not too early for you.'

' "I hope it is not too early for you," she said in that haughty way she has,' said Jary to the Doctor at breakfast two days later, 'as if I was some slug-a-bed who never rose before noon. I can tell you I could have shaken her. Why must she always make plain conversation such a ticklish business? I shall sit mum while she draws me or we shall quarrel for sure.'

'You will have no option. She does not talk while she paints.'

In the event she did not talk at all. She might have addressed six words to him in three quarters of an hour but he could not be sure. He had been shown in, relieved of hat and coat, and had sat quite rigid for twenty minutes while she glared at him and walked about behind an easel. Then she had said she was finished for the morning, would he care to come Friday at the same time, and all with a cool firm politeness as if he were a young boy and she an elderly lady in lace cap and spectacles. He resented it, his quick temper rose, and then Fanny put in her charming head to ask whether he would take coffee. He accepted, but if he had expected Lizzie to unbend, to smile, to seem almost human, he was disappointed. She did not even join them.

'I am not surprised this Captain Jervis left her in a cheap lodging house,' said Jary that afternoon, tramping about the wet and dismal gardens with the Doctor. 'If I had run away with her I would have left her at the first turnpike,' and then, turning his face up to the mass of darkening cloud scudding before the strengthening wind: 'Lord above, I shall be glad when spring comes. It has been a cruel enough winter.'

'He grieves for the baby,' said Lizzie, 'it makes him wonderfully difficult to talk to, he has grown . . . larger and colder.'

She and Fanny had been to the Diddlers with a basket of comforts. Heaven knows they were small enough comforts in all that large misery but nevertheless the baskets from Foley, arriving regularly once a week, sometimes twice, were welcomed for more than their practical value, and Fanny's charity was of the practical kind: her eggs could be eaten or set under a broody to hatch; no, Fanny's baskets would have been welcomed whatever

172

they contained, as Fanny herself was welcomed with whole-hearted, unreserved affection.

Today was a little different, for Fanny had been recruiting. The position at Ramillies for a clean reliable maid was still not filled and though the Diddlers were not clean and nobody had ever put their reliability to the test those were matters which could easily be dealt with. Mrs Farrow, a widow with four daughters, offered the second of them, Kate, for a trial period. The thought of Jary did not trouble her, she had listened to him offering them all dry sound cottages and had formed an opinion then that would stand firm no matter what grim tales and sly stories seeped from the village. The problem at Ramillies was Mrs Fipson, whose young brothers regularly crept about through the alder scrub to lob stones at the goats and geese and the Diddler children.

'I do hope that child does well at Ramillies,' Fanny had said, as she and Lizzie had tackled the steep path up through the wood on their way home, and so gradually they had come to speak of Jary himself and of the pitifully small grave all by itself in that lonely corner.

'If you want your picture,' Fanny remarked as they came down the hill to Foley, 'I daresay I could put a case to the Doctor and he could put it to Mr Savage. Is it all that important?'

'No, not in the least, except she was my grandmother and it was the best picture of them all.'

'How strange he should hang it in his bedroom.'

'You used to have Mr Jewkes in yours, and a terrible great frowning Mr Jewkes, twice life size.'

'Yes, yes, but he was not my grandfather; no, I mean he was not someone else's grandfather. Good Heavens, I would never have a strange man hanging on my bedroom wall.'

They reached the back gate and the Foley geese, who always sneaked into the garden if they were not watched, came hissing down the path, wings outspread. Fanny swiped at them with her empty basket. 'Shoo! Shoo, silly things. I believe we should eat them at Easter, look at

173

them trampling my bulbs. Lizzie, you are sure you want to go to London? You are sure . . . It will not only be painting, my dear, will it? You will have to be pleasant, eternally pleasant, you will have to smile and be so very diplomatic. It is such a strange, shifting, unreliable world, and so many looking for advancement and women always treated differently do what they may, and men of influence only too quick to drop someone even with half the town still in raptures over him . . . Liz, dearest, are you sure?'

She did not speak, but she put her arm round Fanny's plump waist and led her indoors. Only then, taking off her bonnet: 'If I do not go I shall always wonder what it would have been like,' and turning, kissing her cheek: 'Dear Fan, you must not worry. If the world proves too much for me I shall come home. I did before. Oh, Fan, have you forgotten? I did before.'

13

'In the country,' said Mr Fisher, who was crouched on a footstool toasting muffins in the library at Ramillies, 'a temporary affair can last a millenium. You will find they still remember King John, not personally, needless to say, but in relation to how that piece of boggy ground came to be left to Mrs Brown and not Mr Green, and why the road turns right instead of left at the foot of Frenchmans.'

Jary looked startled. 'Good God, you are not about to tell me it was Queen Matilda granted the right to the Whiteleys to put up cottages at the Diddlers.'

Fisher laughed his high-pitched whinnying laugh and blew at a singeing muffin. He was quite ludicrously happy in his cramped position, in charge of a whole plateful of cakes and a dish of butter, for he seldom had a chance to throw off rigid convention or escape his father's censorious eye. He had called on Jary with an offer, a blushing diffident offer of an architect for Jary's cottage project. He had never before dared to dispose of any part of his own money without his father's knowledge and advice, but he liked Jary and admired his plans extremely. He was acquainted with an architect, a good, sound, reasonable man who was all for reform, for pleasant dwellings and good drainage. Would it be in order to engage this gentleman and pay his fee? It would give him so much pleasure, cried Fisher, make him feel useful. Mr Savage could have no idea of the delight of feeling useful.

Jary, who had battled hard to interest the local dignitaries and had come home from several meetings at the parsonage painfully discouraged, saw in Stephen Fisher's eager, hopeful look the very foundation stones of his cottages. For ten minutes or so he thanked him heartily, asked after the architect, mentioned how important the drains were – the Doctor was very strict on drains, spoke in terrible tones of fever and death – and rang for Mrs Clark and the muffins, saying of course Stephen must stay to tea – he may call such a good friend by his christian name, surely? – and more, stay to dinner if he was not engaged already.

Mr Fisher had brought with him, however, not only an offer of practical help but one of information. He remembered old Frederick Marston had once told him that his grandfather had had permission from the squire of Ramillies to put up a shepherd's hut on land just north of Cockshoot – and that was the straggle of alder carr by the river where the Diddlers ford crossed. It had all been grazing land in those days, for earlier farmers, more capable or more desperate, had drained all that low-lying land and put sheep in it during the summer. Since it was still liable to flood the Marstons had built a flimsy dwelling for their shepherd in the shelter of Beke's Wood near a stream that fed the Wiss. This was Ramillies land; in those days there had been a ditch and a stout thorn hedge to mark the boundary.

'I knew the land was mine,' said Jary, 'I knew it.'

'Does it matter?' asked Fisher, and was bold enough to repeat this question to Charles Calloway, who arrived a moment later. 'Does it matter who owns the land if you intend to rehouse the people anyway?'

Calloway looked rather shocked by this happy pair, who had managed to get butter over everything including many of the documents. He was aware he and Jary were not on the best of terms and though he had told himself several times that he did not care, that he did not care for Jary's good opinion, that the man was little more than an adventurer, an ex-pirate, a dispossessed nobody much addicted to expensive whores, he sometimes regretted their inability to get on together and he also regretted the very real possibility of losing Jary's business. He therefore did not reply at once to Fisher's question, and since Jary did not ask him to sit down – a strange lapse in a man usually so cordial – he stood awkwardly holding his notes and sheafs of correspondence, his face heavy and frowning.

'Well' – at last and in a heavy grating voice that matched his expression – 'no, the dispute over ownership is perhaps only academic, for if Mr Savage could prove his absolute rights tomorrow he would still have to house the people where he could for there will be no cottages ready for them until late summer and only then if the builders are goaded with unremitting force. Only Mrs Whiteley is going to make an issue of it now that she has been challenged. She will not rest until the land has been proved hers. She is a determined woman and that vile Pellow, her attorney, has his teeth in the case like a bull terrier and will not let go though we rain depositions on his head. He will use every trick of procedure to avoid a ruling; it will take years, he would see it took years, years even if the case was thrown out at the end. We should all have grey hairs and Ramillies be a ruin before anything was decided.'

'Years?' asked Jary, feeling his muffins sit leadenly as he contemplated a tedious and convoluted law suit. 'Years, Mr Calloway?'

'We have no formal agreement, no deed relating to either the shepherd's hut or the cottages. If one exists, giving the Marstons a right to build, it will be a troublesome business; I only wish such a document had been among your papers, at least we would have known the right and wrong of the matter.'

'But as I said to Stephen before you arrived,' said Jary, 'it all happened years ago, before the Commonwealth even. The document, if it exists, would be so old Queen Elizabeth herself might have read it.'

'I assure you that would not necessarily invalidate it. If the privileges were conveyed to the heirs in title . . .'

'Damn the heirs in title! Damn deeds, and covenants, and Queen Elizabeth! Have I or have I not the right to demolish those cottages?'

'It would be unwise to do so,' said Calloway in the evasive manner of his kind, and with a bow, as if he

177

had long ago learned that the best way to serve up the unpalatable is politely, 'at the present.'

Mr Fisher looked up and saw Jary volcanic and Charles Calloway all brooding defensive gloom, all in all too much emotion, expressed or contained, for one room. He said, 'The thing to do, gentlemen, is to hurry forward with the cottages. I will call on my friend Mr Blake tomorrow at the very earliest moment.'

'It is not the practical solution,' began Jary, 'that worries me, but the principle . . .'

Charles Calloway pursed his lips and looked down at the plate where the last muffin sat, all they had left him. 'I would not stand on principles, sir, it is a risky venture, unless of course your principles have the full backing of the law.'

Kate Farrow having taken fright and not arrived at Ramillies on the day appointed, Lizzie took the trap up Frenchmans and tied up the pony where the narrow path plunged down to the Diddlers. Half an hour later she hurried Kate through the trees and got her into it, jolting back down to Foley and then turning right along Cuckooland.

It was not a pleasant drive, Lizzie was only thankful it was over quickly. Kate was silent, apparently frozen to the seat, and the pony was tiresome going away from his stable, even threatening to lie down.

'The Doctor has a cold,' said Mrs Clark, receiving Kate in the kitchen. 'He has kept to his bed, poor man, packed about with hot bricks. He will certainly sweat it out if he does not die of heat.'

Lizzie suspected the Doctor was unpardonably brutish when ill, the very worst kind of patient, and she smiled, thinking how very many hot bricks it would take before a body would feel warm upstairs at Ramillies.

'He has a roaring fire,' Mrs Clark was continuing, 'any more and the chimney will be alight. Mr Savage had to come out at once, he said it was a Turkish bath, and that when *he* had had a cold the Doctor had prescribed fresh air and fasting, not fires and toast in bed.'

Kate having been inspected and welcomed, turned about for general view in the cast-off dress of Lizzie's, her clean face pale with apprehension, Mrs Clark declared she would do nicely and ushered Lizzie through to the morning room where there was a good fire though nothing like the atmosphere of a Turkish bath; there were draughts all over.

'Good morning,' said Jary, appearing in riding clothes, 'I have just met the poor girl come to help in the kitchen, she ran away like a frightened mouse. Do I look so terrible? I seem to be having the same effect on everyone today, for Hawke has downed his tools and vanished, and the parson positively flew into the church when he saw me riding by, flew in as if he was desperate for sanctuary, yet I thanked him civil for doing the funeral so well and he had all the usual gifts.'

'I expect he feared another of your sermons on the Diddlers. I am sure he only never goes there because he is a timid soul, he would do it if he had the courage.'

'That strikes me as a poor excuse from a man of God. Is he not armed against every evil? Well, if he is not, what hope for the rest of us? Have you had anything? Will you take tea?'

Lizzie sank on to a hard chair. She could understand Mr Odbold's hasty retreat, a Jary filled with optimism was several inches taller than usual, and he was aglow with cheerfulness this morning, having come from a highly satisfactory meeting with Stephen Fisher's Mr Blake, a man after his own heart, a practical, humane man who did not shrink at drains. He was only sorry the Doctor was indisposed and had not been able to meet him.

'Clarkie, a pot of strong coffee for me and some tea for Miss Rayner,' as Miss Clark answered the bell, Kate creeping behind her as apprentice.

'Oh,' said Lizzie, 'if you are drinking coffee, I would prefer it.'

'The last of my own beans,' with a rueful look, 'but there, I shall lay in some more sacks when I go to Helen's Mount.'

Naturally he had to explain why he was going and he thought she grew strangely quiet as he spoke, though he made no great song and dance about inheriting the place, he hardly knew as yet whether he was pleased about it himself. He spoke of it with fondness of course, but more and more he was coming to see that his affection was for its beauty — it had never failed to move him, it was such a lovely house and in so lovely a place — and for what had been there before he was born — close happy family feeling — what he hoped might be there again. He had never believed the thirty years' reign of one crabbed old man, thirty years of drunken disorder, meanness, neglect, the ill treatment of the servants, the general disregard for the well-being of the slaves, would affect his own view of Helen's Mount. Helen's Mount remained and was the house his own father had known, though the garden was unkempt and the furniture was knocked about; the old man was gone and could be forgotten. But since the lawyer's letter had come and he had waited for the expected feeling of joy, yes joy, at being restored his home, he had found that after all it was he who had changed, that Helen's Mount could be set to rights but that Jary Savage could never wipe out those thirty years, that the effect of want and neglect, ill treatment, exile, rank injustice, could never be mended. He did not say any of this to Lizzie Rayner, but he told her a little of his past, and as he spoke unconsciously his voice hardened and his eyes grew darker as the amusement died from them. He had been happiest on his ship, he said suddenly.

The coffee came, brought in by Kate who set it down with a trembling hand but was pink now instead of a dead white. Jary looked across at his guest and saw her leaning to look into the fire, her curls flaming in the light.

'What will happen to Ramillies?' and she looked up quickly. 'I suppose you will sell.'

'Oh, Helen's Mount may come to nothing, a false alarm, a puff of air. There are distant cousins can contest it. I will have to go to Kingston in the spring but there is no question of selling up here on the strength of one lawyer's letter half of which I cannot even read.'

She did not look reassured. Behind her head he could see out of the window and down the avenue, the view he had come to know and love. There was a cold strong wind and the oaks were throwing their branches about under a driving sky.

'Here, drink this. It will warm you through. I saw your pony in the yard, what a sour little thing. Can Mrs Jewkes get nothing better?'

'She is very sentimental about him, my father gave him to her and I do believe, though you must never say I told you, she was a little fond of my father. He is not really wicked, only twenty-five or six, a great age, and he prefers his home comforts to gadding about in a wind. Every year he is to retire and every year he is quite well and sound and gets put in the shafts again.'

In a while they went out to find him, dozing under a sack Millett had considerately flung across him, and he was put in the shafts again and turned towards home.

'She was fairly human today,' Jary reported, entering the Turkish bath, 'I think she does not dislike me quite so much.'

'Who?'

'Lizzie Rayner. What a horrible sight you are, you old rogue. You are going crimson in all this heat. Are you listening? Lizzie Rayner called and took coffee and behaved like a duchess. It was very strange, like having something wild suddenly come to your hand. How can you bear it? Dear God . . .'

Fanny called with cold remedies: pressed beef, bramble jelly, custard tarts. She hoped the Doctor had not been prescribing himself any nasty syrup, any strange pills. She did not believe one could do anything for a cold but cosset it.

'I believe you will find the Doctor of the same opinion,' said Jary, 'at least, so far as he himself is concerned.'

He thought such an irritable, peevish, touchy, quarrelsome animal should not be encouraged by custard tarts, he had been grossly self-indulgent already what with the blazing fire and commanding every hot brick in the house and keeping Kate running up and down with shrub and biscuits, but he smiled at Fanny and said how kind she was and would she not take a dish of tea before going home, privately deciding to appropriate at least the dish of beef.

It was a heavy, cold, overcast day. Fanny's horses had been put up for fear they would take a chill waiting in the drive, and Lussom was snug by the kitchen fire drinking ale by the quart. The time drew on, but Jary did not notice it, he was finding the sprightly Mrs Jewkes an attentive audience and one, moreover, who did not throw cold water over his aspirations. He had been visiting the site of his new cottages, striding about measuring distances, Mr Blake scribbling away from his perch on a tree stump, and they had passed a long congenial morning going over and over the plans, altering, improving, giving rein to their imagination. But at Ramillies what was there? Alex still perspiring to death and unable or unwilling to communicate except in a low rasping God-damn-you voice, a couple of half-trained young spaniels, and for the very briefest moment Mr Stone – who did not even dismount – come with an invitation to dine. There was no one to listen to an enthusiastic description of the cottages, how after this morning's work they would put every other lowly dwelling in Stretfield to shame.

Fanny was cheerfully prepared to admire plans, half-formulated projects, wells and foundations, so long as she could sit by the library fire drinking tea. It was comfortable at Ramillies, and as she had long ago given up the thought of handsome men – she would never admit it, she was always looking out, but hope had died some years ago – it was pleasant having Jary Savage

182

talking to her as if he valued her opinion. Besides, she had another reason for calling than bringing the Doctor some small comforts, and she had spent a long time in front of her mirror making herself look as charming as possible. It was all lost on Jary, who only wanted to talk building, but perhaps a sympathetic ear would achieve as much in the long run.

At some point the fire burned down and Fanny knelt – a most unexpected gesture – to put on another log. From this position she looked up and saw him notice for the first time her artful curls, her artfully darkened lashes, and she said: 'The Doctor, dear man, thinks my cellar – the contents of my cellar – is worth some money. He has given it as his strong opinion that someone who knew a little about wine might find it . . . interesting. I have consulted very privately with Sir James but he cannot see his way to buying even a barrel.' Not even a bottle, she could have said, for fear he is compromised. She had flirted openly with him once long ago when she had been feeling particularly bored, no other man in view, no, not the shadow of another man in view, and that renowned Westdene punch gone to her head. Lady Braile never having forgiven her husband the crime of kissing Fanny's burning cheek in a dim corner of the hall – oh such a chaste, disappointing kiss! – he dare not be found interested in the lady's cellar.

'I wondered, Mr Savage, if you would care to . . . You see, Lizzie is to go to London and must have funds, she cannot wear those dreadful old dresses and every hat she has was her mother's. But you must not breathe a word about the wine, she must never know anyone has even been to inspect it, for she will fly into a temper and refuse the new clothes and will not go, will never meet Sir Whatsit, and Mr Capland or anyone else . . . all out of silly pride. But I may be honest with you, may I not? If I do not sell my cellar I shall be forced to live on credit.'

Jary leaned forward. Her eyes stared directly into his. She was appealing to him and he always hated to resist a woman's appeal. He thought he saw her bottom lip tremble but there was no sign of tears. He thought, in happy succession, of all that matchless spirit in its ancient casks, of the possibility of some excellent burgundies, of the bins of first-class port, of the peculiar brilliance of her eyes, of how long since he had held a woman in his arms, a smiling, consenting woman. He leaned further forward. She was still gazing up, her fingers ashy, tips pressed together. She looked supplicatory and yet there was nothing servile in her posture, and her eyes never left his. It was quite clear – would be clear even to a green boy – that she was offering more than first refusal of her cellar.

He stooped. His lips were inches from hers. He was quite sure he should kiss her, and she knew he was going to, did not draw back, only pressed her hands to her bosom in anticipation.

And into this burning moment the Doctor intruded a long, grey, disapproving face.

'I do not mean to interrupt,' with a startled understanding look, a sudden involuntary foxy grin, 'but Sir James is in the hall.'

'And I,' said Fanny, rising with conscious carelessness, 'should be at home making lists of things Lizzie must take to London.'

The smouldering of disappointed ardour singed the Doctor's conscience, but he gave Fanny a stiff bow and his face was perfectly composed. She smiled at him kindly however, for she always took fortune's reverses with spirit.

But Jary, as soon as the door shut, burst out: 'Damn you, what d'you mean walking in without so much as knocking? It was deliberate. You knew I was . . . engaged.'

'I did not know in what manner you were engaged.'

'But you hoped to catch me out.'

'In conjugo? On your hearthrug? I would have been amazed to do so. But you know, Sir James *is* waiting to see you, he declared he must rouse you out even if you

184

were in your bath. Would you rather he had come in at such a moment?'

'It is something to do with the Diddlers for sure. But Alex, you aren't dressed! That is your nightshirt shoved into your breeches! Good God, what must Mrs Jewkes have thought? At least . . . But no, you are not shaved, not shaved for days,' and then, after a fiery pause, cautiously: 'How are you?'

'Much better. Purged of ill humours.'

And ill humour, I hope, ha ha, thought Jary. Aloud he said: 'I suppose you think me a fool?'

'It had not crossed my mind.'

'Is a man never to yield to temptation, Alex? Do you yourself not feel the need?'

The Doctor cleared his throat, 'I would need to be ten years younger and cast in a different mould before handsome widows knelt at my feet, but supposing I was and one did I might seriously consider her motives before committing myself.'

'You are a cold dog. But I know her motives: she wants me to buy her cellar, she needs the money for Lizzie. And a woman might care for an hour or two of pleasure as much as any man. Why not?'

'If an hour or two of pleasure is all you want there are several young women in Westdene would oblige.'

Jary sneezed, groped for his handkerchief, looked over it with accusing eyes. 'I have caught your cold. I shall be fit for nothing now. But I will buy her cellar, it can do no harm, there is some decent stuff hidden away down there; and there is Lizzie, she cannot trip up the steps of the Academy in a threadbare gown.'

The Doctor laughed.

'Damn you, Alex,' said Jary, and grinned. 'Come and help me talk to Braile. Perhaps the sight of you like that will frighten him away.'

Lizzie was not aware it was Jary's money which bought her new dresses, her shawls, bonnets, travelling capes and dancing shoes, and Fanny made sure that when the dray came for the contents of the cellar, Lizzie was carrying a basket of preserves and pickles to the Diddlers. As Fanny confided to the Doctor when he came for his very last sitting, every devil in Hell would fly were Lizzie to know the true source of a single penny.

'It was why I tried Sir James before I approached Mr Savage,' she told him in a guilty whisper, 'for if Lizzie ever got to know, well, though she would protest no doubt she might come round eventually to seeing it was necessary, but she would never accept being launched by Mr Savage – never! I believe she thinks him a good man, a little rakish perhaps, and she felt for him over the terrible loss of Henriette . . . but she would, oh she would never take a shilling from him she had not earned.'

The Doctor reflected on this as he was shown into the studio, and found a puritan Lizzie in a blue dress high to the neck and her hair in a ribbon, a daunting prospect, every line of her rigid with some emotion and all conflicting. For fifteen minutes she worked in silence and then, with a croak, she flung down her brush. 'There, it is as finished as it will ever be. You may do what you want with it.'

The Doctor stood up. 'I am sorry it has caused so much trouble. I would change my physiognomy if I could, you know.'

He did not raise a smile, not the ghost of a smile. She strode to the window and stood looking out at the bleak country. She did not try to prevent him looking at the picture so he walked round the easel and, momentarily, closed his eyes. When he opened them he was confronted by . . . himself.

He could not say what he had expected but this gaunt, strong, impassioned face was a bolt from Heaven. Yes, it was indeed himself. It was himself as he might have looked in the midst of battle, bloody to the elbows, his voice hoarse with calling for more water, for retractors, for a sharper saw. It was his face as it must have been after he had brought Ann and William together and had sat on in the library smoking, his heart, his hypothetical

186

mythical heart, rent in two. It was his face as he had watched that girl turn away while he prepared to carry the baby down to Jary, a scrap in an old towel, and his face as he had left that same baby a waxen lifeless thing in Mrs Bloy's arms. But it was not his everyday, official, public face. And why had she drawn him *so*, just so, his head half-turned, when she had not posed him like that at all? And when he had been hoping for a respectful, bland, dignified portrait suitable for the august entrance hall of his Edinburgh hospital, supposing they should ever ask him to adorn its walls.

Silence. She had turned to watch him and although he could not see her he could sense her furious energy all concentrated on the back of his neck. He could not think what to say: genius? appalling? is this private side of me so obvious? At last: 'Why have you given me such an intense look as if I was about to bloody someone's nose? And unless my mirror lies my hair is grey, dear girl, quite grey.'

'I painted what I saw.' She was ready for him then, ready to rebut any criticism, for she must know it was a marvellous picture. And if it was unfinished at all it did not show, it was only a little angry in places.

'I wish you had told me what it was to be like,' he said helplessly.

'I did not realize you were expecting a sober head of a respectable surgeon. I simply agreed to paint the man.'

'You have done so indeed. I am thoroughly painted and smoked and exposed. I hoped never to show such an expression, such indignation, such deep lines of righteous fury. I look as if I am about to take a sword to the Army Board and decapitate every last man.'

'I am sorry you are not pleased, but then I never promise to please.'

Fanny came in. She had wondered from the low urgent conversation if they were coming to a quarrel, and her face was a little anxious as she stepped forward to see what Lizzie had done with that pale blob which had been the Doctor's face last time she had seen it. She gave a

187

gasp and plucked nervously at her cuff. 'Dear Liz, how splendid! How . . .' She thought better of 'remarkable' for fear it was misinterpreted; she had nothing but admiration for Lizzie's achievement. This was no blob, no anonymous blob, it was a living, dynamic, angry face. True, the quality of the brushwork in places matched the Doctor's expression, was distinctly aggressive, but . . .

'I never imagined it would turn out so well,' Fanny said, never having imagined it would turn out at all, it seemed to have wrung Lizzie's spirit so. After a moment she realized both artist and subject were sunk in thought. The smell of paint rose about them, the smell of paint and the apple boughs burning in the hearth.

'Oh dear, do you not like it?' asked Fanny.

There was a rustle of skirts as Lizzie flew by, making for the door. 'Of course he does not like it. He wished to be done as a stuffed exhibit, in a wig no doubt, and with a suitably grave expression.'

The door slammed. Fanny drew a long uneven breath. The Doctor rubbed his chin. 'It is a work of art in all truth, and I would be the first man to say damn the conventions, but she is quite right, I had not expected it to be like this. It is . . . I am . . . I am in a state of undress, shall we say.'

Fanny looked, and looked again. 'Oh but she has you to the life. You have spoken of your poor ruined soldiers once or twice with just that expression, and of the shortcomings of your fellow surgeons.'

'A furious and impotent old man, you mean.'

Fanny laughed uneasily, and then came and tucked her hand through his arm. 'Dear me no! Or is that how you feel? Has she struck the wrong note only by striking the right one? Poor Lizzie. She perceives with a . . . with a brilliant eye. But there, I believe you have had your money's worth, she has wept and howled over that painting, it has given her more heartache than anything she has ever done.'

'Oh, I am afraid I have not paid for it yet.'

They had reached the door. Fanny hung on his arm a

moment, deeply serious. 'You must go back to the army, they need you, those poor men, flogged to death at home and flogged to their deaths on battlefields; they need a man who can feel as deeply as that.'

'You are grown very grave, madam.'

'Am I? Ah well, it will pass off, I daresay.'

There was a clatter of cups and Kitty appeared with a tray. Miss Lizzie had gone out walking, she informed them, in only a thin cloak and with no proper shoes.

'It cannot be helped,' said Fanny, 'by this time she will be halfway to Stretfield, she will be going such a pace. There is nothing to be done if she is in one of her queer moods, she will walk it out and come home like a lamb. But you have no pony,' peering out, 'why did you not bring your pony?'

'Jary borrowed him to ride to Westdene, his bay horse – or is it a brown one, I can never tell – is lame, and the black is not eating up or whatever the expression is, they fear he is sickening for something. I have refused my opinion, however, I will not soon forget how they all railed at me about the bull, the anaemic bull.'

'Mr Savage on your pony! His feet will touch the ground!' They were outside. The cold struck them, the bitter wind from the east. 'I hope you do not think too badly of me for encouraging him the other day, Doctor.'

'It is none of my business, of course.'

'But you looked at me uncommon sharp, and well you might. But you are wrong if you think I am a-dangle after a rich man. Lizzie will provide for me in my old age, she will be charging a hundred guineas a picture by then and she will never see me starve. Flirting with Mr Savage is a sweet pleasure, it takes me back to my youth, and it is a wretched long time since I was kissed by anyone so young and handsome. I do not believe you are a man to grudge me that.'

He put on his hat, saying she must go in, it was too cold, too cold by far, and she had the feeling she was lowered in his esteem, that she should not have spoken and made light of it, that neither her behaviour or her

189

subsequent explanation of it to him had been at all lady-like and he felt it and thought the less of her. It saddened her a little because she liked him, but, 'Kisses are not so easy to come by at forty-five,' she said to herself by way of consolation as she went in.

It would have taken a bold horse to get the better of Jary Savage but the Doctor's pony had many an attempt on the Westdene road. Jary, whose feet did not quite reach the ground, but who in one easy movement might have reached to cuff the animal on the nose, grew tired of all this nonsense and brought him home at a gallop, going twice round the park at Ramillies for good measure.

'You oont ever tire him out,' was Millett's comment, taking the reins as Jary dismounted, 'he'd run from here to Norwich and back agin and then some.'

'He nearly had me in the river,' Jary complained to the Doctor, finding him eating bread and cheese by the fire, a grey cat on his lap, 'How you stay in the saddle I cannot imagine. Why is there none for me?' lifting covers and moving dishes. 'Alex, you have eaten my supper. And what is that cat doing? Where did you get it?'

'It is your cat. At least, it's a Ramillies cat.'

'I never knew we had any cats, only in the stables.'

'Did you not? Two have slept on my bed every night: grey mysterious creatures, this one and another with a white paw.'

Mrs Clark sent in more bread and cheese and a jug of ale and the remains of a cold duck. Jary sat eating, toasting his toes, and talking of Stephen Fisher and his architect, Sir James Braile who was being harried by Mrs Whiteley over the Diddlers, and Calloway in a distracted, mumpish mood.

'He is right of course. It is pointless to pursue this case over ownership. I have told him to give it up. We will build the cottages and move the people and that will be that.'

They sank into a kindly drowsiness, talking partridges and ships and coffee beans, for Jary had tired himself out with diplomacy in Calloway's office and was a little bored even by his beloved drains and the new wells. And then, his eyes half-closed, he noticed for the first time the canvas, its back to the room.

'Your portrait? Why is it hiding away in a corner?'

'Because it is still wet. It would have been at Foley yet but the artist could not bear it in her sight a moment longer. I had not been back here two hours before Lussom delivered it in the carriage with Miss Rayner's compliments and if I did not care to spoil it I must stand it undisturbed in some cool dry room for a week or two. We had the devil's own job getting it indoors without smudging it.'

'Don't tell me you have fallen out with Lizzie Rayner?'

Jary reached the picture, turning it round and lifting it to lodge it on a chair, stepping back and frowning. 'Mother of God!'

'It is something wonderful, is it not?'

Jary took another step back. 'Wonderful? Yes, wonderful. She has your very spirit. Do you know, you looked exactly like that when you came down to tell me that poor miserable girl had died, at the inn.'

They looked at the portrait together, in silence, and a mild anxiety assailed them both at the same time: that Miss Lizzie Rayner might find this passionate, animated portraiture too modern for fashionable London as yet.

'Her picture of old Fisher was excellent too,' Jary said, 'but in a more conventional style. That would go down all right at the Academy. But this? I wonder what she is doing with mine.'

They sat and wondered together for a while, and the house settled into its evening routine: Kate sent to bed, Mrs Fipson by her great fire mending linen, Mrs Clark coming in on the stroke of ten to ask if the gentlemen needed anything else. Once Jary cocked his head as if he heard something he had not expected to hear: the distant wail of a small baby woken, perhaps. Now and again a log slipped a little in a shower of sparks. It was all a very long way from the green lawns and fountains at Helen's

Mount, the palms by the beach below the house, his very first home, and from his second, that elderly wooden house where he had run barefoot and forgotten all his manners, and from the mango trees and the clear clear water and his ships and the small hilltop he owned and where he had been going to build himself a summer house . . . It was a very long way too from squalid fields where the dawn only broke to show scavengers and stretcher parties moving about, and from the improvised hospitals, the shacks and barns and noble houses outside which the pile of severed limbs would grow and grow.

'Where will you go?' Jary asked the Doctor.

'Abroad, yes abroad. I will go back to India maybe, I have friends in the Company, I may have some influence there.'

'And all because of this girl in Norfolk.'

'No, no, not all because of her. I have never liked to stay too long in one place. I have never belonged anywhere in particular. I used to believe the desire to be up and away would slacken with age but age is only teaching me that desires of all kinds remain unfortunately keen, perhaps even increase. No, dear Jary, I shall take a ship to India again. If I cannot be of use out there there is no hope for me.'

14

They had closed the trunk. There was nothing to do now but wait for the post-chaise. Outside there was a deep frost, a strange winter stillness, a sky the colour of thrush eggs. Lizzie paused at the window to take it in, seeing the elms stark against the pale land. For a brief moment it all seemed inexpressibly dear and she did not want to leave it. How often she had painted it, either from this window or from further afield, her sketchbook on her knee. For a moment she was aware of conflict in her very soul, conflict between her desire to live quietly in a beloved place and her need to succeed at her one talent. She would not see the black elm buds burst this year and the young green run shivering in the April wind the whole length of the hill; she would not see the gulls drifting down on the first soft breath of summer air, or the lapwings, or the snipe in the marsh by the pool, or hear the pheasants jugging in the dusk. A great tearing sadness seized her and shook her thoroughly, and passed away.

'I believe I can hear the chaise,' she said.

'Lord, then we must get the trunk downstairs. What a price they will charge for being kept waiting.'

Stephen Fisher, anxious and obliging, appeared at the foot of the stairs, consulting his watch every two minutes. He was to accompany Lizzie to London. Though he was dressed with great care for Fanny's benefit – he still hoped, he fed on hope – in his worry he had somehow cast adrift his neckcloth and undone his waistcoat and his hair, so artfully arranged, was falling in his eyes.

'They are never to be relied on,' was his verdict as the chaise pulled up, half an hour late, and he was sharp with the postillion even though the poor man had a perfectly legitimate excuse, for one of the horses had pitched on his knees crossing the ford and Foley had been difficult to find, no sane man would cram a carriage along these remote tracks, no signposts, no obliging natives.

'I will see you in summer, early summer,' said Fanny, gingerly kissing the cold face Lizzie presented. 'Have you forgotten anything?'

There were painting things, footwarmers, extra cushions, blankets, a great basket of pasties and buns and cold tea. Kitty climbed in clutching hat boxes and a little leather bag full of needles, pins, ribbons and lace. They stowed the baggage where they could, and Lussom ran out with grease for the horse's knees.

As a cheerful brisk parting it was a failure: Lizzie looked cold and withdrawn. She allowed Mr Fisher to fuss over her without so much as a glimmer of affront, and spoke very little, always in a dead, hushed voice. She waved, it was true, but it seemed a stiff, perfunctory wave to Fanny, who watched as the carriage drew away with foolish tears filling her eyes. She doubted Lizzie would ever return to Foley, once success and a suitor or two had knocked the memory of it awry, and she was sorry for that, for the house already seemed empty and she was an indifferent letter writer. She decided, as the post-chaise faded from view, that she must do something to cheer herself up or she would sit down and die of melancholy. She decided to put on her best bonnet and call on Mrs Stone, maybe she would be allowed to play a little on the piano, she did so love that little square piano, and all she had at Foley was a very very venerable harpsichord, as temperamental, as unsound, as demanding as a horrid old man, an extremely horrid old man. Since Kitty had gone with Lizzie and she could not take Susan from the kitchen unless she wished to cook her own supper, she ordered Lussom to saddle the pony. He was all that was left in the stables now she had sacrificed the ancient carriage and the two ill-matched horses for Lizzie's sake, and Lussom brought him round with a look of intense disapproval.

'You will have to walk beside me,' Fanny instructed,

'I cannot possibly go alone. The pony might take it into his head to turn round and come home.'

'You'll be lucky if you can make him leave home, the old devil, without a besom up his backside,' was Lussom's comment, half to himself, half to the pony's flank as he bent to settle the girth, but they got him out on the road eventually and set off in the tracks of the post-chaise, very sedately, Fanny clutching her bonnet and Lussom pacing self-consciously behind with a hazel switch and the face of a martyr.

Not long after Fanny had toiled away towards Paradise, Jary came bounding down Frenchmans on the Doctor's pony. He had been visiting the outlying farm, Hopes, where he had been royally entertained to boiled beef and turnips and a tremendous plum cake. Hopes had been bought by the Rayners many years before as a sort of dower house, for there had been a difficult and quarrel-some time when two Rayner widows and four unmarried daughters had threatened the peace and authority of the new young bride at the big house. They had all been packed off to Hopes, a large old draughty house conveniently close to the next village and there they had all lived until age or suitors reduced them to one very old lady and one very young one. The lane that led to the place was still called Ladies Lane.

Jary had stayed longer at Hopes than he had intended, but such hospitality could not be brushed aside. He had smelled the beef cooking as he had stepped in and his hair-raising ride on the pony had made it seem a great while since his breakfast. He had been determined to visit Foley on his way home to wish godspeed to Lizzie and to tell her, quite sincerely, how much he appreciated her portrait of himself, a noble portrait if a little stiff, not how he had imagined himself though perhaps thank God she had not revealed his soul the way she had the Doctor's, poor man. It struck him as he rode down to the gate that there was an unnatural stillness about the place, that he might have delayed too long at Hopes and that Lizzie was already sped.

Susan, emerging very flustered at his knock, informed him he was an hour and a half too late, Miss Rayner had been whisked away long long ago, and Mrs Jewkes was from home. However, there was a young lady in the parlour, a young lady most anxious, most determined to see the Doctor and brought to the wrong house through a series of misdirections.

So it was Jary first set eyes on Lady Gerard.

'Not Mr Savage of Ramillies?' was her immediate question when Susan had retreated after a mumbled introduction.

'The same. I am sorry but your name means nothing to me.'

'I am from High Common in Norfolk. And I am in something of a quandary,' said the slight, dark, self-confident woman before him. 'My friends have left me here in the mistaken belief this was where the Doctor was staying. They will not return until late afternoon. What will this Mrs Jewkes think of me, a perfect stranger and unescorted, occupying her house? What am I to do, Mr Savage? How do I find Dr French?'

'Oh, Fanny would not mind, and she is a great admirer of Alex. Still, you cannot stay, nothing to eat and no company and Alex only a half mile up the road. I tell you what, we must purloin the carriage.'

Oh no, said Susan, roused from basting her ducks, there was no carriage now, it had been sold for a song, poor old thing, seventy if it was a day, and the horses too. She didn't know anything about it except that Mrs Jewkes had mentioned economy, whatever that was, but economy was going to have a hard time paying for all the shoe leather wore out by all this walking, and though Miss Lizzie might go to the ball it would be at the expense of Lussom's knees, his knees always having been weak and him not at all partial to Shanks's pony.

'We are going to have to walk,' said Jary, looking at Lady Gerard's feet, unsuitably shod for even frosty

196

walking. 'We might discover some galoshes. There are patens in the back hall.'

They hunted about for a while and had just assembled the most hopeful looking footwear when Susan reappeared, spoon in hand, to say that if they wanted there was a pad in the stables on which Mr Jewkes's mother, a terrible old lady with no teeth, had ridden pillion for years. At this Lady Gerard sat down on a stool and laughed, her dark curls straying prettily across her wide forehead, and Jary said: 'Well, it would be better than walking, I suppose. But why do you think she mentioned the teeth, how could they have any bearing on riding pillion?'

'Heaven knows,' cried Lady Gerard, clutching her side and gasping, 'but come, quick, before we are given the minute by minute account of the old lady's last illness, there will be no getting away from it.'

The Doctor's pony danced about looking wicked while Jary struggled with the stiff old straps. Lady Gerard did not seem to mind it, and berated him in a tone of voice that made him stand still a whole half minute.

'You cannot expect me to believe the Doctor rides this pony?' she asked when Jary explained the animal's other shortcomings. 'He and horses do not . . . well, they are not compatible.'

'I have noticed. But he has survived so far. I am only afraid that this uncouth wretch has never had two people on his back before and may decide to get rid of us.'

Lady Gerard gave a merry laugh and scrambled up behind him from the mounting block. It was a scramble because she was not in a riding skirt so was rather hampered, but once up and with her hand on Jary's waist she seemed completely unconcerned, even when the pony squealed and lifted his heels. It occurred to Jary suddenly – why had he not thought of it before? – that this was the woman who had wrung old Alex's heart, that large, affectionate, most secretly kept organ he had hoped might never be wrung again in this life. The pony plunged, Jary sent him on with a harsh word and the small hand tightened on his coat. He said: 'No one will see us on this lane, it is very little used.'

'Would it be considered a scandal?' came the breathless voice from behind as the pony leaped sideways again in a proper temper.

'I was not thinking of myself, I was only . . .'

The pony stopped dead and refused to go on. Jary used his legs and voice to no effect. 'If I hit him he may do anything,' he said.

'If you do not we will have to walk,' said Lady Gerard and put her arm more firmly about his waist for extra purchase.

Jary hit him a stinging blow and the pony exploded in a series of bounds, so unsettling Jary never knew how his passenger stayed on, except that he felt that any minute his coat might be detached from its lining, the grip of her hand was so ferocious. They leaped along the lane past Cuckooland, and once Jary thought he heard a little cry of smothered laughter from behind, smothered against his broad back no less.

As they turned in at the gates he was thinking deep thoughts nothing at all to do with ponies, but all to do with women and their inevitable effect on men. Had she truly not known, he wondered? Could a woman, any woman, be ignorant of such effect? Could unwavering affection and concomitant sexual desire remain a secret between close friends? Or had she been too much in love with her future husband to notice? Even that possibility struck him as unlikely. She was not a shrinking girl, innocent and helpless, he knew she had brought a farm, a large farm, back from the brink of ruin, and that she had been married before to a drunken wastrel, and that – he must ask her about it if ever there was a moment – she owned a privateer. It struck him that if he were her new husband he would not care for her to ride pillion with strange men, especially if the dreadful behaviour of the horse meant a great deal of clinging close, and he might have mentioned it, by way of testing her mettle, but Ramillies was in sight.

When they dismounted and reached the front entrance they could hear the furious howling voice of Mrs Fipson accompanied by the harsh acerbic one of the Doctor cursing all women, goosegrease and camphor.

'I do not believe,' said Jary, his hand on the door, 'that we have found him in a sociable mood.'

The Doctor had been attending Kate, whose puny chest had been rubbed raw by liberal application of the cook's grandmother's salve. The Doctor, who had warned Mrs Clark that such a cough would not respond to barbaric remedies but should be carried out in the fresh air and fed with milk and eggs and good beef broth, had thrown the salve out of the window, had called Mrs Fipson a witch and a child-murderer, and had hurried away downstairs. Mrs Fipson had unwisely followed. They were at the foot of the stairs and in acrimonious dispute, Mrs Clark running to join them, when Jary walked in with Lady Gerard.

It is quite true the heart can miss a beat, thought the Doctor, feeling his own do so on the instant. She looked the same yet more mature, more confident than ever if that were possible, more alert. He had missed her more than he could say, she had been in his mind's eye all day sometimes and in lascivious dreams at night, but here she stood like a stranger, Ann yet not Ann; and Jary looking dark, and Mrs Clark confused and reddening, pulling Mrs Fipson away to the kitchen. The Doctor scowled. How he could scowl!

'Why, what a day it has been!' cried Jary, stepping into the breach. 'First I miss Lizzie Rayner, she was away hours before I reached Foley, then Lady Gerard comes to be abandoned at Foley by mistake and after a heart-stopping ride on your pony, your devilish disagreeable pony, finds you out of temper and the house in an uproar. I suppose there will be nothing for dinner either but potatoes and hashed rabbit.'

The Doctor had set his features into a kind of grinning mask, nothing if not deathly, and he murmured several platitudes about the pleasures of meeting old friends and

199

no, he was not out of temper but he had told the woman a thousand times not to use that heinous potion, it was enough to flay a pig.

They retired to the sitting room, a very elegant, chilly, little-used room. The Doctor said 'Lady Gerard?' with a sudden start of surprise at the precise moment Jary, terrified by such a silence, commended the lady's horsemanship; how she had stayed on that pad, sideways, no proper support, and tight skirts to boot he would never know. Perhaps he commended her too heartily, for he roused some memories of a singular escapade she had had on a horse belonging to her first husband, a great black horse troubled by the same temper currently being exhibited by the Doctor. For some reason the recollection of this particular adventure, which had ended in the lady's being decanted into the flowerbeds of the local big house, caused a silence even deeper than the first. Maybe it had taken place in the days before Lady Gerard had discovered her first husband a bigamist and the Doctor had discovered his fatal tenderness for her: at any rate they both looked rather queer. Jary cleared his throat and swung on the bell rope with such fury it threatened to detach rom the wire. Clarkie came at the run, appalled by the dinging below.

'Food? Hot negus, yes. What is there to eat? What has Mrs Fipson prepared, Clarkie?'

Mrs Clark backed away, horrified. She believed dinner was some kind of soup and cold pie, for the Doctor had said he would be out all afternoon and would not have anything on his return and Mr Savage had led them to believe he would be at Hopes all day.

They had banked on his being invited to dinner, Jary thought, and he excused himself, bowing to Lady Gerard and seeing something like alarm in her lovely eyes. Yes, he liked her. But was she asking him not to leave them alone? 'I will not be a moment,' he said, and meant it, though he 'was well aware murder could be accomplished in a moment and the kitchen was a great way off.

Mrs Fipson was roused by Jary appearing on her

threshold with an order to look out the lamb cutlets and wring the necks of as many fowls as she could catch, Lady Gerard and her friends were staying to dinner and must be well fed, the honour of Ramillies dictated it. Oh, said Mrs Fipson, still smarting from her brush with the Doctor, and what about a pigeon or two? They could victual an army with pigeons if an army were to call. Jary told her to mind her tongue and stamped furiously back to the hall, where he paused awkwardly by the sitting room door, wondering if he should stay away for another ten minutes, for half an hour. What was being said? It was not his business what was being said yet he longed to know, longed most childishly, for he was very fond of Alex and besides, thought of him as an example, admired not only his medical skill but his strongly practical nature, his continency, his *morality*. He thought that of all the men he had ever known the Doctor would most decidedly avoid all seven deadly sins, and by conscious choice, acknowledging their existence but stepping deliberately out of their path. He could not see Alex proud nor envious, and though he was often angry it was usually in the face of ignorance and unnecessary suffering, and as to lust, the thought of Alex in a brothel was absurd, though he would not scruple to enter to treat the inmates. On the other hand, there was Ann . . . The Doctor had given no indication he lusted after her, yet deep love and desire were usually bedfellows; a man did not often go about haggard and distressed without some great frustrated longing in the case.

Jary hesitated with his hand on the door knob. What if they were in an embrace? He coughed before he went in but found them miles apart, an acre of carpet between.

'I have settled dinner,' he said, and by the quality of the silence judged that they had been making such stilted, guarded conversation his entrance could only be welcomed. 'My housekeeper is available whenever you wish, Lady Gerard: hot water, mirrors, anything you care to name. Alex, the fire is nearly out. What are you thinking of?'

He rose, and his face quite startled Jary. 'I have something to do,' he said, making for the door, 'I will be back shortly.'

Jary whacked the slow-burning logs with some severity, wishing they were the Doctor's head. What could he say? Good God, and he had invited this woman and her friends to dinner? Friends? Not her new husband?

'You will wish you had not come,' he said, feeling that her troubled reception and all this obvious awkwardness reflected badly on the hospitality of his house, and Jary was a deeply hospitable man, would, as the Doctor had once surmised, treat even his enemies with loving kindness provided they were not two-faced, deceiving dogs. In this case the remark seemed to take on another meaning, more sharp and personal. He realized it as soon as she did not make a reply and looked up at once, contrite. 'I meant that . . .'

'You meant kindly, I know. But you do not have to mind, I am used to Alex's moods and tempers. Even when we were the best of friends he was always unpredictable, flying out for no apparent reason or shutting himself away.' She spoke cheerfully but it was a false cheerfulness, and her 'Even when we were the best of friends' suggested that she felt keenly that though they had been in the past they were not any longer and might never be again.

'I am sorry he did not come to your wedding,' Jary said, 'I give you joy, madam, and the hope of many happy years for you both. I am afraid I never asked if your husband was to be of the party expected for dinner.'

She blushed and looked very strange. Then: 'Of course, Alex has never told you my name, has he? Oh, that would be just like him, and even more like him not to explain when I arrived and we were alone . . . I was Ann Mathick when he knew me first and then against all advice, his included, I married Harry Gerard,' and a peculiar soft look, the ghost of an old, remembered affection passed over her face, 'who died at Copenhagen.'

And was a bigamist, thought Jary, he told me that much, though no names, no other personal particulars. You thought you had never been married to the drunken young pup and then it turned out you had but the other woman hadn't, so she was the one left crying in the cold. So he died at Copenhagen, in the battle. I wonder how that came about.

'You see,' Ann continued, picking at her skirt, 'I should be Mrs Claverden by now, the Doctor was expecting it. But I am not, and he is horribly put about and . . .' Her eyes looked straight into Jary's own, as if measuring and judging the kind of man he was, and she smiled, a small strained smile but a smile nonetheless. 'He is very cross because I am not married. As soon as he knew he grew quite ridiculous, unreasonable. He said I should never have put it off, that I should be safely tied to William, every trouble behind me.'

Jary put down his poker and went to sit, his hands on his knees. He said gently: 'I understand Alex was Mr Claverden's friend.'

'He was, he is. I brought a letter from William – he is in the Navy, has just changed into a new ship, and all correspondence has been going astray for months. Then three days ago a whole bag of letters came, they must have been to Halifax and back or halfway to the Cape, every letter William had written since he left . . . I knew these Norwich friends who were visiting an old cousin in Westdene and I decided to deliver Alex's in person – William enclosed it in one of mine because he had no idea where Alex was.'

'Has Alex read it?'

'Yes' – a small significant yes, and a hurt look – 'he jumped up and accused me of being foolish and inconsistent: why had I put off the wedding till the spring? What was the point? This peace was nothing, supposing war started again and William could not get home in the spring? Do you know' – in a defeated voice, she was not often defeated, he could tell – 'I believe I should not stay

203

to dinner. And my friends are not expecting to, they will be quite cheerful to stop in Bungay.'

'Of course you must stay. Alex is . . . 'But who could say what Alex was? He had been resigned to this marriage and now there was no marriage, at least, there was to be no marriage in the near future, a bewildering state of affairs.

'There is murder being done in the kitchen,' said the Doctor, coming in with a rush of cold air and followed by the better-behaved of the two young spaniels, a black and white, most appealing youngster indeed, who ran straight up to Jary and put his head on his knee. 'Lie down, sir, and be quiet,' was Jary's command, pretending to be unmoved, but the dog remained, wagging its feathery tail and flattening its ears in adoration.

'Jary, did you hear? There is murder afoot in the kitchen. Either Mrs F is slaughtering the boy from the stables or Mrs Clark is going at them both with a hatchet. I have never heard such a row. It is not Kate, the poor flayed child, for she is still in bed. I have just been up to her.'

'I know what it is,' said Jary, fondling the dog's ears, 'young Jack brought the fowls indoors alive instead of wringing their necks in the yard. It would be just like him.'

Ann laughed, and so did Jary, and the dog continued to wag its tireless tail, but the Doctor looked bleak, indescribably bleak, and bowed out and shut the door.

Dinner was unfashionably early because Ann's friends, the Grahams, wished to avoid travelling too much in the dark, and anyway Jary was always hungry and the evening meal at Ramillies swung violently between half past four and six o'clock depending on the state of the kitchen. The kitchen today was in a turmoil, the fire as hot as Mrs Fipson's temper and the stable boy's ears, but the wretched hens, dispatched, plucked, drawn and trussed in twenty minutes, were well on the way to being cooked before the parties were assembled.

Mr and Mrs Graham were bookish people, very devout, kindly and stiff mannered: Jary changed into his magenta coat, caused them something of a shock. The Doctor, who in moments of crisis generally sank to his most odious and disreputable, turned up in his old coat and with gravy on his linen. As if in deliberate defiance his hair stood up on end, he might not have put a comb through it for weeks, and although this was not a formal dinner but only a cheerful, extempore affair and the Grahams themselves were in travelling clothes, he might, as Jary said, coming across him in the hall looking like some shady low character, have put on a decent wig just for once, and a clean shirt and stockings that matched.

It was Ann who saved the occasion, Jary could have kissed her, kissed her thoroughly. And given any encouragement he might well have done so, he had long missed her kind of pleasant female company. She made him talk about Jamaica, drawing in the Grahams as best she could – Mr Graham had once visited Boston, which after all was in approximately the right area of world and on the right side of the Atlantic ocean. The Doctor could only be got to grunt so they ignored him and had a very happy time in spite of him, ranging on from Boston to merchant ships and so to commerce and coffee beans and breadfruit, bearing away for minimum wages and increased prices and the tedious balance never properly achieved between too little labour and too much, and coming home by way of Norfolk sheep and the correct crop to follow turnips in a strict rotation.

'Thank you,' said Jary, meeting Ann at the foot of the stars the moment before the carriage came round, 'I could never have managed that alone.'

He managed, however, to see them all into the carriage, to say his goodbyes, help arrange the rugs, make sure the glass was up. He crushed Ann's ice-cold fingers in his large hand and looked her in the eye, a formidable look, for Jary had a formidable capacity for wishing he could put the world to rights. 'You must not mind him . . . You must not take it to heart. He has . . . he has been crossed

205

in love,' and in a low, low voice, painfully aware the Grahams were listening to every word, 'I . . . I own it did not occur to me at first, he is . . . hmm, old and whimsical and ill-looking, but there are ladies find him attractive, I know; only not this one, this . . . this . . .' A vision of Ann jumping a great black horse over the box hedges of a gentleman's garden was blurred by a sudden recollection of that statue in his knot garden, the lady with the arrows: 'Not this Diana, she is out of reach for so many reasons.'

He stepped back, hoping they would meet again, his house was hers, his house and everything it could provide. She was not pretty, he thought, not beautiful, but oh those eyes and that slow smile and the bold confident lift of her dark head with its soft short hair. Damn it, if he were Alex he would declare himself, risk everything on the one throw. What was there to lose? And this to gain.

'I am sorry it is love,' was her whispered comment, 'love can be such a difficult, troublesome business.'

Jary went in, and found the Doctor and the dog together in possession of the sofa.

'You have behaved very ill, Alex. I never thought to see you behaving so at my table. Get off there, you young . . .' This to the dog who had begun to thump his tail again. 'For Heaven's sake, Alex, stop encouraging all these animals to take life easy, cats on the bed, dogs on chairs . . . He is a gundog, he is to go out and put up the birds and fetch them in when I have knocked them down. He is not to lounge about like Paris, warming his curls by the fire.'

The dog thumped his tail more heartily but Jary yanked him from his soft bed and shot him out of the door, all his silky curls flying.

'She gave no reason for putting off the wedding,' said the Doctor quietly when the door was closed and Jary was standing by the hearth, 'and he only mentioned it as a fact, something agreed between them and almost of no account. He looks forward to May, he says, and begs me to attend unless I am abroad or with the army, unavoidably engaged.'

'And shall you go?'

The Doctor turned a grey face in his direction. He seemed to have become emaciated, shrunken and old. This was how he would look in another twenty years, thought Jary, and all because of an unsatisfied longing for a woman, one woman, when the world was filled with millions of women, most of them more than acceptable and some few exceptional, amazing creatures.

The clocks struck. Mrs Clark came in to ask about candles, supper, the roaming dog who had been up in all the bedrooms and had eaten some tobacco. Somewhere in the middle of all this Jary was aware of the Doctor's voice, low and sad, and although he was not aware of hearing the words properly at the time they returned to him with a piercing clarity when he himself was half way to bed, his shirt in his hands and the Ramillies draughts round his bare shoulders: 'I believe I must not see her again.'

15

'There are eggs,' said the Doctor, 'and eggs. I suppose they will come to resemble the real thing in time. My dear, I mean no disrespect to your pullets but these would be less than a mouthful even for Henriette.'

They were standing in the little orchard at the back of the house, and the pullets were pecking warily some yards off, as if conscious they were behindhand with production, that they risked the ignominy of the stewpot along with their master's wrath. It was two days since Ann had ridden back into the Doctor's life and he was only just recovering his humour, a sour, awkward, straining humour and little enough of that. He had spent the morning with Plesset attending two patients Plesset had given up, one pneumonia and one extensive infection of a fearful wound left to fester. They had nearly breathed their last the moment Dr French came in, he had been like an east wind, ice-cold with disappointment, anguish, self-hatred and despair. A man with no faith in himself, however momentary, has no business trying to snatch others from the pit. But after all he had been skilful and kind, and he was going back this evening to amputate the infected limb, it was all he could do, and if the shock did not break the boy's fragile hold on life then there was still hope, the very slenderest hope.

Jary had noticed this change in the Doctor, this minutest of recoveries. Together they viewed the new hens – the old grey cockerel's new young miserable harem – gave some withered, over-wintered apples to the horses, and walked down to watch Hawke and his men resume the battle of the water garden.

'I will have a mass, a whole sheet of iris,' said Jary, warming to the subject, 'and a boat house.'

'You will ruin the effect if you throw up odd buildings here and there.'

'It will be hardly noticeable, it will be in a clump of willow. The bridge will draw the eye away.'

They stared down into the muddy craters of this rural skirmish, and both were occupied with very different thoughts. Jary saw waterlilies, and wind-ruffled water beneath his lazy oar; the Doctor saw the dead of his actual, long-ago battlefields, not so very different from this one but infinitely more bloody and ghoulishly littered with human remains. He sighed. It would be as well to fight this depression. It was nothing new but it was becoming relentless.

'When will it be finished?' he asked.

'They assure me before June. Next year, of course, it will look much better. I only hope Hawke keeps to the job while I am at Helen's Mount. I shall not be back before winter, and with you away to India – Alex, won't you reconsider, must it be India? – with you away and Charles Calloway set against the whole scheme, who can I leave in charge?'

They gazed again. Two or three of the workmen gazed back for a moment, halting their steady shovelling in the soggier depths. They had the pale blue far-seeing eyes of the northern peoples, of the opportunist invaders whose warships had once pushed their quiet way up the local creeks.

'How strange you will find it,' Jary said suddenly, 'back with scabies and the pox and all those damnable mosquitoes.'

The Doctor poked at a clod with his toe. 'Why should one be so pierced by a woman's smile at such an advanced age? Why does that sort of thing not die away with youth?'

'Advanced age? You? You are scarcely ten years older than I am, and Hawke is half your age again and still hale and sprightly – too much so when it comes to adding figures. And Stephen Fisher is your contemporary and yet thinks of pursuing Fanny Jewkes to the altar; if sheer persistence pays off he is bound to get her there too, I have rarely known a man stick at a cause so long. And . . .' looking about the gardens as if they might inspire him to a more judicious example, 'Alex, there is the parson!'

'Where?'

'Coming up the avenue. I swear it is Odbold. Quick! Perhaps if we are cunning he may not see us. Make for the river.'

Like shady conspirators they slunk along beneath the willows but a faint hallooing pursued them, very very faint but difficult for an honest man to ignore. They held their way doggedly, in silence, and at last came to the pool. The crackling of twigs and a nearer shout told them they were still being tracked.

'Hell's teeth!' cried Jary, plunging into the alder thicket.

'Oh Dr French, I have palpitations!' declared Odbold, clutching at his chest, 'I am faint!'

The Doctor made him sit down in a clump of old rushes, made him draw deep invigorating breaths. The March wind was chilly, spring being young and capricious, and the parson gradually paled from crimson to pewter, a very strained, bloodless, turgid colour, his usual.

'I will walk back to the house with you,' said the Doctor, 'you have had enough exertion for today. Was your errand so urgent? May I be of any help?'

'I must see Mr Savage. I have some . . . oh terrible news, terrible! But was he not with you a moment ago? I thought . . . But then, what with my eyes and the running . . . Dr French, Dr French, the worst has happened, the very worst. Mrs Whiteley has turned out the Diddlers and is this moment pulling down the buildings.'

'Can she do so? Is such an unchristian act within the law?'

The parson stopped, leaning rather heavily on his arm. 'They have not paid their rent,' he said as if that

210

explained all, excused all, and would go some way towards convincing the Doctor how unspeakable the Diddlers were.

'I understood they could not, they are mostly very old, infirm – I have visited myself, there is one case of senile dementia, and the youngest Farrow girl is subject to fits – or very young, and even the able-bodied are refused employment. They pick up stones, I hear, and scare rooks and pigeons. To all intents and purposes they might as well be lepers.'

The Doctor guided Odbold round the piles of earth and the deep holes, and at an appropriate distance from the house raised his voice for Millett.

'I must see Mr Savage,' cried the parson, 'they are his responsibility. Why, the whole village knows he has fought Mrs Whiteley tooth and nail for the rents – the rents they never pay, Doctor, never, and never intend to, the wastrels – and is building them new cottages by Pigg Lane.'

'You are not sympathetic, I see. Millett, help Mr Odbold along. I will open the doors. We must put him in the library, there is sure to be a good fire.'

'They're in my orchard,' squeaked the parson. 'Can you understand, sir? They have come to me – to me! They say I must give them assistance. How am I to assist them? There are sixteen souls to keep and feed, old women and babies and young women with barely a rag to make them decent, and an old man with a rash, a dreadful rash. Suppose it should be contagious?'

'For sure it is a skin complaint, terrible to look at and to have but no great cause for alarm. But did not Christ say: feed my lambs, feed my sheep?'

'It was a spiritual reference. It was not meant to be taken literally in this present age, this year 1802.'

'But was not Christ an eminently practical man? He fed the five thousand, did he not, on very slender means.'

The parson choked. Millett gave a toothless grin. The library fire was blazing and the Doctor made it blaze

211

more, tucking Odbold into a chair with a rug hurried in by Mrs Clark, her eyes popping, her voice very reverent.

'A glass of madeira,' said the Doctor firmly, shooting a glance at the housekeeper, 'a half pint of madeira, and rest, and a pill. I shall make you up a pill. You have had a great shock. Mrs Clark, you will kindly run for another rug and a hot brick.' And there, that will boil all his mean carping objections, that will stew him, the uncharitable scrub, he could have added, but calmly bowed himself out and took hold of Millett's sleeve in the hall.

'Run down to the pool and tell Mr Savage the cottagers are evicted. Tell him the poor souls are camped about the parson's orchard like gipsies and that the parson will surely die if we do not remove them.'

Millett grinned. 'By the pool, your honour?'

'Somewhere by. I left him by the alders.'

Jary rehoused the Diddlers where he could: at Hopes, in two hovels on the Westdene road due for demolition, in a shepherd's hut at Low Paradise. His task was made a little easier by the defection of the Farrows, who had not been seen since Prince Whiteley and the bailiffs had ridden into the Diddlers. Kate said she thought they would have gone to Westdene, there was an uncle there, and the oldest girl Jinny was near her time. She did not seem concerned, she had grown used to life at Ramillies, comfortable and clean for the first time in her life, and her affection for her family was in the nature of an unthinking tribal association: they were not loving or demonstrative but they would stand and fight together if the need arose. And who was the father of Jinny's child? She did not know, it could be one of the charcoal burners or even the eldest Fipson boy who had graduated from throwing stones to sporting under hedges.

'Never mind,' said Jary, 'they are gone to Westdene or wherever and that is five fewer mouths to feed.'

'Sure it is the job of the Parish to feed them,' the Doctor ventured.

'There is some dispute about their eligibility. Would

212

you believe, the parish boundry is in contention now, it crosses somewhere near Cockshoot and the foot of Beke's Wood.'

'How people love to quarrel, or prose away about nice points while their fellows are in want. But then, I long ago decided all committees are made up of idle men, else where would they find time to serve and prattle so?'

'My Aunt Cissie used to say she had never met a philanthropist whose philanthropy was not all in the mouth and mind and never in the legs and hands. I thought it was a deuced odd way of putting it but I know what she meant. Mrs Jewkes, for instance, would not stop to consider, she would march in at once with a pot of jam and six loaves and milk for the baby. I know for a fact she has given away every last one of Lizzie Rayner's old dresses and I saw Tom Moore at Paradise yesterday after a job and looking the gentleman in Mr Jewkes's riding coat.'

They were in the garden and there was a thin drizzle falling. It was a cold damp pale day altogether, enlivened so far only by Stephen Fisher's dashing up the avenue in his whiskey to tell Jary the cottage foundations were in, was it not exciting, and dashing away again for an urgent appointment: his cousin was arriving from Lincoln. And: 'Where on earth is Lincoln?' was Jary's question, surveying the hoofmarks spoiling his weeded gravel.

They inspected the peach trees – not an encouraging sight – and the hens, and the horses. It had become a regular round, a ritual, and even Millett had entered into the spirit of things and now each morning proudly presented the horses, the ponies, the two dogs and an immaculate tack room for inspection. He grumbled in their wake, they were always aware of his defiant beady eyes and that red fleshy nose, but his grumbling was only another part of the ritual, he could not move without grunting and mumbling and finding fault, a silence would have been unnatural.

It was in the quiet of the knot garden, misted over with rain, that Jary pulled back the rampaging box and stared hard at the lady with the arrows, saying as he did so: 'I wish she had not lost her nose. She reminds me of someone I once knew.'

'With or without a nose?'

'You are being facetious. Come on, let's get in out of this wet. I believe Blake said he would call today about the changes to the cottage chimneys. Why, should you think, it is so difficult to design a chimney?'

They went in, and Jary pored over diagrams and mathematical signs and strange equations while the Doctor wrote to Louise Barsham and to William and then to Ann, this last, a most disgraceful, three-line note, a token communication like a peck on the cheek. The drizzle turned to rain and blew against the panes over and over, but neither man looked up, absorbed each in his own world, his own problems. But at last Jary sat back and sighed, and threw down his pencil, and said: 'I believe I will go to sea again.'

'I have noticed some men cannot keep away from salt water once they're addicted. But I thought you were a landsman at heart.'

'I sometimes feel I have spent half my life at sea. I learned to sail when I lived at Montego Bay, just a child. It meant fresh fish for supper and that was something. Then there was all the time I spent in deep-sea ships, merchantmen and the like, and coastal schooners, and a whaler once, but only once, I could not stand that life and the voyages are too long, three years is nothing. I was only glad to be wrecked – there was a fire, we took to the boats, and a good thing we were off the coast of Brazil and not down by the Horn – and picked up by a brig Nantucket bound.' He was lost in memory now, places and people coming alive again before his open inward-looking eyes, and he followed a brief unsentimental description of the Nantucket brig with a sudden intake of breath at a new, more moving vision and: 'I first met Nell at sea.'

The Doctor did not ask who Nell was, he did not have to. He had long been aware that though Jary was an

214

amorous man he was not promiscuous, and that of the women he had enjoyed only one had ever touched his heart and she long gone, fled, married, dead, who knew. So he sat and smoked, his letter to Ann folded in his hand, and he waited, looking into the fire. After a little Jary stirred and said:

'I was only fourteen or so then. She was married to a man called Chevens from an old family in the Carolinas; he was an acquaintance of my uncle and was often in Kingston. He was nothing to look at, tall and dark and skinny, and scarred from some set-to with Indians, but he was good company and could sail a boat within an inch of her life and then get another knot out of her. He had a sloop, a flyer, and he used to bring himself to Jamaica, most of his crew slaves from his estate, black and white, poor devils. I don't believe he was much of a master to them, I know they were afraid of him, but he was more humane than many I have known since. Once or twice I went along for a voyage, it was something to do with learning to be a gentleman and keeping me occupied at the same time because my uncle knew I liked to run about the rigging and play sailor. And Nell was always there.'

She had been in her middle twenties then, at least in her middle twenties, had had two small children. She had been tall and slim and dark and very fine, fine in every way, as loving and loyal and open as she was beautiful and full of fun, and Jary supposed he had always loved her, loved her from the very first moment. Admiration at first, an exquisite sense of shyness making him blush when he looked at her, and then that urgent desire to please, to be noticed, and after a year or two, though their meetings were few, the voyages perhaps twice a summer, a constant almost unconscious adoration, a deep knowledge that she was the best, the truest metal, that he would never find another like her.

'What became of her?'

Jary surfaced, looked about his room as if he had never seen it before, and sank away again into memory. 'She

215

came to Helen's Mount years later as my uncle's . . . guest. Chevens was dead by then, killed in the war. Nell had lost everything: home, land, parents, a child. My uncle took her in, I don't know how it came to be arranged. Perhaps she wrote to him. She was . . . he made her . . .'

'I see.'

'I'm damned if I do' – in a low savage voice, all the old wounds opened – 'I did not at the time and I do not now. Why a beautiful woman like that should take up with a drunken old planter and . . . But there,' with an effort, 'it is all in the past, and who is to say what a woman might not do, no family, no friends, no roof over her head? I suppose he offered her some kind of security, I doubt he ever gave her money, he could rarely be parted from that, and she had the youngest child who had survived, four or five years old by then. Of course he sent her away afterwards, crabbed spiteful old man. I never knew what became of her. I was twenty-two when I got home from Brazil – nearly four years away – and no one would tell me anything, only that she had gone back to the Southlands with the child.'

'I can guess the crime for which you were sent to Brazil but it strikes me as a harsh punishment. You could not blame a woman for growing tired of being an old man's whore.'

'It was worse than you think, I was knocked on the head and delivered to the boat. Jamaica was below the horizon when I came round. I am not sure which of those acts I hate him for most: what he did to Nell or having me shipped away without any choice in the matter. I have often thought of it.'

But the memory of his fear, real hideous fear, and of his blazing desire to strike his uncle dead, of his subsequent hopeless search for Nell and the action-filled years that had dulled his picture of her so much that now he could only recall a vague outline, a way of walking, and her voice; all that was nothing to the one clear vision, of himself and Nell on the verandah at Helen's Mount, a

216

tall ungainly youth of eighteen and a lovely black-haired woman looking deep into an empty wine glass and then up, her eyes great pools of dark. She had not spoken, the look alone was consent. He would never have touched her if she had not given him permission: he did not care for his uncle but his own honour forbade the sharing of a woman like a common strumpet. In any case, she had been much older than him, and experienced, he would never have dared approach her; and on top of all there was his overwhelming distaste, his private anguish, for a woman he had idolized reduced to sleeping in his uncle's bed. It had never left him, the little bitter residue of that disgust, though he could now imagine the circumstances that had driven her to it; no doubt she had never been quite what he imagined, neither so good nor so chaste. It had been with him since the moment he found out, coming on her leaving his uncle's room, confused by disbelief, with him even during that brief night of urgent desire and amazing happiness he had found in her arms. He felt that happiness again now, the pale ghost of it, piercing and sweet, and now as then it was gone in a moment.

But he would always think of her with deep affection.

His mind ran on, to other women, lesser pleasures, lesser joy. Eventually there rose a rather blurred image of Miss Johnson in a pale blue gown and with pearls in her little ears, as quick and accomplished and cultured as any rich young lady from Boston to Buenos Aires, and no kind of hypocrite, quite open about everything. He blinked, trying to imagine her here in this room, but when he looked up he seemed to see a quite different figure with a purposeful, eager walk, and a face full of fierce, eager character: a wide mouth, a most pugnacious nose.

'Oh, damn women!' cried Jary.

Mr Fisher continued to call at Foley though he did not yet have the nerve to press his suit again. Having been rejected once he was in no hurry to be rejected again, and it was pleasant to be friends, Fanny was unstintingly generous to her friends. Often he walked with her to Ramillies to view the great dig, for there was a recognizable pattern to the earthworks now, though Jary's boathouse, newly built on piles, looked like a native hut or a superior kind of hide: it was thatched, with gothic windows. The willows which were to screen it were as yet only a couple of feet high and Fanny, to whom its peculiar eccentricity appealed, dubbed it The Lookout and made a point of walking round it every time she came.

The end of March also saw the walls of the cottages rising, a project now so close to Mr Fisher's heart he was there every day, unrolling the plans and talking over detail with the builder or with Blake. Meanwhile the Diddlers managed as best they could in their makeshift homes, and Jary rode to view the ruins of their old ones with a mixture of relief and fury. Calloway counselled caution, seeing the fire in Jary's eye, but it was Mrs Whiteley who cast them into confusion. She and the vile Pellow discovered a map on which the site was marked as Whiteley land – 'A doctored map, no doubt,' cried Jary, 'I have never known such a grasping woman' – and she put in an audacious claim for all of Cockshoot up to the very trees of Beke's Wood.

'You made her nephew look a fool and this is the result,' said the Doctor over breakfast, when Mrs Clark had come in bearing this unwelcome news from Westdene.

'She will not get the better of me.'

'I am sure she will not, I have always thought you would be a hard man to shift from his principles – but Calloway is no timid fool when he advises you to examine your principles closely. What does it matter if she gains another four or five boggy acres? You will not miss them. My dear, if you wish to defeat her malice while avoiding a long and bloody lawsuit – has it occurred to you she may have even considered beggaring you by this means? – make her a gift of the land, draw your new boundary very black and strong, and present her with the contract – she will be astounded.'

Jary considered. 'It would take the wind out of her sails,' he admitted, 'but what if she refused?'

'She could not, it is what she is suing for after all. She would appear ridiculous.'

Afterwards, when they had strolled out to see the pullets, Jary added, 'Yes, I will do it. I will ride to Westdene tomorrow and see Calloway,' and after a pause: 'I am going to leave Stephen in charge when I go. He has the measure of Hawke and he understands figures, draws up the most careful accounts. They dare not pilfer a single brick from the cottages, he would know it had gone at once. Stone mentioned him yesterday when I met him in the village, he said it was astounding how competent and srong-minded Stephen is become. It is getting away from that rascally old man his father.'

'When do you leave?'

'I thought we could travel down together about the first of the month, you to Chatham or wherever; I have to be in Falmouth by about the sixth. I have a friend, a little bald chubby man – you would never credit the fierce old sea dog he can become in pirate waters – who is leaving for Bridgetown then. He has a schooner, French-built, a fast sailer.'

'And from Bridgetown?'

'Who knows? The whole of that sea is home to me. There will be no trouble reaching Kingston.'

They gazed at the pullets, still touchingly young, and who, to the last and littlest, ignored the old cockerel, who could not do anything for them but pecked alone at a distance. 'Millett says they go for him all together, mad enough to have his eyes out, like a flock of nuns at a man in their parlour. D'you think there's something wrong with them?'

'More likely something wrong with him,' said the Doctor, watching the cockerel move away as the pullets came in his direction. 'Why not obtain a younger, virile mate for your ladies and then perhaps they will quickly tire of their virginity. Either that, or let them do without. He is unnecessary, poor thing, you would still have your eggs without him.'

They walked on to the stables. There were fewer doves since a particularly thorough cull a month back, and those that were left were crooning pleasantly in the sunshine. Jary inspected the horses.

'Have you called at Foley these last few days?' asked the Doctor, watching the aggressive snatching of the black head, the flattening of the ears, as Jary held out some dry bread.

'Once. And if you think there is any improper behaviour you may think again, for there is none.'

'I never thought it. What news of Lizzie Rayner?'

'Oh, she is taking London by storm. They cannot praise her too highly. She is invited out every evening, does not get to bed until four, has a suitor no less.'

'She will not survive.'

'Not survive? Why should she not survive? Is there any special danger in London apart from the soot?'

'There is boredom; there is an invitation a night; there is flattery and deceit and eminent men playing the fool.'

'Oh, she will survive all that,' said Jary with certainty, thinking of many a time she had fixed him with her furious eye. 'She would tell them to get up and be off. She is like my aunts, made of granite. The world would break in two before she did.'

And: 'You were very fond of your aunts,' was the murmur from the Doctor, whose hair in the sunlight had a peculiar metallic brilliance like new-minted money, neither rich gold nor silver, and whose laughing face was suddenly strangely young.

She was bored; there was any amount of flattery and deceit and false, fawning gentlemen; she could not paint, she was never alone; she could not go out without Mrs Barker, Fanny's cousin and her chaperone, and when she did go out it was to more flattery, which she instinctively distrusted, and more fawning, which she despised. She

220

was aware Helen Barker smiled and smiled until her face was stiff trying to counteract her own dark looks, that often Helen spoke for both of them as Lizzie fell silent, rudely, unaccountably silent. It was not a happy time.

It should have been. At twenty she would have been overjoyed to find her portraits the talk of fashionable London. Was it simply age then that tightened her heart and made her acknowledgement of praise so cool? Had age brought world-weariness, absolute cynicism?

'I am an old hag,' she told Kitty one morning, after they had both wrestled with her hair to no purpose, it went its own way as always. 'Look, I have wrinkles.'

'Lord, Miss Lizzie, but so do I,' said Kitty, who had been in Fanny Jewkes's house for twenty years and had often looked at them in Fanny's own mirror.

'They might pass unnoticed across a room, but close . . .'

Who was there to stand close? Even the flatterers kept their distance now, finding her so difficult, so changeable. Even the men who nightly bowed over her hand stepped back at once, encountering her fiery eye. Yes, she had wrinkles, tiny fans of creases at the corners of her eyes and mouth. Age, age, damnable age. And there were grey hairs, she had seen them, squinting reluctantly as Kitty piled up her curls. And there was something else, something as physically present as the lines and shadows: loneliness. Oh the unexpected loneliness, the lack of Fanny with her cheerful, inconsequential flow of news and views, a walking broadsheet of Stretfield. Lizzie had never believed she would miss her in this way, miss even those aspects of her character she had most disliked.

She bit her lip, rising and walking to the window, looking down on the street, the quiet square. It was a dull, cold day. London was mud-coloured, smoky. She missed the view of Frenchmans more than anything.

'The blue,' she said in reply to Kitty's question, but it could have been someone else speaking, her mind was still elsewhere.

'My dear, how charming!' was Helen Barker's first remark as she came downstairs. 'Quite the girl again!'

It was not intended unkindly. She was a woman about Fanny's own age, widowed after only a year of marriage to a Kentish gentleman of some fortune, and choosing ever afterward to live in his town house and lead an independent life, independent . . . but respectable. She was not, Fanny had warned Lizzie, a woman of passionate parts, she was in fact a rather sober moral person, addicted to hymns and what she considered to be serious music and to political intrigue too. Her sitting room was always full of people, she was very popular, but they were not rakish gentlemen, high society beaux, they were generally middle-aged civil servants and elderly noblemen and the flashier sort of parson.

'I do believe,' she said now as they sat down to breakfast, 'you are to have another letter from dear Fanny.' There was the sound of the front door opening and closing, the low murmur of conversation.

The door opened. The letter came in on a tray, very properly, and with the majesty of ancient ritual was handed to Helen for inspection. 'I told you so, it is for you,' she cried, 'but not Fanny's hand. An admirer perhaps.'

It was a man's hand, a dashing, black, aggravating hand. But it was not anyone Lizzie knew, not Sir James, or Stephen Fisher, whose writing was altogether neater and more economical of ink and emotion. She broke it open: it was from Jary Savage. It was Jary Savage in an impulsive, articulate mood, writing to ask her if during the summer when she returned to Foley she could do a painting of Ramillies. He knew she preferred people to landscape, Fanny had told him, but he would be proud to give her the commission. He hoped she was in the best of health, he knew the Doctor sent his kindest regards — no mention of the portrait — and he signed himself her friend and servant, which struck her as a peculiarly Jary-like combination. She smiled as she folded the paper and smiled more widely as she thought of him, and his fountains and the remarkable canal. She knew he had been disappointed with his picture, sensing some fault, some lack even if he could not put a name to it, but he had been gracious and cheerful, paying her for it immediately without being asked. She did not know why she had found it so difficult to paint him, and at another time she might have struggled with him, fretting and furious, as she had with the Doctor. Perhaps it had simply been exhaustion after *that* long long labour and agonizing birth. As it was she had painted the shell and ignored the man beneath, and thus had produced a good sound lifeless picture, a Jary stuffed and mounted and with glass eyes.

'Well, you are cheered up at last,' said Helen, whose curiosity was too great to contain. 'And *is* it an admirer?'

'He admires my work.'

'My dear, so does everyone.'

A pause, while Lizzie crackled toast and the intriguing letter lay folded on the cloth. Then: 'Is he young, Lizzie dear? This gentleman who admires your work – is he young?'

'Young enough and unmarried and exceedingly rich. He fought a duel on my account.'

'Good Heavens! I am sure I never agreed with duelling but to be fought over . . . to be disputed. Well!'

'Oh, I was not in dispute, not bodily in dispute, so to speak. No one was going to propose the moment the shot was fired.'

Helen subsided. It was as well a fresh pot of tea had come in, hot, fragrant, an excellent restorative.

'What a pity,' she said. 'My poor child, what a pity.'

At half past three Helen went forth to leave cards, to call on friends, and to shop. Mrs Hayes, her elderly companion, went with her. Lizzie sat with pen and paper in the sitting room composing a reply to Jary. She was amazed at the impossibility of this simple task, could not think up two coherent consecutive sentences, put down that it was by no means certain she would return to Foley before late July, she had engaged to travel to Brighton with Mrs Barker and to Oxford to paint a duke. Written down this looked sharp and unkind, as if she was telling him her consequence was so great he would have to wait in line, and as she did not mean anything of the sort she screwed up the page and began again, getting no further than 'Dear Sir' and ruining the pen by biting it. As she frowned over the words the memory of Jary rose up, Jary after Henriette had died, that larger, colder man. How she had resented him those first weeks he was at Ramillies, and how that resentment had melted away and yet she had still forced herself to keep up the appearance of it, a strange inappropriate form of self-defence. She had twice been cruelly hurt, had ever afterwards avoided people, making no lasting friendships apart from Fanny, making no effort to be agreeable, rather the reverse. I like him but I will never let him know it, she thought now, knocking over the sand pot with a sudden awkward movement, putting down the pen.

By the time she had to dress for dinner the extent of her communication was still 'Dear Sir' and an unfortunate smudge, and she had to put it away hastily when Helen flew in crying they would be late, late, late and why was Lizzie not upstairs in front of her mirror? After dinner they were to go to a dull party given by and for, not artists, but Helen's closest friends, respectable women and their husbands. The evening did not promise well, might have caused Lizzie some gnashing of teeth, an impolite withdrawal, but a young medical gentleman arrived, a physician in embryo, and seeing her immediately for the youngest thing in the room, worked his way cunningly round the knots of ladies making speedily for the jellied hams and violet creams, saying: 'Good evening, ma'am, and do I have the honour of addressing Miss Rayner, the celebrated Miss Rayner?'

She might have dismissed him with a word, a look, but he was not interested in art and no hand at flattery, he was anxious to ask about Suffolk. Did she know of a Dr Alexander French?

'You cannot conceive how I would like to meet him, to listen to his views. I watched him operate, they gave him a dreadful, a most difficult case – deliberately, I am sure, there is a great deal of jealousy among them – and I swear I have never seen anyone so quick and yet so tender, so skilled, so very skilled. I am so glad you know him. Perhaps ... perhaps I may beg you for an introduction?'

'He is not a close friend,' said Lizzie, 'but I have painted him.'

This possibility had not occurred to young Mr Bliss. He stood a moment in silence grappling with the idea of reproducing that harsh lined misanthropic face, and of such a harsh and misanthropic being sitting obediently for this wand-like lady in grey.

'I admire your courage, ma'am,' he said at last, 'I would not care to paint Dr French. I could not perform an operation under his eye with any degree of coolness. He does not admit mistakes, he does not allow for nerves. But he is a great teacher, a great demonstrator. I learnt more in an hour with him than in three years with my old tutor.'

Lizzie asked him about him ambitions, his prospects for realizing them, and his presence at this party, this dull dull party, for there was to be no dancing and there was a fair sprinkling of people in stages of advanced decay, decrepitude and disability.

'Oh, I was brought by Dr Everitt. I am here by chance.'

'What unlucky chance.'

'No, surely not. Now I have met you, the toast of the Academy, I am told. And you know Dr French whom I admire most sincerely.'

He was a slight, pleasant-looking man with reddish hair, and she allowed him to lead her reluctantly towards the buffet tables.

'The Doctor wishes to go back to the Army, I believe,' she began. 'You may not find him in Suffolk unless you go very soon.'

'Of course he must go back to the Army. The peace

will not last, Miss Rayner, there is no chance for the peace while Bonaparte still lives. Dr French is made for battle, for saving lives on the field and fighting authority off it, his is a stormy nature if I am not mistaken. But then, I hear he has been unlucky in love and in legacies and in his family. It colours a man's outlook, shadows his whole life. Do you not think so?'

'I did not know he had a family. He has never spoken of anyone to me.'

'Nor does he – have a family – that is the very point.'

'And he was never married.'

'I believe not. But a man, pardon my boldness, can be as married without a ring as with one, and come to as much grief and lose as much sleep by it.'

A voice broke in on them, Helen's artificial, social voice. 'Oh, Lizzie, Lizzie, how you monopolize Mr . . . Mr . . . Come, Lady Davey is waiting to meet you and Mr Carbrook is hinting' – a lowered tone, a significant look at Lizzie followed by one of dismissal to the man at her side – 'hinting he wishes to ask you to paint his wife and daughters.'

'Then I must certainly come,' said Lizzie, with a smile of genuine warmth and regret at young Mr Bliss. 'Forgive me, but I hope you will call. I would be delighted to give you a letter for the Doctor. Mrs Barker will give you the direction.'

'Oh!' said Helen.

Lizzie's voice floated back to them. 'If I do not paint I do not eat.'

She painted. She painted two distinguished City men who had made fortunes out of the Exchange and would continue to do so as long as they had wit to multiply and subtract and know into which receptive ear to drop the rumour of the moment. She painted Mrs Carbrook and her three athletic, feline daughters, restraining an impulse to finish them off with whiskers and tails.

'You are working too hard,' accused Helen on a rare foray into the tiny back parlour Lizzie had made her own. 'Everyone is complaining they never see you now, you are shut away with your brushes. I am sure one picture is enough for a few weeks, why must you do three, why paint and paint? it makes you so irritable, and you miss meals and get hardly any fresh air.'

Lizzie accepted the reproof in silence, looking hard at the end of her brush. Helen had been infinitely kind in her own way, infinitely hospitable; without her – though she knew there had been some secret financial arrangement – she would not have been able to come. So she put down her brush and rags and smiled, that rare sweet smile, and proposed as a peace offering a portrait of Helen herself.

'A gentleman below, ma'am, asking for Miss Rayner,' said Helen's maid, knocking timidly for the back parlour was something of a tiger's cave, a dangerous place to intrude if Lizzie was painting.

'Oh, Lizzie, you know who it is . . . Peggy, show him up at once.'

'Yes, ma'am.'

'Oh, what a pity I have to go out. I am sure it is Bennington, I shall give him good morning on my way down. Mrs Hayes will step along, she is so very fond of that young man, she said only the other day that of all the gentlemen who had asked you to dance he was far and away the best catch.'

Helen ran for hat and gloves. Lizzie walked with a determined step to the sitting room, where she could hear voices, at least she could hear Mrs Hayes' strident tones laying down strict rules for the nursing of fevers.

Fevers?

'Good morning, Miss Rayner,' cried Mr Bliss, rising from the sofa where he had perched, hat in hand, 'how pleased I am to see you. I have taken the liberty of calling to beg you to write the note you promised, I am away to Bury St Edmunds tomorrow and if time allows I will go a little out of my way and give my compliments to the Doctor.'

'It will be a great deal out of your way,' said Lizzie,

stepping forward and smiling, 'I will find paper and ink immediately. Mrs Hayes my dear, would you mind stepping out to ask Peggy for a pot of coffee? Mr Bliss looks chilled, there is a bitter wind.'

She sat in the window to write, and Andrew Bliss sat with his coffee and watched her shyly while making conversation with Mrs Hayes – not that he need do much more than grunt, she poured out an endless stream of complaint, symptoms, cures, hardly noticing him, scarcely waiting for his response. He thought Lizzie Rayner was rather fine, a woman of taste and spirit; he had taken the trouble to look at her pictures since they had last met and he knew now how talented she was, worth every last drop of praise. He saw her now frowning over her page, sucking her pen, smiling. Once she looked out of the window and he received the impression, faint but instantly recognizable, of a wild animal pressing itself against the bars and sniffing the free wind.

She was thinking of Foley and the rise of Frenchmans against a riven sky, and the dip to Petty's Bit and Cuckooland and all the flat levels of the Meeting Grounds. The clear, watery, flowing colours were there, and the movement of the hazels and the young birch in the plantation, and the cluck and whirr of the pheasants and the plaintive hooting of the wild geese.

I would take it very kind of you, sir, if you would carry a letter of my own to Suffolk,' she said, turning back, and the white cold light behind her was so strong when he looked up he did not see the sudden shining of her eyes.

16

April had come in with drizzling weather but the work at Ramillies went on apace: all across the Meeting Grounds piles of rubbish from the clearing of the ditches and the thinning of the copses sent thin blue smoke into the dull overcast sky. The house was in turmoil, for the builders were in again, opening up a window that had been bricked in so that even more light, more morning sunshine, would flood Jary's favourite room. And this besides the men, one old, two very young, who were whitewashing the back regions and repainting the whole of the upstairs.

'I will not recognize it when I return,' said Jary happily, 'I have given Mrs Jewkes instructions to see the new carpets in, and Clarkie is to take a whip to those three oddities if they do not get the whole painted by the time I am on my way home. After all, they have the whole summer to do it, they can open up the house, throw wide every casement – if the sun ever shines, that is. I am glad Philip sent to say he was not leaving till the tenth, it has given me time to see the stables finished and the windows in the cottages. Yes, Kate, what is it?'

'A gentleman for the Doctor, sir,' said Kate, grown bold and cheerful after all these weeks. 'Should I show him in the library?'

The Doctor found him there five minutes later, a young gingery man dressed very soberly and bearing a letter addressed in Lizzie Rayner's flying hand.

'And this is for Mr Savage,' said Mr Bliss, handing over the other, taken aback a little both by the Doctor's mean appearance – breeches and threadbare old coat, five days' stubble and uncombed hair – and by the grandeur of the library, which was a very fine room indeed.

'Sit down, sit down,' said the Doctor, waving him to

a chair and breaking open Lizzie's letter at once. 'You watched me operate, you have a . . . yes, yes, I see. I am very pleased to meet you. What was it exactly that you wished . . . Ah, Clarkie, we have a guest. Yes, luncheon certainly. Come, you will stay the night, sir, surely?'

'It is not possible,' was the sad reply, 'I have hired a horse from Bury and I must ride him back in time for tomorrow's coach. He is a poor specimen too, with galls under the saddle. I cannot hurry him, it would be inhuman of me. But I am very sensible of the great honour . . .'

'Great honour, pah!' cried the Doctor, and as a tall, good-looking man twice his size walked in, 'Jary, this young man thinks it would be a great honour to stay at Ramillies the night. If we took him to Westdene early tomorrow do you think he could catch the London coach?'

'I don't see why not. How do you do, sir? You are welcome of course. Any friend of Alex . . . What is it? Not a letter from Lizzie Rayner at last, I had given her up, given up hope of ever receiving a reply, I mean. Mr . . . Bliss, welcome. You have come a long way – did Millett tell me Bury? – and on a sorry nag, you cannot possibly wear yourself out going all the way back. We shall arrange to send on the horse and you will take the Westdene coach. In fact, if you can spare the time to stay another day and night we may all travel to London together. How would that suit?'

Mr Bliss being speechless the Doctor assented for him and roused out Mrs Clark to air the bed. Lizzie had written: 'I believe he admires you most sincerely, you were a breath of fresh air in his stuffy life, I detect a note of disillusion as if perhaps before you burst in on him that one fateful day he was contemplating giving up his profession. He is almost qualified he tells me, a little older than many students because he started late, having been denied the means to support himself by a father set against medicine from the start. I believe all he has is a small annuity from his mother, who is dead, and he

230

manages on this, the father having cut him off and given all to a younger brother. Do be kind to him, I like him very much, I believe he is truly good-hearted and needs only a little encouragement to show of his best. I am so sorry to rattle on, this is the longest note of introduction ever written. I only meant to write three lines when I took up my pen, but the relief at meeting someone so candid and pleasant after so many weeks of such different company, makes me garrulous.'

Lizzie laughing, Lizzie alive with humour and impulsive kindness together, Lizzie in great spirits dashing off lines and lines; the Doctor smiled and thought of her with sudden affection, felt reconciled even to his portrait.

'Come,' he said to Mr Bliss, 'tell me about your studies.'

'It is why I am here, it is why I wished to see you. I need advice, Dr French, oh I most sorely need advice, and I am past the point where I can ask my colleagues, my fellows, or even my teachers. I need an independent mind brought to bear, I need . . . Sir, I am considering giving up medicine.'

So she was right, thought the Doctor, right about that, but how right as to whether you are worth saving, I wonder? And if you are truly good-hearted are you a good doctor too, or have you been struggling all these years in vain?

'Mr Bliss, we will walk about the gardens for a while. Matters are easier to discuss in the open, do you not think? Jary, we shall be back shortly. Will you give Stephen my regards and the inestimable Mr Blake and say I will ride over for the ceremony this afternoon without fail.'

'I hope you will. Perhaps Mr Bliss will remind you of it, if you are not both prattling away about bones and blood.'

The Doctor went out and then looked back in. 'What does Miss Rayner say?'

'That she will do my picture if she returns but it's by no means certain that she will, she has to go to Oxford.

You would think she had swallowed a poker and was sitting on hot coals when she wrote it, every word is . . . stiff. I cannot make her out. I wrote a most cheerful letter, putting myself out to be complimentary, and this is what I get.'

'Persevere, dear Jary, persevere. I believe she is the dearest soul, only she hides the fact as well as she can, poor sweet, she has been so injured in the past.'

'So have we all,' said Jary, 'but we do not all turn fire-eaters, spitting cats, and – what was that woman with the uncommon hair? Medusas. I am almost glad I may never see her again.'

The following night there was a subscription dance at the Assembly rooms in Westdene, the first shot, as Mr Fisher put it, in the battle of the Assizes, that high season of the town's meagre social life. The judge was not due for ten days but by beginning early they could make sure of three whole weeks of festivity, and as the gaol was currently empty they could do so without feeling that they were dancing on anyone's grave.

'Of course we must go,' said Jary, 'a fitting end to our stay here together. We shall change at the Admiral – I shall take a room – and then we may all catch the early coach.'

'I am not a man for cutting a caper,' said Mr Bliss humbly, and begged to be excused, he had no evening clothes, no silk stockings. Jary brushed everything, every last objection aside with: 'How could we leave you sitting by yourself at the Admiral? You are our guest. And as for clothes, I cannot lend you anything, we are not of a size, but the Doctor . . .'

The Doctor lent Mr Bliss his new black coat, a trifle tight about the shoulders but otherwise a good fit, and he lent him smallclothes and shoes and a freshly laundered shirt. Jary prevented him, however, from lending his pony, and told Millett to saddle the brown horse, the gentlemanly brown horse who would look after him like a brother. For the last half-hour before they left he sat at the writing desk in his bedroom, gazing often at his lady in grey, making sure all the necessary papers and documents and bills were correctly filed for Stephen Fisher's use, contracts and plans for reference, Hawke's ill-written letters, lists of repairs needed to the outhouses, notes concerning the servants' wages. He sat there in his finery, his starched neckcloth rather tight as he bent over the books, the close-written instructions, and it seemed to him that every time he raised his head those brown-green eyes, faintly mocking, were looking at him. She was a softer yet more worldly version of Lizzie, a woman who knew herself attractive to men, who had had lovers, an English country Miss Johnson.

Thurza. He would see Thurza again in Kingston. He doubted they could take up where they had left off, so long ago now, and who knew what since then? Marriage? It was not inconceivable. It would be pleasant to think he could mount the steps to her door, and knock, and be shown in, as if no time had elapsed since last he had knocked and been shown in and seen her coming towards him with her hands outstretched, but it was wishful thinking, a boyish dream. A dark, slim, elegant form — perhaps he had always preferred dark women — a light weight on his arm, a kiss, and: 'Jary, my dear, how good to see you after such a time.' No. No, it would not do. Deep affection, pleasure in her company and person, a sincere admiration for her great style, her presence, were all very well but he knew he would never have asked her to be his wife, never would, though he returned to find her free and took up the old enjoyable intimacy. It was a wife he wanted now.

The Doctor knocked. 'Are you ready?'

'I have to lock the desk, that is all. Alex, did you ever come to know the true story of Lizzie Rayner and the redoubtable Captain Jervis? Who was he and how did he come to fly off with her, the poor demented rascal?'

'I will tell you all I know on the way down. Come, come, poor Bliss is waiting, crippled with shyness and my too-tight shoes. He is a great scholar, you know, and a sound man, will make an excellent surgeon, excellent. He never much cared for surgery but I have opened his eyes, he has been asking all kinds of questions, quite insatiable. I believe I have persuaded him not to quit before he is qualified, he only has six months to go, for Heaven's sake, six paltry months.'

'He will pass, I suppose?'

'I devoutly hope so. He knows a great deal more than I did at his age.'

As they left the room Jary glanced behind. 'I am sorry to leave her, I have grown used to that sardonic look. I wondered just now . . . I wondered if I would ever see her again,' and a strange grey look came over his face. 'But there, it must be melancholy, I have grown fond of this old place. And by the way, I took it upon myself to apologize to everyone at the ceremony yesterday, I lied like an unregenerate felon, I said you had the megrim, were out of sorts. It was all done according to custom, they raised some greenery to the roof and cheered and two old men sang a sort of dirge, and that was that, the cottages were blessed, the rites observed, and now the Diddlers can sleep in them without fear of evil spirits. But it was poor of you to miss it and after I particularly mentioned it during the morning. Stephen was quite put out, horribly concerned for your health, worrying about your lungs and your liver, when all the time I knew you were closeted with young Bliss rambling on in the most gruesome way and showing him your dreadful specimen jars and probably dissecting rats or bats and the like on my dining room table.'

'I am sorry I put you to the trouble of excusing me with a lie.'

'Well, I thought of saying you were detained by a medical colleague, which sounded nearer the truth, but you had been most particularly invited, they all looked so hangdog when I rode up without you. I could not let them think you preferred the company of a colleague and had forgotten all about them, forgotten to send apologies. But look, tell me about Jervis as we go.'

Outside rags of cloud obscured the moon, the wind was rising. Mrs Clark wiped away a tear as she said goodbye and in the back door Kate stood looking desolate by Mrs Fipson's shadowy bulk, watching them ride away.

At the Admiral they found the yard smoky with flares and a great bustle of carriages and horses and even sedan chairs, and a solid stream of people making their way to the Assembly rooms across the market square, not to speak of servants and dogs and even an audacious piglet which neatly tripped the Doctor as he was about to go through the inn door.

'A pig!' cried Mr Bliss, astonished. Though there were many pigs in the back streets of London he had never seen one trying to attend a social function before.

'The devil it is,' said Jary and caught the Doctor as he fell.

'I think we should take some madeira before we walk over, there is going to be an infernal crush. I only hope my cousin has had the good sense to stay at home.'

He hurried off to see about the madeira and the trunks which had been sent on that morning from Ramillies ready for the London coach. The Doctor and Andrew Bliss sank gratefully into the small sitting room, looking at each other's stockings with pursed lips and anxious frowns. And: 'You have riding breeches on,' whispered Bliss in horror, 'they are brown.'

'Have I? To be sure no one will notice, there will not be an inch to move. I have been to these country extravaganzas before,' and then in the brief interval before Jary returned he explained a little of why Mr Savage hoped his cousin would not be present, a vain hope he felt.

Half an hour later they crossed the square, seeing a great many people but no one they knew until Stephen Fisher darted from the doorway and wrung Jary's hand. 'And Doctor, how are you? Are you recovered?'

'Recovered?' The Doctor looked at a loss.

'Of course he is recovered,' said Jary strongly, 'if a

doctor cannot put himself to rights what hope have the rest of us? May I present Mr Bliss of Guy's Hospital?' and he herded them all inside continuing introductions and explanations, cheerful, irresistible, his blue eyes shining, though there was one moment, catching sight of the Doctor's brown breeches, when his aimless flow ceased abruptly and the blue eyes took on a darker hue.

It was certainly a crush. The Doctor bowed to one or two people Jary did not know and explained vaguely that he had met them while in Plesset's company, whether as acquaintances or patients he did not say. Jary spotted two of the Stone daughters, both of whom saw him at the same moment and retired giggling into the main room. And then there was Fanny, in a restrained green dress and with a single green feather in her hair, a single rope of pearls about her neck. She was fighting her way forward with difficulty, her hand reached back for that of an elderly woman in mouse brown whom they recognized with surprise as Miss Pawle from Hopes. It was Miss Pawle who had served up the excellent beef Jary had eaten on his first and subsequent visits to the farm, and Miss Pawle who had lodged the Lasts and Mother Henham in the empty quarters above the stables, and all for a feverish, shameful, desperate love of the man. Jary, unaware that Miss Pawle's feelings were any more than those of any tenant for any landlord, only noticed that she blushed when she spoke to him, something he found strangely off-putting in an old maid.

'You will never guess,' said Fanny, grasping his offered arm with relief, 'Ma Henham has put a spell on the Hopes poultry. They are laying so well there are eggs and to spare so Miss Pawle has been forced to give awwy a good many to the Diddlers.'

'I never heard such nonsense!' said Jary, elbowing through the crowd. 'It is all the young green to eat and a feeling of hey-nonny-no. Why, my heifers have been cavorting about the park like madwomen and all they are doing is looking for the bull. It is the natural thing in spring.'

'Hush,' said Fanny, as several curious faces turned their way, 'what gentleman would prate of bulling heifers at a ball? Look, there is your cousin, there in the dark grey with the emeralds. Dear me, I would give a great deal for a necklace of such quality, and to think that boy will have it all and toss it away on the ears of a horse.'

'Ears?' asked the Doctor, reaching their side after a prolonged struggle and catching only the last few words.

'Newmarket,' said Fanny mysteriously. 'Wait and see.'

The main room was lit by more candles than were strictly necessary even to make a show and in the brilliant light two hundred people, drawn from twenty miles around, chattered and laughed and waved fans and swayed back and forth in one direction or another.

'There is Sir James,' said Fanny, turning to find Miss Pawle, who had disappeared. 'Doctor, where is Miss Pawle?'

'Oh, I am very much afraid I let her go, we had such an entanglement with a military gentleman and a lady in pink.'

'She is sunk without trace,' said Fanny, casting her eye round, 'she will never forgive me.'

Jary bowed, was greeted rapturously by Lady Braile and Eugenia, who had been much plagued by the elderly Mr Fisher in a wanton mood, no more an invalid than they were themselves. They bore Jary off with them to meet some gentlemen of their acquaintance who were all for landscaping and rearranging nature and another who had recently been on a long and terrifying voyage where his ship had tried and tried to round Cape Horn and had not done so, had been forced to retreat, battered and exhausted. 'I have known it happen,' said Jary.

Fanny, seeing Stephen Fisher for a moment as the crowd parted, edged the Doctor into a quiet corner and put up her fan. 'Goodness, the heat! Do you see that pasty child over there in the pale blue? That is the second oldest Stone girl, she has been living with an aunt for two years and only just returned. Oh, there is Miss Pawle, the poor dotty old thing, and she has a glass of something . . .'

'And a gentleman in a red coat with whiskers.'

'I never did think a great deal of military men.'

They stood and watched the faces pass for a moment, and then Fanny said: 'I am very worried about Lizzie,' giving a small laugh when she saw the Doctor's surprise and continuing: 'I have known her so long, you see, since she was a very little girl; if I could not read between the lines after such an age I would be ashamed. She is not happy, not at all happy.'

'But she is applauded, feted, sits with great men.'

A long, level look. 'You and I would not mistake all that for happiness. Happiness is an altogether more difficult, elusive thing. She *ought* to be happy, because at last she has achieved recognition – a splendid thing in itself – and then it also means she can be independent for the first time, not leaning on friends or feeling obliged to marry was someone to ask her. That is no small consideration. It must weight with her, it must mean something, she was all joy and light and pleasure when the first letter came about the Admiral's portrait, but there is something deeper than disillusionment now, a . . . restlessness too. I have known her like this before and it worries me.'

'I have known homesickness so virulent it could drive a man distracted, depressed, turned in upon himself. Is it that, do you think? She was undoubtedly attached to Ramillies – and to you.'

'Oh, pooh, she would never get herself into a state over me. But look, there is Mr Savage again and with a lady on each arm.'

He relinquished the ladies as soon as he could and brought over two glasses of thin pale wine. He had met his cousin, he told them, and she had actually inclined her head though it would have killed her to speak. He had hoped they might be done with acrimony now, the new boundary drawn, Pellow dismissed, everything settled between them, but it was clear that was not to be. She would have struck him dead, said Jary, had she had anything to hand and as it was she did the job with her eyes, the old harridan.

'Speaking of the Whiteleys,' said Fanny, touching his arm, 'there is dear Prince and in tremendous spirits, he has been drinking deep for certain. He would be quite unsteady was he to let go of that strumpet's arm.' And behind her fan: 'She is supposed to be the sister of one of his Ipswich friends and so she may be, but the way she encourages him and helps him along while showing off her bosom to the entire room is not the behaviour of any decent woman. Thank God, thank God Lizzie did not marry him. At least one good has come out of all that unhappiness.'

The eyes, the dark, beautiful eyes of Prince Whiteley's lady companion suddenly fixed on Jary, and her little tongue showed momentarily between her lips. She had been expecting a boring evening, for although Westdene boasted some distinguished invalids most of them were not fit enough to appreciate a pretty bosom when they saw one, or were too old, and besides, her escort was drunk and she did not care for him drunk, he became peevish and irritable and ridiculously arrogant. She was also annoyed with him tonight for stepping on her train and tearing it, and for not telling her his aunt was to be here, the aunt she had come to believe was little more than a recluse, and there had been a girl in the market square, a thin little drab not more than fourteen, who had hung on his arm, his very arm, and whispered in his ear, and when remonstrated with he had only said: 'I know her, there is no harm in it. Stop whining so,' and had brought her in white-faced and furious as the girl had run away. Now she saw a tall, elegant, astonishingly handsome man staring at her with apparent interest and she felt the unpromising evening was taking a turn for the better.

It was much later, when Prince Whiteley was drunker than ever and, on coming face to face with his aunt, had thrust the girl aside with a sharp 'Madam, I beg you' as if they were strangers and she had importunately seized his arm, that she escaped, slipping away among the revellers. Dances at the Assembly rooms were seldom stately and serious affairs for long; it might have been the sea air, or the preponderance of old men who had not thought to dance again and now felt they could, or the fair sprinkling of navy coats and military ones, or simply what the Doctor called bucolic frenzy: the determination of a remote and isolated people to make the most of infrequent celebration. Whatever it was, the girl found no difficulty in putting a whole room and fifty perspiring beings between herself and her dear Prince, and after a moment, seeing Jary just finishing a punishing country dance with Mrs Stone, in gliding to his side.

She actually reached his very side and, as he nearly tripped over her, dropped her fan and gave an exclamation. It was very prettily done. He stooped to retrieve it at once and as he rose her eyes shone brilliantly into his. It seemed to him the message he read there was rather bold, but perhaps he misinterpreted it, he had drunk shrub on top of the madeira and more than enough of the thin indifferent wine. He told himself he must have been mistaken about the invitation in the girl's eyes; drink and lascivious anticipation – he had only a moment ago been thinking of Thurza, the welcome he might expect after all, the way she might shut all others out just while she greeted him – had got the better of him. But she curtseyed deeply, thanked him in a warm and husky voice, did hope he would forgive her for causing him trouble, but was not the crowd dreadful, was not the heat unbearable, quite quite unbearable . . . He saw her sway, put a steadying hand on her arm, her bare arm above her glove. Perhaps she should sit down, he said, or take a breath of air in the square. Why not the garden? in a small voice, but he was already steering her for the main entrance where a liveried servant was renewing some of the candles. No, thought Jary, he was damned if he was going to walk Prince Whiteley's partner up and down the grass in the garden, for although it was lit by hanging lanterns the soft light only made it more mysterious and private, the very place for lovers. No, he would let her walk about the market square until her head cleared, in public, where it was quite obvious a man would not go if he wished for intimacy and clandestine kisses.

'You have been most kind,' she said when they reached the centre of the cobbled open space, sad heaps of wood that were the dismantled stalls of the Tuesday market all around them, 'and you a complete stranger, Mr . . . Mr Savage. My brother never has the least idea of chivalry.'

'Your brother?'

'Oh, you are wondering what my brother has to do with it, because I was with Mr Whiteley? You see, Mr Whiteley is my brother's friend.'

She hung upon his arm, close, confiding. She did not care for Mr Whiteley, she began, to tell the truth she detested him, but her brother had been his friend these many years and found some pleasure in his company though she could not; and what was a girl to do who had no mother and no chance of an evening out unless she accepted her brother's terms? She lived with an elderly aunt too ill to go out, there was only Tom to chaperon her, and if Tom brought along his friends, several friends, some undesirable and downright rakish, how could she object?

Jary smiled, listening to the glib lies. Still, she had looked genuinely flushed and uncomfortable inside even if she had cast down her fan on purpose, and while listening he could enjoy an untramelled view of her bosom, her lovely shoulders, her neck and the lobes of her little pink ears. Discounting her occasional over-bold looks she was a charming creature, he was flattered she had cast her fan at him, but as to carrying things any further, he would as soon have paid his money in a bawdy house, a thing he had never done in his life.

'Come,' he said at last, as they walked back, 'I must take you in, the night air is quite cold. And I must find my friends.'

At this she laughed, saying she could suffer any amount

241

of cold air for the pleasure of being in his company, and began to walk slower, until all of a sudden there was a scuffle in the door and a strangled shout made them look up.

It was Prince Whiteley holding on to two friends for support, and as he caught sight of Jary he yelled again, and staggered forward, swearing. It was the girl's scream which attracted the onlookers: an interested clutch of Westdene spinsters, some boys, a party just about to step into a coach. The girl gave another cry, quite unnecessarily, and clung to Jary's arm.

'Damn you, sir' – Whiteley let go of his companions and swayed to within a few feet, his eyes bulging – 'first you try to kill me and then you try to steal my land and now you take a . . . a lady from my side without so much as . . . You are an impudent dog, a . . . a most impu . . . Lucy, come here. I shall . . . By God, I shall kill you if ever I get the chance.'

The situation took on an air of unreality. A carriage came out from the Admiral and turned down the street, two men on the far side of the square began to laugh at something, a dog trotted by without looking to right or left. Jary, judging the advanced state of Whiteley's drunkenness, thought it prudent to keep quiet. He detached the girl – her fingers were biting into his arm – and set her away from him, saying mildly: 'The young lady asked me to bring her out for air, we were this minute returning. It is a simple enough matter as she will explain herself. Good evening to you, sir.'

But Whiteley, incensed, grabbed him as he passed. He was too unsteady for such a manoeuvre, however, and he fell, pulling Jary half over with him. 'Let me go. You are drunk, Mr Whiteley. Have you no sense of shame or decency? Take the young lady in, for God's sake, and behave like a gentleman.'

Whiteley heaved himself up, swearing again, waving aside his embarrassed friends who came to offer their arms. He looked ridiculous, so angry he could hardly frame his words, and there was spittle on his chin. Put

Jary did not underestimate him for his malevolence was almost tangible, and a weak man badly drunk, especially a weak man with a score of imaginary grievances, can be unpredictable and dangerous.

'I will kill you!' he shouted. The little crowd of watchers took a united step back.

Jary made no reply, no sensible or effective reply suggesting itself, and began to walk towards the entrance. As he reached the step he heard the movement behind him and turned just in time to fend off Whiteley's arms with a sudden cold fury of his own, a violent exasperation. This was enough to make Whiteley collapse again, pouring out a stream of filth, howling about revenge.

Jary beckoned to one of the hovering friends. 'Take him home, why don't you? He has caused enough uproar already and over nothing. His aunt is inside. How will she feel if you let him go on in this manner?'

They picked Whiteley up, trying to brush him off, but he flailed them away again and lurched after Jary. 'I will kill you!'

They were in full hearing of the avid audience above. Several more people had joined the ladies by the door, staring and looking shocked. Andrew Bliss's face appeared, Jary saw it quite clearly the moment before Prince Whiteley's hand caught at his sleeve.

'I would be careful what you are about, Mr Whiteley.'

Irrational, devouring hatred. 'God damn you!' said Whiteley.

'He will damn you first,' declared Jary, losing his temper, 'of that I am very sure.'

The Doctor saw Jary coming and the first thing he noticed was how the people fell back on either side. The second thing was Jary's face – usually full of light, smiling, cheerful – closed and dark and threatening. 'It is all right,' he said to Andrew Bliss, 'he is not an intemperate man.'

'He was intolerably provoked.'

'I wish to God I had never come,' said Jary as he

reached them, 'I shall go across to the Admiral directly. Were you there? Did you see?'

'No, but Andrew here ran in to tell me Whiteley was trying to fight you. Come, sit here a moment.' And seeing Jary's hands shaking; 'Is there anything I can do?'

An emphatic movement of his head. 'No. No, unless he follows me in here in which case you had better restrain me, I shall surely knock him senseless. He is drunk, roaring drunk, threatening my life. I did my best out there, anything I said maddened him, and I could not decently hit a man who could barely stand. His friends could do nothing with him. He is a lunatic, Alex, what harm have I ever done him?'

'A self-centred, jealous mind finds its own reasons for outrageous behaviour. He did not like you from the start and he is afraid of your influence over the old woman.'

'But I have none.'

'He made sure of it. He probably fed her scandal simply to make sure she would refuse to have you in the house. It was he engaged Pellow, Mr Stone told me earlier this evening, he had heard it somewhere – and it is a rumour I can well believe. I suspect his aunt might have challenged the wisdom of this recently, she is not an absolute fool, can add figures as well as any, no doubt. Pellow was expensive and an embarrassment. What is more, she must have known she could no more prove a claim to the land than you, and that shortly you would both be engaged in a futile battle that might last years. I believe she seized on your offer of those few acres – your surrender – and signed the contract within hours, knowing when she was well off. Maybe she and her nephew quarrelled subsequently, for believe me, avaricious though he is, he would never have set his own name to any proposal of yours.'

Jary leaned forward, hanging his hands between his knees. Was it his imagination, or was the chatter, the laughter, a little subdued? He could see Braile quite clearly some way off and he was looking in his direction, looking grim and troubled.

'Alex, good night. I don't have the heart for any more of this. Mr Bliss, your servant,' and he rose and went away through the thinning crowd.

'Doctor, Mr Bliss,' said Fanny, 'what is all this about Prince Whiteley trying to knock Jary down? It is the talk of the evening.'

'Where is Mrs Whiteley?'

A certain triumph shone from Fanny's face. 'She has just this minute ordered her carriage, she is leaving. She would not speak to him. He is in disgrace.'

'It will only serve to make him more bellicose.'

They strolled together about the room saying their goodbyes. They met the Brailes, Eugenia smiling most particularly at the Doctor and also the pink Mr Bliss, and two of the Stone girls locked to the bosoms of hearty young men in the last dance, and a very merry Miss Pawle, but they did not see Whiteley or his friends. At last the Doctor took Fanny's hand and bent to kiss her knuckles. 'Dear lady, I have to catch the early coach and besides, I am too old for such late nights. May I see you to your carriage and then bid you good night?'

'I have sold my carriage, do you not remember? I am entirely at the mercy of Miss Pawle and old John Stoker from Hopes who is more used to driving a wagon than a gentleman's carriage. I will not say anything except goodbye,' with a smiling, affectionate look, 'for I do so hate protracted partings. I hope you will come back to see us again.'

The Doctor and Mr Bliss made their way to the Admiral and found Jary still up, a bottle of port at his side.

'Ah, it's you. Will you take a glass?'

'We are away to our beds,' said the Doctor, 'there will be time for three hours' sleep before the coach.'

'In Jamaica . . .' began Jary, lifting his glass and looking into it closely, 'in Jamaica . . .' But they were never to learn about Jamaica, for he suddenly seemed to shake himself and said in a much more normal voice: 'It

245

is absurd in a grown man to let such a paltry thing cast him down. What is the matter with me, Alex?'

'You are tired, you are already anticipating problems in Kingston, and forgive me, dear Jary, but you are certainly drunk. In the morning your sense of proportion will return and your spirits will rise. Andrew, pour a glass for both of us, we shall toast Ramillies farewell and look to the future. I have to step out a moment to give a message about the horses.'

He found the old man who was to ride them home to Ramillies, red-faced, red-eyed, slumbering uneasily in a corner of the yard under a blanket, waiting for the first coach. He touched his shoulder. 'Friend, would you tell Millett the chestnut pony is to go on to Norfolk? Here is a note for the housekeeper at Ramillies setting out the arrangements.'

The horseman put the note and the Doctor's silver in his bosom and grinned at him kindly, and then Pamela came across the yard with a lantern. 'Why, Doctor, 'tis you. Do you go in, John, mother has a mull by the fire, it still wants fifteen minutes till the coach. Doctor,' as the old man shuffled away, trailing his blanket, 'is it true? They are saying Mr Savage means to kill Prince Whiteley.'

'My dear, you must never believe all you hear.'

And he led her in, telling her that if men took serious note of all they heard in tap-rooms they would never have found out the earth was not flat. But he was sorry Jary's last evening had made him so miserable, he would be glad to be on the road to London.

17

At four o'clock there was a muffled knocking at his door. From a long long way down the Doctor stirred and turned over. Then cautious footsteps and a hand on his shoulder, the dull flickering of a shaded candle in the doorway behind.

'Doctor, Doctor, you are needed below,' and the round face of Mrs King swam into blurred focus, a face usually shining with good nature and laughter and now pale and oddly composed.

'Below? Below?' For a moment he felt time slip unaccountably and he thought he must be back on a ship, that his poor doomed soldiers were crying out for him from the cruelly confined spaces where they had been packed to be out of the way. He sat up, and his room at the Admiral came into view, displacing the other so very clear in his mind, and he said testily: 'Yes, woman, yes. What is it? What is it o'clock, dear Lord? Is it morning? Is the coach arrived?'

'No, no, Doctor,' and she bundled his clothes onto the bed. 'Please, sir, will you dress? Sir James Braile is downstairs and asking for you. There has been an accident.'

'What kind of accident?' He could see now that it was Pamela in the doorway with the candle, her face staring and shocked. 'I have not been asleep above an hour and now to be roused out . . .'

'It is four o'clock, Doctor, but no one is astir. Please make as little noise as you can, Sir James does not want the whole house awake. He is very impatient, shall I tell him you are coming?'

'Tell him. Tell him indeed. But please to go out while I dress, Mrs King.'

In five minutes he was at the foot of the main stairs.

Sir James was there with two solid, cheerless men whom he guessed were constables. They too looked as if they had been dragged from comfortable beds, one stifled a yawn as he looked at him and the other had definitely tied his stock in a tearing hurry. Sir James stepped forward. 'Doctor, I thought you would never come. Will you step outside a moment? Just round the corner, the length of a street. I will tell you everything as we go.'

'Will I need my instruments? My bag?'

Sir James rubbed his nose. 'Bag? No, no. It is too late for that.'

They went out into the new morning, the very new morning, grey mist dispersing even as they hurried through it, across the market square and into the narrow mouth of a narrower lane that led straight down to the low cliffs and the beach. Here the houses leaned inwards and their feet rang on the stones, here another alley intersected and another. Into this second one Sir James turned with an impatient noise, his cane tapping the wall of the nearest cottage. All was darkness except for the shaded lantern one of the constables carried and round this corner he held the light up so that they could all see what there was to be seen.

'He was found an hour ago, nearly an hour ago,' said Braile, looking down with distaste. 'Luckily I was still awake when they sent and rode back as soon as I could. They had called Plesset but he is confined to bed, has some chest complaint, and he said send for you. Well?'

'He has been stabbed. Hold the light closer.'

Crouched on the damp ground, moving the dead man's coat aside to see where he had been struck, the Doctor felt a strange light-headedness. He reached over to close Prince Whiteley's staring eyes.

'I believe it would be best if you took him indoors somewhere near, there will be people about very shortly. Can it be arranged? I would be grateful if someone could be sent back to the inn for my colleague, Mr Bliss, who would be of great assistance, and I will need my bag after all.'

Sir James Braile leaned forward. The sound of the sea came to them as they formed their awkward group around the body. There was daylight in the main street and over the cold grey beach, but here in this cramped and sour-smelling corner there was none and the lantern was still needed even when Whiteley had been picked up and carried into the last cottage down the lane, a quick, furtive, embarrassing undertaking.

'I ran,' said Andrew Bliss, coming upon the Doctor in the tiny parlour, the curtains drawn, the body laid out on the table, 'they did not tell me he was dead. Good God, it is the man who threatened Mr Savage last night.'

'It is, God rest his soul.'

'He has been murdered.'

'Hush. The poor old woman whose house this is believes she has an injured man in her sitting room, not a dead one. Sir James has gone to make arrangements to shift him as privately as possible, else the whole town will be agog. Tell me, was Mr Savage on the coach?'

Bliss was frowning down, his face still pink from his sprint across from the Admiral. He had all the appearance of a man who had flung on his clothes anyhow and was still not properly awake, and also of a man grappling with the potential of this unexpected turn of events. 'Mr Savage? No, sir, he was not. He was just awake when they came at a run to fetch me, there was a great deal of whispering and shushing and creaking of boards. It must have roused him, he was only next door, and he came in while I was looking for your bag. I said you had been called out to an injured man and that I was needed too, and he laughed and said something whimsical about Prometheus, but I do not think he was himself. He mentioned that he would inform them we must forfeit the seats on the coach and take a later one, he did not seem put out by it, only resigned.'

'He is used to reverses of fortune.'

'Mr Savage? I would not have guessed it.'

'Oh, he has led an adventuring life, leads one yet I fear, for there are those will connect this business with that stupid quarrel last night. Here, let us ease off his coat before he is quite stiff and examine the wounds properly. It is all one to him and to everyone else no doubt but at least we will be able to tell Sir James whether he was stabbed from the front or the back.'

They worked together for a bare ten minutes, speaking quietly when occasion demanded, speaking Latin once or twice, grunting, turning the body with the ease of men who have long been used to handling corpses.

'Both,' said Bliss at last, 'he was attacked back and front. Or wounded when he was down.'

'Two people. We must make Sir James aware of the possibility, the strong possibility, of his being killed by two people. I will find him if I can. Stay here, keep the old woman out, and I will have some breakfast sent over from the inn – you will not mind eating in here, will you?'

Outside a cool windy day, April without the sun. The mist had blown away but a marble greyness was everywhere, a dim light like the last flight of winter. The streets were busy, it was cattle market day, and small boys with sticks were driving great bulls and reluctant groups of bullocks and snorting dashing heifers into odd corners.

'Oh Doctor, there you are. Should I heat you something? The coach went two hours ago, 'tis a shame and you all set to leave us. Mr Savage is in the little sitting room eating his breakfast,' said Pamela, who was flying up the passage, jug in hand. 'Ring hard if you need me, I shall be serving the drovers and men and every gentleman farmer in the county every last minute and all day,' and she had gone with a flash of petticoat, hailed distantly by her mother's voice calling for fresh linen.

'Oh there you are,' said Jary, looking up. 'You look tired. Here, try this coffee. No one will tell me anything. Mrs King looked in to see if you were back yet, she said she was sorry she had to wake you so early and you only just in bed but Sir James said she must, spoke quite cruelly. She will not forgive him for a while, I fancy, the poor woman. She is not used to being ordered about like that in her own house. What is it all about? Who was injured?'

The Doctor poured some coffee. He said softly: 'I am afraid I have some disagreeable news. It may keep us from catching the next coach or any coach for some considerable time. Jary, Prince Whiteley was murdered last night.'

In the silence the clink of Jary's cup was unusually loud. Then: 'How could he have been? He was alive at one o'clock shouting insults at me.'

'But now he is dead, and a nasty, brutish, miserable death too, stabbed several times, a frenzied attack I fancy, at least frenzied enough – one thrust would have done the job, two to be sure, eight was excessive in my opinion. I have left poor Andrew by the body and am on my way to see Sir James.'

Jary sat looking at the coffee pot. His face had a strange, drawn, introverted expression and he was biting his lip.

'I am sorry he is dead,' he said, 'though it is no surprise he ended in a drunken brawl. He could not hold his drink, it made him quarrelsome. It is not even true aggression, that sort of waspish humour, it is like a cowardly dog snapping and snarling because of some momentary courage, freak momentary courage. Lord knows I have separated enough fighting seamen and carried home enough drunks in my time to know the difference. But of course a man like that is just as dangerous as a real tough once he has a weapon in his hand, perhaps more so because he is unpredictable. I am sorry a man brought up a gentleman and with every advantage should come to it though, it is something to do with idle hands and all that, idle hands and too much money. Still, I am sorry. What will that doting old woman do without him?' And then, looking up suddenly in a blaze of astonished blue: 'Alex, they will say I killed him.'

'My dear, as if I had not already thought of it,' thought of it hurrying down that damp sea-breathing lane in the half-light, the lantern at his back, the knowledge of what

251

he was to find dull in his mind, thought of it as he had turned the body over with that oddly familiar dismay, not dismay at death itself but at the absolute certainty that all passion came to this in the end, all feeling to this irremediable blank. 'Perhaps it would be wiser to go home to Ramillies for a few hours. As soon as I have finished here I will join you. I had rather join you,' and this in a low low voice, 'at Ramillies than sit in this inn with all the coming and going and constant noise.'

'The horses have been taken already.'

'All to the good. Forgive me, but I do not think it would be wise to ride down the main street this morning, rumour is everywhere in spite of Sir James's precautions, and you are a noticeable man, you could not slip away unseen. Take a chaise, go straight home. Ah, Mrs King,' as that lady answered his bell, 'some breakfast for poor Mr Bliss, he was obliged to go out. Shall I carry it to him? I am dashing off this minute but will return before you have cooked the sausages; chops, bacon, toast, a flask of coffee, that should do. Put it under a cover, I shall hurry it across to him.' And at her strange knowing look: 'I left him comforting a poor old woman, the dear soul, a widow.'

'I do believe I threw her off the scent,' he said with satisfaction when Mrs King withdrew, puzzled, 'but I must not delay. Go home, Jary, take my advice: go home.'

Jary stood up, stood to his full height and stretched, then reached down for his coat. 'Home? I begin to see I have never yet found a place I may truthfully call home. But I shall be at Ramillies, I shall do as you say.' And then, with a hard look: 'I did not kill him, Alex.'

'Do you think you need to tell me? Of course you did not. Come, I shall tell them you want a chaise in ten minutes, the sooner you are away and admiring your canal the better.'

In four hours there was not a soul between Westdene and Stretfield who did not know Prince Whiteley had been murdered, that the constables had dragged his mutilated body from a midden down the end of one of Ⓡthe fisher rows attended by Sir James Braile in his capacity of magistrate. Indeed, Sir James was hard put to it to reach Mrs Whiteley in time to prevent her being told of her nephew's death by one of the labourers or a man mending the road. She took it badly, as might be expected, and rumour had her vowing vengeance on the felon – it was commonly believed Mrs Whiteley had an unlimited capacity for revenge.

Dr Plesset rose from his sick bed to attend a formal examination of the body where it lay in the town gaol – it had been pushed there on a hand bier in a plain elm coffin without exciting any comment – and he had subsequently crammed into a chaise and four with Dr French and young Mr Bliss for the short journey to Sir James's house for an interview mainly remarkable for the restrained good manners of all concerned while discussing the violent death of a man none of them had liked. They trod on eggs, as the Doctor afterwards told Jary, careful to voice no opinions but only the unvarnished facts: such and such a possible time of death, this wound the cause of death but all wounds bar one desperately deep and likely to have proved mortal within hours, body exactly where it had fallen, not dragged, not robbed – there were guineas in the pocket – and no sign of a fight. And: 'I see,' said Sir James, his fingers drumming on the table top. 'Gentlemen, you have been very thorough and discreet, I must congratulate you. Will you have something to drink?' and he rose to pour madeira, remarking that it was the hour for luncheon, a meal he did not despise, for he breakfasted at seven and they did not dine until six. He sat down in his chair again, and sighed.

'We are not used to sensational murders,' he said, 'and this one must be handled with tact.'

'I fear Mrs Whiteley is incapable of tact,' Dr French remarked, running a hand across his bristly chin and sinking his face in his drink in the hope of banishing the strange fetid chill of that room in the gaol.

'Mrs Whiteley need have no fear, justice will be done if justice can be done, but she must expect the law to take its course.' This suggested to his listeners that Mrs Whiteley had not been too overcome to rail at him and tell him his duty. His momentary sour look was a reflection of the memory.

For a time, while the clocks ticked and the madeira went down and footsteps passed and repassed outside the door, Sir James scratched down in a spidery, cramped, ornate hand everything the Doctor knew about the incident at the Assembly rooms, everything Mr Bliss had witnessed. The clocks struck, Plesset sank deeper in his chair and began to snore gently, a wizened, faded, worn-out old man, too ill for all the excitement. Sir James looked up at him and frowned and looked down again, sanding the final line. He said: 'I like Savage myself, a sound, straightforward sort,' and then, staring straight at the Doctor: I know you are his friend, I do not mean to divide your loyalties, but would you consider him capable of this?'

The Doctor's reply was flinty: 'Not in the least. Never. No.'

'It is only fair to tell you, suspicion falls entirely on him at the present moment. They were seen to have a quarrel, they threatened each other. Between half past twelve and three where was Mr Savage, pray? Do you know?'

'At the Admiral. Mr Bliss and I spoke to him when we returned from the Assembly rooms at one.'

'And was he in a good mood, was he on his way to bed, playing cards, drinking? What was he doing?'

The Doctor looked blank. Mr Bliss cleared his throat. 'I believe,' he said, 'Mr Savage was taking a last glass of port. Dr French and I joined him to toast to the success of his voyage to Jamaica.'

The Doctor and Mr Bliss exchanged a glance. The younger man's plain, honest face glowed with indignation: he could not have said how it had come about but he felt that he valued Jary extremely.

'A last . . . glass of . . . port,' said Sir James, writing on. 'Of course, you will be required to write your own statements but I must have notes, I must have my own notes: the sequence of events, the witnesses.'

'What happened to his party? The girl, his other friends?' asked the Doctor. 'Why did they let him go off alone?'

'God knows. It is a damnable business. But no doubt we shall find out. I have not yet discovered where any of them lodged, or even whether they had come in a carriage and so departed in it. I have not begun any general inquiry, my time has all been taken up with Mrs Whiteley.'

'He was her whole life,' came Plesset's thick voice from the depths of his chair, 'she will become more of a recluse than ever.'

'She has the ear of the Lord Lieutenant, that I do know.' Sir James was gloomily studying his page, his damning page. 'And she will not rest until we find the culprit.'

For a long time they all sat in morose contemplation of the empty grate, until the distant slamming of a door brought them to themselves. 'You will take a bite to eat,' said Sir James, rising, 'I shall tell Meg. Excuse me,' and he went out to find his wife, feeling in sore need of some pleasant sympathy. He had had a trying morning, attending the constables with their macabre humours, their unabated gloom punctuated by unexpectedly light-hearted and coarse remarks as they had supervised the removal of the body; then hurrying to break the news to that sour old woman in her dull, cold drawing room, prepared for anything: hysterics, fainting, screams; but not for what he found: cold, furiously cold hatred and the instant thought, the strongest hope, of revenge; sitting in his study putting in motion the ponderous wheels of the law while all the time the body of that unattractive man lay in the guardroom at the gaol and most vividly in his mind's eye. Over and above his natural revulsion, his natural concern, and his natural dislike of such grim

255

duties, was another more instinctive revulsion and concern and dislike. He had never cared for Whiteley, a light-headed, spoiled, dissolute young sprig, a trial to any family, but he would not have wished him murdered, nor tumbled in a stinking alley, nor laid out in bloody state on the gaoler's table. A wish, vague but profound, that it had never happened, or that it had not been Whiteley, or that Jary Savage, whom he had begun to admire, should have nothing to do with it. A fear, as vague but as real as the wish, that it might be his unpleasant duty to commit a man he liked to trial.

'What a study we are in,' said Plesset, when they had sat waiting some time and had begun to wonder if Sir James and his wife were having a difference of opinion over luncheon and three unexpected guests. 'I would be sorry, you know, if suspicion fell on Savage. I thought him very well behaved at the duel, the fault entirely Whiteley's; and the business over the Diddlers, why, he was always gentlemanly. He is a man of honour, I am sure.'

The Doctor scratched his lean jaw. 'What is honour worth, sir? Can honour set to a leg? No, no. He is foreign and eccentric and he comes from the abode of pirates. Honour will be as smoke in the cold blast of English prejudice.'

'I don't grasp your allusion to legs,' began Plesset.

'It is Shakespeare,' said Bliss.

'Shakespeare, by God! I never cared for Shakespeare,' and after a pause, 'I am damn sure Whiteley would not have cared for Shakespeare either, he did not have a leaning to the theatre: actresses maybe, but not spectacle or poetry. Yes, actresses, horses, the chase... Gentlemen, gentlemen...' And on a fading note: 'I do not feel well. Will you have the goodness to see me to my house.'

'She hev the character of a witch,' Hawke was saying to Jary as they paced the riverbank contemplating the strange effect the canal was having on the original watercourses. A full acre of reed beds and alder carr lay exposed to the roots and the river was reduced to a determined stream between the mud flats.

'Oh, I knew Ma Henham cooked herbs and scanned palms,' said Jary, 'but I would not have given her credit for charming away whole rivers. There must be something happening upstream, the mill regulates the flow in these lower stretches. If they have closed up their sluice the moment I open my new one I am not surprised the water has fallen to such a level.'

But Hawke, who had been put out to find Mr Savage returned when he ought to have been well on his way to the west country and thence to Jamaica, dismissed all scientific theories, all practical explanations, and clung to Ma Henham. 'She do know every herb as sprouts a leaf and what they cure, and what they kill. You should have seen her old cottage at the Diddlers. It had a rare stink.'

So did the river, what was left of it. There were two disconsolate herons on the far bank eyeing the waste of fine silt and the stranded weed. Jary said: 'I suppose I shall have to ride up to the mill and see what has happened,' and he eased one boot out of the mud and grasped at a tussock, more appalled by the wilderness than he would let Hawke see, doubly appalled perhaps after the accumulated miseries of the long dispiriting night and the shocking morning. 'Is that not the Doctor, home at last?' as he reached firmer ground.

It was; the Doctor on foot, grey and more lifeless than Jary had ever known him. Hawke made his apologies, he was needed at the sluice, and he went off at a great rate for his stomach was complaining, he had a beef sandwich in his bag and it was already far far past noon, nearly two indeed though the grey overcast day looked substantially the same as it had at nine and would at five.

'You have not walked from Westdene?' asked Jary, amazed, looking at the Doctor's untidy hair, his damp shoes.

'No indeed. Sir James sent old Plesset home in his

257

carriage, the poor man was far from well. Andrew and I accompanied him and were set down at the gates. Andrew walked on a little to look at the church, he is very much devoted to antiquity. But tell me, where is the river gone?'

'Into my canal. I arrived back to find they had opened the sluice at six this morning, and this is the result. There has been a miscalculation.'

'There has, there has. Will they not complain in Westdene? Their harbour will disappear, and all their fishermen will be left in the mud.'

'Oh, it looks worse than it is, I expect. And the canal is a success. Come and see for yourself.'

It was a perfectly acceptable canal, full of muddied, greyish water, and it looked as bleak and cold as a marl pit. The Doctor pursed his lips. 'Well, it is wet,' he said at last.

'It will do very nicely when the greenery is restored.'

'So it will. But what about the river?'

'We have to adjust the sluice, it will be perfectly all right. I thought of riding up to Cockshoot to the mill to see what Blake is about, he can only be letting very little water through today to cause such a shortfall.'

'Well, I bow before your optimism. Such a terrible sight as that would give many a lesser man a quaking of the heart. And if the sluices, having been adjusted, do not answer?'

'Then we shall have to make the canal into a sunken garden and drain the water back where it came from.'

The Doctor gave a short laugh and they began to walk up to the house side by side. He had the feeling Jary would have liked to ask about events in Westdene but he said nothing, only pacing on with a dark troubled look, his hands in his pockets. At last: 'Have you eaten?'

'No, I regret not. We were about to be offered a mutton chop when Plesset was taken queer, he should never have attempted the journey and all that standing about in a miserable cold room at the gaol: the least exertion may kill him and he knows it, I had the feeling he wished to hurry home simply in order to die in his own bed. Sir James was most concerned. He was not feeling well himself, he takes his duty very seriously and is finding it disagreeable. It has made him bilious. I have to make him up a pill. He said he would call later in the day to speak to you.'

'In his official capacity?'

'Just so.'

They had reached the gravel. Jary flung back his head and looked up at the mellow brick of the house, at the shining windows. As always he thought of Henriette as his eye roamed up to the nursery floor, and it occurred to him again how hopes and ambitions go bewilderingly awry, how seldom a course of action keeps to the one straight path, how frequent are the doublings back, the detours, the arrivals in strange places. Had Henriette's death been the end of his strong hope for a new kind of life at Ramillies?

'Forgive me,' he said, 'I feel low today' – a quick sideways glance – 'and you look it. Are they saying I murdered him?'

'There are all kinds of rumours abroad, most of them fantastic.'

They went round the house and skirted the orchard to see if the pullets had laid any eggs. They had not. Jary glared at all his ill-natured birds but a hen's expression is difficult to read. He sighed. 'You ought to eat. I shall ask Clarkie for something. Your young medical friend should be here any minute.'

He came in just as they were sitting down in unprecedented gloom to bread and cheese and a pot of coffee, and he too was grave and rather quiet. He had seen the parson, he said, a strange thin man, vehement, and *he* had known for sure Prince Whiteley had been clubbed down on the beach, left for the tide to take out. 'Where do people get such stories? I let him ramble on, I could not disabuse him without giving away more than was necessary, but his whole tale was invention beginning to end. Perhaps he made it up himself, he seemed a cheerless

259

soul who might take refuge in that sort of borrowed excitement. I am so sorry' — with a hasty anxious look at Jary — 'I hope he is not your friend.'

'Not at all, though I believe he means well. He is a constrained, misanthropic man, uneasy in the company of others.'

'I am surprised he became a parson then, but I suppose he was put to the cloth the way some men are put to shepherding and making shoes. His church is in a sad way, it seems to be sucking up water from miles around, there is green mould like cheese on every wall.' There was a silence broken only by the strong chomp of Mr Bliss's jaws and the mewing of one of the grey cats outside the door. Then the Doctor stirred, leaning forward to lift the lid of the coffee pot.

'Ask Clarkie for some more,' said Jary, and as he spoke the door opened on the knock and Clarkie herself came in, wearing an expression of doom, a remarkably taut grey worried look for a woman usually so animated and cheerful.

'Pray excuse me, sir, but Mr Calloway is here. I have showed him into the library.'

'Ten to one he has come about his bill,' said Jary, rising.

'Well, he will have to wait until I have finished this. Clarkie, more coffee for the doctors and you had better send young Kate upstairs to air the beds, we shall not be leaving for a day or two. Oh, and tell Millett I shall need him to ride to Westdene with an urgent letter, it must go directly, I will never get to Falmouth in time for the schooner.'

At the closing of the door he walked over to the window and stared out at the moist and dull green garden. It could have been October, there was so much wet and greyness. He was quite sure Calloway had not come about his bill, and he thought that probably the two men behind him were equally sure and correctly surmised why he had come, the bloody-minded Pharisaical prophet of doom he was.

'Do you think Calloway suspects I may be taken up for murder?'

'Of course not,' said the Doctor, 'but he has heard Whiteley is dead and that you quarrelled with him before he died. Natural curiosity and a desire to serve his client as best he can have brought him at the gallop.'

The thought of Calloway with or without good intentions seemed disagreeable to Jary. He found the lawyer a difficult man to have a natural conversation with, inclined to throw him into a wretched humour with no more than a line, a gratingly cautious: 'Have you considered all the possibilities?' or 'Would it not be more prudent to wait upon events?' and since he was feeling less than diplomatic today the thought of that touchy, patronizing manner, that dark and disdainful gaze, made him feel more miserable than ever.

'I am going to write my letter,' he said, 'I will let Mr Calloway kick his heels until I am done.'

He went up to his room and opened the door on amazing tidiness, no trace of himself anywhere, the room cleaned and put straight and closed up. He opened the window, though all that came in was a draught of damp air and the smell of the distant mud. Then he turned and looked up, meeting the familiar challenge in her eyes. She reminded him so forcibly of Lizzie Rayner he wondered now why he had not perceived it from the first: the Doctor certainly had. He had not thought of Lizzie Rayner for some time, not for a whole day at least; he found she often walked uninvited into his mind with much the same vigour and air of belonging she showed while actually walking in his park, and he would be aware of a brief urgent desire to know how she did, how she really did, and whether Lizzie in fine clothes taking commissions from duchesses was recognizable as the Lizzie who had delivered Kate Farrow willy-nilly to his door, her temper and her curls astray.

He sat down to write his letter and as he wrote, regretting he could not sail with an old shipmate, regretting not being able to get away for the foreseeable future, regretting everything, it seemed to him that his mental picture, his sharp memory of Helen's Mount receded as he wrote, so that by the time he signed his name with a sudden bitter flourish it was still visible but blurred and very distant, very very distant, like a house in a dream or an ideal, something longed for and lost, never to be his.

Sir James Braile shut himself away with various influential people, some half dozen legal gentlemen of unquestionable acumen, and now and then sent for his constables, all his witnesses, and the town reeve. Depositions, statements from here and there, points of law, a welter of circumstantial evidence; he drank coffee, smoked, smoked and considered, considered. Then he commanded his clerk to ride to Ipswich to take statements from Miss Lucy Stanley and Mr Horace Stanley and Mr John Coble and anyone else who had been at the Assembly rooms that night, and when the close-written sheets came back he sat over them smoking and considering far into the night. Eventually, with the weariness of a man who has run a great distance and still has not outpaced the enemy or found a secure hiding place, he took up his pen and scribbled a note to Dr French at Ramillies, begging him to call at his earliest convenience.

His earliest convenience was the afternoon of the following day and he arrived like the east wind, dry and cold. He was – most strangely – impeccably dressed. Sir James had never seen him so clean shaven, so perfumed, so elegant. And he seemed to have put on an unassailable authority with his fine black coat; his glance was very keen as he said: 'I suppose you wish to tell me you must arrest Jary Savage.'

Sir James, in the act of motioning him to the most comfortable chair, looked astonished, astonished and embarrassed. He stood, a big awkward lump of a man, wrestling with his conscience, his duty as magistrate, his personal feelings, and everything in him that was gentlemanly suddenly at war.

262

'I am striving to avoid it. You know, Mrs Whiteley has the ear of a higher authority, I have had two letters now urging me to action. Doctor, I have looked at all the evidence, such as it is, and the plain facts are these: Mr Savage and Mr Whiteley quarrelled, Mr Savage returned to the Admiral – he was seen, served a bottle of port – two bottles I believe – while Mr Whiteley said goodnight to his friends, he did not want to go with them to the White Hart, he had business elsewhere. He did not say what business. He was last seen by them crossing the market square towards the Admiral. Then you yourself, Doctor, and your Mr Bliss, return to the inn. It is one o'clock. You share Mr Savage's port, you retire to bed at one thirty. Put what does Mr Savage do? It is presumed he sat on over the port. Mrs King did not disturb him, he had said good night to her anyway and she was eager to get to her bed, she had to rise early. I have to tell you – Heaven knows I am sorry to have to tell you – that between one thirty and three nobody set eyes on Mr Savage.'

'But of course not, he had gone to bed.'

'I am not trying to be difficult, but you have only his word for it. He has said he went to bed soon after the clock struck two, he was dozing, he had drunk too much; he has said he did not meet anyone on the stairs or in the passages.'

'That would not be unreasonable. I believe Mrs King locks the front door and discourages revellers at such late hours. The Assembly rooms crowd had gone home long before.'

'She locked the door about five minutes after you and Mr Bliss arrived at one. She was late doing so because it had been a lively evening.'

Sir James took out his pipe. No, the Doctor would not join him. There was bright sunshine outside the windows, spring at last, and every so often a beam slanted in through the window and fell on the faded Persian rug at the Doctor's feet. He stared at its intricate pattern, pondered its long journey to this undistinguished resting place, by camel and slow fat merchantman, sails bellying in warm oragnge-scented airs . . .

'He could have left the inn, Doctor, killed Whiteley and been back in bed in half an hour.'

'You have no witnesses . . .'

'To prove it one way or the other, no. But I have found an old man in one of the cottages down the lane who heard running feet just before two and saw a tall figure making for the market square.'

'He saw a man clearly in that pitchy thoroughfare? And how did he know it was just before two, pray? He consulted his watch perhaps. It is more likely your constables have been over-zealous and asked leading questions with the result the old man is convinced he saw what he feels they want him to have seen.'

'Dr French, the judge arrives in four days. I have to decide whether to commit a man for trial.'

'What kind of trial, Sir James? I have been in Westdene this morning, I have heard the talk. In a very few days, even if the murderer confessed at the market cross, he would not be believed: it is Mr Savage who is condemned. He is condemned because he is a foreigner, because he has strange manners and the occasional want of tact, because he wishes to remove dirt and disease and unnecessary hardship from his cottagers, because he is too tall, too dark, and altogether too incomprehensibly generous. Mrs Whiteley is not liked but she is known, her nature is understood, and she has been letting the cottages fall down and their occupants die of avoidable fevers for years. She must also be allowed a natural desire for revenge, and if she chooses to avenge her nephew on Jary Savage the people will stand by her, it is only fitting. Prejudice, my dear sir, will gather force so quickly there will be no chance of a fair trial this side of Colchester.'

Sir James puffed at his pipe. The clocks ticked on monotonously. A distant bell ringing, and female voices, and faint faint laughter came from other parts of the house. The Doctor sat back, considering his slender brown hands and the clean linen at his wrists, and then he looked up and in his face was an expression Lizzie Rayner would have recognized, for she had painted it into his portrait.

'You believe him guilty yourself, Sir James.'

'I am not so dishonourable as to prejudge a man. You do me wrong, sir.'

'But it would be human to have an opinion. In your opinion he is guilty.'

'Damnation! I think perhaps they met and continued their quarrel and that Savage was provoked.'

The Doctor took out his beautiful watch and shook it, holding it to his ear. 'I regret I must leave you, I have another appointment. I believe your case to be a pack of cards, sir, a pack of cards. If such ardent hypothesis – and, I may say, wishful thinking – is the best you can produce, you and your learned friends, then I hope you are laughed out of court. I hope so indeed,' and he bowed, his gaze so cold and distant the other man was momentarily transfixed. 'Your servant, sir. '

'Dr French . . .'

'No, sir, you should not have asked me here, hoping I would defend him while you played devil's advocate, trying out your theories. I do not envy you your position and the responsibility, but it is always a sad spectacle when an educated man clutches at straws even the most ignorant would recognize for what they were. I will take no part in your speculation and your surmising, I was not aware anyone other than pot-boys and travelling tinkers would ignore so many facts for the sake of such a fiction.'

'I am afraid I have insulted Sir James Braile,' said the Doctor, shown into Charles Calloway's rooms half an hour later.

'Not intentionally, I hope?'

'Very much so. I classed him with pot-boys and travelling tinkers. He is an honest man, crippled by the desire to do the right thing, but God save us from honest men who cannot make up their minds. For all his anguish and

265

his turning the facts over and over he will come to the conclusion others wish him to come to – he has done so already if I read the signs – because finally he will take as justification for his decision the opinions of other men. He is very weak. He has always resisted Mrs Whiteley in the past because there was nothing much at issue, but Mrs Whiteley and the Lord Lieutenant along with a dozen other landowners and attorneys are too many for him. He is grappling with his conscience, sure, but he will win, he will most certainly win, his conscience will be chased off.'

Calloway's sombre face darkened even more at this, but after all it was no more than he had suspected, he had been sure from the first that if a case could be made out against Jary a case would be made out, though it was cobbled and patched and a disgraceful piece of contrivance. So he forced a smile and showed the Doctor to a chair, noticing the Doctor's elegance and aware too, instinctively, of the Doctor's deep dismay. His smile grew gradually more natural and his voice perceptibly warmer.

'I am sorry Mr Savage flew off at me when I came to Ramillies,' he said. 'He kept me waiting a very long time and seemed off-hand, obstructive, when he came in. I am afraid I did not show my best side – and nor did he.'

'He was not in the mood to appreciate your wishing to help him. I have come tonight to offer, as it were, an olive branch.'

Calloway looked momentarily as if he was not in the habit of being offered olive branches, nor, in a universally distrusted profession, any concessions at all. He became more conciliatory at once, and said he would send out for dinner – surely Dr French would stay to dinner? In general he patronized Mrs Lowe in Becket's Row, hot meals at all hours, pastries, fresh bread, the only draw-back being there was little or no choice, it might be rabbit or it might be broiled beef or it might be fish of some kind but most certainly it would not be all three.

'Fate,' remarked the Doctor as the plates steamed in,

most definitely broiled beef, tender and juicy, 'Jary believes in fate.'

'So does Mother Henham,' said Calloway drily, 'perhaps we should ask her what his might be.'

18

'Another letter from dear Fanny,' said Helen, dropping it on the bed, and after a suitable time: 'Well, what news from the country? Not . . . bad news? Oh Lizzie dear, surely not bad news?'

Lizzie read the letter slowly for the third time. There was a savage, irresolute, chaotic look in Helen's direction, a crackling of paper as it was swiftly folded, and: 'Bad news, yes. I must go home at once.'

'Go home? But my dear, how can you go home? Why, you have engagements for a month and your pictures, Lady Mc . . . McWhatsit coming to sit for you next week. And Madame Le Brun . . . Lizzie, you cannot possibly go home!'

Of course she could, said Lizzie, and what was more she was leaving at once, at once as soon as she had packed and swallowed her breakfast, as soon as a post-chaise could be got to the door. She burned about the room, flinging open the wardrobe, dragging out the drawers of the matching chests.

'But what is it? What has happened?' cried Helen. 'My dear, do calm yourself. Not terrible news, not catastrophe? Not dear Fanny . . .'

'Fanny?' throwing shoes from under the little scrolled sofa. 'No, not Fanny. Mr Savage.'

'Mr Savage?' faintly.

'He has been taken up for murder.'

'Murder?' More faintly still; 'Murder! Whose murder?'

'Mr Whiteley's.'

'Mr Whiteley whom you always wished to . . . to the devil?'

'The very same. It was perhaps the only point about which Mr Savage and I wholeheartedly agreed, but now it seems he and not I will hang for it.'

'Lizzie! Lizzie, how can you say such things? But why must you go? Mr Savage is . . . is an acquaintance. He can make no claim on . . . on you. It will look so strange, as if there is a . . . connection.'

Lizzie was brushing her hair back, snatching up a towel and bending over the water in the basin. 'Remember, he fought a duel on my behalf.'

'That makes it look worse, Heaven knows! Are you very sure you should go? Think of all the trouble before, the unkind talk when you and Captain Jervis . . . My love, how can you mean to travel today?'

'You may come if you like. Fanny would enjoy a guest, she frets for the wider world.'

'Oh! Oh, how could I come? I cannot just shut up the house. Lizzie, you are not yourself.'

But she was herself at last, herself again. Her glowing face was testimony to it. Helen fell back and subsided onto the bed.

'You must say I have been called away,' came the authoritative voice from the washbasin, 'there is . . . there is illness in the family.'

'But you have no family! Oh yes, yes of course I will do my best but. . .'

'And I will write to the Academy, and Madame Le Brun, and to Lady McLean.'

For a while there was only the flurry of Lizzie dressing, and of Kitty coming in and out quite flushed and confused, and the noise of the trunks coming upstairs, the bags and boxes coming down from the attics. Now and again Helen would rush in begging them not to forget the silver-backed hair brushes, the new sunshades, the silk chemises. 'How Fanny will love your new things,' she said, poking odds and ends in the trunk before they closed it, 'but how little you have spent considering, I mean considering how much you earned for that last portrait alone.'

'I have been stupidly extravagant in truth,' said Lizzie, looking at the row of hatboxes, 'I should have saved every penny. I have a great deal to repay Fanny, years and years of debts I once thought I would never clear. You cannot imagine the relief of seeing myself square at last.'

They went down for breakfast, a servant sent to order the chaise, the food coming in and Lizzie not eating it, toying with cocoa and a slice of bread. It was a dull drizzling morning and when London was grey it was uncommonly grey, spring might have been unheard of there, but even so she viewed the coming journey with deep anticipatory delight, a bubbling happiness. She had not realized how desperately she had longed for an excuse to leave, how wearisome the last weeks had been, how much her orgy of painting had been simple escape. Now, in this strange mood, this joy, she found memory heightened to an almost unbearable pitch: Foley by the burnished levels of the Meeting Grounds, the flaking paint of the elderly garden seat where she had often sat and watched the bats, Fanny's dread bats, and the barn owls from the hayloft like ghosts over the hedges; Fanny playing the harpsichord on spring evenings, the windows open and every waft of air apparently throwing it out of tune, a spirited crescendo broken off with 'Oh just listen to it, the rogue, every third note out of true!'; Jary Savage dancing with her, the step and counter-step, the serious measure, the sure touch of his warm hands.

'Lizzie,' came Helen's anxious voice, 'Lizzie, are you listening? I was saying that you do not know ... Mr Savage might well turn out to be ... to have done it.'

'Not him. But I tell you, I would have killed Prince Whiteley had I thought I would never be found out.'

'Oh Lizzie, Lizzie, what a terrible thing to say!'

'But then I am such a terrible woman. You have said so often.'

There was a knock. The chaise had arrived: should they load the trunk? Lizzie rose and ran out, a feverish look in her eye, a mad desire to be on the road. Yes, there it was, four good horses and a decent carriage, better than average. Kitty appeared in a cloak and sober bonnet carrying a bag, asking if they would need more

270

than a snack for the coach, were they going to stop on the road? No, said Lizzie, no they were not going to stop, they were dashing straight back to Suffolk, there was not a moment to be lost.

'I still do not understand why you should care that this man has been accused of murder, why you should find it necessary to rush back to Westdene,' said Helen, in the brief interval Lizzie spent in front of the mirror tying her bonnet. 'How does it affect you, pray?'

'Let us say it affects Ramillies,' said Lizzie non-committally, and then turning in a rush of contrition: 'Helen, you can have no idea how grateful I am, how very very grateful for all you have done.'

'I was pleased to have you, pleased to do Fanny a good turn.'

Kitty was in the doorway. The man wanted to know if they were going to start directly, his horses were catching cold. 'How disgraceful!' exclaimed Helen. 'To think they charge so much a mile and are so disobliging. My dear, you must stop overnight, you cannot keep travelling in the dark, why, anything could happen.'

But Lizzie was determined nothing should happen to keep her from Foley. To begin with she sat in silence watching the mist roll away from the carriage as it crept through the traffic, a great din of shouting and horses' hooves muffled by the wet glass. After a while trees appeared, pavements vanished, and rather shoddy small houses in uniform rows loomed up and fell away, and then open country, the bleat of sheep mingling with the blast of a mail horn as a coach came furiously from the opposite direction. On and on, woods, hedges, gates, hills, valleys, glimpses of water; for a while there was driving rain and then it eased, showing more woods, more hedges and more water. At the third change of horses, getting down to ease her stiffening limbs, Lizzie grew imperious: she wished to be in Suffolk, not kicking her heels at a post-house. They went on. They went on in a different carriage and with less regard for life and

271

limb; bread and cheese and salt beef were posted through the window to them, and a flask of cold tea.

The dark came. The lights were ineffectual in the streaming gloom, rain and wind now as they drew nearer and nearer the margin of the land, and once or twice they checked for a great lumbering wagon even worse lit, or kept well to their side as a mail coach passed, or pulled up steaming at a tollgate. Kitty slept, the tea flask clutched to her chest, her mouth open. Lizzie sat and stared into the blackness, the rain flying at the window. At one change of horses, pulling up abruptly, the surprise of being motionless after so long rocking and swaying bringing her round from a light sleep, she wondered why indeed she was hurrying back to Suffolk. Was it only for herself, to escape London and the tedious social round she so disliked?

The window was tapped, the door opened a fraction. A man's face, creased and confused, looked in. Would the lady care for anything: food, drink, hot bricks, more rugs? He was taken aback to find the lady alone except for her snoring maid, but she was a proud-looking piece, as he afterwards reported to his wife, with a commanding voice. She wanted nothing but a bottle of wine, wine and two glasses. When he ran back with them she had taken off her bonnet and the light fell on her soft hair turning it amber. He gave her a bold look but she was not having any of that, paid him and dismissed him with a word. They trimmed the lamps, the postillion mounted, and the chaise rolled on again.

Drinking wine in a moving carriage was a new experience, Lizzie nearly spilled the whole down her new grey travelling dress. She had hoped it might make her drowsy instead of which it brought more memories, much older ones, into her wakeful mind. She had the oddest feeling that she was in some state of suspension between two lives, between two stages of life, that this uncomfortable scramble through the turbulent dark was a necessary transition. She had longed for recognition, for the wealth that might accompany it, and now she found she liked neither the recognition nor the tendency for a preoccupation with guineas to lead to a singular obsession, an all-consuming passion for them to the extent that an artist might base his price upon his client's status, thus making a portrait of a duke ten times that of a country squire. To be sure there might be rich men who did not consider any object worth looking at unless they had paid a great price for it, would treasure the meanest china plate worth twopence if some mountebank had sold it to them for two hundred pounds, who would not look at a horse under a hundred guineas though it was the Godolphin Arabian himself; yes, to be sure, there were always fools of that sort, and besides, to obtain the highest price for one's talent was only good business, but to Lizzie it could be carried to extreme lengths and end by debasing the artist, the man and painter both. She had found that there were limits to her pursuit of wealth, natural and moral limits; she could make a great deal of money and she found she did not care to, which was strange seeing how she had longed and longed to escape her circumscribed, modest life at Foley, to escape that keenly felt obligation to Fanny whom she loved dearly and who shamed her by asking nothing in return. Was it then that the other reason for earning great quantities of money had gone, that she accepted now that Ramillies was out of reach?

What would she be left with, the mainspring of her life gone?

They were drawing up. She leaned forward and pulled down the glass: a tollgate, a candle winking in the gloom, a door closing, a woman's voice saying this here was a heathen time to be on the road, two in the morning and the weather a pig's breakfast, rain, rain, wind and floods. As the carriage moved forward again Lizzie saw a pudding-shaped figure with a tarpaulin sheet held over its head, calling goodnight and good riddance. A moment later there was a finger post, unreadable in the swirl of dark and wet, but the chaise swerved right-handed,

273

slowing down appreciably in the deeper going away from the turnpike.

Long long afterwards, jerked from a sort of waking dream of Ramillies and youth, youth and disillusion, Lizzie saw the lights and heard the familiar cries and the rattle and crash of yet another inn yard. This time there was no great hurry to change the horses, they were led away steaming to be rubbed down and the coach left momentarily forlorn, mud-splashed to the very roof. Then a liveried servant was at the door: would the ladies care to step inside for breakfast, there was anything hot they cared to name; it was with great regret, the most abject apologies, he had to inform them the inn could not provide four fresh horses, they were very short of horses altogether, this not being a regular posting place and a remarkable upsurge in business having reduced their stock. In half an hour the lady might have a coach and pair, a new, well-sprung coach and a fit, well-rested pair at present eating up their beans as fast as they could lay teeth to them.

A coach and pair would do, said Lizzie, shaking Kitty awake, but please to see that the baggage was all transferred and properly secured. For herself she would not care for breakfast but her maid might like a bite to eat and something hot to drink. The servant bowed and held up an umbrella. Lizzie stepped down. There was the thick greyness of coming day, the lull between dark and light when the wind falters, and the strange sweet tang of the sea.

'You are two miles from Westdene, ma'am,' she was told as she came in to the atmosphere of woodsmoke and spilled ale and tobacco, 'for your offside leader cast two shoes in the mud and fell lame so that the boy stopped here instead of going on.'

'We are two miles from Westdene,' said Lizzie to a grey, half-dead Kitty who appeared in the door, and saw her face, momentarily blank with bewilderment, suddenly break into the most breathtakingly enormous smile.

*

Effusive greeting, kisses, embraces: she had been sorely missed. Fanny had been sewing, an occupation she detested, trying to thread her needle for the tenth time in the early morning twilight of her little parlour while she waited for the breakfast to be brought in. She had risen when the door had opened, glad of the interruption, and there had stood Lizzie, muddy hems, wild hair, exultant joy all over her face.

It had taken an hour for Fanny to calm down, sitting with a jug of cocoa and a great pile of toast amid the remains of the paper and string in which her presents had been wrapped: scarves, gloves, combs, silk underwear. She could not have been happier if Stephen Fisher had changed overnight into the handsomest of men and offered not only marriage but forty thousand a year and a house in Portman Square. She beamed, she laughed, she talked.

'But why did you come back, my dear?' after a long sobering moment, watching Lizzie stoop to pick up some of the debris. 'Oh I am so glad, so glad, but . . . What was it brought you home?'

'Mr Savage and Ramillies, I suppose, or Ramillies and Mr Savage. Who knows? The house was safe with him and now everything will go to ruin again.'

'Dear Liz, can you really believe he killed Whiteley?'

'No, no of course not. But that does not mean he might not be found guilty.'

Joy drained away. They looked at one another. Lizzie saw her dear plump friend with a little moustache of cocoa and wide anxious eyes; Fanny saw a vital, elegant Lizzie, her hair cut off and all the soft curls that were left tied up in a simple ribbon.

'The law is very strange,' Fanny began, 'there is something odd about his counsel, he can cross-examine witnesses but not speak on Mr Savage's behalf. Oh, I scarcely understand it, but Charles Calloway has matters in hand, has found a sound, elderly, respectable counsel well known on the eastern circuit or whatever it is. You know, sometimes I think it is all just a game they have

275

invented to keep themselves occupied and not . . . not anything to do with justice at all.' And then: 'Oh Lizzie' – reaching forward to take her hands – 'oh Lizzie, how good to have you home.'

Lizzie tossed her hat on the library table and stooped to see what was in the twenty-three specimen jars ranged in the cold hearth.

'Do mind,' said the Doctor, 'mind the poor chameleon.'

'How hideous it is, pickled.'

'But it is the only one I have. We would all look hideous pickled, dear Lizzie. There is no need to rock the jar!' And he had reached her, was grasping her arm, leading her away, installing her in one of the high-backed chairs. There she sat and looked up at him, beads of rain still caught in her hair where she had dashed in from the garden, her hands folded in her lap.

'You called me Lizzie.'

'It was improper. I beg your pardon.'

'You do not give a fig for my pardon.'

'But I apologize for the liberty.'

'I did not say I minded it.'

They smiled at each other. This was an unorthodox visit, so very early in the morning, and lacking even the barest minimum of conventional behaviour. The Doctor groped among the jars, lifting them one by one on to the long table where they displayed their gruesome contents in the dim watery light of the dim watery day. Lizzie stared, rose, walked up and down, stared again, asked quietly if that were not a hand, and that a toe, and that . . . something else. And when he nodded and said yes, and the hand was fresh, Dr Plesset had carried it over in his pocket not three weeks ago, an unlucky accident in a saw-pit necessitating a hurried amputation, she swung round, pale and breathing hard, and asked in a hoarse voice if Jary were well.

'As well as any man who is kept confined for a crime he did not commit. He is subdued but not unnerved. I see the jars distress you, perhaps we could go to another room. I had them sent up from my London lodging, all except the hand. Old Plesset thought I would like it, being out of the ordinary – there is only a vestigial thumb, you know . . . But what brings you back? I was told you were shortly to leave for Oxford, that you would not see Foley till October. And you look knocked-up, white, finished. When did you set out?'

'Yesterday morning. I arrived three hours ago.'

'And have not slept?' She shook her head. 'You do not mean to tell me you have left London, left your future wealth and happiness and a myriad opportunities, all the sincere admiration, to gallop to Stretfield because Jary Savage has been put in gaol?'

'Oh, as for London, you may grind it to dust and scatter it across Diddlers Ground; as for sincere admiration, I met with very little; and as for happiness, it is not found by looking, nor born of wealth and flattery.'

'Well, that is certainly true.'

She walked to the window: the old familiar view. The rain fell steadily out of a dismal sky. 'This has been an unlucky house since my father died,' she said quietly, 'or before that, since . . . since he killed the peacock. They all said it would bring bad luck. There was my engagement to Whiteley, so foolish, so ill-considered; there was father breaking his neck; there was losing the house and all the land, not even having Hopes to live in . . . I used to tell myself it was all the fault of the peacock, it was a kind of comfort. But now this: perhaps the house is cursed after all.'

'Nonsense! You cannot believe it.'

She swung round to look at him, more graceful than he remembered, more thoroughly alive. The short hair suited her, and indignation had always done so. 'How right I was,' she said, 'to paint you as I did,' and then, more softly: 'I am only sorry I did not do justice to Mr Savage, I have seldom done such a bland, meaningless picture.'

'Why so?'

'Oh, who can say? I believed I disliked him, wished

very much to dislike him, and I suppose I knew I did not dislike him in the least. The picture was . . . it was an exercise in indifference.'

The Doctor smiled and held open the door. 'Let us repair to the morning room, it is always warm and cheerful.'

The portrait of Jary hung above the fireplace, and though to anyone who knew him well it was apparent that four-fifths of his character were missing from that dark face with its pleasant, serious gaze, nevertheless it was a striking piece of work. They both stared at it for a moment, lost in very different thoughts and then, as if she had asked him to, the Doctor began a brief and lucid account of the events leading up to Jary's arrest – a strange, ill-managed affair which had actually taken place in Charles Calloway's office – Calloway had been incensed, almost ferocious – and the arrival of the judge and his officers for the Assizes, a sobering sight, several members of the local gentry riding in carriages to meet him and a great many small boys with catapults doing the same, all mixed with a dozen of the prettiest young women Westdene could provide, armed with baskets of flowers, an airing of the venerable, discoloured, cumbersome snap-dragon that usually lived close up under the reeve's ceiling on hooks, and a general air of celebration and simple good cheer. Since the gaol could render up only two prisoners, Jary and a young, timid, mousey fellow caught throwing stones through the windows of his rival in love, it did not look as if the judge would be long delayed in Westdene this year, however many morris dances or eight-course dinners or pretty young women they threw in his way. The upshot was that the poor stone-throwing boy had been tried this very day – he had no idea of the sentence, the verdict was a foregone conclusion but the sentence was a matter for Mr Justice Fielder who apparently loved his port, his dogs and his daughter and very little else. He certainly did not care much for the common run of humanity, which paraded before him endless variation on the seven deadly sins, nor did he care for meeting the same gentry, the same magistrates, constables, counsels and even jurymen over and over through the passage of many years on his tediously familiar circuit. His sentencing reflected these feelings; he had the reputation of a hard man, if not exactly a hanging judge a very near miss indeed.

Jary's case was to come up tomorrow, said the Doctor, everything hustled along at great speed for the judge's convenience, he could not hang about eating Mrs King's veal pie and taking the sea air for ever, or even for a week. Charles Calloway said it was a disgrace, they had no time to prepare a case, but as they had no case, strictly speaking, he had become resigned to it during the last twenty-four hours and had primed Mr Frost as counsel the very best he could, seeing he had nothing to prime him with but the truth: that Jary had gone to bed at two and had been asleep when the murder was committed.

'It does not seem to be much of a defence,' said the Doctor sadly as he drew to a close. 'Charles and Mr Frost shake their heads and grind their teeth over it, crying woe and damnation. When I point out that it is the Crown's duty to prove Jary did step out and stab Mr Whiteley seven times without bloodying himself in the process or being seen leaving the inn or crossing the square they shake their heads even more, the gloomy killjoys, and say look at this heap, this Olympus of circumstantial evidence. It is all air, the case against Jary is all air, but Charles says he has seen men hung on air or put in the pillory, or transported.'

'How cheerful you all are. Is there nothing to be done?'

'Short of finding the real murderer which I fear we shall never do, no, there is nothing. If only' – running on deep in thought – 'he had taken some wench to bed, Pamela perhaps, a good sturdy shameless wench who would stand up in court for him.' And then, with a start: 'Forgive me, it is just that I have been reminded these last three days of something I once said to Jary after Henriette was born, that in such remote places you can depend on it, they will resist change and kill anything

279

unusual. It is a melancholy thought. It has begun to haunt me.'

Lizzie rose and pulled the bell. When Mrs Clark came she ordered tea with a smile, tea and biscuits and for the Doctor a bottle of sherry, it was a cold morning, too much weather altogether for the time of year.

The Doctor had partaken of some strange meals in his time, hurried snacks punctuated by the banging of big guns and the crackle of muskets, moonlit suppers which had to be energetically preserved from rats, ship's biscuit soup at sea which had often ended up in his lap, and odd picnics in coaches and post-chaises, an excellent curry in a Colonel's coach in Calcutta, flying fish in a pie; but he had never sat down to such sour sherry, such dry biscuits, and in such a funereal atmosphere, and it appeared Lizzie's tea was very far from perfect, she looked inside the pot suspiciously and then pushed the whole tray to one side.

The handle rattled, the door opened hesitantly. Mr Bliss was on the threshold. 'I do beg your pardon, Doctor, I did not know . . .'

'Come in, Andrew, come in. I believe you know Miss Rayner.'

'But of course. She was kind enough to write a letter of introduction to you, have you forgotten?' It was clear the Doctor had forgotten, he looked bewildered. 'Miss Rayner, how do you do? I little thought when I begged you for a note that I would end up most thoroughly concerned in a murder trial, quite possibly called as a witness.'

'I am sorry for it. Do sit down. I would offer you a dish of tea but I guarantee you would not like it. I believe Mrs Fipson has taken leave of her senses, Mr Savage being away, housekeeping gone to pieces, the kitchen in chaos. I shall have to send Fanny over, she is no house-wife but a great manager, a great setter-to-rights. I am sure Mrs Clark would not mind, she seems positively distracted. Doctor, will you pour Mr Bliss a glass of your sherry?'

'I would not touch it,' was the reply, 'it will give you the gripes. I believe the best thing would be to ride into Westdene and eat at the Admiral. Perhaps afterwards we might stop by at the gaol.'

'Your pony is much admired in Norfolk, I hear,' said Bliss with a smile, and then to Lizzie, 'Did you ever see the Doctor's chestnut pony? I have never known quite such character in a horse's skin before, though I am no expert, I am only used to hirelings. The Doctor, having decided to go to India, has given his pony into the safe-keeping of an old friend, a Lady Gerard: Millett rode him up two days ago. And would you believe it, the lady was enchanted, slapped a saddle on the cunning little beast and was away.'

'Lady Gerard evidently has nerves of steel,' said Lizzie, with a wicked look at the Doctor.

'She has indeed, but only when riding a horse. At all other times her determination is of the usual temporary nature, she has the feminine trick of changing her mind as often as her petticoats.'

'Why Doctor, what a sour remark! It is not worthy of you. It is the peevish complaint of a rejected lover, quite unjustified, and throwing more light on the nature of the complainer than of the lady.'

It was a bold stroke, and although she was in the act of rising and shaking Mr Bliss's hand, she saw that it had gone home. So it *was* this mysterious Lady Gerard who had driven him to deepest Suffolk. Lizzie said her goodbyes, brooding on this, and at the outer door, reaching for her umbrella: 'I hope I have not said anything to offend you, I would hate to do so.'

'It is nothing, dear girl, nothing. I am too old for romantic notions.'

'What a great deal of nonsense,' and then, gazing out at the dismal rain, the grey, monotonous rain: 'I thought I was too, but perhaps we are never safe. Perhaps it is given to everyone to love one or two others deeply, even unthinkingly, more than life itself, and it is just chance whether we meet them early or late or not at all.'

He looked at her, but she was smiling. 'Will you be in court?' he asked.

'No, I believe not. I do not want to see him harried and torn about – I have sat in at the Assizes before now, it is not an edifying spectacle even when the crime is the most serious; there is an air of unreality, posturing, theatre. I suppose . . . Do you think he would see me if I called at the gaol tonight? Are there restrictions?'

'There is an hour at which the gaol is locked, but it is purely theoretical, it never strikes. I have sat with him two evenings until midnight and let myself out as easily as through the front door at Foley. Would you like me to take you in?'

'Would you? I would be most grateful. Of course, he may not care to see me. I am prepared for that.'

She was prepared for anything. He had never seen her so like Jary's lady in grey. There was some difference in her he could not put a name to, some profound change.

'Until later,' he said. 'Seven o'clock in Ship Street?'

'Seven o'clock in Ship Street,' she answered, and raising her umbrella, stepped out into the rain.

19

Ship Street was a smelly lane that ran up from the old quay and petered out at the openings to several of the narrow alleys and fishermen's rows. When the Doctor stepped out of Charles Calloway's office on the waterfront and made his way up it, deep in thought, it wanted but five minutes to seven and he could see the dark shape of the hooded gig drawn up by the wall halfway along. The wall was a very old one, the windowless side of a building whose chimneys poked at regular intervals through the fancy parapet. Built as a merchants' hall when Westdene was at the height of its prosperity not long before Agincourt, it had afterwards been used as council chamber, courtrooms, corn exchange, and gaol. It had been added to and altered almost every decade and as the town – shifting about because of the silting river and the encroaching sea – had crept up to and round it, a great wall had been built on the two sides previously left open to what was now Fore Street and Friday Walk where the main entrance was currently decked with greenery to welcome the judge.

Lizzie stepped down from the gig. 'Kitty will hold the pony,' she said at the Doctor's startled glance at the driver, 'Fanny sold the carriage for my sake, do you remember? We were rather hard pushed to find anything on wheels at all. I borrowed this from Paradise.'

'I did not think,' said the Doctor forlornly, 'I should have remembered. There is the coach at Ramillies standing idle.'

'But nothing to pull it since you and Mr Bliss had purloined the only horses. Never mind, I am here now and to the hour.'

He gave her his arm and led her a few yards to a low

wooden door in the wall. It opened, and they stepped through.

'Charles Calloway has begged I bring you for something to eat and drink after you have seen Jary,' he said as they picked their way across a courtyard and made for a low door opposite.

'I expect he thought Fanny would be with me.'

'No, I don't think so.'

'Dear Dr French, are you aware of the nature of my relationship with Mr Calloway? We were friends as children, you know, his father was my father's lawyer. But after we grew up we had a great many differences of opinion, and he hated my engagement to Prince Whiteley though he told me we were well-suited, we were as feckless and bad-tempered as each other. Then I ran away with Murray Jervis and it confirmed his worst fears, Miss Lizzie Rayner was unspeakable. Now he dislikes me so thoroughly I always think he might one day have a fit when we meet, a sort of hysterical revulsion. I cannot believe he asked you to take me to his rooms. He would die rather than let me cross the threshold.'

An inner door was opened by old Quarel, all the turnkey there was, wiping the froth of his beer from his upper lip with a large red handkerchief. Beg pardon, he said, he had not heard the Doctor coming, there were two of the judge's clerks and a constable and a sergeant of militia in the guardroom playing cards, a terrible serious contest and a heap of money on the outcome. A coin changed hands. 'We will see ourselves up,' said the Doctor, and ushered Lizzie to the stone stairs.

'Mr Savage did not eat his supper,' said Quarel with a knowing look, 'though that young Pamela from the Admiral brought it over herself on a tray and under a silver cover, the judge himself could not have better service. He is in a fit of the melancholy, asked only for paper and ink. I hev known prisoners before turn literary on the night before their trials.'

Up and up, stone steps worn shallow in the centre, a musty smell, and then a little landing, two doors off it,

284

and the Doctor took Lizzie's arm. 'He does not know you are coming. I cannot say what kind of mood he will be in.'

It was a small square room, the best in the place in fact, the best a country lock-up could afford, it being used only to a general hugger-mugger of petty thieves, bastardy cases and disorderly conducts. There was a chair and a table and a low-bred sofa and a truckle bed. There were washing things in a corner, a jug and basin, half-hidden by a screen, and over all a grey, utilitarian air, as if it was a monk's cell – except that there were bars at the one small window.

Jary stood up. He had been writing and his fingers were inky. He had had great trouble with his pens, scratchy inferior things, and too-thick inferior ink. He had just damned the twentieth blot and had shaken sand all down his front in his hurry to finish at their knock, and his look was cold, a cold, quiet, furious stare of something very close to hatred.

Lizzie might have ducked before it, crying to be let out again. But the anguish of being unjustly persecuted, wholly defeated, was too well known to her not to recognize it even in competition with a dozen other warring emotions. She may have quailed inwardly but her face was composed. She held out her hand, saying: 'I can see you are shocked, you were not expecting visitors tonight. But I will not stay a moment, I have left Kitty in charge of Fanny's old pony.'

Jary had got over his horror at seeing her, and his own hand came up automatically, but before it touched hers he saw the great stains of ink and he snatched it away. 'Forgive me, there is ink everywhere . . . Alex, pull up the chair for Miss Rayner. Has the rain stopped at last?'

'At last, but it is no mild spring evening,' replied the Doctor, bringing the grandfather chair to a vacant spot near the hearth, 'no birdsong and westering sun. There was talk at the Admiral of the night coach getting stuck in a ford and all the outsides swimming for it.'

Jary waited until Lizzie was seated and then resumed

his place on the joint stool by the table. He was in a buff-coloured suit, imperfectly shaved – the turnkey shaved him, he was not allowed sharp instruments, it was a rule of the gaol – and he looked grave and preoccupied which was only to be expected. He did appear very large, however, in relation to the room, and larger still due to a superabundance of damped-down emotion.

'I came to bring you this,' said Lizzie, extracting something from her bag, a small paper rolled up. 'You wrote to me in London about the picture of Ramillies. I had not forgotten. This began as a rough working for a big canvas but then I began to fill it in and turn it into something in its own right. I am afraid it was done from memory and I think memory played me false in several respects: the attic windows are quite wrong and the entrance is more central. But I thought perhaps you might care for it anyway.'

He unrolled it. It was extraordinarily well-worked, a perfect sketch, and in the foreground fountains and the play of light on water. 'It is very good,' said Jary, but his expression was somehow absent, a deathly blank.

'The painting will be better.'

He looked up at her and noticed for the first time her cropped hair, the smart London hat, her altered face. Was she thinner? Or was it, not that her eyes were larger and more brilliant, but that there was an expression in them that compelled attention? A new life? No. A new serenity, a calm, smiling look, all the restless frustration vanished.

It occurred to him that the Ramillies he held in his hand was the idealized Ramillies of her homesickness, very little different from his own created by nostalgia for Helen's Mount. There had never been such a place, and never would be now.

'Goodbye,' said Lizzie, rising, 'I shall probably find the pony has run away with poor Kitty, or eaten her.'

'I have not even offered you a glass of wine.'

'I did not expect you to,' and she took the Doctor's

arm. 'Come, Dr French, I must not be late. Fanny thinks I am playing the piano with Sophie Stone.'

Jary held the door, the door which should have been kept locked and never was, and he was about to say something when footsteps approached up the stone steps and Quarel came panting into view. A great crowd of people had just arrived, he whispered, mostly legal gentlemen, court officials and the like, but Sir James Braile was with them and the Reeve too and a savage-looking cove what was a constable from Ipswich, a hard piece of goods, an ex-Bow Street Runner.

'I must put on the lock,' Quarel told them, 'I am sorry for it, Mr Savage, but it is the rule. Doctor, Doctor, you must take the lady out at once, creep down, they may not see you.'

'Lizzie,' and Jary took a step from the room and held out his hand. She turned, saw it, reached back her own, smiled, and was gone.

They crept, ears straining for the first indication of approaching authority; they hurried down the cold stone passage and into the courtyard, the faint hum of conversation from some inner room rising and falling behind them. In the yard were three carriages, their lamps lit, their drivers in a guilty group, glancing about perpetually, throwing dice. The little door to Ship Street was locked, there was nothing for it but to brave the main entrance.

They braved it, walking straight up to the pasty youth hovering by the minute foot gate and asking to be let out. He had had no orders, he said, Mr Quarel had not mentioned the Doctor nor no lady. When he had opened the great gates for the carriages a gentleman had leaned out and told him that on no account was he to open them again before the judge arrived in the morning.

'But the gentleman said nothing about opening the little door,' said the Doctor reasonably, pointing at it. 'What he meant was, you are to keep people out, not keep them in.'

'But it is a gaol,' said Lizzie when they had passed

through the tiny hole and stood in the street at last, 'of course he must keep people in. You have confused him most wickedly, poor boy.'

They were now in Friday Walk, the market place to the right. They turned left towards the sea. There were some people about and one or two gave Lizzie curious stares. She put up her chin, nearly putting out the Doctor's eye with the crown of her London hat.

'Oh where is Kitty?' she cried when they reached the junction with Ship Street; the gig had vanished.

They went on, making their way to the quay and the row of old merchants' houses fronting it. In one of these Charles Calloway had his rooms and his office.

'You must come in,' said the Doctor, 'we will send Charles's boy out to look for the gig.'

They went in, ascended the narrow stair and opened the door on a scene of industrious chaos: papers, large books, briefs, boxes open and closed. In the middle of all this sat Whimble, his clerk, a thin, stooping, aged man, but they had no sooner entered and he had stood up and begun a greeting when the inner door flung wide and Charles Calloway came out. 'Doctor, come through. Miss Rayner, good evening.'

It was a bachelor's sitting room, furniture and ornament very sparse, a great deal of pipe ash in the grate, a surprising view of a long green garden with plum trees and rose bushes.

'I have sent down to Mrs Hawke for refreshment,' said Calloway with an embarrassed air. Lizzie was already at bay, had been since she passed the door; she did not exactly curl back her lip and show her teeth but it wanted only the smallest provocation and she would do so. He looked at her anxiously. She was still recognizably Lizzie, London fashions could not disguise her to a man who had pushed her out of a tree at eight years old, yet there was something changed. He found he rather liked her smile — always spontaneous and wide, it now seemed softer and more kind — but he pulled himself up at this point and showed her to a chair with a rigid politeness, pulling on the bell again, wondering where Mrs Hawke had got to, disobliging female that she was.

She was so disobliging as to refuse to answer the bell, and Whimble had to be sent down to the basement kitchen to inquire the reason; twenty minutes passed, and night hid the garden from view. Lizzie, who had very little to say to Charles Calloway, mentioned Kitty and how very worried Fanny would be if she were not home at Foley by nine o'clock.

'I shall step up to the Admiral and hire a carriage,' said Calloway, 'then you may return in style.'

'You are very kind,' said Lizzie in a voice that suggested she thought otherwise, thought that twelve years of perverse feeling, hard words and mutual disapproval could not be dismissed in twelve days of reconciliation, never mind twenty minutes, 'but I must find out what has happened to Kitty and the gig, I cannot go home without them.'

Further ringing brought no response. The Doctor stirred, rising out of a strange lethargy and seeing Lizzie and Calloway seated either side of the room but with more than a room's width between them, much much more. The Atlantic ocean, he thought sleepily, could not have put a more impossible gulf between them than all this undignified misunderstanding and assumed disdain. He pulled himself to his feet. 'I shall away to seek Mrs Hawke,' he said, 'and poor lost Mr Whimble. Could the lady be any relation of Jary's Hawke, the canal builder?'

'Oh, they are all related somehow,' said Calloway drearily, 'they are all cousins at some remove or uncles or half-brothers, or even several combinations at one and the same time. Which reminds me, Hawke has sent to say he has an urgent job at Pointers Hill over beyond Sir James Braile's and cannot do any more at Ramillies for the present.'

'It is all cock and bull, a fabrication. He is worrying about his bill and when it might be met.' And then, cocking his head: 'Is that not a hammering on the front door? Perhaps the boy has found Kitty.'

'What boy?' demanded Calloway. 'The child who helps Whimble has gone home for his mother's funeral.'

'No, no, this was a ragged bruising boy with a bent nose who was lounging on your step. I said he could have a shilling if he found a hooded gig with a very frightened lady inside.'

'Rest assured he will do so for a shilling, even if it is not the right gig and the right lady. Sixpence would have been a fairer rate for the task.'

'But for sixpence he would have shambled along and for a shilling he will run, a great difference. Excuse me, I shall go down.'

He had reached the top of the stairs when he met Whimble toiling up with a tray. 'A froward woman, Mrs Hawke,' said the old man, leaning against the wall to catch his breath, 'she would not lay a tray for Miss Rayner, not Miss Rayner, says she, the hussy. And when I remember how Miss Rayner was brought up, what carriages, what clothes ... and all lost, all lost and through no fault of hers; and her father kindness itself, God rest him. I must say' – with a sudden brightening, his colour returned to normal' – 'he would have thought it ill done, all his gardens dug about.'

'Oh that ... I assure you the finished effect will be ... will be romantic. I believe the old squire would approve.' And then at the renewed drumming below: 'I must go down, it is the boy for sure.'

The boy stood on the step. He had found the gig parked at the Admiral and the lady inside as snug as you like and sipping gin and lemon. A plain brown square cove was with her, a gentleman by his clothes if not by the company he was a-keeping, sitting down with low wenches in a public room.

The Doctor paid his shilling and went back upstairs.

'Kitty is found, safe at the Admiral with Mr Bliss. Oh, I am so sorry, I did not wish to interrupt a feast ...' For feast it was though of a somewhat catholic nature, buns and pork pie, cheese and egg custards jostling uneasily together. Lizzie, who had got over her brief but difficult interview with Jary and three quarters of an hour in the prickly company of a man she did not think she liked and who most assuredly did not like her, was doing justice to the beef she had found lurking by the pie and to the buns, which were sweet, with sugar on the top. She had a fine haughty look about her, not so much snarling resentment as a furious contained energy; her tail was lashing, thought the Doctor, in a moment she would spring and bite. Instead she continued to eat, and eat as if she had missed every meal since flying back from London, not bothering to speak, not bothering to hide her obvious hunger.

'I wish you all luck for tomorrow,' said the Doctor, turning to Calloway, whose expression as he looked at Lizzie was not easy to read but was not indulgent nor even very kind. 'What time does the case come on?'

'Ten o'clock. But Frost and I will be closeted from half past six, going over the notes. I have invited him here for breakfast. He is staying at the Fox out on the Saxmundham road and if ever a place served indifferent food it is that vile pinching pot-house. I did not want him to go into court without a hot meal to set him up and some strong coffee to clear his head. He is an honest, reliable man and the judge is used to him, which is practically everything, but a night among fleas and a breakfast of dry toast and ale will hardly set a man up for a long long day in an atmosphere of prejudice thick as a London fog.'

'His function is to cross-examine?'

'It is. And since it is all we can do we must do it thoroughly, though it is a mystery how they are going to make out a case against him without a witness to say he was seen away from the Admiral after two o'clock.'

'You do not think they mean to produce one?'

'I have had no word of it, if so. But who was there to see him when he was safe abed?'

'A rogue may be got to lie for a guinea from any taproom in the country, I fear. But let us hope that if such a rogue is produced Mr Frost may soon confound him.

291

Miss Rayner, we ought to be leaving if you are to reach Foley by nine.'

They took their leave. Calloway saw them to the door, as formal, as polite as ever. As soon as he had withdrawn and they were alone: 'What was it all about?' Lizzie demanded. 'What is he up to, Dr French?'

'Up to, my dear?' Yes, there was the boy again, as tough as ever, a gappy smile spreading as he saw who they were. 'Surely you do not think Mr Calloway is up to anything?'

'Then why did he ask me there? It was almost improper. If I had not been with you I could not have gone – though Heaven knows I have no reputation to lose in this censorious place – and as it was he disapproved as strongly as he could, he offered hospitality yet thought the worse of me for accepting it. Why did he do it? What was it for?'

'I thought it was a genuine attempt to patch up your old friendship. He gave no hint of any ulterior motive when he asked me to suggest a visit to you when I met you at the gaol. But perhaps, my dear, it was simple curiosity, he wished to see how you had got on in London.'

'Whether I had improved?'

'You are very hard on him. His is a difficult temperament. Those taciturn, dark-browed men often suffer the most dreadful low humours, find the world oppressive, are fearful pessimists; and Mr Calloway is further crippled by his conscience, for he is a just and honourable man, and where others can smile at natural lapses and little peccadilloes, the imperfect condition of the human race, he must adhere to his rigid code, austere and righteous, without a moment's pause.'

'I hev a light, man,' said a familiar voice, and a lantern on a pole swayed towards them, stopped, and rose to show them the boy again. 'The night is dark,' he added hopefully, by way of explanation.

'Lead on then,' said the Doctor, smiling. The night was indeed dark down here on the quay, though there were lights aboard the few small vessels alongside and fainter lights beyond where the harbour faded away into the mud flats. The Doctor and Lizzie had been walking in the dim glow cast across the cobbles by these irregular pinpricks, too absorbed to notice the black holes and slimy steps and wandering drains into which they might have fallen by straying inches to right or left. Now, at the bottom of Friday Walk, the sight of a carriage coming down at a sedate trot in a positive blaze of candlepower – for there were two link boys running ahead, laughing – only served to show up the impenetrable gloom beside and behind. Away from the luminous sea a man could not go three strides without falling on his nose in the dark.

They hurried on, the cool air, scented by woodsmoke and ale and the unsavoury rows and alleys, lifting Lizzie's fine skirts and getting under the Doctor's hat. The boy skipped merrily in front, his lamp showing up the uneven pavement and the drains, the blank faces of the better houses – this had once been a fashionable street – and the cracked panes of the poorer ones. There were very few people about. Westdene generally shut itself indoors by seven except in high summer and on market days, and it was already well past half after eight.

'I thought you would find us,' said Mr Bliss as they entered the Admiral; he had led Kitty out to the great square hall with its smoke-encrusted panelling and its wide shallow Jacobean staircase and had sat her down on a bench while he consulted his watch and wondered what to do next. 'I thought Miss Rayner would be safe with you, I told Kitty so. She has been sobbing' – in a lower voice and with an exasperated glance over his shoulder. 'The pony brought her here, just turned itself round and trotted off, she had no say in the matter.'

'No doubt Mrs Jewkes puts up her trap at the Admiral whenever she comes into Westdene. I have always found that ponies in particular never forget which side their bread is buttered.'

'No indeed,' said Lizzie, 'they never do, greed is the

293

middle name of every one I have ever come across. Kitty, dear Kitty, I am so sorry you were run away with . . .' and she went to speak privately, her hand on Kitty's arm.

'Miss Rayner looks tired,' said Mr Bliss, gazing after her. 'It is the effect of all the travelling, no proper rest. Would it not be better to hire a chaise?'

'I do not think Miss Rayner would agree. But you and I can ride with them and see them safe to their door.'

The pony was put in the gig, Kitty bundled in her cloak. As they stepped from the door every clock in the inn and several in the town chimed nine.

'Good Heavens,' said Lizzie with a low laugh, pulling on her gloves, 'it is a good thing I had no reputation to begin with for I shall certainly have none now. Out at night dining with single gentlemen, having taken a gig under false pretences and put about a story I was practising piano music.'

'And the gig has only one lamp,' said the Doctor.

'It took three quarters of an hour to cover the three and a half miles,' he told Calloway the next morning. 'Mr Bliss fell in the ditch and the pony got his bridle over one eye by some trick and we did not notice until the bit fell out of his mouth. We went very gingerly, as if on ice, for one small candle is nothing in a very black night. I thought Mrs Jewkes would run out and berate us most thoroughly but instead she threw open the door and said please to come in, was it not a cold night, would we care for a glass of rum; never a word of censure, though she told Lizzie – told Miss Rayner – that she would be better off in bed she looked so weary, and the dear girl retired at once, like a lamb.'

'I have never known Lizzie Rayner like a lamb,' with a harsh disagreeable note of dislike. 'But tell me, has Mr Savage mentioned his will to you?'

'Only that he intended to make another since Henriette is dead.'

'Well, he sat up half last night making it. He did not say a word to me, not one word. You are his friend, to be sure, none closer – but I am his attorney, should he not trust me? Why did he not ask me to draw it up, pray, as I did the last?' A pause, but before the Doctor could think of any sensible remark, Calloway plunged on, very much in the throes of a woeful indignation, a feeling of being slighted, his advice not even sought. 'This morning at seven a boy comes from the gaol: could I go at once, Mr Savage wishes to see me. I had to leave Mr Frost here' – a nod in Mr Frost's direction – 'in the middle of a most serious, involved discussion, all our preparatory work, and dash off not knowing what I was to find. And then I am made to stand in front of his table like a misbehaved schoolboy while he tells me what he has done and calmly asks me to destroy his previous will as soon as is convenient. He has surely taken leave of his senses, Doctor.'

'Are you asking me if he is sane? His will is his own business, should you be speaking to me about it at all?'

'He said I should. He said as he would not have a chance to see you before the trial I was to explain what he has done. He said you would laugh. Laugh! I tell you, it was quixotic enough to leave his estate to that bastard child, but to leave Ramillies and a fortune to that . . . to that woman! What is he thinking of? What sane man would do it?'

'What woman? Not Miss Johnson of Jamaica?'

Mr Frost gave a snort and then extracted a grey handkerchief to blow his nose. 'And who is this Miss Johnson? I do hope she is not relevant to my case.'

It was half past eight. He was still busily consuming Mrs Hawke's prodigious breakfast, plate after plate, a tall, lean, tired man in his fifties, learned, capable, pleasant, but currently much occupied with kidneys and bacon. He had several documents propped against the coffee pot and the water jug which he read over the top of his spectacles, read and re-read and frowned at and finally threw down on a heap of similar discarded documents at his feet.

'Not Miss Johnson, no – though she is still to receive

a thousand pounds, she will not be left in the cold. Surely you understand, Doctor? It is Lizzie Rayner will inherit everything.'

The Doctor laughed.

'It is no laughing matter, sir. Why, I almost believe you connived to wreck his sense of proportion. What did she say to him last night to achieve such a bounty this morning? I had not formed the impression she was anything at all to him but perhaps I have misunderstood. Pray enlighten me, was that accursed duel something more than a tilt about bad manners? Is Jary Savage attached to the lady?'

'I am quite sure he is, but no, no,' catching sight of Calloway's thunderous face, 'not in the way you mean. He is very attached to Ramillies and Lizzie Rayner may not be *detached* from Ramillies, if you follow me. He cannot love the place without being conscious of *her* love for it, and her loss of it. It is so like him to give way to his romantic nature and take delight in restitution.'

'Romantic nature be damned! I was not aware he had one, whatever it may be, only that he has a great deal of money and spends it unwisely. I have begged him to tear the will up, to reconsider, to write afresh. I have argued that even in the extreme unlikelihood of his being found guilty it is seven to three against his being hanged and the nature of the case is such it would be a very harsh judge indeed who would intend the sentence carried out. But he will not listen to argument, he says that if he is not to have justice through the law he will make sure Lizzie Rayner at least has justice through his will. He says he believes it is fate. Have you ever heard such poppycock and from a clever man?'

It was a clear sunny morning, a foretaste of summer. Calloway strode to the window and looked down at his garden, seeing nothing but Jary's implacable face. 'He says,' more quietly now, 'that the lady does not know and is not to be told. He says that if, as we all suppose, he is acquitted and returns to Ramillies, marries a wife, begets legitimate children, then he will write a more

296

conventional document, will destroy this amazing piece of folly.'

'Well,' said the Doctor, 'it all sounds perfectly sensible.'

'Sensible! My God, sensible! Lizzie Rayner is unworthy of such an inheritance. Do you realize the extent of his fortune? And now he stands to gain this Helen's Mount, a vast plantation, two hundred and fifty slaves, Heaven knows what else, not to speak of some shipping interests of his late uncle's: two large schooners, two brigs, a ketch. And then there is his privateering, a despicable business in my opinion and hardly likely to be profitable while the peace lasts: what would a woman want with shares in a privateer?'

The Doctor said nothing, his mind wandering away at once to that old house in Norfolk and the lady who inhabited it, who had clapped a saddle on his pony and ridden, laughing no doubt, all about the water meadows; the lady who owned a privateer entire, a most rakish dangerous vessel, unbelievably expensive to fit out and keep afloat.

'Gentlemen,' said Mr Frost, 'I believe time is getting on. I must hurry over to the courthouse, that so-charming antique building: I do believe even the smells are medieval. Will you lend me Whimble, Charles, to help carry the books?'

'I shall do more than that, I shall carry them myself. Doctor, forgive us, we must walk across. No doubt I shall see you this evening if the court does not sit late.'

'Mr Bliss and I are at the Admiral all day,' said the Doctor, bowing, 'I do not wish to see a friend humiliated.'

'Oh, it will hardly be any sort of scrap,' said Frost, though not with the full-blooded conviction his words ought to have conveyed, 'Mr Savage will suffer very little, we hope. They cannot make too much of his bad character for he is a stranger, to be judged on his behaviour the last six months in this place. A man called Fisher is to speak for him if we can contrive it, will make much of his charitable works, his new cottages, his concern for these rough dispossessed people from the woods. Even if we cannot get him called I doubt the prosecution will bloody his nose very easily, they will have to stick to time, place, motive, weapon.'

'You sound optimistic,' was the Doctor's remark as he followed them out.

'Oh we are,' said Frost, 'we are. But if you are a praying man, Doctor, I would not mind an Our Father or two.'

'Do not mind him,' said Calloway, turning to bid him farewell, 'it is only that he knows the old judge very well, knows his humours, his likes and dislikes, and in this case he is not sure if we shall have him on our side.'

'I thought, forgive me, that a judge was generally considered impartial.'

'You are a man of the world, Dr French. My father used to say that only a corpse is impartial. We must hope for the best, that is all, hope that Mr Savage makes a good impression.'

The sea was very blue. The Doctor strolled beside it, along the quay to where the hard road gave way to a muddy track that climbed the gentle cliffs the far side of the harbour. There was an old man in a small old boat to row people across the Wiss and the Doctor paid his halfpenny and sat in the stern with his feet in two inches of grey cold water, watching the green land come nearer and nearer. The track carried him up and out of sight of the town, a headland dotted all over with suspicious sheep cut off even the church tower for a moment, and then he dropped down across the springy turf to find a low pebbly place where he could reach the beach, a flat grey-gold beach that stretched away as far as his eye could see. It was sheltered in the lee of the sandy cliffs and he sat a long time with his hands clasped round his knees and his face turned up to the first strong sun of the year, and as he sat he thought of Jary back there in the court, Jary who always seemed to belong in the open, in the clean, sweeping air, either because of his size or because of the impression of enormous energy he gave:

he seemed too large for any normal house. I will step in this afternoon, he thought, I will show my face so that he knows I have not run off to enjoy myself, that I am his friend when he has need of me but that I do not think it proper to watch him at bay, all that legal pack snarling round him.

Then he thought of Ann, whose letter he had received that morning, a short kind letter thanking him for the pony – 'Of course I will keep him for you if it means you will one day knock on my door again to reclaim him' – and saying how sorry she was Mr Savage was in such straits – 'a strong, compassionate man, I liked him immensely' – and not mentioning William or marriage or any domestic arrangements at all. Perhaps she is not the woman I once thought her, went through his head, perhaps I have been so overwhelmed by her sense of purpose, her courage, her impulsive charity – taking Tom in, her dissolute old uncle's natural child, daring the whole district not to accept him as her cousin and respect-able, an enormous undertaking and pulled off with dash and determination – perhaps all this has blinded me to her faults. There is her quick temper, she will not suffer fools, and there is her weakness when someone she likes makes an appeal to her heart: her first husband, Tom even, her appalling domestics. In all that she is something like a female Jary, as easily touched, as easily frightened off, as easily wounded. But what if she is also fickle and cold, what if she is selfish? There might be another man knocking at the door at Thorn; she is still young, and is good-looking and has a decent fortune. Suppose that is why she does not mention William, why the wedding has been postponed – because she has found another and prefers him.

It would not be like her to carry on an affair in secret, to entertain a man while engaged to another. It would not be Ann to do such a thing. He could not love her if she was capable of it. Yes, he could love her. He would be hurt, disillusioned, lost, but he would still love her; though the love were changed and disillusion never left him he would love as fiercely. It was a sad thought, this resignation to his fate – he did not want to love her, what other word could he call it? The sun on his face did not seem so warm after all and there were little wispy clouds blowing in from the sea. He stood up, settled his hat on, and began to walk back.

The tide had turned in the hour he had sat under the cliffs and there was a small waste of glutinous mud where the ferryboat ground its bow. He took a huge leap, fell short, and sank to his ankles.

'Gentlemen generally take the bridge,' said the old man, pocketing his halfpenny and nodding upriver to where the Saxmundham road crossed over on squat old arches.

'You are a terrible sight and you will catch a cold if you do not change your shoes and stockings at once,' said Lizzie Rayner, meeting him as he toiled up from the bog to the road.

'I did not bring any clean ones,' was his forlorn reply.

'Never mind. Mrs King will wash and dry those, or perhaps Mr Calloway will lend you some.'

'Mr Calloway is in court.'

'Yes, how silly. I forgot. Still, Mrs Hawke is there, no doubt. Goodness, you cannot walk through the town looking like that, or smelling like it either.'

They climbed the steps, knocked, were admitted at long last by a scandalized Mrs Hawke who wanted nothing to do with saving the Doctor from inflammation of the lungs. They might have been there all day and reduced to beg on their knees but Whimble returned from the courtroom for some mislaid papers and took them up to Calloway's rooms at once, producing a vast bunch of keys, a more striking bunch of keys than old Quarel's at the gaol. Of course Mr Calloway would think nothing of it, would roast Mrs Hawke at her own spit, the roguish, disobliging, cantakerous old ... He broke off but his eye glittered, remembering past slights. Mr Calloway would be honoured to lend his stockings, would not hear of the Doctor slopping up Friday Walk to the Admiral advertising his distress to half the town. And what a crowd of gaping, curious, ill-mannered louts were about today, God knows, cramming the market square – and it was market day too – and parading past the gaol, peering in, bowing to the judge's coach or pelting it with mud and excrement depending on their mood and station, barefoot boys all over, pockets being picked, ladies distressed, gentlemen sworn at.

'They are stuffed in the public gallery like herrings,' he ended, groping in a drawer in some inner room and coming back flushed with triumph, a pair of good white stockings in his hand. 'Here, Doctor, let me have your shoes. They will wipe over and be as good as ever. Miss Rayner, do sit down, do. I have forgotten all my manners.'

She smiled at him, the kindest smile the Doctor had ever seen her give. 'Dear Whimble, you could never do that.'

The Doctor retired to wash his feet and put on the stockings. Whimble produced a bottle of sherry from a deep cupboard and insisted Lizzie take a glass 'to set you up, my dear'. She looked at him over the rim: 'Dutch courage?' she asked. 'I did not intend to go to the court, I meant to keep at Foley and sit sketching in the garden. But I could not sketch a blade of grass today to save my life. Mrs Jewkes was driven distracted. Then Mr Fisher called for one thing and another, had been to Stretfield to see Mr Blake and the cottages, offered to bring us to Westdene in style if we cared to come. Fanny would not, she said she would rather go to bed and draw the curtains round her until it is all over and he is acquitted and home again – in reality she is spring cleaning, turning out every box and cupboard to relieve her feelings. Anyway, I got into the carriage and here I am. I really don't know why I came.'

'They did not take long over the formalities,' said Whimble. 'Old Fielder never hangs about, bless him. He does not care for Poynter, the prosecution man, a sullen drunken fellow who lets his junior prepare the case and then takes the credit – it is well known – but then he don't care for foreign gentlemen neither, throwing money about, upsetting the status quo as you might say, and shooting at the local gentry.'

'It will not be over today?' cried Lizzie, aghast.

'No, Miss Elizabeth, no indeed. They are bringing in a great many witnesses to say all they can about the ill feeling between Mr Savage and young Whiteley but Mr Frost has brought them down a peg or two, showing how a great deal is surmise and hearsay: oh a droll, laconic way of going on has Mr Frost. I suppose by dinner time we may come to the real evidence, the few facts, but Mr Fielder is no enemy to sitting till midnight if the mood takes him, the Doctor may not be called till then.'

The Doctor emerged in stockinged feet and accepted his wiped-over shoes from Whimble's hand, looking down at Lizzie and her sherry.

'Mr Bliss is at the Admiral,' he said, 'in case they should want me in court and send a boy across. Will you come back there with me now and have some bread and cheese, a veal pie? You cannot walk about the town all day alone, it is not proper. As Mr Whimble has pointed out there are crowds of gawping strangers and a great many wicked boys about. I believe Mr Fisher is to be there at half past two and he has a cousin with him, a very correct lady indeed if my memory serves me right. You will not be condemned to eat with a parcel of men.'

'I have heard Mr Fisher's cousin is formidable.'

'Yes,' hesitantly, 'yes, perhaps that is the word. Mr Fisher finds her so. The only joy is that so does his miserable father and for once, I believe, the old gentleman is put firmly in his place.'

Poor Mr Bliss had also been put in his place, a very low place by the look of it, and Lizzie and the Doctor walked in to a very strained atmosphere at the Admiral, Lizzie unfortunately laughing as he opened the door of the private room for her so that the formidable lady in question had a general impression of almost coquettish

302

gaiety and an undisciplined sense of humour, a bold, fair, flirting woman in the most outrageous hat.

'My cousin Miss Bridges,' said Mr Fisher nervously, 'Miss Rayner the artist, Harriet, the lady who painted that splendid picture of. . . .'

'Yes, yes, of course I remember,' still looking at the hat. 'I conceive that is a London fashion, Miss Rayner, not yet percolated to the country.'

There might have been more awkwardness, a general deterioration into incivility, if Mrs King had not chosen this moment to launch herself through the door followed by Pamela and one of the clean, busy, little maids bearing trays of pies and cheese and pickles and plates and dishes and napkins and a huge rack of toast for Mr Fisher, toast and anchovy paste.

Eating restored their spirits and a more normal conversation began to flow, or perhaps not *flow*, for all the men and Lizzie were deeply concerned with the outcome of Jary's case and were not up to their usual cheerfulness by a long way, and Miss Bridges was quite jealous of the London hat and gazed at it often in preoccupied silence. Andrew Bliss also gazed at it, and quite as often at the face beneath it, at the definite nose and wide mouth. He had just noticed that she had a sprinkling of pale freckles along her high cheekbones when a knock on the door heralded the messenger from the court: could the Doctor run across at the double, they was almost ready for him, and could he stop by to see Mr Whimble in the anteroom afore he got into the box, Mr Whimble had a note for him.

'I will come with you,' said Lizzie, rising and throwing down her napkin. Mr Bliss jumped up at once.

'Let me come too, you will find the public gallery a terrible place, you know. You will have to clear a space by brute force and that does not seem proper for a lady.'

'Oh I may not go up there,' she said.

'They will not allow you to hang about below,' said the Doctor. 'Let Andrew escort you up if you care for it. Do not go alone, my dear. Mr Fisher, Miss Bridges,

303

goodbye. I hope we meet again shortly when this wretched business is behind us.'

They passed in through the small door, crossed the yard, pushed through a score of unknown, semi-official busybodies: clerks, runners, valets. In through another door and up a strange corridor, wide, echoing, peopled by two men in wigs, a gentleman with a gold-knobbed cane who nodded to them as they passed, and a boy who smelled of fish in the clutch of a costumed usher, the boy who had found the body, a terrified, trembling child.

They gave their names. Mr Bliss offered Lizzie his arm; the stairs to the public gallery were immediately on the left. A subdued murmur through a closed door straight ahead was Mr Frost calling some bold statement into question and the rising swell of sound that followed some emotional upheaval among the spectators. Lizzie turned back to the Doctor suddenly. 'I believe you are right,' she said, 'the best place to be is out along the cliffs, damn shoes and stockings, damn everything.'

If you knew, he thought, if only you knew, a fortune and Ramillies, a vast plantation, two hundred and fifty slaves . . . Out of the corner of his eye he could see Whimble approaching, Whimble looking grey and old and clutching a white paper and a bundle of red-ribboned documents.

'Dr Plesset cannot appear, he has had a fit,' were his urgent, whispered words, drawing the Doctor aside. 'Poor soul, he has not much longer in this world. We thought it only right to warn you though, Poynter may try to call your medical evidence into question since they know you are Mr Savage's friend. You are wearing two hats, Dr French, and I am very sorry for it.'

'But the medical evidence is irrefutable; besides, it is written down and signed by Dr Plesset and myself.'

'Oh indeed, indeed. It is just that you must be prepared for anything, Doctor, anything at all.'

'Can you see?' asked Bliss into Lizzie's ear. He had never hoped to get so close to her but he could not even stop to consider the pleasant sensation it gave him, not here, not in this place, Jary Savage in the dock on a hanging charge. It was odd how life often did that, he thought, realized one's deep desires in a perverse, disagreeable way, so that what had been perfect in a dream was damned uncomfortable in the reality.

'Yes, I can see,' replied Lizzie, who was crushed up against a pillar behind a gross woman in black. The gallery was certainly full, and it certainly stank of close-pressed human bodies, some of whom shuffled and wriggled strangely for there was not room to scratch. Yes, she could see. The body of the court was filled with wigs, and filled with piles of papers and a gross of quills, and also filled with an indefinable atmosphere of polite restraint, as if things were not going according to custom or to the wishes of the majority of the wigs.

The judge was a very small, thin, wizened man, hardly worth a second look. Lizzie stared at him in surprise. What had she been expecting, a judicial Jary Savage, large and commanding? Another closer examination showed her the shrewd, keen little eyes, the mind obviously wide awake though the features only twitched occasionally: a sort of amiable rodent. And there was Jary, utterly self-possessed, dressed in a dark grey coat, immaculate linen.

The fishy boy, a wreck of nerves, told the court in fits and starts how he had found a body up Sprats Row, how he had had nothing to do with it, nothing at all, he had only been running home to his mother in the fish huts on the beach. He had not known what to do, had run home anyway, he had never been in trouble, he did not want to be taken up for scragging a gentleman for a guinea or two. But his mother, a law-abiding soul, and compassionate – what if the gentleman was still alive? – had hurried to rouse the constables by way of Joe Salt, the herring man, who kept his business along the end of . . .

'And did you go back to see if the gentleman was dead?' asked Poynter, scratching under his wig.

'No, sir, but Mother did.'

305

'And she said he was dead?'

'Oh yes, sir. And she should know,' with a sudden air of defiance, 'for she does lyings-in and layings-out, sir.'

Mr Frost rose slowly and begged the boy to try to remember if he had perhaps heard the sounds of a scuffle as he had been walking home down the lane, or a cry, or the patter of running feet. What had made him look in the alley, a blind alley, a poky hole used as a rubbish tip? Why should he look in the alley if he had not heard something suspicious?

An objection from Mr Poynter. The judge snapped at both of them from his much greater height, scratching something down at the same time. Mr Frost apologized, re-phrased his question, got the same reply he would have got anyway: no, no noise, no indications of a fight, no, no reason to go up the alley but the boy had looked in, seen a dark shape, wondered what it was.

'It is very dark in the alley,' said Mr Frost reasonably. 'You mean to say that in the dark – we have heard, gentlemen,' addressing the court, 'that it is always dark in the lane and the rows that run parallel with it and run into it for this is the oldest part of the town and the cottages and buildings are very close together, over-hanging, tottering, one might say, one upon another – so I ask you how, Mr Gill, you managed to see a body in the alley? You had no lantern, you have already said so.'

Young Gill looked petrified. 'Answer the question,' said the judge, jabbing his quill over the side of the bench and scowling at it. 'What made you look into the alley, boy? How did you distinguish a dead man in the dark?'

Silence. Then: 'I saw his stockings, sir.'

Frost played about a little longer but nothing came of it, the boy, in spite of his trembling, was adamant. He is either stupid or has been thoroughly frightened into his story, thought Lizzie, who sensed a great deal left unsaid. But then Gill was dismissed and the Doctor took his place, a very sober Doctor in spectacles and a remarkably clean, new, handsome tie-wig – where had he come by either in those few moments outside? Had he had them in a pocket? Had Whimble had them in his?

Lizzie drew deep breaths of hot reeking air, fifty times breathed, and leant more heavily against her pillar. She was aware that Mr Bliss was forced to lean more closely than was proper against her other side, was aware through some sixth, seventh, eighth sense that he rather enjoyed doing so, was aware also that he was a dear man, a gentleman, and had no thought of molesting her. But oh it was hot! How could Jary stand there, so cool, so composed, practically unmoving, apparently unmoved? And now Poynter's disagreeable thick voice and the Doctor's quiet, succinct replies, the rustle of the medical report, notes explaining Dr Plesset's absence, notes between Charles Calloway and Frost, Frost and Whimble, the judge and a small man in black with a hare lip who sat directly below the bench.

The Doctor was a good witness, good in that he answered clearly, confined himself to the questions, translated the medical language into simple plain English, refused to be ruffled by Poynter's sudden ugly reference to his having an 'interest' in making it seem that Whiteley had been set upon by footpads – had not the Doctor lived a great while with Mr Savage at Ramillies? – parried the crude jab with a look of utter contempt so that Frost, who had been rising to his feet, subsided again with a secret smile, and looked most unusually sober, respectable and learned.

The Doctor had not been a witness to the quarrel at the Assembly rooms but he had seen what state Mr Savage was in immediately afterwards. Could the Doctor describe Mr Savage's state? What did the Doctor mean by angry and disappointed? What could have caused disappointment? Was disappointment not inappropriate to the occasion?

'Mr Savage had hoped there had been an end to the bad feelings caused by the difference of opinion over the Diddlers. He had hoped that in future he would get along more happily with Mrs Whiteley and her nephew.'

'Yet how could that be? He was not welcome at the house, was he?'

'No, but he had several times sent invitations to Mrs Whiteley to visit his own, all of them unanswered. He is an amiable man, he did not care for such continuing bad feeling.'

All eyes turned briefly to Jary, who looked very far from amiable. He looked grim, set, exhausted. The long day had told on him, the realization that they had been talking six hours and had still not come to the point, still not brought off the expected acquittal, was telling on him now. He looked a hard man, the Jary of the big, swift-sailing, ferocious privateer, the man of action, sword in hand. He did not move and his face, expressionless all day, remained expressionless, and yet he seemed to grow even taller and to grow insensibly more forbidding, a man quite capable of killing another down a dark alley. There was not a man in the court who did not shrink from provoking him, seeing those dark, fixed eyes, that strong jaw.

'And you said good night at that hour, that hour exactly,' Poynter was saying, 'and remember nothing more until Mrs King roused you at four to come downstairs to Sir James Braile?'

'That is correct.'

'You did not think to knock up your friend at that moment?'

'I did not,' with a hard stare, a hard, disdainful stare, 'I had been asked to come quickly, I was aware there was a need to be swift and silent: Sir James did not wish to wake the inn. In any case, Mr Savage was sleeping at the end of the passage, it was not as if he would have been accidentally disturbed and merited an explanation.'

'You believed he had been asleep since you left him in the small parlour?'

'I did.'

'You had not the slightest cause to think otherwise?'

'I did not.'

You will not get the better of him, old cock, said Mr

Bliss to himself, staring down, he is used to tougher birds than you prancing and posturing and trying to get him at fault. A man who can answer for five hundred prime soldiers, whisked away, isolated, dosed, returned to fighting trim, and all in direct opposition to the commands of the Army Board, of every committee sitting, of every senior officer, of every whoreson laced and ribboned idiot in England or without, is not a man to buckle at the knees when faced by a single unattractive, sly, miserable cove in a horsehair hearthrug.

'I wish to leave,' said Lizzie, turning her face up to his. 'Could you see me to the stairs?'

He saw she looked pale, looked very pale. Perhaps it was the air, or rather, the lack of it. But outside on the top step she said quietly: 'Did you see the jury? I know some of them. They are all men will condemn him out of hand, old-fashioned, close, insular men who cannot bear anything out of the ordinary. If Poynter said Mr Savage's very presence was enough to make the price of their corn drop they would believe it and would hang him with their own hands.'

'Come, you are overwrought. I am not surprised. I will see you back to the inn. Would you like me to order a carriage?'

No, she did not want a carriage, she did not know what she wanted, a dull, cold premonition had seized her and the world was grey, a strange, grey, alien place. It was grey enough in reality, the sun long gone behind a haze of darkening cloud, and a vigorous little wind got up and surging up Friday Walk to the market place. As they hurried along a carriage drew up at the corner in front of them and a familiar face appeared in the window.

'Dear Lizzie, how are you?' asked Mrs Stone. She could see quite well however that Lizzie was not at all as self-possessed as usual, her face was bleak.

'Are you returning to Stretfield, ma'am?' and Mr Bliss took off his hat, lifting a pair of hopeful eyes. 'If you are, would you have room for Miss Rayner? She has been to court, is tired out, and has no carriage.'

Mrs Stone smiled benevolently. 'There is room and to spare,' she cried cheerfully, 'and I am going home directly. As it is I will be late for dinner.'

Mr Bliss held open the door. Lizzie climbed in. Then she turned and said quickly: 'Will you tell the Doctor I shall call at Ramillies for news in the morning? In the morning early.'

'I will indeed. And if he is not there I shall be, or there will be a message, you may count upon it.'

'My dear Lizzie,' said Mrs Stone as they rattled away from Westdene at a fine pace, mindful of Mrs Stone's cooling dinner, 'what a singularly attentive young man. How he glowed when he looked at you. What a very great pity all the nicest men are practically penniless.' It occurred to her as she spoke that Jary Savage was not penniless and was a very nice man indeed, open and amiable and unaffected, but then his amiability was of a different quality, he was a seasoned, experienced sort of man, had been virtually a pirate.

'They are going to find him guilty,' said Lizzie abruptly in a low, furious voice.

'Oh my dear, surely not? Why, how could they? There is no evidence,' and then, after a moment's reflection, a glance at Lizzie's strained, lined face: 'But even if they did they would never hang him.'

Lizzie did not reply. She turned her head and the little brim of the London hat hid her expression. She saw the gates of Ramillies through the glass, and then the churchyard wall, the yews, the church. She thought of Henriette, the new year's grass growing on that bare little mound, and she closed her eyes feeling the silly hot tears, a great lump in her throat. What they were for she did not know, unless it was the loss of something precious, of untold promise, almost before it had begun.

'You will soon be at Foley,' said Mrs Stone, 'you will soon be home.'

20

Lizzie came down to breakfast in her old green dress. It had been put aside to give to the servants and Fanny had hoped never to see it again except on fair days or at harvest home.

'I am going to paint,' said Lizzie.

'Paint! Good Heavens! Paint what?'

'Ramillies.'

'But . . .' Useless to say 'why bother?' Useless to refer to the weary, bitter Lizzie of the previous evening, the Lizzie so sure Jary Savage was to be found guilty. It was not that she had changed her opinion with the new day or become cheerful and optimistic, it was simply that she was in one of her wild, unpredictable moods. It was more than possible she would walk it out on the way to Ramillies, or if not, paint it out when she got there.

'Where is my straw hat, Fan? Where have you hidden my straw hat?' she called from the porch, rooting in the wicker hamper.

'Oh dear. You know it was so old and shapeless . . .'

'Give me my hat this instant, Fanny Jewkes, or I shall go without one.'

She strode along the lane, head down, skirts brushing up gentle clouds of dust. By the old lost avenue she turned into the park, sitting to rest only once on an old pile of sheep hurdles, putting down her painting things and looking up through the sun-dappled leaves to the clear clear sky. It was still very early.

The door in the wall yielded to her steady pull: she had the trick of it from years ago. Inside was her mother's garden, weeded now and newly planted with pinks and lavender about the sundial. She crossed to the stables thinking that Millett would give her some news but Millett was not there and only the grass-cutting pony

311

looked up as she entered the long empty row of stalls. For a moment she stood leaning back against the wall. It was years since she had been in here, years. A strange light sick feeling came over her. The smell took her back, took her back in an instant . ... Yet it was only an ordinary stable smell: leather, horse, straw, ammonia; she had stood in the stables at Foley and felt nothing like this. She closed her eyes. You could not tamper with a smell, could not twist it out of true as you could the memories that owed their all to other senses: a whiff and an immediate transportation, ten thousand miles, fifty years crossed in a blink. This was where her very first pony had rolled with colic until Tredge had come running at her father's shout and they had pulled him on his feet, a little hairy animal like a large dog, and had walked him about, sweating and staring; this was where she had hidden to cry for her dead rabbits, her sick dog, the tubful of kittens old Tredge had drowned; this was where she had kept her nearly tame jackdaw and her hedgehog and the baby owl a much younger and less grumpy Millett had found for her; and from this door she had watched them bear her father's body across the yard on a hurdle, covered by an old horse blanket, covered right over so that she had known at once that he was dead.

Her eyes, grown used to the dimness, picked out the feather where it lay in the dark corner. She stooped over it. There was an eye on it, faded but unmistakable: it was a peacock's feather. She snatched it up, another memory rising, rising, blotting out the rest: her father with something under his arm, cradled like a baby, and holding it out for her to touch the soft, lustrous breast, the vivid, vivid blue. 'Lizzie, my love, I have shot him by mistake, the poor old bird. Do you think we should bury him with Meg and True and all your lost fledgelings?' But they had not buried him, some other business had come between them and such honourable intentions, some business that had taken her father from home. She had not wanted to bury the peacock herself, she had admired but never loved him, being rather frightened of

312

his disdain, his reserve, he would never come to her call, had no appearance of affection. It seemed to the young Lizzie that laying such a bird to rest in the grassy corner where her pets lay was not something she could accomplish alone, it would be a macabre ritual, not a true ceremony and tearful farewell like that accorded the dear dogs, the cats, the treasured featherless scraps of doves and swallows and ducks. So the peacock had lain forgotten in the stables, in the old unused loose boxes at the end of the row of stalls where now and then the visiting bull would be penned, snorting and heaving, before they drove the heifers off the park into the temporary pound by the back gates.

Lizzie ran out into the sunlit yard, the feather in her hand, and nearly collided with the Doctor, who had just dismounted from Jary's black horse – a most unsuitable beast for the Doctor, a nice horse turned sour through indifferent treatment and therefore as unreliable as he could be – though Lizzie had not heard the ring of hooves on the stones, she had been so many years away.

'My dear, what is it? What has happened?' as he dropped the reins and caught her shoulders to stop her falling.

'It is a peacock's feather,' she said. 'You must know . . . It is bad luck to bring them indoors.'

'So I remember being told long long ago when Jary first moved here. To be sure they are a sacred bird to some. I believe there was a whole bundle found in the coach house or some corner or other and they were burnt on the kitchen stove, a terrible crime apparently, Mrs Fipson tried to decapitate the boy for it.'

'Then they have been in the stables all this time.'

'Dear Lizzie' – he had an arm about her but she did not notice it, and he had regained his reins, pushed the wicked black nose away with a growl – 'You surely do not believe a heap of peacock's feathers the cause of all the ill luck of this house for twenty years? I know you are a child of Ramillies and come from a long line of Suffolk countrymen, but such credit given to foolish superstition is beyond an intelligent man's understanding. Why, you may as well believe in Mother Henham's predictions.'

'Perhaps I do. Perhaps the second sight or whatever you care to call it is only instinct developed to its highest pitch, and instinct speaks true though it is inexplicable '

'Oh I never sneeze at instinct, sweet, no indeed. But come inside, come in do.'

'Not with the feather.' She still held it in her hand. 'I will walk down to the river and . . . and launch it. It will sink or swim to Westdene; anyway, it will be gone.'

'I will put up the horse and join you.'

When he had taken off bridle and saddle, a long fiddly business, he had never been clever with bridles and girths, and given the anxious beast a meagre feed of oats and chaff, he set out across the lawn, skirting the pond, the canal, the Lookout, and found Lizzie on the riverbank, her hands empty.

'It is gone,' she said. He looked downstream but saw nothing, only the normal ripples, a half-submerged branch, a female mallard. She stood very still, strangely pale and withdrawn, as if she had just performed some religious service or a magic ritual, and he remembered from far back his first sight of a body being launched upon the Mother Ganges, the people too poor to afford the wood to burn it, a small wasted body, no doubt a child.

'Dear girl, come back to the house. We shall badger poor Clarkie for something strong and hot. After all, I have good news,' and he paused, finding her clear piercing eye on him, an eye to which he could not strictly lie. 'Well, it is not bad news, at any rate. They worked their way through what facts there were last night – there were very few, very few of a solid incontrovertible nature – and very late Poynter stood up and said he wished to call another witness, a man who had heard the fight in the alley. It was too late, however, even the judge had had a long enough day of it, and the fug with all the candles lit and people coming in from the pot-houses was indescribable. Anyway, Andrew and I rode there straight after breakfast this morning, anxious about this fellow who was going to lay Jary by the heels — oh that was the intention, why, of course it was, Poynter is prosecuting, he will only bring witnesses who speak against the prisoner — but we need not have bothered, not to ride there in a lather, our hearts in our mouths. Mr Frost was in great form, as cool as you like, and he dissolved the witness like an ice cream in the sun, a sort of . . . a sort of slow steady glow of righteous indignation that anybody could come out with such a gabble of rubbish in a court of law. You saw his way, quiet and persevering. "You are under oath," says he at the finish, "let me ask you again: did you see Mr Savage running from the alley?" And no, of course he had not. He had seen a tall dark man at the *top* of the lane, a tall dark man in good clothes, but after this there was even some dispute as to the direction in which this supposed gentleman was walking, whether he was coming out of the lane or simply passing its mouth, and as to its being unquestionably Jary Savage — well! The poor poxed fellow — forgive me, I speak in the heat of the moment, though he was indeed, the doomed rascal, syphilitic as I am a true judge — the poor fellow was a miserable liar and in the end, asked so politely over and over to speak up, to let the jury hear him clearly, he broke down, grew confused, I thought he should weep. It only took half an hour start to finish, from Mr Frost rising to his sitting down, and I saw the judge give such a look at Poynter, such a very hard look. Of course it strikes me as a very strange system, Jary in effect must defend himself, Frost may only ask questions, not . . . not sum up on his behalf.'

'Does the judge do so?'

'I am not familiar with the law and please God never will be. All I can say is that it is unlikely Mr Fielder will say much in defence of Jary when he speaks to the jury, he will be quite happy to see him found guilty, he is out of patience with Poynter for bringing a slow, sorry case of it.'

315

They had turned from the river and walked up again through the water garden. 'The sluices answer,' said the Doctor, looking about. 'There will be irises and lily pads and pretty ducks.'

She did not smile. There was a deep deep furrow between her brows. After a moment: she had forgotten her painting things, they were in the stables. And where was Millett? Where was the boy? Gone to the court, said the Doctor, both of them sneaking off as soon as he and Mr Bliss had cleared the avenue. They had footed it all the way and had been spotted in the public gallery sitting very low and near the front, heads down, crouched, like men avoiding tipstaffs. If they thought to get away with it they were mistaken.

'I think Millett is very fond of Mr Savage,' said Lizzie as they went indoors. 'He was very attached to my father who saved him from the press in Lowestoft when he was quite a child – Millet, I mean, only about twelve – by saying that he was his own servant boy and by God he was not going to donate him gratis to His Majesty's Navy, not if he had to lay them all out with his stick. He could never have done it of course, he had a silver-topped cane, a gentleman's toy, and they were all rough huge brutes with clubs and ropes, but he faced them out and he was obviously well bred – possibly well connected – so that although they didn't believe a word they left him alone. Millett was always . . . contrary, and he took to the bottle very early on, Father could never break him of it and threats of dismissal came to nothing, they were too used to each other and my father was too good-hearted. But I do not think Millett went to court to gloat nor out of curiosity, I think he wishes Mr Savage home again, he really does.'

'That is the most romantic flim-flam I have ever heard from you. I would never have expected it. Ah Clarkie, Miss Rayner has had a shock, no, nothing at all, a . . . a stumble, a feeling faint. Can you bring tea and something to eat: muffins?'

'What a dreadful lie,' said Lizzie as the door of the

morning room closed, 'as if she does not know I never feel faint. I feel much better now, anyway. It is all thanks to you.'

'Nonsense. Nonsense.'

She was in the window. The sun fell slantwise on her hair and lit it up; she had dragged off the straw hat, dragged off pins and all. She still looked remote, as remote as she must have done that day her father died and she had begun to realize what it meant, perhaps looking from this selfsame window. He looked at her and saw the depredations, the bitter wounds, of all the years since she had been turned from this house; how much she had resented it and how little resigned she had become as time passed, struggling, ageing, closing in on herself.

'Are you sorry you did not marry the Captain?' he asked. He asked before he could stop himself, before he rightly knew what he had said, he had simply spoken his thought aloud. Her face turned, the eyes very wide for a moment, her lovely mouth pulled straight, and before he could beg pardon or in any way soften the blow she said: 'No, not in the least.' And what is it to you, said her direct look, what kind of friend could drag back those old old painful memories?

'It is a sorry world,' he said. 'How many men must daily use and abandon the women who trust them.'

She walked to a chair. Out of the sun her hair took on its usual lustre, soft light brown, nothing extraordinary. 'I was not used, Doctor, not as you . . . as you meant it just now, nor was I abandoned. I think we both regretted our impulse before we reached Ipswich. I thought I was in love with him, he paid me such attention. Looking back I believe that was the trouble, nobody had ever paid me attention before, no personable young man anyway.' She could not say how bruised she had still been in those days, bruised by grief that had never had the opportunity to ebb naturally, only heightened by her being bundled off to Woodbridge and to a house of unsympathetic strangers; bruised by Whiteley's rejection, the thunder-

317

clap of knowledge that told her men did not always woo for love and nothing they said could necessarily be written anywhere but on sand. 'We took a room at an inn in Ipswich, ordered dinner, but he looked rather strange, said he must go out to see about something. . . . something to do with our marriage in the morning, and I suppose I thought of the night to come and what he might hope for, and of how I no longer hoped for it, nor for marriage, nor for leaving Stretfield behind for ever. So I put on my things and crept out before he came back, and walked about all night – how I was not taken up by the watch or mistaken for a . . . Oh well, perhaps we get on better in this bad old world when we are innocent than later on, when we know too much. I dared not take a seat on a coach, I thought he would find me out, so I walked a whole stage and got on a country cart, a carrier's, coming up to Westdene. It took three days and we all slept under haystacks – there were a couple of old women and a child – and I have never been so glad to smell the sea' – until the other day, until she stepped out of the chaise and recognized that taint in the wind. 'Fanny was astounded, took me in, prepared a footbath and continued the true friend she had always been. Dear Fan, she has had a great deal to put up with, a great deal.'

The door opened. There was Clarkie with the tea. Behind her Kate Farrow had hold of the painting things fetched from the loose box.

'There is no news,' said the Doctor to their dumb inquiry, 'and the trial will go on all day and probably tomorrow. Mr Whiteley's young lady has been delayed coming from Colchester.'

'Lord, Colchester,' said Kate, who had never heard of it, it might have been Java or the Galapagos.

They sat over their tea a good while, talking of ordinary everyday domestic things, of Ma Henham and her herbs, of Stephen Fisher and his unwavering desire to marry Fanny, of the cottages, the first thing in modern design, being plastered out at this moment, of Henriette whose face looked at them from the wall and whose brief life they would never quite forget . . .

'Perhaps now the feather is gone Mr Savage's luck may turn,' said Lizzie at last, when ten o'clock had struck.

'A rational man does not put his faith in peacocks' feathers,' replied the Doctor.

'But there is nothing else, is there?' she said, and bent to pick up her box, her discarded hat. 'I shall go down on the lawn to paint.'

At midday the Doctor walked across the grass and stood behind her, his head on one side. She was working with an ardent rapidity at one corner of her canvas so that it was beginning to look as if a tempest was intended.

'It is a beautiful day,' he said, 'there is summer in the air.'

It was a warm, enchanted day; there was a great noise of pigeons in the trees and the constant flutter of the rascally sparrows in the shrubs growing against the house. A fragrance of bruised grass and sun-warmed box wafted across.

'Will you be here all day?' she asked, her brush poised. She was far advanced on the background, trees like vague phantoms, a charging sky.

'No, my dear, I shall be away in less than half an hour. I must return to see if that saucy Miss Lucy has arrived. She does not speak for Jary but what she says may do him some good. The real sky is blue, dear child, blue as a blackbird egg, deep deep blue; why is yours like blustery autumn?'

'Oh I am in that kind of mood, I am blustery myself,' with a sudden smile, a sparkle of her eyes. He saw that she wore the oldest dress, ages old, green silk very faded, certainly her mother's or even her grandmother's, it did not even give a nod to present day fashion, being tight in the waist and very full in the skirt. She had tied a piece of once-white sheet about her middle to guard against the paint and her hat was put on crooked, her beloved, misshapen straw hat. 'They will never know who did it, will they?' she asked, dropping her brush into the little pile of rags at her feet. 'If only there was the slightest hint of someone else, someone who had a reason to quarrel, to take his life . . .'

'His acquaintance was wide and mostly disreputable. A poor witless fellow he once cheated on Newmarket Heath – he was often there and not always with his fast set – may very well have met him by chance or design and taken his revenge. But I think not,' rubbing his bristly chin, 'I think not. That young puppy Gill heard or saw something, of that I am sure, and so are Frost and Calloway: local sailors? young toughs? At any rate he had been well taught and properly frightened,'

She was gathering up her things. 'Dear Doctor' – standing up – 'you rode back this morning because of me, did you not?'

'I had promised to be here or to leave you word.'

'You are too good,' and to his surprise she leaned forward and kissed his cheek, 'oh far too good. But you see how virtue has its reward? You have nearly cured me of my fit of temper, my . . . my humdudgeon. Fanny calls it that. She used to call it that when I was eight and she still does. She threw some tea at me once when I was being perfectly obnoxious but then spoiled it by laughing because I looked so drowned and indignant.'

They walked to the house; she had her arm through his. The sun found the last gold hairs on the Doctor's grizzled head and shimmered on the green silk. 'I have resented him, you know,' she said very quietly, as if aware he was scrutinizing her, 'Jary Savage. I have inwardly disparaged him. And all the time I liked him, admired him even. I am glad Ramillies is his, I am glad he has dug up the lawns and means to have fountains and gazebos; I am glad he is to build another score cottages and dig new wells and pay for a new bell in the church. I suppose I gave him that silly little sketch of the house to tell him so but how could he understand unless I was to put it into words? He thinks me disagreeable and disputatious. He has probably heard all the gossip and thinks it is true, that I am a proud, quarrelsome, independent little cat with a cat's morals. No, do not try to look shocked. There are plenty of people who say such things,' and then, as they reached the door, looking back: 'Will he ever see it? Will he ever punt his boat up and down among the pochard? Fanny said the Lookout was ideal for picnics . . .'

'And you truly do not grieve for the old lawns, the view you remember? '

'Not any more,' with a level, considering look way down to the river, a wandering line of green reeds and the tell-tale copses. 'You do not destroy a place by digging a few holes, and these were scarcely lawns, they were hayfields, and I would rather have Jary Savage in a punt than an acre of twitch and bindweed.'

You are very lovable, he was thinking, difficult and nervous but remarkably lovable; you have hidden your light under a bushel too long. 'I must shave,' he said, 'I must spruce myself up. But first let us circumnavigate the garden, take a last peaceful view of Ramillies.'

'You astonished us all yesterday,' she told him as they walked. 'Where did you get the wig? A wig! I thought you had thrown yours away for ever?'

'I have too. I am liberated from wigs, my dear. But giving evidence in a court of law, a capital charge, my friend, a great many pompous, scribbling, stuffy fools looking me over head to foot . . . I could not have done less than appear as correct as possible. The wig was found by Mrs King, left on a wigstand by a titled gentleman was her story, believe it if you like.'

'And the spectacles?'

'Oh they were mine, are mine. I have them here. I bought them many years ago to impress the senior officers – or rather not to impress them, to make them think me a harmless, short-sighted fellow best humoured and left alone. I regret the disguise, I regret I stood in that dock and though I did not lie, God help me, I was not myself. Do you know, I love this old part of the house best, it has a homely dignity, it does not aspire to grandeur, it does not cry "Money!"and figure away like a little madam in a new dress.'

'What a strange simile! No, I suppose it does not. Yet it was a vast place, a great deal was knocked down when the other front was built. It was a mansion in its own way.'

They paused by the sundial a moment. The pigeons stopped their chant. It was noon, a June-like warmth, the smell of green things growing. 'You have a grasshopper in your hair,' she said and reached to brush it off, and then she turned, ran lightly up the three shallow steps, crossed the sparse gravel, and put a hand on the old front door: 'Is it locked?' but as she spoke it swung inwards on the dim cool hall, the chequer of the tiled floor, the great oak staircase. By the time he reached the door she was at the top of the stairs, the green silk going swish swish in the heavy silence.

'Lizzie?'

She was in the room at the end of the passage, standing by the window looking out. He knew at once it had been her room. It was here she had come after her dog had died and the kittens had been drowned and they had told her she must pack and go to Woodbridge. This room had seen all her grief. 'All these years,' she said, 'I would have given my life to get Ramillies back. How very foolish we are in general.'

'And now? Would you give a fig for Ramillies, Lizzie Rayner, were you to be given it tomorrow?'

She laughed, her fingers braced against the little lattice panes. 'It was a day like this when I found out I would have to leave here. Would you believe it, I had never even thought of such a possibility?'

'And how you minded, how very desperately you minded. Of course. And you blamed it on the peacock.'

'I could not blame it on my father, not then. I did not know about his borrowing, about his harbour scheme, about the money lost on the Exchange or lent to friends who were no friends at all. All I knew was that Ramillies was a little shabby, that jobs were put off, that the replanting in the park was never done; but I always had new dresses and books and paints, and we had four carriage horses and two hunters and my pony. I was very innocent, very ignorant, Doctor.'

'You were very young.' Had she raved, screamed, run wildly in the gardens when they had told her, when Charles Calloway's father had stepped gravely in with the news she was no heiress, was nothing, was dependent on the charity of others? He could not imagine it, and yet . . . And yet such a nature must have found an outlet.

'What did you do when they told you?'

'Do?' The ghost of a smile. 'Oh I said yes and no and how kind of my relations and of course I could be packed by Friday.' A deep, lost look. 'Of course I can be packed by Friday,' the very words. 'And then when they had all gone I ran down to the bridge and wondered if I could throw myself off.'

'But you have told me you can swim.'

'I know' – a wry smile this time – 'it would be so tiresomely difficult to drown, and especially in water that scarcely reaches the knees. And there again, my nature is too robust for such a caper. That was what old Calloway told me, that I had a robust nature, that I would rise above my altered circumstances and find happiness and prosperity. Yes he did, he truly did, pontificating in the middle of the library; he was quite as parsonical as Charles, as preaching, as strait-laced. Do you think I have a robust nature?'

'I do indeed, though I hope I would refrain from telling you in such circumstances.'

'Of course you would. You are the kindest, most sensitive of men. You growl about like some poor unkempt old tiger, a very moth-eaten tiger to be sure, behaving most strangely, keeping bottled dormice in your pockets and dissecting things in the bedroom, unmentionable things, I have had it all from Mrs Clark, you know. There is nothing secret in a place like this. And all the time you are very shrewd and very good. I don't know,' and she paused as if she had become aware that such a speech

323

was very foreign to her, she had never spoken like this to anyone before, except to Fanny perhaps during the bitter crises of the past. 'I don't know if Mr Savage will ever have a better friend.'

They went back downstairs. The door still stood wide open to the sunny garden. 'I must run back to Foley,' said Lizzie, 'it must be very late. I may see you this evening. Will they sit late again do you think?'

'I do not know,' as they stepped out into the blinding light. 'My dear, I do not know.'

She paused, while the pigeons stopped and began again, two or three together. 'If they find him guilty I shall go away. I could not stay here thinking of how Whiteley has blighted my life, alive and dead. My God, alive and dead!'

And: 'Doctor! Doctor!' cried a loud, roaring, disagreeable voice, 'Doctor, you are wanted, sir, now this minute and quick as you can!' and through the stable gate came Millett, panting and hobbling, a crash of hooves behind him witness to the brown horse he had left loose plunging about to find his friend. 'Sir, sir, Mr Frost is all knocked to pieces. You must come at once.'

'How did it happen? Calm down, calm down, I will go in for my bag. No, Lizzie dear, you run for it, it is only in the hall. I must get out the horse. Millett, you old devil, tell me what has happened?'

'The judge give up, sir, he rose the old boy and said it was all done till this young wench come up from Colchester. It might be four o'clock says he or even five. Well I see Mr Frost go out with young Mr C, off for a bite to eat I reckon and good luck they deserve it, and down Friday come this here shay, like smoke, sir, like smoke. It swerve 'cos of the crowd comin' out of the gaol but it was all out of control, the boy with a face like chalk . . . Howsoever, it catched Mr Frost a wallop with the nearside wheel, threw him back four paces. He lay on the ground, sir. Mr C he catch sight of me and yells "Go fetch the Doctor, take my horse"and so I come.'

'Thank you,' said the Doctor to Lizzie, taking his bag.

'It seems Mr Frost has been struck by a runaway post-chaise. I expect they already have a surgeon to him but I will go and see whether I can assist.'

She stood looking at him. It was as if all her spirit had been suddenly extinguished, she was so still, so shrunken. Then she leaned forward, offered her cheek for his kiss.

'Well,' said Millett, watching the Doctor mount – a tedious business involving much backing up and strong commands and scrambling about – 'Well, I never seen *her* in such a mood, meek as Mary and letting old coves peck her cheek.

'She don't look herself,' he remarked aloud as they sped up the avenue to the gate and cantered out on to the Westdene road, 'she look like a girl in love,' and he looked sideways to see what effect this remark might have. These queer-looking quiet clever coves were often secretly lascivious in his opinion, he had known many a husband cuckolded by such drab little men.

But the Doctor only gave a short laugh and clapped his heels into the black horse so that he drew away, his bag bumping beside him, both hands – both hands! – twisted deep in the full black mane.

21

Jary had dined on dry biscuits and a glass of rum, very little for a man who had had nothing since breakfast, but he was in a state of unbearable tension, he had really begun to believe he could not face any more of it, any more of this terrible stalemate, the same facts reiterated so slowly, slowly, and all building up an atmosphere of guilt, his guilt, yet there was not the slightest proof he struck the blows and never would be.

'How is he?' was his first question as Quarel shepherded the Doctor through the door and clanged it shut behind him.

'Cracked ribs, I think, three or even four, nothing to upset yourself about; but he is in great pain, cannot breathe easily yet nor will do for some days, so cannot speak easily either. You know what it means?'

Jary sat down on his stool. He had taken off his coat for the little room was uncomfortably warm, and he had loosened his stock. He looked hot and tired and something else: nervous? Not trembling nervous by any means but in a strange heightened mood, his reserve momentarily broken, as if the news of Frost's accident had knocked him shrewdly.

'There is only this girl to testify,' he said, 'I believe I shall manage to question her decently enough supposing she says anything worth challenging. What can she say? She was with him that night, she was the last to see him alive, she let him kiss her hand and climbed into her carriage. There is not going to be much meat on those bones, Alex. Dear God, they have not made a case against me, they have only proved I had the opportunity, that I might have wished him dead. Half Westdene may have wished him dead for all I know and I was not the only one with opportunity. They even said this morning that

I must have walked coolly to the end of the lane and tossed the knife into the sea. I could feel the jury looking at me in a body at that moment, wondering how hideous a man must be to deliberately carry a bloody knife forty yards and throw it off the quay, wiping his hands on his coat tails no doubt and saying "There, that's done for him, the devil". They are all against me, every man, and the judge . . . My God, no wonder so many men are hung if they are not allowed a counsel to conduct the whole case, if they have to wrestle with court procedure and rely on the help of miserable, sour, mean little men half asleep under their wigs. If I was illiterate and in rags, how would they treat me? How would I have a fair trial?'

There was no answer to all this, every question being rhetorical, and the Doctor knew the wisdom of sympathetic silence, he had sat by the beds of patients suffering just such desperate moods though generally for other reasons. Amputations often caused this flying out, this bitter railing, not immediately but after the initial strength and courage had worn down, leaving the man fractious and resentful. It was only natural. In most cases it would pass.

'It is four o'clock already,' he said gently, getting out his watch. 'If she is coming by post-chaise it is an uncommon slow one. Calloway said he would come up to fetch me if the court was about to sit. By the way, I have been with Lizzie Rayner, she wishes you all the best though she cannot put it into words, did not even try to send a message, she thought it might be thought presumptuous, that you might suspect she was secretly glad of your misfortune. Nothing could be further from the truth. I do like that girl, Jary, I do indeed.'

A lift of those dark eyebrows. 'You did not tell her?'

'I hope I never break confidences. I join Fanny Jewkes in that sentiment. What good would it do, pray, to tell her she might inherit Ramillies and a fortune? Yes?' as the door began to open, and then hurriedly: 'Do you think she would be pleased, be overjoyed, knowing it would be hers only when you swung at the rope's end? Yes, Quarel, what is it?'

'Beg pardon, sir, but I thought you should know, the judge is on his way in. That Miss Stanley has arrived at last, charged into the Admiral like a rocket my boy says, has just stopped to change her hat and is running over.'

Jary gave a harsh laugh. 'Women! It would not surprise me if she said he had an appointment to meet me in the lane, I did not behave as gallantly as she had hoped and there is some old saying about Hell and women scorned, is there not?'

'I heard something of the sort once but you were never a cynic, Jary dear, never at all. Women do not lie any more than men, I find, perhaps less, and they bear their woes with more fortitude, do not go all aswim at the sight of blood. It is only men think them into poor weak inconstant creatures, jealous and unpredictable. Speak to Miss Stanley kindly as you would any human being, speak to her direct and cheerful, and you may be surprised at what she has to say.'

There were rumours running all over the parish, scarcely credible. They had come from Westdene on the evening coach to Beccles, the same sort of antique, ponderous vehicle which had brought the Doctor and Jary to Ramillies in the first place, and since it had already picked up twice in the few miles before it reached Stretfield and it put down a young chattering fellow at the Paradise turn, by eight o'clock half the village knew that Miss Rayner was to have Ramillies and twenty thousand a year.

The news reached the Stones by way of the coachman, the cook and Mrs Stone's maid, who passed it on while dabbing spilt wine off her mistress's dress. Mr Odbold was a guest to dinner and he pooh-poohed any such suggestion with a look of scorn: how could Mr Savage, without being deranged, without growing insane, leave his money to Miss Rayner. Miss Rayner! He had been confounded by rumour many times, he said, he did not trust rumour in the least. Mrs Stone said boldly nor did she, but she prayed this was the truth, the very truth, for such a romantic gesture was a rare and precious thing, men in general being unromantic creatures and tight with their money. For her part she would be overjoyed if there was the least particle of substance to it, and she wished Lizzie as much gold and property as she could get.

Mr Odbold passed an uneasy night at the parsonage and over his porridge and his weak tea his old servant told him that she had heard from Joe King who had it from a Fipson boy who had it from Dick Plaicey who was in Westdene all day yesterday and heard it with his own ears, that if Mr Savage was not hung he and Miss Rayner were going to make a match of it so that either way Ramillies would rightfully be hers again, either way she would come home. This was too much for Odbold, who saddled his mule, a squat, anxious mule with all the nervous hesitation of an animal that was neither one thing nor the other, and trotted away to Paradise and Foley.

By the time he reached the ford, however, having met a man clearing a blocked culvert and a small boy with some teggs and more of the ubiquitous Fipsons, the sum had risen to thirty thousand, Ramillies and half Jamaica, marriage for a certainty. By Foley he was wondering what it would be next: Ramillies and the entire spice islands? Fifty thousand pounds? Five hundred slaves?

'What is it all about?' he cried to Fanny, tying his mule to the gate and seeing her cutting flowers. 'Who started such a tale? Who is responsible for such nonsense? My dear Mrs Jewkes, what does the young lady herself say about it?'

'What is it, Fan?' said Lizzie's frowsty morning voice – it was barely past seven, no time for morning callers – and her face appeared at an upper casement.

'Mr Odbold says you are to inherit Ramillies and fifty thousand pounds, Lizzie dear, or if Mr Savage don't hang – bless him, I never entertain the thought of it – you and he are to be married with the same result.'

329

The face wavered and vanished. 'My God!' came faintly from within.

'You have surprised us before breakfast,' said Fanny, not without a note of reproof, 'but pray step in and join us. La, how people do speculate. It only goes to show how the thought of money runs to our poor weak heads. As to who started the rumour, well, who indeed? Who started the rumour little Henriette was Mr Savage's own flesh and blood? Who started the rumour that Lizzie was ravished by Captain Jervis and abandoned in a common lodging house? No, you will never find the source, it would take you till Judgement Day.'

The parson looked flushed and angry. He hesitated on the step, protested in a low voice that he had had his breakfast, he would not intrude, and added: 'But is there any truth in it, Mrs Jewkes? There must be some foundation, a rumour does not spring out of air. Miss Rayner *did* gallop away in a chaise, ma'am, and did not return for several days; if what was bruited about the village was not the truth at least one can understand how it came to be thought the truth.'

'Just as any fool can understand how Mr Savage *might* have killed Mr Whiteley. I am surprised at you, sir! Where is your charity? You have hurried here panting to know if this tale is true because you are worried for your bell, sir, your precious bell. You are afraid that if Lizzie has Ramillies and the money you may never get it, you have treated her with such disdain and condescension. I will not have you in my house, sir! Go away!'

'Good Lord,' said Lizzie, looking through the parlour window, 'he is scuttling up the lane as fast as he can go. What did you say to him?'

'Oh, nothing I have not been aching to say a very long time,' and then, with a shrug: 'Only I am very glad I am not a papist, Lizzie dear, for I would be very reluctant to go to confession and say I had sent a parson packing, almost boxed his ears. What penance would they give me, do you think?'

But Lizzie was laughing, overcome, and not only at

330

the sight of Mr Odbold, or the thought of Fanny in a confessional, but at the ludicrous, ludicrous rumour, the idea that Jary Savage should leave her Ramillies and his fortune. And 'Would you give a fig for Ramillies, Lizzie Rayner, were you to be given it tomorrow?' came a voice, and she stopped laughing, sober in a moment, wide-eyed.

'I am going to Ramillies,' she said.

'Lizzie, Lizzie, it is not half past seven. They will be still abed.'

But she had run away already, calling for Kitty, something she did very rarely unless she was going to take trouble, to make an impression. A quarter of an hour passed while Fanny chewed solemnly on her toast and thought of Mr Odbold's scandalized face and wondered at herself for feeling so cheerful and unrepentant though she could never show it, never, she must stay looking grave as if conscious of her sin. Then the door opened and Lizzie was back, looking very fine in dark blue, a dress Fanny had not seen before, a small blue hat on her head.

'My love, you are dressed to kill! Why are you going to Ramillies?'

'I have to see the Doctor.'

'Mrs Stone thinks you and the Doctor have grown very close.'

'Mrs Stone is a tittle-tattle as you well know. It was probably she who started this absurd notion about Mr Savage's will.'

All along the lane she walked with a fierce concentration, her head down, her good skirts held up with exaggerated care. When she came to where the cattle stood warming their backs in the first real sun of the day she stopped, and looked up. Already there was the deep full green of midsummer, though midsummer was far off. In the great old trees the wood pigeons were beginning their daily round: take two cows, Taffy, take two cows . . . Under the young spreading leaves she could see the ghosts: herself as a child riding on the hay wain, as a girl walking with Whiteley in a white dress knowing even then she was not as happy as she should be though he offered unthought-of delights and a new status combined with preservation of the old; her father riding to Paradise, drawing rein to speak to her, his great horse restless and all foamed about the mouth; her father's smiling face, a little florid and well-worn, pouched about the eyes, but essentially the face of a weak, charming, generous-hearted man; then another Lizzie Rayner, blotched with weeping, the skin round her eyes tight and shiny, running to hide in the secret rushy places of the lower Meeting Grounds before she had to pin on her look of proud indifference and step into the chaise that was to take her to Woodbridge.

The cattle shifted, licked each other's coats. Lizzie lifted her head and looked up at the clear promising sky and breathed deeply, and smiled. The past faded, slipped back into its rightful place. There was no ache about her heart. It seemed to her that she had grown up at last, a process arrested when she had left Ramillies that fateful summer; she had only matured in part of her mind, part had still clung to the old house, the old lost security, the memories. Now it seemed Jary Savage had set her free, but by doing . . . what? By being what? Himself of course. Another man might not have taken Henriette as his own, it was just like him to be so quixotically generous; she could believe, yes, she could believe he would will her Ramillies and a fortune, he had a strong sense of justice and of fate. It had all begun with those secret visits to Henriette, the afternoon she had sat in the nursery drawing that silken fuzz of black hair, that rounded cheek, the great eyes. She had never thought of having babies of her own until that afternoon. All the babies she had ever held had been just babies until she picked up Henriette. It came to her, thinking of Jary and his deep grief – still with him, she was sure – and the little stone in the churchyard, that Henriette had a great deal to answer for: if Henriette had not died Jary would never have considered changing his will.

I am not his kind of woman, she thought, walking on.

He likes his women soft and generous, intelligent yes, but only intelligent enough to know that what he requires is a sort of genial devotion, not true companionship, not that joyful lack of reserve that marks the best marriages. He has suffered from lack of a mother – *I* know what that means – a superabundance of strange, adoring aunts, the continual cruelties of a depraved old man. He would be wary of complicated commitment, all his senses engaged.

She reached the door in the wall. Inside was silence, a drift of perfume from the little lavender bushes warming in the sun. For a moment she stood there, looking at the house. No, it was not a sudden thing, it had been growing for months, perhaps ever since Jary Savage had arrived: she did not want Ramillies any more, it was a fine house and had been a happy home but it was not hers, it was Jary's, she was glad it was Jary's.

'Miss Rayner, why how lovely to see you,' exclaimed Mr Bliss, pulling the napkin from his throat and standing up, 'I am afraid the Doctor has left already, he is to call on poor Dr Plesset and then visit Mr Frost who has been moved to the Admiral. But do come in, sit down, may I offer you tea, chocolate, coffee? What would you like? Mr Fisher will be here in a moment, he is going to drive me to Westdene. Mr Savage's horrible black horse cast a shoe coming home last night and grew very sore on the stones so he is laid up again. He spends a very great deal of his time in the stable, the monster.'

Lizzie sat and allowed him to pour her coffee. He was very pleased to have her company but because it was so unexpected and he felt he was not looking his best he grew pink and anxious, pressing her to another cup before she had finished the first and glancing several times at the clock in case it should be time for Stephen Fisher.

'Miss Stanley?' he said in answer to her inquiry. 'What a goings-on! Apparently her brother sent over a note – we were all in court by then just waiting for the judge – to say she did not feel very well, that she begged to be excused. Mr Calloway nearly had a fit, said you could not be excused unless you were practically dead, but anyway the judge took a different view, was charmingly sympathetic. We were all dismissed till ten o'clock this morning.'

'Does it not allow Mr Frost time to recover?'

'Oh no, unfortunately there is no chance of that. I mean, he *is* recovered, yes indeed, but very sore, dosed with laudanum, not taking proper breaths. It was the hub struck him I think: he had already been pushed over in the general scramble to get out of the way and it must have been the hub caught him a cruel blow. It was a wonder he did not fall under the wheel or have his ribs stove in.'

Mrs Clark knocked. 'Mr Fisher has turned in at the avenue, sir. Kate has just run from upstairs to tell me. You asked to be called as soon as he arrived.'

'Yes, thank you, Mrs Clark. Could you look out my hat? I tossed it somewhere in the hall. Miss Rayner, do forgive my leaving you like this, but I promised to follow the Doctor as soon as I could.'

They stepped out into the sunshine. 'Oh Miss Rayner, how glad I am to see you,' cried Stephen Fisher from the carriage. 'Please tell Mrs Jewkes I will call this evening, I will bring her the verdict in person. But you look so well, my dear. You must come and dine next week, my cousin would like that. What with the trial and all this toing and froing we have not entertained at all since she arrived.'

Mr Bliss climbed in and closed the door. 'May I call on you with Mr Fisher?' he asked through the window, very hurried and anxious, and in the next breath: 'Forgive me, but you must have walked over to see the Doctor urgently — what have I been thinking of? Is there a message? How can I make amends?'

'Oh, it was nothing,' she said — apart from asking him if there is any truth in this rumour, this amazing wicked rumour — 'it was nothing at all.'

The coach drew away, rattling between the oaks. 'Have you heard this story going about in Westdene?' asked Mr

Fisher, settling back in his corner. 'Oh the dear girl looks so well, so very well . . . It must be that, it must be. I was in half a mind to wish her joy but you can never tell with Lizzie Rayner how she will take things and of course there has been no official announcement. But how romantic! What a charming solution!'

Mr Bliss's frown deepened. 'I am sorry, sir, I do not follow you.'

'Why, they say Miss Rayner is to marry Mr Savage.' Mr Bliss drew a ragged breath. He felt a stab of unreasonable jealousy, deep and sharp enough to make him look a little queer for a moment or two, and he could not help himself saying bitterly: 'If Mr Savage is not hung.'

'Oh.' Mr Fisher's eyes grew round and horrified. 'Oh, how can you think it? They would never hang him, never.' And after a long long reflective pause: 'How could they do so, with no evidence?'

'The Doctor says it is not evidence will hang him but prejudice.'

The Doctor was in the front room of the Admiral watching the crowds in the market place. There were several hundred sheep in pens and two score geese looking disdainful, and the usual mix of countrymen and seamen, small barefoot boys bobbing in and out.

'Oh sir, is it true?' asked Mrs King in a hushed voice, bringing his breakfast coffee. 'Is it true what they say about Miss Rayner?'

'What do they say about Miss Rayner?'

'That she is to be married to Mr Savage or if not,' lower still, 'if the worst happens, she is to have all his money.'

'Mrs King, Mrs King, what a parcel of old gossips you all are. Ah, there is Mr Calloway, I am expecting him. Please to bring another cup.' And across this other cup as he poured he asked quietly, 'What is all this about Miss Rayner? Are there strange stories flying in the wind?'

'In the wind! The news is all about the town, has been since last night apparently: Lizzie Rayner is engaged to

Savage and if things go ill with us she will have Ramillies anyway. God alone knows where it started. No doubt Savage will think I had a hand in it. Who else knew about his will?'

'I wonder,' remembering Quarel at the door, such a delicate moment. 'But marriage? How people love a happy ending, if marriage can be said to be a happy ending, which in ninety cases in a hundred I would doubt, sincerely doubt. I wonder what Lizzie thinks?'

'Oh she will be cock-a-hoop, it is all she has ever wanted – Ramillies, I mean, not marriage. I do not think Lizzie Rayner is a marrying sort of woman.'

'It is a quarter before ten, sir,' said Pamela from the door, 'and there is a great crowd by the gaol gates, Buckton says; oh, and Mr Bliss is returned, sir, he is in the hall.'

'Doctor! Will you walk across? We will not be allowed in if we dawdle. Mr Calloway, good morning.'

'I cannot come, Andrew, I must away at once to poor Plesset. I have been to the apothecary's, the Chinese down Market Street, and laid in a store, such a store, of necessaries. Would you believe it, his drug cupboard is bare, quite bare. What little he had that greasy young upstart Fowler has taken; Fowler is looking after his patients now, and rising from lowly assistant to chief has done him no good, no good at all, a self-opinionated know-nothing, a braggart, hot air, no skill, no feeling, no whisper of intelligence, Sill, I must away. I shall return as soon as possible.'

Mr Bliss groped in his pocket. 'This came not fifteen minutes after you left. I did not know if it was urgent so I took the liberty of bringing it along. Perhaps, Mr Calloway, I could accompany you across to the court? Doctor, goodbye, I hope Dr Plesset is recovered.'

He will not be, thought the Doctor, stowing Ann's letter in his bosom; he will not be, the stubborn old man, nor will ever be till he closes his eyes on this world. And as he passed out of the door and called the boy holding the brown horse: which he will do very soon, may already have done, God help him. He mounted, bundled up the reins. Oh for his little chestnut, those familiar in-curving ears. He felt too far from the ground on this beast, perfectly satisfactory for a man of Jary's height and weight but too much horse for him, far too much horse in all respects. He jogged along precariously, clutching the mane or the saddle.

Later, noon or thereabouts, coming out of Plesset's house into the dull warm day, he thought of Ann's letter, still crackling in his shirt. It was not the time and place to read it now, the old man dead upstairs: as he looked up, thinking of the end, the old servant flung open the casement. Yes, he thought, yes, let his soul go free, he did his best for his people within his limits. He heard the small muffled noise of one or two women weeping in the house. Would anyone in High Common weep when he died, he wondered, if indeed, he was to die in High Common.

He rode to the church where they had told him he would find the parson. Mr Odbold was in the vestry surrounded by moth-eaten vestments, torn books and two half mice.

'Poor man,' he said, 'poor man. I shall go along at once. There is a Miss Plesset to be informed, I believe, a very elderly lady in Bath.'

Why did country vestries always smell of the tomb, wondered the Doctor. He watched the parson scoop up the dismembered mice with distaste, shovelling them outside.

'Cats! Cruel! Cruel!' came back through the open door.

'Well, good morning. I must get back to Westdene.'

'To the trial?' the parson came in again, seizing two books and banging them together furiously so that dust rose in clouds. 'It must be nearly over. Do you think they will find him guilty? It is terrible what man is capable of, is it not, Doctor? I could not conceive of stabbing a man to death yet so many do it, and do it lightly we must believe, for spite or a handful of money or in a drunken rage. Dear, dear, it is very sad. I suppose the ladies at

Foley are very concerned with Mr Savage's fate; how I do not understand women, temperamental women. It is independence is the cause of such frowardness, such unbecoming boldness. A woman who is not thoroughly domesticated is so often saucy, even brazen.'

'Do you speak of Mrs Jewkes, sir? Are you saying that Mrs Jewkes is froward and bold and saucy?'

'Ah. Ah no,' catching sight of the Doctor's glittering cold eye. 'Umm. I cannot think it would be a good match, they are both somewhat impulsive young people, strong-willed.'

The Doctor walked out into the air, putting on his hat which had now, to add to its other peculiarities, a rim of canonical dust. There was the sound of tearing grass, of gluttonous munching, of a large voracious animal destroying something succulent: the brown horse was eating the creeper about the porch.

'Oh!' cried Odbold, flapping his hands. 'Oh! Oh, it was a tender rare marvellous thing from China, I have tended it like my own child. Shoo, shoo!'

The horse moved away without haste and stood finishing its mouthful. 'It will grow again,' said the Doctor, 'it will recover. Even in China it might expect to be ravaged now and again. They have a great many horses in China, not to speak of bears.'

But: 'He has trampled the Rayner graves, he has been gnawing the stone,' came the high-pitched, infuriated cry as the parson flitted to and fro across his churchyard.

'I am sure it was not the horse, He has an iron digestion without doubt, but stone? No, good sir, 'twas not the horse gnawed the stone.'

The horse, whose bit had a strange dusting of white powder, much as his rider's hat had its sprinkling of vestry dust, trotted away cheerfully.

He tied it to the gate at Ramillies and sat down under the first oak in the avenue to read his letter.

Dearest Alex
    A note, a brief note to let you know how the pony

338

does, how we all do. Lady Barsham says she has not heard from you for several weeks – how can you square it with your conscience? The lady loves you dearly. Here is my first news – I make it first because it is agreeable and the other is not – Tom wishes to become engaged to Charlotte. Well, it was not unexpected, but they seem so piteously young. Or is it that I am growing old so that they seem younger than they are? Anyway, Lord Barsham has no objection provided they wait another year. Tom is incensed, but I have pointed out that it is more than he had any right to expect, it is not every titled gentleman would let his favourite daughter marry a man who is a. illegitimate b. not exactly wealthy c. totally uneducated. I believe they will be very happy, they will weather the year with no trouble, underneath all the youthful impatience and cries of 'Not fair!' they are remarkably stoical people. I have told Tom that Charlotte is a dear, that if he ever makes her unhappy he will answer to me. But I suspect you cannot get through marriage without some unhappiness, it would not be natural – you notice how philosophical I have become after my own experience? Of course you were right when you said I had brought it on myself. If I say I think I had more unhappiness than I had looked for in such a short marriage I do not complain, merely hope to explain in part what I have to write next.

I am not going to marry William. I went to Portsmouth three weeks ago and met him, he had very little time ashore, poor man, he was being sent to the West Indies, Heaven knows why. He was glad to go, said it was a miracle he should keep in a ship when so many good men are on the beach. Then of course he must have been glad to go because I had disappointed him. Do not ask me why I did it, I cannot put it into any kind of words, but I have known it was coming for a long long time now and resolutely closed my eyes to it, telling myself I was in love with him – which perhaps I was for a week or two, he is a fine man, a worthy man, and I do not mean that in a dull, patronizing way, I mean he is good and strong, I would like him for my friend. Perhaps that is the sticking point: he and I could never be friends. It came to me the other day that we do not laugh at the same things, that we are always pleasant in each other's company but it is a kind of false pleasantness. Do you recall how we used to quarrel? We have not quarrelled since I said I would be his wife. I never thought of it till recently but then it seemed a very strange thing, for he still tries to check me, to curb my most ambitious schemes – oh, probably quite sensibly – but before I would fly out at him and he at me. Anyway, we have parted amicably, he has never never been less than a gentleman. I am sorry for it though know it is for the best. I felt I must write and tell you myself – a ridiculous, foolish, garbled letter is it not? – because you are his friend and brought us together and were my friend and I hope might be again.

I was so sorry to hear about Mr Savage. I hope and pray everything goes well for him. Will you write before you go to India? If only to scold? there is so much I would like to tell you, so many confessions and explanations and, no doubt, excuses, but I am not at my best in a letter. Perhaps I have said too much already, straying from the point, using two words where one will do.

Your friend
Ann Gerard

P.S. Mr Savage led me to believe you had a broken heart, which no doubt I should not mention, you will not bless me for it, but in the unlikely event of this being the truth – you told me once you did not believe in such a thing – I hope it is mended, or at least is mending, and that you will find happiness, in India if not elsewhere. She cannot value you to break your heart, a good woman would not do it and a hard, capricious woman is not good enough for you. There, I have read my sermon. I have presumed too much. You are cursing me roundly or laughing or wishing I may fall off your pony and break my bones.

A mixture of feelings: anxiety, sadness for them both, both Ann and William, exasperation, even anger, and underneath, far underneath, the slow steady burning happiness, an unworthy joy because she was free.

But not free for him. He could not ignore the twenty years that separated them, nearly twenty years. Some men would think nothing of them, would rejoice to lay siege to a much younger woman, but the Doctor was not one of these and in any case, there were so many other objections: he had very little money, he had been a bachelor a very long time, and not least perhaps, he was not at all good-looking, rather the reverse.

'We are both old fools,' he said, remounting the horse and turning its head towards Westdene, 'for I am despicably glad William is not to have her though I cannot – how low we sink, how far below civilized behaviour, below human kindness – and you will surely have the bellyache from all that Chinese greenery, there were berries on it, strange transparent berries.'

Westdene: the smell of the sea very strong, the first drops of rain falling, fewer people in the streets. The Doctor was conscious of hunger, of being tired and out of spirits. His shameful happiness had burned away and left him only a shade less miserable than before.

'Oh Doctor, how late you are,' and there was Pamela with a tray, elbowing through the crowd in the bar, 'Mr Calloway was asking after you an hour ago. Mr Bliss is in the snug, shall I bring you anything there?'

'One of your mother's pies, dear girl, and a bottle of port,' and reaching the quiet corner where Bliss was sitting with a pipe and newspaper: 'Has there been a verdict?'

'Verdict? No, no. The jury begged leave to retire, is

out now, we are all on tenterhooks. That girl Lucy Stanley came up with the information that Whiteley had been called aside by some waif as he arrived at the Assembly and when quizzed said he had to meet a friend later in the evening. When he handed her into the carriage she thought that was where he was going, to meet this friend.'

'Some friend, to stab him seven times and so furiously.'

'If it was the friend. The judge was not overcome by her evidence for all he asked her three times if she was faint, the courtroom was uncommon hot, and sent for a glass of water for her, smiling down at her all the time. In his summing up he said the jury must not automatically assume this unknown friend was the murderer. Whiteley could quite easily have met someone, passed some time with him, parted from him on good terms, and then been killed by a different party. Of course it was sense, he was obliged to point it out, I suppose, but it looked bad, it somehow dismissed the only piece of evidence that was possibly in Mr Savage's favour.'

'And how did Mr Savage look?'

'Cold, hard, reserved; he has looked so all day. Dr French, you do not really think they might find him guilty?'

'Thank you, my dear,' as Pamela brought the port and pie. 'It has always been a strong possibility, Andrew.'

There was a murmur, a rising murmur. Someone at the door said: 'The jury is coming back in. There is a terrible crowd in Friday Walk, a sheep couldn't get through.'

And: 'Come,' said the Doctor, jumping up, abandoning his meal, 'I must be there.'

22

The general impression from the public gallery was of heat and noise, too much of both. The sun having deserted, hiding away behind the building clouds, and strange intermittent rain showers rattling the windows, candles had been lit, the great many-branched lamp that dangled over the clustered wigs.

'Here he comes, the old warmint,' said a voice directly behind the Doctor's left ear. 'How he do strut along.'

It was true, the judge had an officious walk; it was a defensive action, the Doctor decided, like that of a small cock in a run full of very large hens. There was the expectant hush, the ritual pause, a moment when all the wigs were facing one direction waiting the nod, and then a great shuffling and clearing of throats and Mr Justice Fielder sitting down with great dignity, casting a deliberately cold glance at the jury benches.

Why have I not looked at Jary yet, wondered the Doctor, letting his eyes move round. Because it is a damnable intrusion staring at another's pain, and in a public place along with this avid rabble, these sensation seekers. I do not wish to be associated with them; least of all do I wish him to look up and see me here and believe I have come, like them, to see him hunted down.

Yes: cold, hard, reserved. He believes in fate but will not knuckle to it, will avert it if he can with his dying breath; he does not lack courage. He should be in charge of Ann's ship, it would be more his element, he is not cut out for a country squire, a useful, circumscribed life. He has an over-large heart, God knows, rescuing that girl and her baby, leaving his all to Lizzie Rayner; his sense of natural justice would not be everybody's. Yet I have heard only good things said about him between the Admiral and this dreadful place, a great deal of laughter, commendation, cheerful agreement. Perhaps after all his instinct to do right as he sees it is only the basic human urge – in those of us not altogether lacking in moral fibre – the urge many of us overcome with cold logic, with so-called rational argument, the 'I would have helped him if I could but there was no time, no means, I was not well' of those who make a practise of walking by upon the other side. If so this would account for his apparent popularity this morning, there is no doubt this move to reinstate Lizzie is applauded. He is not the disobliging stranger he was yesterday. A street boy selling buns, a stunted little thing, tough as any human being I have ever met, told me last evening that this Mr Savage was a great black man who had once been a slave on an estate in Africay. He was most certain he was horrible and uncivilized, a cannibal perhaps, for he was only called Savage owing to the fact he landed in England with no surname, the heathen cannibals of Africay not going in for such polite touches; yet a few moments ago when I saw the selfsame boy by the gaol gate he greeted me like a brother and said how he wished the cannibal well, he had a spark of goodness in his soul, had he not?

A spark, to be sure; it is not much in evidence now. He has his duelling face on, Mother of God. He does not even turn to look at the jury – are they hanging their heads, damn them, or is it imagination? – as they shuffle in. That fat, bald, prosperous devil is the foreman, he likes his own voice, look how he is waiting for the judge to speak so that he can have the pleasure of replying in the loudest, most pompous tones he can produce. Let him be acquitted, let him be acquitted. I have not prayed for anything for a great many years, I lapsed long ago into prayerless cynicism, into determined atheism, but please God let him be acquitted. Hot, so hot, poor Bliss has sweat running down his cheek. It is not possible for so many people to hold their combined breath for so long . . .

'Not guilty,' said the foreman gravely, and behind him the other eleven grinned from ear to ear, as pleased as if

344

they had just discovered the New World and all her riches. 'Thank God!' cried Bliss, squirming round to see the Doctor. There was a great hubbub of congratulation, huge content. Only the man in the dock seemed aloof from it, as unyieldingly sober as when he had come in. It would not be human to suppress a smile in the circumstances yet he did not smile, and if that whey-pinched look was relief it was strange relief. All the wigs were bobbing and colliding, from the far left of the gallery came the beginning of a ragged cheer. The judge was about to knock for silence, a growing disgust adding to the rigidity of his features.

'Hooray,' said the voice in the Doctor's ear. 'Hooray Mr Jardine bloody Savage, you can hev a good wet and go on home.'

'Hooray indeed,' said Bliss, fighting the two feet to the Doctor's side. 'Lord, what a crush! Look at Calloway, he is grinning from ear to ear.'

The judge raised his voice to an imperious pitch. There was a reluctant silence broken by witty observations from the ladies in the front row who encouraged him to get on with it, they were waiting for their dinner and so was Mr Savage no doubt who thought he might never have another one.

'You did not expect a different verdict?' asked Bliss, amazed. 'Doctor, you surprise me.'

'Let us simply say I do not put my faith in the Law, the Law is a strumpet, Mr Bliss. And if you want my opinion for what little it is worth I would say that it is Lizzie Rayner has won this victory, not evidence or the lack of it, not arguments, not justice.'

'But there is no substance in this rumour of marriage.'

'No, no. Though if I were an advocate of marriage' – which I am not and never was, and this recent affair between Ann and William showing me how cruelly one may get stung if one meddles – 'if I were, say, I would not oppose the match. They are both headstrong and resilient, both past the bloom of youth. They would spit and curse, part enemies, kiss and make up. It would be a difficult relationship but it would survive, I think, survive and maybe flourish.'

They emerged at the foot of the stairs to an even greater crush, ®a gathering by the doors of the court, a press of faces turned for the first glimpse of the man from Africay.

'Africay!' cried the Doctor, and then, seizing Mr Bliss's sleeve, 'Andrew, forgive me. I cannot wait here, the world and his wife hanging about to wring his hand. What hypocrisy, what repellent hypocrisy. They would as soon have cheered at his hanging. I am away to the Admiral. If you see him, speak to him, tell him I have ridden back to Ramillies, that I wish him joy of his acquittal, the sincerest joy.'

'Hurrying away, Dr French?' asked Mr Stone, meeting him in the populous yard as he half ran to the street. 'A patient no doubt. How is old Plesset now?'

'He is dead,' said Dr French, ducking though the little door, not looking behind.

He is dead, he is dead, he died in the courtroom, I do not know how or when but it happened. Was it the last of his boyish innocence, the cheerful open optimism that had survived a life afloat, repeated injustice at his uncle's hands, reverses of fortune here there and everywhere, lack of funds, lack of food, lack of affection, was it that which died at last? Certainly it was as if a light had been put out, a light that had long been shining through all manner of huge storms. In a strange way I am afraid for him. Will he ever be the same, dear, impulsive man?

'He is acquitted,' he said aloud to Fanny, seeing joy spring across her face. There was a gratifying uproar in the court. It was a popular verdict, God knows.'

'Thank God. Thank God for it. There were times when I wondered . . . I did not have absolute trust in the process of the law, in that young puppy Calloway and all those devious attorneys. Thank God.'

He had ridden straight to Foley. He had not intended to, intending only to leave Westdene and seek peace and quiet, a breath of good clean air. He had had enough of the devious attorneys, tap-room speculation, of the mob. But the sight of fresh flowers on Henriette's grave as he came to the church – he had been obscurely drawn to the church – made him think of the two ladies who had most likely put them there and he had trotted on, thankful not to be accosted in the village, though Mr Blake ran out from the new cottages as he passed, cock-a-hoop as a boy when he heard the news.

A capricious late afternoon, now and then a vigorous wind and sometimes rain on it, great spattering drops, and then a brightening, an almost-lifting of the massed clouds, and a lull. No birds sang. The horse seemed subdued. Was there a storm to come? The Doctor crossed the ford and there was Foley, low and homely, smoking from both chimneys.

'Oh how Lizzie will fly out when she hears she has missed you,' said Fanny, hurrying out the madeira and calling for cakes, 'she has been at Hopes nearly all day, Miss Pawle has been very low, poor thing, had a letter from Bombay to say her sister had died. It was a very sad blow to the old dear even though they had not met for fifteen years and ten thousand miles is a prodigious great distance too. Lizzie took up some cheese, and marmalade – for the Diddlers.

'It was Lizzie saved him, the thought of Lizzie reinstated.'

'Stuff! When she was twenty-one, an innocent slip of a thing, they could not say enough poisonous things about her, some have never invited her to their houses since. Mrs Whiteley was one, of course, the old . . . the old . . . Well, never mind. I always grow heated about it and all to no purpose. There is no way to treat such people except by ignoring them. It is no good their veering round like weathercocks now she is a crabbed old maid and making out they always had a kindly thought for her. Stuff and nonsense! I will say it again. What they really care for is the fortune, the fortune and Lizzie's success at the Royal Academy. Hearts they don't care a fig for, Doctor, only guineas and fashion.'

He laughed. He remembered her at Ramillies about to commit that indiscretion, smiling even through her discomforture, never holding it against him that he had poked in his nose at the wrong moment. He offered his glass for more madeira, and raised it.

'To you, my dear, and the last of your admirable cellar.'

'Oh but you should drink to Mr Savage. And it is not the last of the cellar for I must confess he had it all, every last barrel and bottle and pipe and hogshead or whatever they are called. Lizzie found out, you know. I believe my friend Mrs Barker in London was disgracefully indiscreet, though I forgive her for Lizzie probably went at her hammer and tongs once she had wind of it. She went at me hammer and tongs, I never knew the meaning of ranting and raving till then, why had I sold it, a Tom Fool thing to do, she never minded old dresses, she had had no intention of cutting a figure at my expense – oh on and on. And then she burst into tears. I had no idea what to do. It ain't natural in Lizzie to sob and I have never looked for gratitude.'

Lussom came in. 'A message come down from Hopes,' he said, with a scowl at the madeira, which he hoped they had not drunk to the bottom as he had promised himself a glass in the kitchen, 'Miss Rayner is staying for dinner.'

'Oh thank you, Lussom. And Lussom, open the good ale, the strong brew, and drink to Mr Savage's health. He is free, he is coming home.'

'I am glad of it, ma'am.'

'Dinner at Hopes,' exclaimed Fanny as the door closed. 'The poor dear, how she will hate it. They keep a good table at Hopes but even the best food is not improved by being watered with tears. Poor Lizzie, how she must wish she had stayed here or gone to paint at Ramillies. She would have gone to paint but the weather was so changeable. Doctor, you look worn out, do have another glass. Why, we could be very wicked and finish the bottle. It was not more than three-quarters full.'

A squall of rain blew up against the windows. 'Oh,' said Fanny, 'I hope it does not mean to set in like this for the night. They will not have sat down to eat at Hopes yet and it is a goodish walk back. If it grows dark early and keeps on raining she may have to stay at Hopes till morning.'

The Doctor appeared to drag himself back from a great distance, jerking up his head. 'Forgive me, you have reminded me of my own case. I must away to Ramillies.'

'Of course,' and she actually put up her soft powdery cheek for his kiss. 'Of course you must be there when he returns. And you must give him my sincerest regards, my best wishes, all joy for the future. Lussom, Lussom,' running to the door, 'Lussom, where is the Doctor's hat? He is leaving.'

'His hat is on the peg, ma'am, and I have to report his horse has trampled in the garden, it untied itself.'

'Untied itself! Oh. Oh well . . . Perhaps,' in an undertone, 'it was not tied properly to begin with, the Doctor is not handy with horses,' and then louder: 'Still, it is a blessing it has not galloped back to Ramillies, to its own stable. Horses do that, the inconsiderate things.'

'Not he,' said Lussom lugubriously, 'he's a-chewing on that little shrub by the gate. Do you go and look.'

Of course she had always been welcome in the cottages, she was the true daughter of the Squire, that good old man who, for all his shortcomings and they had known them all, had always done his best for them, had never seen them hungry. She was not quite what they would have preferred, being too awkward and energetic and forthright for a comfortable guest, but there was no false pride in her, no queenly reserve, and over the years she had called in regularly with pots of this and jars of that and good milk from Foley – they had long ago lost their cows – and old clothes and offers of work. And besides, she and they had a common bond, as strong as that of the ancient feudal obligations, for both she and they had suffered at the hands of the Whiteleys, losing everything in the process, she more than they it was considered, for she had lost her character and position as well as the roof over her head.

At the moment when Fanny believed she was sitting down to roast duck in Hopes she was actually poised on the edge of a hard old chair in a miserable crooked little building called Swinyerds in the corner of the Hopes stackyard, drinking agrimony tea.

'It work miracles, it do,' said Mother Henham, turning over the cards. 'There's no call for making faces, Missy.'

'It has a strong taste.'

'Not your Hyson, no, not off your pretty tea bushes. But that sets you up, you'll feel the better for it. Do you want me to read your palm if you don't care for the cards?'

'I came to see how you were, not to consult you.'

Miss Nose-in-the-air is it! Do you hide your palm, gal, or shan't I tell you a story. But there, a woman's life show on her face for any child to read. Or a man's.'

'Some men's lives and some faces. What about . . . Mr Savage? He was a wild lad, Fanny says, frivolous and inconstant. I don't see any of that in his face.'

'He always hev a good heart. Good hearts won't be hid.'

Lizzie eased herself on the hard chair, feeling the strengthening gripes of her stomach. Damn politeness! Damn agrimony, miracle brew or no! A question rose, formed itself, dissolved away again. But Ma Henham had read it in her eyes.

'I hev seen him,' she said softly, 'riding up the avenue at Ramillies.'

'When?' cried Lizzie.

'Oh, not a quarter of an hour since. Come and look at my hens. I had them from that higgler with the saucy eye and the stiff-legged mare . . . Look, look, there they run, the dears.

Lizzie looked out and saw six small black shapes pursuing the much larger Hopes Poultry with a furious intent until, in a twinkling, the stackyard was theirs entirely and a very small black cock got upon the gate post and crowed with wicked joy.

'I am so glad they had the sense to lend you an umbrella,' said Fanny as she came into the hall at Foley some hour and half later, 'I hope Miss Pawle was not too dreary. What did you have for dinner?'

'Nothing. She was certainly too dreary to eat.'

'But we had a message! The dear Doctor was here, he had brought the news . . . Lizzie, Lizzie, he is free!'

'I know. Ma Henham told me. She had seen him at Ramillies that very minute.'

'Rubbish!' said poor Fanny, who felt it was a shabby thing to do, it had quite spoiled her pleasure at being first with the news. 'How could she have seen him, pray? He is probably dining at Mr Fisher's or something. I know the Doctor hurried away to Ramillies in case he should be there but . . . She is a dreadful old woman. She saw nothing of the sort!'

'Still, she gave me six eggs from her magic fowls. I said we had a broody so I was pressed to take them. Do you think they will hatch into dragons?'

'I wish you would not tease,' said Fanny, with a suspicious glance at the little white eggs in their straw nest in Lizzie's handkerchief. 'They are perfectly ordinary. It is all nonsense to suppose black hens are anything but black hens.'

'Then I will take them to the coop directly and tell your broody we expect six ordinary chicks and no dragons.'

They met again in the parlour where Fanny was drawing the curtains. The fire had been lit all day and burned up brightly. There was a suspicious-looking bottle on the side.

'You have been drinking,' said Lizzie, astounded.

'Only a glass of port after dinner. And I had some madeira to toast Mr Savage, I could hardly do less. But tell me, why did they not feed you at Hopes? Surely Miss Pawle being indisposed does not mean you must go hungry, and after you had been invited.'

Lizzie laughed. She was in a curious mood, half elation,

half dark brooding. She looked tired too, and some of her curls were a little damp.

'The whole house seemed to be in mourning,' she said, 'and they had heard about Dr Plesset and he and Miss Pawle were once young things together, it had come as another shock. And anyway, I did not really feel like eating when it came to it. I told dear old Sally Parker to put everything away, to sit down and have a dish of tea, I would walk back here. Then I met Ma Henham and she gave me some agrimony tea.'

'Good God, agrimony! And what does that cure, pray?'

Lizzie smiled. 'I believe I would rather not know.'

He made straight for the morning room, it was most particularly his own. There was a fire lit too, seeing it had been a chilly, unpredictable afternoon, and he felt in need of warmth, warmth and solitude. He felt strangely cold, strangely lost. It was a feeling that had come to him on the first day in court and had been growing stronger every hour since and if he had hoped it might fade and die with triumphant vindication, with release, he had been mistaken, it stayed and stayed.

'I am not at home,' he said to Mrs Clark as she bobbed in her head to ask if there was anything he wanted, hardly able to keep the look of triumph and gratitude from her face as she did so, the triumph and gratitude that had wreathed her in smiles ever since they had heard of the acquittal an hour ago. 'If anyone should call, I do not mind who it is, do you understand, I am not at home.'

He walked to the window and looked up the avenue. No, he was not at home. The conventional phrase, the stark reality, troubled him. He felt weary, physically weary, as he might have done after an action at sea, but in this case there was no much-needed rest, no instant oblivion and then the cheerful waking, refreshed. He felt restless and irritable, kept remembering the ignominious and hasty retreat from the courtroom through a back door to avoid the crowd, the dash into Ship Street where Stephen Fisher's carriage was waiting, his own harsh, ungrateful orders to set him down on the Stretfield road, he wished to walk home across country; Stephen's face, hurt, confused, resigned; the mass of people in the market place jostling and shouting, his own name cried out several times, the words 'Not Guilty' reaching them through the glass, the drawn blinds, laughter, drunken singing, the coachman swearing as people ran under the noses of the horses.

'If you are sure, Jardine,' Stephen had said as they drew up a bare half mile from the Ramillies gates, 'if you are sure you do not want me to take you up to the house . . .'

A handshake. 'You have done enough. I shall always be grateful.' Mother of God, to get away, to be alone.

'But what shall I say to Mr Calloway? I had invited him to dine thinking you would be there too.'

'Say I am not in a fit state for company, I am not myself. I shall make a point of seeing him tomorrow. Give him as many apologies as you like. Forgive me, Stephen. I wish to walk.'

The pasture running down to the river, sheep dotted about and moving away at his approach; clouds banking up and then blowing on, a few drops of rain, a shower, a gleam of restored sunlight, more clouds. There was no bridge between Ramillies and the sea but a little downstream from the park there was a watering place where the banks had crumbled and the bottom was gravelly and level: he took off his shoes and waded across, the cold water the first real sensation in a week. Once on the other side a hundred yards brought him to his own boundary, a young wood of oak and ash planted by Lizzie's father as a youth, walking out with his own father on fine dewy mornings. There was a miniature valley here, a deep vee-shaped hollow where a tiny beck ran down almost unseen to meet the river; the ground was a little soft in the bottom, nothing more. From the top of the far slope he knew he would be able to see the house.

This was where he had paused, sitting halfway up, not

giving a damn for the damp, for the cold in his wet feet, for the threat of another shower. It was a quiet, secret place, this hollow, green, and he could see some kind of bog flowers in bloom down in the marshy stretches. There were no birds singing except now and again a furious blackbird, a challenge cut off in the middle, but the trees moved, he could hear their leaves; he could hear the wind in the grass.

He sat until the full force of the shower drove him on, up to the shelter of the first of the great oaks on the rise. From there he could look down on Ramillies, the river away to his right, the sudden crowing of a cock floating up through the urgent patter of the rain on the oak leaves. It came to him as he stood there, an entirely disembodied, involuntary thought, that this was how Lizzie Rayner must feel, a stranger in her own home.

'Do you wish to be alone?' said the Doctor, opening the door of the morning room. 'Mrs Clark has given instructions you are not in to anybody, not even King George.'

'Dear Alex, you know I would never exclude you.'

'Oh there are times when we would exclude everybody, even our dearest friends. I would quite understand. It was why I left as soon as the court was dismissed, I could not face company at such a moment. I just looked in to say . . . nothing in particular, for some things are so awkward to get into words. I shall go away again directly and write some letters.'

Jary bent to put another log on the fire. 'No, no, don't go. Stay and talk. I have missed our talks these last few days. I am afraid I have wounded poor Stephen deeply, not allowing him to drive me in triumph up to the front door. I made him put me down before the park.'

'So I assumed, seeing Clarkie scurrying about with your wet stockings.'

'He had a celebration dinner planned; he had killed the fatted calf. I felt a scrub turning him down. But I could not have done it. Apart from not being hungry I could not have sat in company and talked any sense.'

There was a silence while they both sat and looked into the fire. Then Jary looked up at his portrait and a wry smile made him suddenly more human. 'She did not paint what she saw, did she? She was afraid to, she thought it would give offence. She saw an insensitive, overbearing foreigner playing the merry devil with her beloved Ramillies.'

'Nonsense. She saw nothing of the kind. She has told me so. She was sorry to leave out so much, to make you a mere shadow of yourself, but she was in a state of war with her feelings, she could not bring herself to like you on principle and was too honest to pretend she disliked you – hence your face up there is bland and non-committal, she was trying hard not to do you an injustice.'

Jary's smile widened. His blue eyes – how remarkably cold such very blue eyes could seem at times, the Doctor mused – narrowed, intensely amused.

'The lady has opened her heart to you, I see.'

'She has taken to wearing it on her sleeve, I assure you, but people are so unused to the thought of her having one at all it passes entirely unnoticed.'

'On her sleeve?'

'It is a figure of speech.'

'I am aware of that. Lizzie Rayner in love?'

'Not exactly perhaps. It is not a sensation she is used to, she will refuse to acknowledge it as long as possible.'

A pause. The amusement left Jary's face slowly. 'Has she mentioned this rumour that yokes us together? Calloway, who can scarcely bring himself to speak of her since I changed my will, told me outside the court that it was the rumour swayed the jury, for everyone knew the judge wished for a conviction, his summing up was a marvel of partiality. I thought it was all over then.'

'The judge is a bilious man, I could recommend a draught to cure the discomfort and I would warn him off an over-indulgence in port on top of scanty meals. It is indigestion makes him crabbed, and a keen sense of his inferiority, of the fact that he is not a good judge. To be sure there are not many good judges, all in all, but few of them know their own weaknesses with such painful clarity, or admit to themselves how much they dislike their role of God.'

'You are saying that my life depended on the state of his stomach.'

'Great things often turn about such frivolities, as you well know. Shall I ring for port? Neither of us over-indulge, we can be allowed a bottle surely?'

The Doctor shifted his gaze to Jary's face and saw the great weariness there, physical weariness and mental too, but his brain was turning over and over the events of the last days and perhaps the apparent suspension of feeling during the trial meant a furious onrush of bewildering emotion now. He could sympathize, he knew what it was like: he had felt like this after reading Ann's letter.

'I am going to bed,' said Jary suddenly, rising as he spoke. 'Never mind the port, Alex. I shall be myself in the morning.'

'Would you like something to make you sleep?'

'No. No, I shall sleep. Sailors can always sleep and wake at will, and I am more a sailor than anything else perhaps. I did not know it before but I was always happiest at sea.'

Up in his room he lit two more candles from the one he carried, and stared about. It was all put ready for him, the bed warmed, his nightshirt laid out; it was as if he had never been away, never contemplated the journey to Helen's Mount. He looked up by force of habit and the lady in grey looked back.

She had run away with Jervis but it had not been a happy experience, she had come back. What had she been like then, so much younger and perhaps even more disputatious, running full tilt at anything life offered? He wondered if she would ever be content but doubted it as he doubted it of himself; in Lizzie's case the world itself did not suit her, it implied level ground when the whole world to her was mountains and chasms; in his own case it suggested inactivity, and inactivity he could not bear.

There is a critical point I suppose, he thought, looking about him, where we make a more or less conscious choice to go on as we are or to make sail and bear away to new horizons; an ignoble thought suddenly: to cut and run?

A more or less conscious choice. He stared up at Lizzie's grandmother. He was very fond of her. He had once or twice been struck, as he had come through his door, by the wish that she was a living person standing there with whom he could discuss the frustrations and achievements of the day, whose contrary spirit not only challenged his own but fulfilled a need, infuriated and gave immense joy at the same time. It is all air, he thought now, like wishing to make Ramillies a home. What a fool you are, said another inner voice scathingly: you have Ramillies, you most probably have Helen's Mount, you have good friends, you have your ships, you have your life, God help you, and all you can do is stand here feeling sorry for yourself because things have not turned out the way you expected.

The candles flickered. He could hear the slow, deliberate, light footsteps in the passage that was the Doctor going to bed. Unless he was mistaken he too had taken some kind of knock and was at a loss how to deal with it, there was a grim, closed look about his face, a deliberate withdrawal. But the morning would bring relief, with luck, a new day, maybe sunshine. He would be a long way down in needless misery if he could not respond to sunshine after being so closely confined. He began to pull his shirt off over his head and as he did so, caught in an awkward position, his eyes, tight closed, opened on the lady in grey, and his drawn, tired face broke immediately into a loving smile.

The next day brought the longed-for sunshine, watery but steady, and it also brought three notes of congratulation, one of which was from Sir James Braile and included an invitation to dine, one of which was from the Stones and included a postscript from Mrs Stone wishing him joy of his forthcoming marriage.

'How will I face that Lizzie?' asked Jary of the Doctor when they met by the canal at mid-morning, frightening the mallard who had already taken possession. 'How do we stamp out such a damned tale?'

'By the time you get to Jamaica the district will have forgotten all about it.'

'You mean, just leave, say nothing?'

'My dear, you cannot be held responsible for a rumour.'

'But how they will all speculate, the cats, when I am gone, quizzing Lizzie Rayner till she runs mad, no doubt. I cannot leave her to face that sort of ignominy. It would be kinder to put a formal announcement in the paper.'

'Announcement? Good God! Of marriage?'

'Of course not. Of . . . of our having no intention of marrying.'

The Doctor rubbed his chin. 'There are ducklings in that clump,' he said, 'look. Six or seven. If I were you I would consult with Lizzie before doing anything so rash. You have a tendency to jump from sound rock into quaking bogs without a moment's thought. Look, there they go, the poor frail innocents. Your canal is an ocean to them.'

'I am glad the sluices answer. I was afraid I would be damned the length of the river for interfering with the course of nature. It would be one more thing to hold against me.'

They took their usual stroll about the house, stopping to pay the customary visit to the pullets – hens now, matronly and self-possessed – and to the horses. Millett's screechy voice raised in song amid the clank of buckets and the restrained cooing of the few remaining doves, and then the sound of carriage wheels, urgent hooves: 'Damn!' said Jary, retreating at once. 'Alex, see who it is. Send them away. I am out. I am ill. I am dead.'

'For shame, Doctor, you are not shaved and have a nightcap on,' said Fanny, leaning from the window, presuming on friendship. 'It is half past eleven o'clock, you know. But then I daresay you sat up late into the night talking. How you must have talked!'

'I am taking Mrs Jewkes to view the cottages,' said Stephen Fisher, getting down and wringing the Doctor's hand. 'She was kind enough to say she would come with me when I called at Foley just now to ask how she did. I have asked her and Miss Rayner to dine the day after tomorrow and I did so hope you and Mr Bliss and of course Mr Savage could join us.'

'I fear Mr Bliss is away to London tomorrow. He has already been absent far too long. He is at the Admiral now getting his affairs in order, bespeaking his place on the coach.'

'But you and Mr Savage . . .'

'I cannot speak for Mr Savage. I will ask him when he returns. But I would be most happy to accept. It will be in the nature of a farewell dinner for I am leaving for London myself the day after that and have just written to secure a passage in a ship to Madeira.'

'Madeira. I did not know you were going to Madeira.'

'It is by way of being a stepping stone. From Madeira I may go to India or America.'

'But what will you live on?' in a shocked, anxious voice, and then, aware he had been rude, remarkably rude: 'Forgive me. But when you were an army surgeon you had your pay. Without official standing there can be no regular income. I would not care to think of a friend alone upon the ocean with his pockets empty, his well-being dependent on the winds of chance.'

The Doctor ushered him back into the carriage. 'You are very kind. I shall not forget such a generous thought. But I have a little money of my own, you know, I shall survive. Believe me, we are most of us subject to the winds of chance. Mrs Jewkes, I hope you enjoy the cottages. Good morning to you.' But a thought struck him as they were about to move off: 'Where is Miss Rayner today?'

'Oh,' said Fanny with an arch look that failed to come

off, going bright red, 'oh, I believe she said she wanted to finish the picture of Ramillies. She set off very early. Is she not here?'

You know very well where she is, thought the Doctor, why will you not say? Then it came to him: she was fishing, fishing in Ramillies waters.

'I have not seen her,' he replied with studied emphasis, and saw Fanny's quick suppressed grin, Mr Fisher's innocent stare, and the carriage rolled forward and trundled away up the avenue.

'Where are they off to?' demanded Jary, emerging from the shelter of the stables.

'To inspect the cottages. Poor Mrs Jewkes will have to endure an hour of minute detail, every inch and angle expounded, every modern convenience, every fireplace and closet. It is not like her to ride out with Mr Fisher; perhaps she is softening towards him. He has certainly been less under his father's influence of late and he has a good heart, after all, he deserves her indulgence.'

'But not her hand in marriage, she is far too good for him, worthy man that he is. And where is Lizzie? *She* would not write me any note to say how glad she was I am not condemned to the rope or Botany Bay.'

The Doctor hesitated. He had dabbled in matchmaking before and look where it had brought him?

'She is probably down by the pond,' he said at last, not meeting Jary's eye, 'hooking your precious fish.'

Lizzie was not the only one abroad for stolen fish: she met the Fipson boys, who should have been at Miss Sankey's school, creeping along the hedge up the poacher's path from the river. Will Fipson had a fish in his pocket, he pushed its tail out of sight with a guilty jerk. Fishing was good by the new sluice, he said in answer to her questions, a shy, envious eye on the good rod over her shoulder.

Fishes might have risen for small boys with optimism and stale bread but Lizzie found they would not rise for her. She sat on the bank and sketched a strangely distorted willow on her pocket pad, and now and again her glance would stray to the quiet water and her untroubled hook and then away through the trees towards the invisible Ramillies, which she could see in her mind's eye as clearly as if it had been fifty yards along the bank. After a while she took some bread and cheese from her pocket and ate it, and pulled off her straw hat and unpinned her hair.

The heat grew. There was a murmuring summer quiet; it might have been June. The river flowed gently towards Westdene at its proper level. Only a moorhen broke the silence, leading her babies through the reeds to swim, and once the raucous scolding of the jays from the woods on the far bank. Lizzie lay in a tangle of grasses, her shoes off, her face to the sun. She was a child again: often and often she had lain like this in other warm springs, other summers. She was a child, loved and protected; the world turned, the days marched on in kindly, undeviating procession: lessons, riding, walking to church, fishing on the sly, a new puppy, new books, painting, painting, picking gooseberries, jam pudding, simnel cakes, her first glass of wine.

'It is all yours again,' said Jary's voice in imaginary conversation, 'I give it all to you.'

'I do not want it. It is not the same, it can never be the same.'

'Of course you want it. You have always wanted it.'

'No, no, no . . .'

The anxious repetitive tooting of the moorhen did not disturb her, she had fallen asleep, her arm in the crook of her elbow and the shadows of the leaves dappling her bright hair.

23

He ducked under the elder bush and came upon her lying there. She looked very young and touching which was something new in his experience, and he was suddenly loath to wake her. But as he stood undecided her line twitched and he crept down to the water's edge to pick up the rod and pull it in, a delicate operation, hampered by the rushes, the dangling branches of willow, and the soft unreliable bank.

'Damn!' he exclaimed as the line snagged, twisted, and he felt the fish jerk free.

'You have not lost my fish? That is really too bad of you, and after I have waited all morning for a bite.'

She was sitting up, pretend indignation hiding her confusion. As he looked she clapped on the straw hat, pushing her hair off her face.

'I rather think it was *my* fish,' he said with a smile.

'I suppose it was. Are you going to make a fuss about it?' And suddenly, leaning forward with her hand raised in warning, she added, very low: 'There is a wren in the willow.'

There was, and it crept from twig to twig until it was directly over Jary's head when it paused.

'How did you find me?' asked Lizzie, and it flew away.

'I was walking about enjoying the sun when I came across a curious child with no front teeth and no hair. He put me on the right path for the river "and Miss Lizzie". I had difficulty making out what he said. For a moment I thought . . . But never mind. I am glad to see you again and looking so well.'

'It was Jo Fipson you met. He has had the ringworm.'

'Another Fipson?'

'There are eleven, and then the cousins, and two

362

outcasts, half-brother and sister, I think, who went to live at the Diddlers.'

'Incest?'

'Well, I suppose it is. Mr Odbold says there has been some mistake, otherwise it would be an abomination. He is rather too particular for a country parson, I am sure there are times he should turn a very blind eye. He and Fanny have fallen out, you know.'

He did not know, he was sorry to hear it, though he had long been under the impression Mr Odbold did not visit at Foley. Nor did he, said Lizzie, putting on her shoes, and nor would he ever now.

'He had heard this rumour that you had left me your fortune,' she said, and her voice had an edge to it as if she was determined to speak though she would much rather remain silent. 'He was horrified, flew over to Foley to find out if it were true. Fanny told him he only cared about it in case he did not get his new bell or the building work done on the tower or whatever. She grew quite passionate and he slunk away deflated.'

Jary handed her her rod. She took it and began to follow the little path back through the trees, stopping to disentangle her skirts once or twice.

'I had left everything to Henriette,' Jary said as they broke from the trees and found themselves by the park fence, 'but as that no longer served I thought you might as well have it all; well, not quite all, there were some odd legacies to friends.'

She turned on him, dropping her rod without even noticing, a strange, white, passionate face. 'How romantic you are! How like you to leave everything to a woman you do not like simply because it seems just. Or had you been drinking Fanny's brandy when you came to your decision? Oh yes, don't think I do not know why her cellars are empty now, nor how she used the money to buy my gowns and keep me in fine style in London. Well it is a good thing I have the means to pay her back, I have made enough money to keep Foley for a year or two. And did you think, did you even stop to think, whether I would take Ramillies, twenty Ramillies, when you must die to give me it?' The words poured out, furious, low-pitched, her mind running faster than her tongue, and just as he had thought she was done she began again, lower, if anything more furious: 'I would not take any of it on such terms. I would not take a penny.'

She had drawn a breath, he could speak. He said quickly, angry himself now: 'But you love Ramillies. And who else was there? Alex would not want it. I have no close relations, no wife, no children. You would restore it, make it a fine house. You love it.'

She burned in front of him, consumed in this strange, desperate emotion; the bright curls sprang from under her hat, her eyes were greener than he had ever seen them. 'Not as much as I love . . .'

And it was as if she had been extinguished. She fell silent, stooping at once to pick up the rod, walking away without a backward glance.

'Come up to the house,' he said abruptly, standing still. 'You have not wished me joy of my acquittal.'

She hesitated by the gap in the fence, her hand on the rail. 'I congratulate you most sincerely. I was never so glad in my life.' And after a little because he did not speak: 'It meant I should not have to worry about your damnable will,' in a strained, harsh voice that was supposed to be light and mocking.

He caught her up, put his hands on her shoulders. Her heart contracted: there was no other way to express that sudden tightening in her chest. She would not turn round.

'What about marriage?' he said. 'Does it appeal to you?'

'Not in the least. I would fall so very far short of the ideal.'

'Alex says he does not recommend it, but then as I point out to him he has never married, he cannot speak from experience.'

'I could not bear the hum-drum business of rubbing along, of sacrifice and compromise, of being a sort of domestic appurtenance, a respectable slave. The duties and obligations seem so heavily weighted on the one side.'

'Ah,' said Jary.

He said it so forlornly that she forgot her resolution and turned round. He gave her a rueful smile and shrugged. 'I know when I am beaten. You and Alex would suit each other much better. I cannot cope with such cynicism.'

By so little, a pause for breath, the lack of a suitable word, chances and opportunities are lost. She could find nothing to say and he was already turning to walk back to Ramillies.

'I do hope that was not a proposal,' she said at last when he was twenty yards away.

'No, it was not' – still walking – 'I am leaving for Jamaica at the end of next week and while I am there I am going to visit an old friend' – an unnecessary emphasis – 'a Miss Johnson.'

'To ask her to marry you?' She had nearly caught him up, trailing her rod, her cheeks pink.

'She is not the marrying kind.'

'You will change your will before you go? If you do not I shall live in fear and trembling in case your ship goes down or one of Miss Johnson's other admirers pistols you to death.'

They had come across the grass to the avenue and beyond them was the lawn, the water garden, a man with a wheelbarrow far down by the river – a wheelbarrow full of water plants.

He was thinking about a gazebo, said Jary; it would only be a little gazebo, room for a man and a cat, or should he say book? The Doctor, no doubt, would be the kind of man to take a book to a gazebo.

'I always thought one sat and gazed from a gazebo,' said Lizzie, turning about and shading her eyes to see where the Doctor might read his book.

'That would be up to you. I only thought that if it were built of the same red brick as the house, and was

365

round and roofed with the old tiles, with a honeysuckle or two and some roses . . .'

'I have never met a man like you before,' said Lizzie solemnly, 'I have never in my life met a man who could sincerely imagine a little round gazebo with roses all about it.' No wonder Fanny adores you, it is just the kind of thing she would think of herself.

They wandered here and there about the grass and came to the Lookout, climbing its flight of wooden steps and standing on the upper floor looking out of the gothic windows.

'There is Hawke,' said Jary, 'he came back the moment the verdict was announced. You cannot blame him being worried that his bills would not be met. Horses have to eat, as Millett is always telling me.'

'I suppose he wrote you an appealing letter, he begged your kind understanding, such a delicate matter, children to feed, Mrs Hawke unwell . . . I do not believe you can resist a direct appeal, however false. The Hawkes are all opportunists, extremely selfish and with a strong sense of moral superiority. He will find a thousand ways of making you part with your money. If I were you I would ask old Jack Fipson to build your gazebo. He would do a fine job and charge a fair price and it would wipe Hawke's eye, so to speak, it would let him see you are not to be trifled with.'

'You are giving me advice,' with surprise.

'Well, you do not have to take it. But remember, there have always been Hawkes in Stretfield and they have all been cunning and all died rich.'

'While you are in the mood for counselling: what do I do about a wife? Would you suggest I carry off one of the Stones, or sweet Eugenia? There is no time for a proper courtship, it would have to be a runaway wedding.'

'You would sully your newly restored reputation, which would be a shame,' said Lizzie, looking through the glass at the appearance, unaccompanied, of the parson's terrible mule, who trotted briskly across the front of the house and vanished towards the orchard. 'And carrying off a highly excited young woman is not always the easiest of tasks, or the most dignified. It will not be like courting her under her father's roof, with her father's blessing. Girls who gallop away with men whom they profess to love can turn shrewish and difficult after only an hour or two. I speak from experience, and you may ask Fanny, I can be more shrewish than any female alive.' A pause. Behind the mule came Millett, hobbling as fast as he could, ⓡand behind him Mrs Clark, holding her skirt with one hand and her cap with the other. 'There is also Miss Johnson. You are asking a great deal of an innocent girl from an orderly country house to expect her to understand you have a mistress you do not mean to give up.'

Jary laughed. He lodged himself on the sill and laughed. It was the first time he had looked even remotely like his old self and the change was marked too by the sudden release of tension, a dissolving of the last awkwardness between them.

'I never said I would not give her up.'

'I think perhaps she will only grow more dear once you have learned the restraints and disappointments and domestic chores of marriage.'

'There you go again, damning it out of hand. And you are as much the hypocrite as the Doctor, for you never married either.'

The sun made dusty lozenges on the floor. Dr French appeared by the house and stood a moment, looking about.

'The parson's mule is in among your hens,' said Lizzie, 'there is a great deal of running about.'

'If the mule has any sense at all he will retreat, those hens are the most savage, perverse, unnatural creatures this side of the jungle. Lizzie Rayner, will you marry me?'

How graceless she could be in a fiery, defensive mood. She became all angles, physical and mental, from the suddenly aggressive chin to the brittle warning note in her voice. It came to him abruptly that he would like to make her smile again more than anything, that he loved her smile. It moved him more than anything about her, it was so rare, part of the young and tender Lizzie so knocked and battered by circumstance. He moved to stand beside her by the window, looking out at the green, the sunlit garden. He was as aware of her as she was of him, but since they both felt constrained by complicated inhibitions they simply stood in silence, while the mule, Millett and Mrs Clark swept by in procession on the gravel and vanished towards the stables.

'I have thought a lot about you recently,' he said slowly, 'I saw you in court, you know.'

'I did not come to gape.'

'I know you did not. It was something else entirely on your face.'

'It is all the fault of this mad rumour,' she cried, 'but you must not feel obliged by your overdeveloped sense of honour to put matters right by making it come true. I do not want a husband, and no man in his senses would want me: I will never give up my painting, I will feel an obligation towards Fanny till my dying day, and I would never never countenance any Miss Johnson, I would flay her alive.' And then, with a start: 'They are coming back again. Look, the parson is with them this time.'

'The devil!' said Jary, watching. 'The cunning old brute has no intention of facing the hens again, he is away over the park.'

'You know, you need a woman who will always smile at you, always be tender and happy, who will give you all the outer husk of marriage without troubling herself – or you – with the essential core. It is so much more amiable, so much more peaceful, than becoming entirely involved. Think how happy you were with Miss Johnson. I am sure you were. She did not ask you to love her or be constant or to understand her when she flew into a passion, she did not set you impossible goals or hold up her own virtue when yours fell short.' Her head tipped forward; she was looking down at her fingers: they had traces of paint about the nails. 'I am not like that,' she added.

He turned her to face him and she looked straight up into his eyes – how very blue they were and fringed with black lashes as appealingly as a child's – and she smiled because words had failed her, and he kissed her.

A crashing below and shouts, Millett's roar – a very breathless, depressed roar by now – 'God rot your soul, you . . .' and the parson's shriek, Mrs Clark's 'Oh sir, do sit a moment, catch your breath' and the furious snort of the mule.

'We must be married before I go to Jamaica,' Jary was saying, 'and come with me, else you will sit here twiddling your thumbs and wondering about my virtue and Miss Johnson.'

At which point the mule, mounting the steps, put his head in at the door.

'I have been in tighter spots,' Jary told the Doctor when they met him in the knot garden a little later. 'There was a time in Brazil I believed I might be cooked and eaten, and had just got to the point of hoping I might choke them to death for it when they called the whole thing off and we all had to sit about eating fruit and drinking something filthy from a gourd. But I have never felt such sheer terror as when that wretched animal's head with all those yellow teeth poked through our only bolt hole.'

'I told them not to run after him,' said the Doctor reproachfully, 'you would expect Millett to have more sense.'

'Lizzie cuffed him on the nose and told him he was a horrible beast and should be ashamed of himself and he backed out so quickly he fell off the steps and winded himself, lying there like a dead thing.'

'He made me so angry,' said Lizzie, 'interrupting.'

'I believe I can guess what he interrupted. I am so glad Jary took my advice. There is a side of him would succumb to the advances of even the most obnoxious old mule but you, my dear, will see them all off and Jary's

369

heart and fortune still intact. Come, walk with me to the house and tell me, did you catch any fish?'

She put her arm through his. 'I wish you would give up this idea of India,' she said. 'Go back to Norfolk, lay siege to this Lady Gerard, it would be a miracle if she were to resist you; I could not resist you myself and nor could Fanny, she has told me so. She says you do not make enough of yourself.'

'You are being indiscreet.'

'Discretion be blowed! We are all fond of you. We hope you may be happy.'

® 'But I am so much older than she is, Lizzie dear, too old to cut capers with a lovely young woman.' Though in her company I am no better than a boy of sixteen, crippled with shyness, wretched with desire. How cruel this hot, desperate, unwonted longing that had stirred up his complacent middle age. It must be the result of such long celibacy, or at least such long celibacy had heightened it to unbearable pitch.

'But you love her, deeply, deeply,' and there was a sudden involuntary lift to her voice, her hand tightened on his arm. 'I shall never be loved like that. It is a very rare thing.'

She turned her head so that their eyes met. She knew more of him than Ann, he thought, understood more, appreciated what she found. She admired him; the portrait told him so. More than that, she could not understand why he was afraid Ann might not love him. Look at him today: perfect black coat, dazzling linen, brushed hair, the softer, cheerful look that made him ten years younger. She knew all about his still-active vanity and could not think why he must always damp it down for Ann, making more of his age than was necessary.

'I hear what you say,' he replied now, putting his hand over hers, 'but India will be best. You must come indoors a moment and say goodbye to Mr Bliss, he is leaving shortly and he is too shy to approach you, I think he is in love.'

She laughed, hanging on his arm. 'It is all too much

for one day,' she said. 'Do you think I will carry off the position of mistress of Helen's Mount?'

'I think you must resign yourself to his selling it, it holds more unhappy memories than he will ever say. But he will not settle at Ramillies, not permanently, he will return and fly away again with distressing regularity. He will probably go back to sea when this war gets into its stride again and be knocked on the head and leave you a rich woman.'

'God forbid!'

They walked into the house, laughing.

Mr Bliss was in the morning room gazing down the avenue. He blushed in spite of his resolve and held Lizzie's hand a fraction longer than he should by way of saying farewell to foolish wishes.

'Pray, what are those little brown birds all crouching down pretending they are invisible?' Pointing.

'They are partridges.'

'Are they so? I have never met one with his feathers on.'

She craned round him, smiling wider and wider. 'Dear Dr French, come and look.'

They all looked. Under the oak trees, advancing on Ramillies under a pink sunshade, were Fanny and Stephen Fisher, hand in hand.